Kate High a graduate [...] Faber Academy, contemporary artist, working in metals. She has exhibited internationally, with her work having been shown at the V&A, the Design Council, and also selling through outlets such as Liberty's and Chelsea Crafts Fair. Kate is a former voluntary branch administrator for the RSPCA and she co-founded a charity that aims to support older animals, Lincs-Ark.

The Cat and the Corpse in the Old Barn is her debut novel and the first mystery in the Clarice Beech series, which is set in the Lincolnshire Wolds.

Also by Kate High
The Cat and the Corpse in the Old Barn

KATE HIGH

THE MAN WHO VANISHED AND THE DOG WHO WAITED

CONSTABLE

CONSTABLE

First published in hardback in Great Britain in 2021 by Constable

This paperback edition published in 2022 by Constable

1 3 5 7 9 10 8 6 4 2

A CIP catalogue record for this book
is available from the British Library.

ISBN: 978-1-47213-176-8

Typeset in Caslon Pro by SX Composing DTP, Rayleigh, Essex
Printed and bound in Great Britain by CPI Group (UK), Croydon CRO 4YY

Papers used by Constable are from well-managed forests
and other responsible sources.

Constable
An imprint of
Little, Brown Book Group
Carmelite House
50 Victoria Embankment
London EC4Y 0DZ

An Hachette UK Company
www.hachette.co.uk

www.littlebrown.co.uk

For Steve, Edna, Margaret, Stephen and Michael

Chapter 1

The morning was still. Except for flies and bees, nothing moved within the boundaries of the old walled garden. The sky was an unbroken cloudless blue and the air, heavy with heat, was honeyed by the perfume of flowers.

Clarice Beech reclined in an old blue-and-white striped deckchair, her long legs in calf-length denim jeans stretched out onto a perfect manicured lawn. Her auburn hair, cut short into a bob, was concealed under a floppy sunhat and most of her face was hidden behind a large pair of sunglasses. Her bare arms, exposed by her yellow T-shirt, matched her freckled, sun-bronzed legs.

While she awaited the return of her hostess with coffee, Clarice surveyed the garden. Behind her, the double doors of the conservatory, leading to the kitchen, were open. In front stretched an elongated lawn with flower beds on either side, ending in a low hedge behind which was a wall with a locked gate and spaces to park cars.

It was rare to find such a large garden in this part of Lincoln. Alford House, a Grade II listed property, and the walls that enclosed this private sanctuary had been built in the mid-eighteenth century for a wealthy miller and his family. The property had gone through several owners until, in the early part of the twentieth century, it was bought by the Montgomery family. Displayed in the sitting room were framed wall-hung photographs taken over the last century of family events and gatherings held in the garden. Although many were in black and white, the images were almost identical to Clarice's current view, the only exception being those taken during the years of the Second World War. The headline above one framed press cutting proclaimed: *The Montgomerys Lead the Way*, the article explaining how the family had dug up their lawn and flower beds to plant vegetables as part of the war effort. The newspaper picture showed a man named as Sir Henry Montgomery, smartly attired in a tweed jacket and plus-fours, pointing his pipe towards evenly spaced lines of seedlings. Clarice had smiled at the image; she could not imagine that in the mid twentieth century, a man of Sir Henry's status would roll up his sleeves to dig and plant potatoes. The old wealthy families retained servants to perform those tasks, but she appreciated that the article was of its time, dutifully depicting the Montgomerys' patriotism.

She moved her eyes along the deep herbaceous border that stretched from the wall to meet the lawn, trying to remember the names of the vast army of plants gathered, upstanding, in small groups. Blue and white *Scabiosa*, deep blue *Aconitum*, often known as monkshood, *Alcea*, commonly called hollyhock, and the yellow daisy-like flower *Doronicum*. Her host, Lady Jayne Montgomery, had obviously given thought, in the planting of the various varieties, to height and requirements for sun or shade. *Lythrum*, with its lance-shaped leaves and purple-red flowers, and *Polygonatum*, with curving fronds under which hung masses of white bells, were planted in the shadow of a large loganberry tree.

Further away, enjoying the benefit of the full sunlight, were bright pink and yellow *Potentilla* and mauve and purple *Phlox*. Clarice briefly half closed her eyes and looked through her lashes, a game she'd played as a child, to view the white *Gypsophila* as rolling, floating clouds. The garden was Jayne's passion, and getting it to this point of excellence must have been an almost full-time occupation.

Turning her attention to the bricks in the old wall, most of which was hidden behind tall plants, shrubs and climbers, Clarice imagined the craftsmen labouring day after day to hand-make each brick, and then others working to construct the wall itself.

Jayne had offered Clarice the use of her walled garden for a fund-raising open day, to take place on the coming Sunday. There would be chutneys, jams and bread, a book stall and a tombola. Refreshments – tea, coffee, home-made lemonade and cakes – would be served at small tables by volunteers. The beneficiary, Castlewick Animal Welfare, or CAW for short, had been founded by Clarice when she began to take in waifs and strays of the four-legged variety. All monies would help to pay for veterinary and food costs: she hoped, if the weather was like this, to get an excellent turnout.

The main attraction, for inquisitive visitors to the private residence on the lane leading to Steep Hill in Lincoln, would be the walled garden itself. Clarice was aware that further up the hill, near Minster Yard, was where the more prestigious homes sat. But the beauty of this house would make up for any lack of status compared to its more elevated neighbours. It was rare

3

for the thrice-married Jayne, now in her mid-eighties, to allow members of the public into her private domain. She was, as she had explained to Clarice, the custodian of the exquisite house and garden for her remaining lifetime. On her death, it would be inherited by the eldest son of her late husband's first marriage.

Jayne and Clarice had first met five years earlier, through Amanda Jenkins, a mutual friend. Jayne's third husband, the retired circuit judge Sir James Montgomery, had died suddenly following a heart attack. Six months after his passing, her only remaining companion, Libby, a Miniature Poodle, had had to be put to sleep. She was, Amanda had explained, inconsolable; might CAW have a small, older dog available for adoption, to fill the sad gap?

Clarice had introduced Jayne to Basil, an eight-year-old Terrier/Springer Spaniel cross, who had recently lost his mistress after she'd been taken into a nursing home. Watching their first meeting, Clarice had witnessed love at first sight – the two oldies suited one another exactly, a perfect match. After his adoption, Basil had supplied amiable companionship, and Jayne had provided him with an ample lap, combined with the services of an ear scratcher.

Clarice had been secretly amused by Basil's upwardly mobile trajectory. Adopters were never told who had given their animal up for adoption, but Clarice knew that Basil had gone from a home in a busy run-down estate in a town on the east coast to the swanky area below Steep Hill in Lincoln. The factor that remained constant was the love he received in both places. Now, at thirteen, although rather portly and sedate, his pace suited that of his mistress. The garden was her obsession, and as she worked her way around to plant or weed, Basil would always be close at hand.

Clarice had asked Georgie Lowe, the head of CAW's fund-raising committee, to accompany her today, to look at the garden and discuss the forthcoming event with Jayne: timings, setting up, and how many small tables with chairs might be required. Georgie, who was both nosy and an incurable gossip, had welcomed the opportunity to look around Jayne's home and garden. But she had phoned early that morning, the disappointment in her voice palpable, to say that Jessica, her eleven-year-old daughter, had fallen ill with a stomach bug, and she would not be able to attend with Clarice.

When Clarice, on arrival had explained Georgie's absence, she realised that Jayne, rather than being disappointed, was pleased that it would be just the two of them, and immediately understood the reason. Although she would have been horrified by the suggestion, Jayne shared Georgie's penchant for gossip, and she had not had an opportunity for a proper natter with Clarice since the latter had reunited with her husband, Rick.

'Coffee!' Jayne came into the garden bearing a round floral-patterned tray. She was a short woman, with broad hips and a large chest that jutted out like a ledge over the crockery she carried. Despite her age, her skin was smooth and creamy, and her pale blue almond-shaped eyes might have seemed cold were it not for the laughter lines around them, her face when she spoke alert with good humour. Following a few feet behind her waddled Basil.

On the tray were not only cups with coffee, a jug of milk and sugar, but also what looked like flapjacks.

'Have you been baking?' Clarice eyed the flapjacks greedily.

'Yes, these are sultana and apricot,' Jayne beamed. 'We can eat them while you fill me in about that gorgeous husband of yours. I want all the nitty-gritty.'

'It's been six months.' Clarice spoke as she picked up the pink-patterned bone-china cup filled with black filter coffee. 'It's old news now.'

'Not to me,' Jayne protested. 'How you ever let that delightful *tall* man slip through your fingers I'll never know.'

Clarice laughed. Although she was actually over six feet tall, she never admitted to being more than five foot eleven. Rick, at six foot four, was taller than her by three inches.

'You'd have had to settle for a midget if you'd let him go,' Jayne continued. 'I mean someone quite small by your standards.'

'I'm not going down that route, thank you,' Clarice smiled. 'Anyway, Rick still spends a lot of time in the house he rents in Castlewick. The new-build estate. He always refers to it as number 24. The moment has never been quite right for him to move back into the cottage with me.'

'Why did he not give it up when you decided to get back together?' Jayne looked puzzled.

'It was what we both wanted.' Clarice spoke pensively. 'We wanted to get back to being a couple, but slowly; to rediscover each other again.'

'Sounds sensible.'

'Yes, it's worked like a second honeymoon.'

'That's perfect.' Jayne sounded genuinely pleased for her.

'And life has become manic for Rick – he's just finished one complex case and is on to another – so it's just easier for him to keep the rental for a while longer, and it's so convenient for his office at HQ.'

'Well, if that's what works for the two of you . . .'

'It isn't a matter of choice,' Clarice said, 'but we'll get there once he's less busy.'

'What's he working on now?' Jayne enquired. 'If you're allowed to say.'

'A suspicious death; a man who died at a printing factory, crushed in a press.' Rick had only just begun work on the case, and Clarice hoped to find out more about it later in the day.

'The Ben Abbot case? I read about that,' Jayne said with interest. 'It was reported this week in the *Lincoln Herald* as an accident. Abbot's the printers have been in North Hykeham for years. Ben's father only died a few weeks ago, and there's a brother.' She looked at Clarice reflectively. 'If Rick's working on the case, it must be suspected murder.'

'I couldn't possibly comment,' Clarice said, though she smiled as she spoke.

Jayne nodded, understanding that her friend would not be drawn further on the subject. 'Is he coming on Sunday?' she asked hopefully. Despite her age, she was an incorrigible flirt.

'I think so, work allowing.'

'Good.' She gave Clarice a sly smile. 'I'll look forward to it. I expect he's going with you to the opening of your London exhibition?'

'Yes,' Clarice said. 'It's a group exhibition, with three other makers. I do one every third year in London, the next year in Norwich, then a year when we have a break. We'll set up on Friday morning – it's open from six to nine in the evening.'

'So you'll have a lot on, with this fund-raiser on Sunday.'

'Fortunately the gallery's manned by staff – included in the cost, which isn't always the case. I'll set up and be there for the opening, stay over on Friday night, and then home on Saturday.'

'Are the other makers all ceramicists?' Jayne asked.

'Yes, but we're not competing. These group exhibitions

highlight our differences. Jerry, one of the makers, works on miniatures – cups and saucers, teapots, really quirky stuff. Ros does flat plates, and John's work has a 1960s Scandinavian look about it, with a contemporary twist.'

'A nice contrast to your tall vases.'

Clarice nodded as she scanned the garden. 'Now, thinking about Sunday, can one of the volunteers bring some folding tables and chairs on Friday?'

'No problem, I can store them in the garage until we need them. Just make sure they phone first to guarantee that I'm in.' Jayne followed Clarice's eyeline. 'Tables for teas and cakes at this end, nearer the kitchen?'

'My thought exactly,' Clarice agreed. 'Less of a walk carrying trays.'

An hour later, after finalising the arrangements, Clarice gave both Jayne and Basil a hug and said goodbye.

Walking from the house to her car, she mulled over the conversation. She wondered if her upbeat responses about her estrangement from Rick might one day no longer be an act. Could she stop remembering the loneliness of the break-up as a distressing spasm rippling through her body? It was, she determined as she reached the car, surely only a matter of time.

She found her mobile phone on the front seat of her dark blue Range Rover. There were three missed calls, all from Louise Corkindale, an old friend who lived in the Wolds outside Lincoln.

While she'd been away, the car had heated with the sun. She rolled down the windows to allow air in. A group of children racing each other down the hill, their voices shrill, reminded her that the school summer break had started, and made her think again about Georgie, wondering how she was getting on with Jessica. She hoped Seth, older than Jessica by four years, had managed to avoid the bug.

Louise picked up on the second ring. 'Hi, Louise!' Clarice said. 'Have you been trying to reach me?'

'Clarice, yes.' Louise sounded breathless. 'Thank you for getting back to me. I need to ask for your advice. It's about Susie, Guy's dog.'

'Ah, lovely Susie the Boxer.' Clarice picked up a sense of alarm in the usually level voice of her friend. 'Nothing wrong, I hope?'

'Well, yes, there is. I have Susie here with me, but I need some advice about where to board her. Guy's wife Charlotte asked me to hang on to her myself, but Milo, my Westie, is fifteen now; he won't tolerate another dog on his territory. And Susie has a nasty cut on the back of her leg.'

'How did that happen?' Clarice asked, confused by the direction of the conversation.

'I don't know, she just turned up on my doorstep. She ran off while Charlotte was occupied, so she didn't realise she'd gone.'

Clarice wondered if the cut was deep, and why her friend hadn't taken the dog to the vet. 'Louise, I'm just about to leave Lincoln; can I call in on my way home? I'll be with you in half an hour.'

'Yes, thank you, Clarice, if you could.'

'Where is Guy?' Clarice asked. 'Is he back in London on business?'

'No, that's the problem. He's gone.'

'What do you mean, gone? Gone where?'

'I don't know,' Louise said, her voice suddenly tearful.

'Charlotte says he left home around seven yesterday morning with someone he described as a business acquaintance, and he's not been seen since. He's simply vanished.'

Chapter 2

Driving along Silver Street onto Monks Road, Clarice concentrated on the heavy traffic, but picking up the route out of Lincoln, she began to relax. The sun, which had dazzled between the buildings in the city, now lit up the undulating, dancing fields of wheat, turning the vista into a golden haze.

She was troubled by the fear in Louise's voice. Her friend of many years was usually steady and unflappable. How was it possible for her son to simply vanish? If he'd been unhappy with his marriage to Charlotte, he must have shown signs before packing his bags. Or was it more sinister, something work-related? Guy was a defence barrister, operating from chambers at Lincoln's Inn in London.

Louise, a widow, was in her mid-seventies. Clarice had never known Martin, her husband, who had died while Guy was a child. After his death, Louise had expanded her hobby of growing herbs into a small market-garden business. It had worked well: she was able to fit her business commitments around her domestic life and had always been at home during school holidays. The company had thrived, and now employed three full-time staff members. Louise's situation put Clarice in mind of her own parents: her father had died suddenly, leaving Mary, her mother, to bring up Clarice as a single parent. Both women had managed admirably.

Guy was only a year younger than Clarice, and their paths had crossed in the pub in Castlewick when they were in their late teens. Later, Louise had taken an interest in Clarice's animal charity, by which time Guy had moved to London to begin his career. By all accounts, he had been a pleasant, intelligent young man. And now he was a successful lawyer. Clarice and Louise had several friends in common, amongst them Jonathan Royal, a vet, and his partner Keith Banner, a solicitor, both with businesses based in Castlewick. Clarice thought once more about the cut to Susie's leg, wondering why Louise had not already taken the dog to Jonathan's surgery.

Stuck behind a slow-moving tractor pulling a wide load, she reminded herself methodically of the details of the Corkindale family. Guy was forty-one and married to Charlotte, who was a similar age. They had their main home in Lincolnshire and a small flat in London for Guy when he was working there. The oldest daughter, Tara, from Charlotte's first marriage, was fifteen, and the two younger girls were eight-year-old Angel and six-year-old Poppy.

Clarice watched with relief as the tractor in front indicated and turned left, allowing her to pick up speed. The landscape changed as she progressed deeper into the Wolds, the lanes becoming narrow with snake-like twists and curves. Twenty minutes later she dropped a gear to slow the car as she turned on to the single-width unmade track leading to Louise's home. Opening the windows, she felt the warm breeze against her skin, carrying with it the earthy smells of soil, grasses and wheat. The narrow track presented no problems for most of the year, but in winter, with rain, ice and snow, it could become perilous for travellers. On either side were deep man-made dykes, currently filled with summer grasses, which allowed water to drain from the land. Louise drove an old Land Rover, heavy enough to avoid the skidding and dips encountered by the drivers of smaller cars.

Clarice could see from a distance the neat rows of plastic tunnels used for growing the herbs, arranged like shiny alien vessels against the backdrop of the landscape. Louise's three employees included a couple in their early fifties, Ian and Judith Roberts. Judith had come first, fifteen years ago, to be joined by Ian five years later, after he had been made redundant from his previous job. The third employee was Gavin, a young man taken on straight from school as the business expanded. The Robertses now knew as much about the running of the business as Louise did. She often commented that if she took a week or two away, everything continued to glide smoothly along under their watchful eyes. Judith had asked if they might have first option to buy the business and the cottage if Louise ever decided to sell up and move away. She had agreed, but told them that she loved her home and still enjoyed working, so that point might not be reached for years. Still, Judith and Ian had been satisfied by her response.

As she curved around a small wooded area that was part of Louise's garden, Clarice came to the front of the idyllic eighteenth-century cottage, partly hidden by large shrubs and climbing double-headed white roses. As she pulled to a halt in the driveway, she was reminded of Jayne's garden, the smell of newly cut grass mingling with the scent of flowers and the chattering of garden birds. To this was added the fragrance of

13

herbs and, in the depths of the open country, the unceasing monotonous grumble of farm machinery.

'Clarice, so glad you could come.'

A small, slim woman with neat features, her white and grey hair cut short, emerged from the cottage, walking towards Clarice with open arms. They hugged, and Clarice followed as Louise led her inside

'I'm all over the place, Clarice,' she said. 'It's silly really, I'm sure there must be a rational explanation, but I'm just so worried.'

'Has he ever done this before?' Clarice asked.

Louise raised her shoulders and grimaced, in an exasperated gesture.

After passing through a short hallway, they had arrived in the sitting room. Two small rooms had been merged to create this space, an archway in the centre indicating where the dividing wall had once been. The room was the heart of the house, its plaster walls a beige grey, the doors and floor oak, as were the wooden beams overhead supporting the low ceiling. Around the room were antique tapestry-backed chairs, and a chintzy three-seater sofa and matching armchairs were arranged before an unlit wood-burning stove. To one side in a small nook sat an oak bureau, passed down to Louise from her parents.

Milo came forward slowly to greet them, the movement of his tail random, his coat dull, the muzzle he pushed into Clarice's proffered hand damp and snow white.

'Poor old man.' Clarice knelt down in front of him and talked as she stroked. 'You are looking your age, but I bet you get lots of TLC.' The dog sat upright in front of her, his head to one side, observing her through milky, clouded eyes. From another part of the house came the sound of barking.

'Yes, he's slow and very arthritic.' Louise leaned over to stroke Milo's head. 'He's also deaf, rather short-sighted and a bit doddery, bless him, but I do try to give him lots of love.'

'Being a bit doddery's allowed at fifteen,' Clarice smiled as Milo turned away to clamber up into one of the armchairs.

'It's just as well they're low enough for him,' Louise said. 'That one's his favourite.'

'I assume that's Susie barking?' Clarice spoke as the barking paused and then resumed.

Louise nodded. 'She just wants some attention, but I can't let her in here – she's far too full-on for Milo. Her tail's like a whip when she's excited. I love that she's got a proper one, though. I remember years ago Boxers had theirs docked – horrible.'

Clarice followed Louise to the sofa and took a seat next to her. 'Start from the beginning, and tell me what happened.'

Louise brought her hands down to rest in her lap and inclined her head down momentarily; when she lifted it, she was composed. 'I don't really know.'

Clarice nodded, puzzled.

'The family often use the route between their house and mine to exercise Susie – we're only two or three miles apart, and it's a good walk for the children and the dog. They follow the course around the river and take the small bridge at Miles End. Susie's a bright girl – she could find her way here blindfolded.'

Clarice nodded again. Though she had never been to Guy's home, she knew the course of the river and the route Louise described.

'I was in the garden at about ten o'clock this morning when I heard barking. I went round to the front and Susie was there, limping towards me.'

'A cut on the back leg?' Clarice asked.

'Yes,' Louise confirmed. 'I knew Guy had been home for the weekend – I saw him on Saturday – and he was due to return to London early yesterday morning.'

'But he didn't?'

'Apparently not. When I found Susie, I telephoned the house. According to Charlotte, Guy had said he needed to discuss a problem with a business acquaintance before he left. The man – Charles something; Charlotte didn't know his surname – came and picked him up at about seven a.m.'

'Why did Guy not just invite him into the house to talk?'

'It's school holidays,' Louise said. 'The children are at home. I expect, if it was a serious business meeting, he wouldn't want them interrupting. But he didn't come back. His bag is still packed and in the hall.'

'Charlotte didn't phone to tell you?' Clarice asked. She had met Charlotte on two occasions at social gatherings at Louise's home and found her to be polite but not overly interested in small talk. She had sensed that having been invited on numerous occasions by her mother-in-law, the woman would see it as a duty to make an appearance once or twice per year.

'No, she said she didn't want to worry me.' Louise glowered. 'Like I wouldn't want to know if there was a problem concerning my own son.'

'Doesn't Charlotte usually take him to the station?'

'Yes, she does, but she said he had done this once before, so she wasn't worried.'

'So it's not completely out of character?'

'No, I suppose not entirely.' Louise sounded unsure. 'I can't remember exactly what happened, but I recall something years ago. There was a lot of joking about Guy not keeping his eye on the clock.'

'But on that occasion he did come back?'

'Yes, he was very late getting to his chambers in London, I think, and late for meetings.'

'But yesterday he didn't arrive at work at all?' Clarice asked.

'No,' Louise said. 'He didn't turn up at his chambers or the flat. In case of an emergency we know the number of his neighbour, Stuart; they have keys to each other's flats. Stuart says he spoke to Guy on Friday afternoon before he left to come home for the weekend and he's not been back since.'

'And what about Susie?' Clarice asked. 'How does that relate to Guy disappearing?'

'Charlotte said she thought something must have panicked her.'

'Noise or activity?'

'She didn't know.' Louise shrugged. 'She said the children were in the garden yesterday evening with the dog. The girls came in when she called them, but Susie had gone.'

'That is strange,' Clarice said reflectively. 'Guy going missing in the morning, and then the dog in the evening.'

'Yes, I thought that – and wherever did Susie go overnight?'

'At least she came here this morning. What have you done about the cut to her leg?'

'I cleaned it up, and she's got a sock over a bandage to keep out any dirt, but she really should go and see Jonathan.' Louise sounded deflated.

Clarice glanced at the row of silver-framed photographs arranged on the bureau: Guy looking shy in his first school uniform; wearing a mortarboard and gown for his graduation from university; in wig and gown as a barrister. There were several of him with Charlotte and the three children. In the centre, in pride of place, was a recent photograph of him and Louise in the garden, his arm around his mother's shoulders.

Today Louise looked unwell, drained of energy. Clarice remembered how attractive and vibrant she had been when she was younger. Now she looked like something put through the wash too many times, limp and colourless.

'It's no good making yourself ill,' she said. 'Let's go through what you've already done.' She looked at her watch – nearly midday; he'd been missing for almost thirty hours. 'Have you contacted the police?'

'Charlotte said that if he doesn't turn up by early evening, she'll ring them. If it's under twenty-four hours, they won't be interested, apparently.'

'Is there anything you've not told me?' Clarice asked.

Louise hesitated, and in that brief pause, Clarice sensed that there was indeed something her friend was reluctant to discuss.

'It's better to say now, Louise. The police will want to know everything when you contact them,' Clarice said urgently.

'Yes, I do see that, but what if I talk about him, say things he would prefer others not to find out, and then he turns up and is cross with me?'

A silence hung between them, while Clarice's mind bounced from one thought to another, speculating on what it was her friend couldn't tell her. 'If you don't want to talk about it, I understand,' she said eventually. 'Some things can be too personal.'

'I was thinking before you came how old-school I am.' Louise spoke quietly.

'In what way?'

'Mental health issues.' She shot out the words. 'I think Guy was suffering from depression; he's not been himself for weeks.'

'There's no shame in being ill, physically or mentally,' Clarice said. 'It can happen to anyone; depression is very common. Has he spoken to his GP?'

'No, he insisted that he didn't have a problem. I'm worried that it's my fault. I was initially very much of the mind that he should pull himself together.'

'You say initially.'

'I realised finally that whatever the issue was, it was serious, not something he could just snap out of.'

'What does Charlotte think? Have you talked to her?'

'She thinks it's the case he's been working on – he's on the defence team on the John Bream case.'

'I know the name,' Clarice said thoughtfully. 'He's been charged with money laundering – large amounts?' She looked at Louise, who nodded.

'Millions. Guy believes him to be innocent; he thinks he was set up by his business partner, Mick Housman. Housman laid a trail to Bream that would be hard to miss, and he's the one who will benefit from him being found guilty.'

'Louise,' Clarice said with concern, 'this makes his disappearance very worrying. You should have contacted the police immediately – I'm surprised someone from his chambers hasn't already done it.'

'Charlotte has asked that we wait until later today, but I think James Wright would agree with you. He's a good friend of Guy's – works in the same chambers. I rang him before you came. He said the Bream case comes to court next week, and if we don't contact the police today, then he'll do it himself.'

'Quite right,' Clarice said.

'But Charlotte said that if we get the police involved, it will put his career at risk if they decide he's not of sound mind. He's worked so hard to get where he is.'

Clarice looked at Louise for a few moments. 'If he is mentally ill, don't you think you should try to help him to get treatment and support?'

'Yes, but it might not be that serious – we may be overreacting. He may still turn up!'

'I'm sorry, but I think the police should be informed.'

'I'm not sure . . . I don't want to ruin his career. Let me talk to Charlotte first.' Louise stood up hurriedly as she spoke.

'No,' Clarice said, 'I've got a better idea.' She rose to move and stand next to Louise. 'If I can catch him now, let me speak to Rick. You've known him for years and you know he'd never steer you wrong.'

Louise looked hesitant before nodding.

'And we will follow his advice.' There was steel in Clarice's voice.

Louise nodded again.

Chapter 3

As she drove away, Clarice glanced in her rear-view mirror. Louise was standing motionless in the driveway, watching her departure. Clarice had sensed her friend's desolation, noticing her lack of eye contact and the tremor in her voice as she held back the threat of tears. The sparky, entertaining woman she had known had changed suddenly into this helpless, lost creature, trapped by her own indecision. When Rick had told her that Guy's disappearance must be reported and investigated, Louise had sunk into another frenzy of uncertainty.

Clarice felt herself physically tense. Had she been unkind, pressing Louise to make a decision? Her heart had said not to push it, but her head had told her there was no other choice.

In the rear of the car, separated from Clarice by the dog screen, Susie turned her head back and forth, looking first at Louise and then at the back of Clarice's head. The striped, earthy tones of her brindle fur were more noticeable against the background of a beige blanket.

Once it had been decided to contact Rick, Louise had taken the house phone and led Clarice into the conservatory at the back of the cottage. Susie had stopped barking when they entered, pressing herself against first one then the other in her glee at their arrival. Clarice was lucky; catching Rick in his office, she'd briefly explained what had happened before passing the phone to Louise to go into more detail.

As Louise spoke to Rick, Clarice observed Susie. The dog was not putting weight on the damaged back leg, but craving attention and high with excitement, she whipped her body around in frenetic three-legged dance moves. 'Susie . . . Susie . . . Susie.' Clarice gently caressed the dog, and with her voice low brought her to a state of calm.

She had called Jonathan before leaving. Although it was outside his official hours, he suggested she meet him at his surgery immediately. The drive to Castlewick took less than twenty minutes.

Jonathan and Keith lived in a white-fronted three-storey house, one of many built in the town at the turn of the twentieth century, on a side street leading away from the main square. The small squat building attached to it had been added in the 1940s, and was used by a chemist before it became a veterinary surgery. Clarice parked the car behind the surgery and, lifting Susie out, went to the open back door of the house.

'Hi, Jonathan!' she called.

'Clarice, my lovely!' Jonathan Royal appeared suddenly as if on a spring. He carried a large quantity of boxed dog food that threatened to spill from his arms.

'Can I help you?' Clarice asked.

'No, dear girl – no problem.' He tipped his load onto a kitchen surface. 'Let's go next door.' Then, to the dog, 'I'll have a little peek at that poorly leg.'

The consulting room as always was shiny clean. Jonathan

quickly typed in details on a computer to bring up Susie's past history. Half an hour later, after Clarice had explained what had happened and he had examined and bandaged the dog's back leg, Jonathan propped himself against the consulting room table, arms folded.

'Poor Louise.' He leaned in towards Clarice, his voice a conspiratorial whisper. Jonathan, much like Georgie Lowe, loved gossip, especially when it was fresh.

'Remember, Jonathan, it's not for public consumption,' Clarice said sternly. She was aware that if he was told something in confidence, Jonathan would only repeat it to his partner, and as a solicitor, Keith knew how to keep secrets.

'But Louise did tell you to tell me?'

'Yes, she didn't want to lie about what's happened. She's aware that if Guy isn't found soon, everyone is going to know.'

Susie, on the floor between them, looked up, her eyes fixed on Clarice, her tail moving ceaselessly.

'Well, yes, I can see that.'

Clarice always thought of Jonathan as an affectionate Labrador. In his late forties, he was short, rotund and smiley. His reading glasses more often than not were balanced on the top of his head amidst his abundant pure white curly hair. He could move from serious business to banter in an instant, with his wicked sense of humour. But today the news about Guy had left him sombre.

He nodded. 'He was such a serious little boy, and he's turned into a lovely bloke,' he said thoughtfully.

'Yes,' Clarice agreed.

'Rick insisted the police should be involved?'

'Yes, because of Guy's work, although it will probably have

no connection.' Clarice, limiting the information on a need-to-know basis, had not told him about the Bream case or Louise's fears about her son's depression.

'Now,' Jonathan crouched down, 'keep that bandage on, Susie, or you'll have to wear the bucket.' He gave the dog a friendly pat.

'Thanks, Jonathan,' Clarice said. 'If she starts to chew it, I'll put the plastic collar on her. Hopefully with it being the back leg she might leave it alone.'

'The cut is in a clean line, and it's deep. I can't say what caused it – not a knife cut, it's too wide, but it might be from something she caught herself on, perhaps a piece of jagged metal. She's had an antibiotic jab, and I'd like to see her again at the end of the week.'

'Friday?'

Jonathan nodded.

'I'll ask Bob to bring her in on Friday morning for the general surgery. I'm away really early to London.'

'Yes, of course,' Jonathan said with enthusiasm. 'It's the opening of your new exhibition – you must be so excited. I want lots of pics of the grand event. And if Bob can't manage to bring her, come over on Saturday afternoon when you're back from London. Just give me a ring first.'

'Thanks,' Clarice said, 'you're a real pal.'

'I imagine it happened while she was out overnight.' Jonathan looked at Susie reflectively. 'I wonder what spooked her to do a runner – she's a typical Boxer, living in the fast lane doing everything at ninety miles an hour, and she has a sweet nature.'

'Louise couldn't shed any light on it.'

'And Susie's moving in with you and your mob,' Jonathan said.

'You mean my four-legged family,' Clarice laughed. 'I think she's confused enough without the added turmoil of going into kennels. She's always stayed with Louise when Guy and his family have gone away, although not in the last year, because of Milo.'

'I bet Rick'll be delighted by another addition.' Jonathan's eyes glinted with mischief.

'He'll come around to the idea,' Clarice said. 'He generally does.'

They walked out to the car together, with Susie hobbling between them.

'Rick and I are looking forward to supper here tomorrow. Who's cooking?' Clarice said as she opened the boot. 'I know you did all the cooking after Keith's hip operation, but you're back to sharing now, aren't you?'

'It's Keith's turn,' Jonathan sniffed. He and Keith were ruthlessly competitive, both believing themselves the better chef. 'The op was five months ago, Clarice. I'm not in charge any more. Still – more opportunity for me to have a drink. We're trying out some blue gin.'

'Blue!'

'It's from South Africa; the blue comes from the infusion of blue pea, which turns pink when tonic is added.'

Clarice raised her eyebrows in amusement. 'I'll tell Rick. It's my turn to drive.'

'Poor you,' Jonathan said with mock sincerity.

Chapter 4

Rick Beech reclined in an armchair in the living room, with Clarice stretched out on the sofa opposite. His favourite cat, Muddy, a five-year-old tabby, had spread herself across his lap in a way that ensured that no space was available for an interloper. Next to his feet on the floor, Big Bill, a large ginger tom, eyed her with contempt.

Clarice followed Rick's gaze down to where Susie had fallen asleep. To one side of her, the two family dogs had also succumbed to slumber. Jazz, a small, brown and white long-haired mongrel with short legs and an extraordinarily long tail, snored noisily, her head resting on the back of Blue, a black Labrador cross with a large splash of white fur on her chest. Both dogs had come to Clarice as rescues, with histories of neglect and abuse, destined to be rehomed. In the process of nurturing them, she had become emotionally attached, and with neither being pretty or photogenic, when suitable homes could not be found, she had kept them as her own.

'It's only a temporary arrangement,' she said, knowing Rick was not happy with the addition to the household. 'And I'm sure Louise understands why you thought it necessary to contact the police immediately about Guy's disappearance.'

'You should put Susie into a kennel; there's no shortage around here.'

'During the summer school holidays?' Clarice queried.

'Ah yes.' He paused, thinking. 'But I worry that you're taking on too much – mainly other people's problems. You've got eighteen cats in the cattery, if you include the kittens, plus the fund-raiser at Jayne's and the ceramics exhibition opening on Friday.'

Clarice gave him her sweetest smile. 'Don't worry about me, I like to be busy.'

She looked at her husband. He was a big man, tall and broad, with grey-speckled brown hair cropped close to his scalp, his face darkened by a permanent five o'clock shadow. She imagined his appearance might often intimidate, which in his profession, as a detective inspector with Lincoln police, was possibly a bonus.

'You look tired.' She spoke softly. 'Can't you stay over tonight?'

'Not tonight. I'll get back to number 24 – I need to be in before the crack of sparrow fart tomorrow.' He tilted his head back and yawned. 'If I can move things along, I can stay over when we get back from Jonathan and Keith's tomorrow evening. I'm not working on Sunday, so I can help you with the fund-raiser. Plus, I've booked holiday leave to go to London with you on Friday.'

'Great.' Clarice sounded enthusiastic. 'Two nights and a Sunday afternoon.'

'It's always difficult midweek – I mean going to Jonathan and Keith for supper.'

'It's difficult any time,' Clarice said, then, as an afterthought, thinking she didn't want it to sound like a criticism, 'especially when you've got a big case.'

'Well, there's always something on the go. We don't finish one case, draw a line and start another; it's never-ending, unlike those TV detective shows, where it's always so neat.'

'The one you're starting now – the Ben Abbot case? Jayne mentioned that it had been reported in the local press as an accident.'

'It looked like an accident – it was supposed to. But the SOCOs have done their work, and the pathologist has put it down to murder too.'

'I thought the body had been too badly damaged to tell?'

Rick nodded. 'It was a mess, yes, but luckily for us, the skull was recovered almost intact, and there was evidence of trauma. He was hit with a hammer.' He ran his fingers absent-mindedly down Muddy's spine as he spoke.

'Pretty conclusive, then.'

'Yup.' He stretched and yawned again. 'Decent bloke by all accounts, hard-working, and according to his late father's neighbour, he kept an eye on his old dad.'

'Jayne said the father only died a few weeks ago.'

'He was a widower; the mother died years ago. The father started the business in the 1960s.'

'With all that going on, I'm sorry to have added to your burden with Guy's disappearance.'

'Hardly your fault,' Rick shrugged. 'I would have been upset if you hadn't made Louise contact me.'

'She did tell you that Guy had done something similar before?'

'It wasn't the same,' Rick shrugged. 'It was apparently years ago, and he'd lost track of time, but he did turn up later on the same day.'

'But it's not really your department – missing persons.'

'No, it's Tony Simpson's, but it would cross the dividing line if it became a murder inquiry.'

'Let's hope it doesn't go there,' Clarice said, drawing her knees up to her chest and wrapping her arms around her legs as she spoke in an involuntary defensive gesture. She hadn't wanted to consider the possibility that Guy might be dead, but the thought had been lurking like a dark shadow.

'Yes, let's hope not. You know that people who go missing invariably turn up within twenty-four hours?'

'Yes, but that's passed!'

'Seventy-two hours is the timescale that makes us panic. The longer it goes on, the more there's cause for concern.' Rick sounded solemn. 'But Guy's not a missing child, and according to Charlotte he knew the person he was meeting.'

'How did the visit to Charlotte go?'

'Tony said she was understandably upset, but he felt she was trying to put on a brave face for the children. You've met her; what did you make of her?'

'Intelligent,' Clarice said, the words coming slowly, 'hard-working and successful. I think the face she reveals to the world would be super-important to her.'

Rick looked puzzled.

'A successful couple with the perfect family,' Clarice continued. 'I'm thinking of those TV commercials where everyone is permanently sunny and well-behaved. In reality we know that's only a marketing ploy; flawless families don't exist.'

'You didn't particularly like her?'

'I didn't *dis*like her,' Clarice tried to explain. 'She wasn't unfriendly; more . . . aloof. She struck me as being the really focused type – on her career, her husband's career, her home, the children – not one to waste time on someone who had no value to her.'

'Such as you?' Rick gave a lopsided sardonic grin.

'Such as me and the other country bumpkins at Louise's fund-raisers,' Clarice agreed. 'I imagined she'd put aside a set amount of time to spend there, and that her attendance was from duty not pleasure.'

'A cold fish?' Rick asked.

'Not cold exactly,' Clarice said. 'She was quite animated with the people she engaged with, a kind of low-key working the room; charming but detached.'

'OK.' Rick sounded reflective.

'I'm seeing her tomorrow afternoon, in fact,' Clarice said.

'Clarice.' Rick's eyes hooked into hers. 'Don't go poking around in police business.'

'I'm not,' Clarice said, her voice matter-of-fact. 'I've simply asked Louise if she thought the children might like to come and see Susie. It's bad enough that their father is missing – I felt seeing their dog would be a comfort.'

'If Louise is bringing the three girls here, why do you have to visit their mother?'

'Two girls. Louise asked Charlotte if they wanted to come over for a couple of hours, but apparently Tara, the eldest, isn't coming.'

'And you have to see Charlotte because?' Rick's voice was suspicious.

'Because Grandma Louise has a doctor's appointment and can't take the girls home, so I said that I will.' Clarice's expression was innocent.

'Don't stick your nose in,' Rick said, holding her gaze. 'And I really don't understand why Charlotte can't look after her own dog!'

'Because according to Louise, the wheels have dropped off. Charlotte isn't coping.'

'She works from home?' Rick asked.

'Not at the moment. She's a freelance textile designer, but she's cancelled all her work commitments.' Clarice paused. 'The thing that's really niggling away at me is why Guy didn't just invite this man Charles into the house.'

'Did you not say that Louise told you it would have been too noisy with the children about?'

'Hmm, I don't buy that.'

'Go on.' Rick folded his arms and leaned towards her.

'I'm sure they could have asked Tara to amuse her sisters upstairs for an hour. She's fifteen – old enough for a spot of babysitting.'

'You think Guy didn't want Charles in the house?'

'Don't you?'

'I can't say the thought hadn't crossed my mind.'

'I don't really know Guy, but from everything I've ever heard, he's a straight, decent man.' Clarice deliberated. 'It does point to the John Bream case – he's been worried and depressed recently, and then he didn't want his visitor to come into his home, so near his family.'

Rick nodded, leaning back deep in thought.

He had, Clarice realised, already moved on from his warning of a few minutes ago that she should not stick her nose in. She felt a frisson of excitement – the game was on.

* * *

Later, after Rick had left, Clarice put Susie on a lead and took the three dogs out for the last walk of the day. Jonathan had instructed her to keep Susie calm for a few days and not allow her to jump or run around until her leg had begun to heal. Given the Boxer's personality, it was a task of gargantuan proportions. Blue, carrying an old rubber ball, its colour undefinable, ran back and forth with Jazz as they worked their way around the perimeter of the garden.

The cottage, which had been Clarice's childhood home, dated back to 1855, and had been subsequently enlarged over the years by various owners. A large part of the garden was a wildflower meadow, and there was a well-tended vegetable patch and a herb garden, the summer crop netted to protect it from rabbits. Further on were several outbuildings: Clarice's ceramics workshop, which looked like a small bungalow; a barn that had been converted to a garage and another semi-derelict barn. To one side of the wildflower meadow, accessed by a stone pathway, was a long, low building surrounded by an external enclosure, a temporary home for cats.

When Clarice had been in her late twenties, studying ceramics, her mother Mary had been diagnosed with terminal cancer and Clarice had returned home to nurse her. After Mary's death, she had remained at the cottage, developing her skills and reputation as a ceramicist and selling her work through galleries and exhibitions. When, almost twelve years ago, she had married Rick, then still a sergeant, it had seemed only natural to continue living here as a couple. When the relationship had broken down, it had been a shock. Rick had blamed himself, but Clarice had to admit that it was as much her fault as his. His work schedule was often gruelling, but her own was also hectic.

Earlier, as the sun was setting, the sky had been split into uneven lines of blue and yellow, with a blood-coloured slash that had flatlined onto the horizon. Now the light was disappearing. Clarice stood still for a moment to relish the beauty of her surroundings. It was becoming chilly, and the cold air wrapped around her bare arms and legs. She watched Blue and Jazz as they did an exuberant lap of the workshop before following her and Susie to the large willow tree. Dressed in its summer garb, its branches copiously leafy, it stirred gently with the night breeze.

Her thoughts went to Louise, and how she must be feeling. Then, as she turned to return to the cottage, the name James Wright came to mind: Louise had said that he was a good friend of Guy's. Tomorrow she would ask her for his contact details. Being in London at the end of the week presented an opportunity – if it could be arranged – to meet up with him and get his thoughts on Guy's disappearance and the possible reasons behind it. Once the arrangements had been made, she would tell Rick, though perhaps not until they were on their way to London, when it was too late to cancel.

Chapter 5

The following morning, having already walked the dogs and fed them and her own felines, Clarice was in the cat barn by 7 a.m. The building had been one long room until one of the charity volunteers, a builder by trade, had divided it into three. The small end section, having its own outside fenced space, was for the full-on feral cats. She fed the eight cats in the central part of the barn, plus Elsie, the feral, before going to the lactating queens and their litters.

The two sets of kittens were at different stages. Roma was black and white, with long hair, and had five almost-two-day-old kittens, their eyes not yet open. She had a big appetite, and left them for a few minutes to eagerly eat every scrap of her breakfast before returning to lie down and allow them to plug in for their feed. On the other side of the room was Ruby, a sleek, small black girl of about nine months. Clarice always felt sorry for the young mothers, not much more than kittens themselves, though luckily Ruby was turning out to be maternal. Black-and-white Riley and tabby-and-white Ryan, having taken their first steps five days ago aged three weeks, now staggered clumsily around like a couple of drunkards.

Both mothers had come in as pregnant strays and were friendly, used to being handled. When it came to choosing names to identify the animals, Clarice worked through the letters of the alphabet. She was currently on R. Elsie, the feral cat, had been named by Jonathan, who called any nameless creatures who came into his care after characters past or present from *Coronation Street*. Ena, the feistiest of Clarice's cats, had originated from him.

If Roma and Ruby had not been friendly, Clarice could not have put them together. Semi-feral cats that could be brought around came in regularly. Fully feral ones, and those too old or set in their ways to be rehomed as family pets, were destined to be placed as farm or barn cats. She wondered, looking at Roma and Ruby, if once their kittens had been adopted and they had been neutered, they might be rehomed as a pair. They got on so well together, it would be the perfect solution.

Returning to the larger room, she collected the empty dishes. Unlike the smaller rooms, this area had a sink with a drainer, a fridge and a corner table with a kettle, a jar of instant coffee and a small radio permanently tuned to Radio 4. The queens and their youngsters would progress here when the kittens were about six weeks old and were eating independently of their mothers. Socialising with the other cats would build their confidence before, depending upon their size, at between ten and twelve weeks, they were put up for adoption.

After washing and drying the dishes, Clarice checked the level of the water bowls and went to the three cats in various parts of the room to stroke and talk to them, then wandered outside into the run. The sun was bright in an almost cloudless blue sky, with no wind or movement in the trees and shrubs in the main garden.

The outdoor enclosure was netted with wire on all sides and the top so that the cats could come out into the safe space during the day. Both inside and out were boxes with large holes, hiding places for shy animals, used at the moment only by Polly, an extremely timid chocolate tortoiseshell in long-term foster care. The other four cats were arranged on top of the boxes or on the grass. Having just been fed, and indifferent to Clarice's presence, their main interest was their personal grooming.

Clarice knelt on the grass outside Polly's box and said her name, to be rewarded by the emergence of the cat's dark head. Although she was confident with Clarice, her extreme shyness made it difficult for would-be adopters to bond with her. Clarice remembered other cats with personality traits that had made them difficult to rehome. The longer they remained with her, the stronger the bond, and she worried about their futures, especially in the early hours of the morning, the time when, half in and half out of sleep, anxieties surfaced.

As she left the enclosure through the double gate, Clarice heard the approach of a car being driven down the incline from the road. It would be Sandra and Bob Todd, friends and volunteers, who helped with the animals. In the time it took to walk across the garden, they had beaten her to the kitchen, and as she entered, Sandra was already filling the kettle to make tea.

'Mornin', darlin',' she called over her shoulder, her east London voice carrying the giveaway rasp of the ex-smoker.

'Hi, Sandra,' Clarice said, going to one of the pine units to take out three mugs. The kitchen was bright and well lit, the walls decorated with framed posters of ceramics exhibitions in different parts of the UK and abroad. The bright red spiral staircase in one corner matched the Aga. A Victorian dresser, bought by Rick and Clarice the first year they were married, held wedding and family photographs, including one of Clarice's parents Mary and Frank. Clarice had known Sandra and Bob since her childhood; Sandra had been one of her mother's closest friends.

Bob, short, round and ruddy-complexioned, came in from the sitting room, followed by the dogs, Blue carrying a black sock stolen from the laundry bag.

'This one up for adoption?' he asked as Susie did her three-legged jig around the kitchen, showing her best moves, before stopping in front of Sandra.

Sandra bent to scratch her back. 'Hello, darlin', you're gorgeous.' The dog responded by throwing herself down on the floor, stretching out to reveal her belly.

'Aww, you got a poorly leg?' Sandra knelt beside her and began to gently rub and scratch with both hands.

Sandra was smaller than her husband, and at seventy-four, a year older. Her hair was dyed black, her eyes darkly made up and her lipstick her signature deep pink: she always carried a lippy in the back pocket of her trousers.

Clarice looked at Bob. 'She's just come to stay for a while – family troubles.'

'She's lovely,' Bob said. 'I wondered why you'd shut the dogs in the sitting room.'

'I didn't want her running off. I was trying to beat you to the house when I heard your car – she's got form as an escape artist. Let's have a cuppa,' she added, seeing Bob's puzzled expression, 'and I'll fill you in.'

Half an hour later, the three of them were still sitting around the pine kitchen table, their mugs empty in front of them. Blue rested her face in Sandra's lap, where she had deposited the now damp sock. Clarice had given them the same information about Guy she'd given Jonathan.

'Poor Louise,' Bob said. 'Hope he's turned up by now.'

'Me too.' Clarice sighed. 'But I'm not optimistic. Louise would've called if there was any news.'

'It'll be good for the kids to come over and see their dog,' Sandra said.

'It's something, but they must be upset and confused.'

'Have you fed the cats?' Bob asked, moving the conversation briskly to the normality of the daily tasks.

'Sorted,' said Clarice, then, more thoughtfully, 'I do wish Polly could get more confidence – she seems to have stopped making progress.'

Sandra collected the mugs and walked with them to the sink. 'She's a little belter, but nobody ever gets close enough to understand that.'

'She came to us from an old lady who led a very quiet life. When her health declined, she had to go into a care home.'

'I remember. You told us the neighbours didn't even know she had a cat, so nobody knew her name,' Bob said. 'That was the house with all the dishes?'

'Yes, dishes, saucers, plates,' Clarice said, her voice forlorn. 'At least ten in every room. Poor old Mrs Higgins, her dementia was getting worse and she couldn't remember if she'd fed her, so she just kept putting more down and never picked them up again.'

'Polly's age is against her,' Bob said. 'Jonathan thought she'd be around ten.'

'That's not bleedin' old!' Sandra protested. 'Cats can go on to twenty.'

'I know that,' Bob shot back, 'but how many people want the older ones? That's why Clarice always has so many – she ends up keeping the problem ones nobody else wants.'

'I do get what Bob means,' Clarice said. 'We know ten isn't old, but most people want kittens, so they won't even look at the older ones.'

'I know how he means it, darlin',' Sandra said, smiling at her husband.

He nodded affably.

Clarice smiled. Anyone who didn't know the couple might think they didn't get on. But both felt comfortable bluntly disagreeing with the other on any subject. Their relationship had lasted for over fifty years and given them two daughters and much companionship.

'What needs doing this morning, Clarice?' Bob asked.

'Your favourite job,' Clarice said with a cheeky grin.

'Cash and carry?'

She nodded.

'Good,' Sandra laughed. 'I get the mums and kittens for their next feed – *my* favourite job.'

'Have you checked what we need?' Bob said, getting up.

'No, although I do know we're low on dry food for the cats. I've left the checking to you.'

Later, as Bob was leaving, he asked, 'Is Georgie coming in this morning?'

'No, I phoned her last night and Jessica's much better, but she won't be in until tomorrow. She has the use of her husband's van on Friday, so she's going to take the small tables to Jayne's.'

'And we're doing the tea and coffee at the fund-raiser?' Sandra asked.

'Yes, if that's still all right with you.'

'It is,' Sandra said, 'and Friday night we're staying over while you and Rick are in London.' She turned to Susie. 'And we'll remember not to leave the door open so *you* don't get out and do a runner. Though let's hope your master's turned up by then and you've gone home.'

Chapter 6

Later, after a lunch of sandwiches and fruit cake, Bob and Sandra left and Clarice went into the workshop, leaving the dogs in the cottage. Usually Blue and Jazz, used to her routine, would accompany her. On entering she would switch on the radio, while both dogs climbed onto a small sofa in the corner of the workshop. But though Susie had settled well inside the cottage, the workshop would be a new space for her and today Clarice didn't have time to keep an eye on her, needing to focus on checking what she would take to London on Friday.

The eight large vases she was exhibiting were all new designs, immediately recognisable as the work of Clarice Beech. Like most artists/makers she had over the years developed her own style. Mary, her mother, had been an amateur hobbyist ceramicist, learning her skills at local evening classes from the late 1960s, when those who produced kiln-fired items in clay were described as potters. Mary had loved the work of Clarice Cliff, and when her daughter was born had stolen her Christian name.

The vases, all between two and three feet in height, in dazzling reds and oranges, had gone last week, together with the display plinths they'd stand on to bring them to eye level. John Jackson, one of the four makers in the exhibition, had access to a Transit van belonging to his father, who used it for his flower-growing business in Spalding. John had collected Clarice's work and that of Ros Ford. The fourth ceramicist, Jerry Caldecott, who produced miniature items, would take his own pieces directly to the gallery on Friday morning to set up.

Clarice brought out a large red plastic box and began going through its contents: a poster, in colour, with an image of one of her large vases, below which was an artist's statement; her leaflets, giving a short CV, with several photographs of pieces that had been sold over the years; labels produced on her home printer to identify each piece, Blu Tack, price lists and her business cards. There was also an unused visitors' book, where those attending the preview or the week-long exhibition could comment on the show, or leave contact details.

She repacked the box and added some unused ballpoint pens to go with the visitors' book. She felt the familiar twinge of nerves, her stomach twisting. It was part excitement, part fear. Would all the pieces so carefully bubble-wrapped and packaged in boxes arrive intact, or might one or more reach the gallery with a chip to its surface or, just as bad, a fine crack? Would her new work be well received, and how would it stand in comparison to her fellow makers? Despite having participated in many exhibitions over the years, each time was always like the first. What she was putting out there was part of herself, from the first thought to the full design, and then the production of each piece. It was like standing naked in a room full of strangers and asking what people thought; her work came from and was part of her being.

Back in the cottage, she went to the utility room store cupboard off the kitchen. After a short search, she found two Frisbees, a football, two racquets, five shuttlecocks and a small kite. Laying out the paltry collection on the kitchen table, she realised that now that most of her friends' children had grown up, she rarely had young visitors and the stock of items on offer had never been replenished. She could not imagine that Guy's daughters, with their sophisticated London mother, would find anything to interest them.

Going into the garden, she set to weeding the vegetable patch. She always watered later in the day when it was cooler. Usually while performing these tasks she would be thinking about cats that needed rehoming, or designs for her pots, but today her thoughts were on Guy.

At just gone 2 p.m., as arranged, Louise's green Land Rover pulled up outside. Making sure that she closed the kitchen door firmly to keep the three dogs inside, Clarice went out to meet her guests. Louise climbed out before helping her granddaughters to remove their seat belts and jump down from the back of the vehicle. Clarice smiled at the children. It was easy to see they were sisters. Both were leggy and had shoulder-length blonde hair with a fringe and blue eyes. Angel, however, taller by a head, was stouter and robust, while Poppy was thin and wiry. They looked, Clarice mused, like smaller versions of their mother.

'Hello,' they chorused, both looking up shyly through their tousled fringes.

'You don't remember me,' Clarice said, 'but I met you when you were little.'

They looked at one another, and then at their grandmother.

'I told you Clarice had met you when you were staying with me while Mummy and Daddy were in London – it was about three years ago.'

'You were toddlers.' Clarice nodded in agreement.

'I think I can remember,' Angel said.

'I don't think so,' Louise said, laughing.

'Our daddy's gone away,' Poppy said.

'He's working,' Angel said sharply. 'He'll come home at the weekend, like he always does.'

Poppy looked at her sister but did not reply.

'Were you always big?' Angel said as she raised her hand higher and higher until she was standing on her toes.

'Clarice is tall, Angel,' Louise said, 'but she's not big – she's amazingly slim.'

'I would remember you if you were *always* tall,' Angel said.

'A giant,' Poppy said, 'more tall than my daddy.'

'Taller,' Louise corrected.

From the kitchen, the gang of three began to bark.

'Is that Susie?' Angel shouted, clapping her hands.

Clarice nodded, going to the door. 'Shall I let them out?'

'Yes, yes!' both girls chanted.

'Now be calm and hold my hands, or you'll overexcite them,' said Louise. 'Remember there are three dogs.'

'Yes, Grandma.' The girls, restraining themselves obediently, took the proffered hands and stood still.

Once the door was opened, the three dogs bounded out joyfully, Blue in the lead, carrying a red rubber bone, followed by Jazz and Susie. After a couple of minutes of excitement, Clarice called her dogs to order while Susie went to the sisters, who wrapped their arms around her. She calmed immediately

44

and stood perfectly still, apart from the incessant swishing of her tail.

'She is so good with the children,' Clarice said, impressed.

'I know Boxers often have a reputation of being overexcitable, but Guy insisted that if they had a dog, it must be trained to be gentle and obedient around children,' Louise said.

'I'm with him on that,' Clarice said. 'I rarely get a bad dog come in needing a new home, but I do sadly meet a lot of bad owners.' She mentally ticked another box: Guy had managed to turn Susie into a well-behaved member of their family. 'Let's go and sit in the garden.' She led the way. 'I'll go inside and get some drinks in a minute.'

'This was such a good idea, Clarice,' Louise said an hour later as they sat at the wooden table in the shadow of the cottage, watching the two girls.

They had walked the boundary of the garden before coming back for home-made lemonade and cake. The girls were now throwing the bright orange Frisbees for Blue and Jazz to retrieve while Susie watched on a short lead, Clarice stroking her head to make up for the fact that she wasn't allowed to join in.

It was the first opportunity they had had to talk alone.

'How is Charlotte coping?' Clarice asked.

'Not good. Tara's been a godsend – I don't know how she'd have managed without her.'

'She's from Charlotte's first marriage?'

'That's right, though she was only a toddler when Guy and her mother married. Her father moved to Australia with his new wife but sadly died in a car accident. Guy has been the only father she's known. He adores her, although ...'

Clarice waited, her expression puzzled.

'She's made Paul – her birth father – into the absent hero.' Louise raised her eyebrows in exasperation. 'I hope it's a phase that she'll get through. Guy told me that if he refuses her something, she says her *real* father would have let her have it.'

'I guess that's a way to get what she wants. All children must try it on at times, in whatever way they can.' Clarice smiled. 'She didn't want to come today to see Susie?'

'No.' Louise laughed. 'How to say this to someone who runs a rescue? Tara is not an animal person.'

'Not a dog lover?'

'Not dogs, cats, rabbits – whatever. She wouldn't do anything to harm them, of course. If she was told that Susie needed feeding or taking for a walk because her mum and dad were busy – she'd do it.' Louise paused. 'She's a good girl, you know. Please don't mention to Charlotte what I told you about her. I don't think she'd like it if she thought Guy had been criticising his stepdaughter to me.'

'Don't worry, I wouldn't repeat what you've said. My lips are sealed.'

'You'll know that Charlotte had a visit from a police officer – DI Tony Simpson,' Louise said. 'Do you know him?'

'Yes – a decent bloke and an excellent officer. You're in good hands.'

'I don't want to be in good hands.' Louise was suddenly sharp. 'I just want to know my boy is safe.'

'Yes,' Clarice said, 'of course. You're in such a horrible place – I can only imagine what you're going through.'

'I appreciate that, Clarice.' Louise's voice had lost the snappish edge. She watched her grandchildren as she spoke. 'People say all the right things, and sometimes they try to empathise, but if they've never been in that position themselves, it rings hollow.'

Clarice waited, feeling that Louise needed to talk.

'It happened when Martin died. His death fell two days before Christmas. You'd be amazed how many people were crass enough to say, "What a terrible thing to happen at Christmas".' Louise gave a shrill laugh; the children turned momentarily to look and then went back to playing. 'As if the time of year had any relevance. Easter, the summer holiday, it would have been the same – ridiculous!'

'My own father died in December, so I do understand what you mean,' Clarice said. 'People are uncomfortable talking about death, and sometimes they say stupid things because they feel awkward, but I'm sure most mean well.'

Louise turned to face her. 'Yes, I remember. And you were only a couple of years older than Guy was when his father died.' She was thoughtful. 'You're right, of course, but at the time, when you're in that sad place, it's so hard just to get from one day to the next. It was Guy who kept me going.'

'Do you have other family?'

'Only an older sister, Madge; she and her husband live in Yorkshire. And like you and Guy, Charlotte's an only child, so there are no aunts, uncles or cousins for the girls.'

A silence fell between them, and they both continued to watch the dogs now being chased by the children.

Clarice broke the silence. 'Have you had any more thoughts about why Guy might have disappeared?'

'I've thought about nothing else.' Louise stroked the tabletop absent-mindedly. 'I believe there can only be one reason: the man he went with – Charles – must be connected to what he was working on.'

'You're ruling out the depression.'

'Not entirely. But going with this man, someone he obviously knew and trusted, and then just disappearing . . .' She looked directly at Clarice. 'What else can we conclude?'

'Would you have any objections to my contacting James Wright?' Clarice asked. 'I'm in London on Friday with Rick.'

'Do you think it would help? The police will surely have spoken to him already.'

'It's a long shot, but as I'm going to be there anyway . . .'

Louise sat in silence for a few moments, as if weighing up the suggestion.

'I'll phone you with his contact details when I get home,' she said, a new resolve in her voice, 'and you will let me know what he says – truthfully?'

'I promise, I won't hold anything back.'

Looking at her friend, Clarice could see tears running down her face. Louise stood, turning so that her back was to the children, brushing them quickly away. 'I don't want the girls to see me crying,' she said. She suddenly reached out to clutch Clarice's hand. 'Help me find my boy, Clarice. I need to know that he's safe – it's killing me thinking the worst.'

'I'll do my very best,' Clarice said quietly.

Letting go of her hand, Louise turned to the children, her face alight with a fixed smile. 'Grandma has to go now to see the doctor,' she said. 'Be good girls for Clarice – best behaviour – and later she'll take you home to Mummy.'

Chapter 7

As she was adjusting the seat belts and strapping the girls into the back of her car, Clarice realised that Rick had not phoned. He'd returned to a routine familiar before their estrangement, calling her on his mobile when he had a quiet moment. It didn't bode well; it meant he had been too busy to take breaks. Clarice tried to think optimistically – maybe he was saving his chat for tonight, at supper with Jonathan and Keith.

She lost her train of thought as Poppy, for the fifth time, asked why Susie couldn't go with them. Clarice repeated that Susie would come home soon, and that before that, they could visit again to play with her.

'It's because her leg is sore,' Angel informed her sister bossily.

The subject changed when Poppy noticed there were sheep in a field they were passing. This rapidly moved to the different types of farm animals, and the noises they made.

Following the route dictated by her satnav, Clarice found herself outside the small village of Heathby, which she had driven through many times. Two miles past the last house, she turned onto a long road, green fields full of grazing sheep on either side, along with the occasional cottage. And then, as she rounded a tight bend, a dazzling of the sun against glass drew her gaze to the left, and she had her first glimpse of Lark House.

She felt an immediate connection to the contemporary property, its clean contours nestling in a green hollow. Louise had told her that it was a barn conversion, a modern architect-designed building, but this far exceeded her expectations. She slowed down to a crawl to take in the rectangular design, which incorporated slanted roofs, concrete and glass. It had unspoilt aspects from all four sides, with views across the undulating countryside and, at the back, over rising woodland that covered between three and four acres. She imagined, however, that the house would not be to everybody's taste: many of her friends and neighbours were traditionalists and would see too great a conflict between the lush, bucolic splendour of the Wolds setting and this modernist building. To turn the bend in the road and come upon the property would be for them like finding a tree wearing a Vivienne Westwood dress.

'It's here, Clarice,' Angel informed her from the back seat, impatient, not understanding why she had slowed the car. For the sisters, this was their home – normality – not something new and exciting.

Yes,' Clarice said, 'I can see.'

She drove across a bridge over the river, reaching the entrance a few yards along on the other side. Slate in a steel mount to one side of the gateway announced in hand-engraved lettering: *Lark House*. On the other side of the open wrought-iron gates, the plum-coloured bricks that made up the driveway stretched seemingly endlessly, drawing the eye in a straight line to the house. To the left, below the woods, the river curved around the garden boundary.

As Clarice parked next to a new white Mercedes whose personalised number plate indicated Charlotte to be its owner, she considered how much this house must have cost in building and maintenance. Given Guy and Charlotte's professions there would have been no financial problem, though, and Charlotte might also have brought inherited wealth to the marriage.

As she unbuckled the children, Charlotte emerged from the house, a thin woman with a perfect tan, wearing a green silk sheath dress and gold-coloured sandals. Her well-cut blonde hair hung to just above her shoulders, swinging as she moved her head.

'Have you had a good time?' she asked as she came towards the children.

'Yes!' the sisters chorused.

'How are you, Clarice?' She put her arms wide, not touching but encompassing Clarice to air-kiss somewhere near her left ear. 'Thank you for having Susie, and for letting the children come over. Did Louise get away to the GP on time?'

'Yes,' said Clarice, 'with time to spare.'

'Good, come in and have some tea with me.' Charlotte turned as she spoke, with the unquestioning assumption that Clarice would follow.

Inside, the house was light and airy. The ground floor incorporated a kitchen, dining and living area. The kitchen units were hardwood, with quartz worktops, and there was marble flooring throughout. The furnishings were sparse but adequate, the centrepiece six matching Arne Jacobsen steel and plywood chairs arranged around a marble-topped dining table. At one end of the L-shaped open-plan space was a staircase, its thick open treads made of recycled sanded railway sleepers.

Clarice's second thought, her first being a mix of admiration and envy, was to wonder how, with two young children, Charlotte kept the place so tidy.

A chubby teenager with short curly hair, wearing jeans and a T-shirt, came from the kitchen area to greet them.

'Hi, I'm Tara,' she said, giving Clarice a smile. 'Sorry I didn't come over today. I had things to do. It was kind of you to include me in the invitation.' As she reached her, she offered Clarice her hand.

'It's so nice to meet you,' Clarice said, thinking how unusual it was for a fifteen-year-old to be so confident. At that age she would not have thought to formally introduce herself.

'We played with Clarice's dogs,' Poppy informed her half-sister.

'And Susie,' Angel said, then after a moment's pause and a glance at Clarice, '*our* dog.'

There was, Clarice realised, an apprehension in Angel that she might not get her dog back.

'Clarice's dogs are called Blue and Jazz, and Jazz has the longest tail in the world,' Poppy said, 'even longer than Susie's.'

'Wow, that must be long,' Tara smiled.

'Earl Grey OK with you, Clarice, or do you prefer green?' Charlotte called from the kitchen.

'Earl Grey would be lovely,' Clarice said, walking over to her. Builder's tea clearly wasn't on the menu.

'Come on, let's get your drawing box out and we can show Clarice how clever you are,' Tara said to the two younger girls.

'She's so good with them,' Clarice said in a low voice to Charlotte as she watched the girls go to a small cupboard to bring out a blue plastic box containing paper, crayons and pencils. They took it to a stainless-steel and glass coffee table and sat down on a woven rug on the floor in front of it.

'Yes, she's fantastic,' Charlotte murmured. 'I don't know how I'd get through without her.'

Clarice fleetingly saw the distress in her eyes, then, with a blink and a movement of her head it was gone, her eyelids shutters to hide the pain. But her jerky movements, uptight and controlled as she moved about the kitchen, gave her away. Like her mother-in-law, distress was not far below the surface.

At the coffee table, three heads bent together, Tara's brown one next to the younger girls' blonde. While Angel and Poppy were unquestionably their mother's daughters, Tara, Clarice thought, must be more like her father, Charlotte's first husband, with her heavier nose and chin. The two younger girls had tanned skin, while Tara's face and arms were pink where she had caught the sun.

Charlotte, as if reading Clarice's mind, said, 'Tara takes after her father, my first husband, Paul.'

'Louise told me that you married Guy when Tara was quite young,' Clarice said.

'Yes, I knew it was a mistake with Paul from the beginning. He moved to live in Australia with wife number two.'

'I understand he died there?'

'A car accident.' Charlotte spoke without emotion.

'How awful for Tara!'

'She didn't know him. I met and married Guy when she was two, and to all intents and purpose he's her father. They're very close.'

'A happy ending.' Clarice, remembering what Louise had told her, realised that Charlotte had a firmly fixed view of the relationship between her daughter and husband. Either that or she wanted the world to view her family as serene and unconflicted, whatever the reality.

'It should be.' Charlotte, wrapping her hand tightly around her mug, moved her head and blinked again, as if a wave of angst had suddenly engulfed her and she had to fight to curb the emotional turmoil, to keep it under control. The situation would be, Clarice reflected, painful for anyone, but for someone as buttoned up as Charlotte, it must be sheer hell.

'Have the police told you if they've found out who Charles is?'

'No.' Charlotte looked at her mug of tea rather than at Clarice. 'I knew he was coming to the house. Guy needed to talk to him about some business, but I didn't take much notice. I thought he would be back quite soon. You would not believe how guilty I feel.'

Clarice glanced at her, surprised at her frankness: she'd had the impression Charlotte wasn't the type to open up, especially to someone she hardly knew.

'You can't know all his business contacts,' she said. 'Why should you?'

Charlotte shrugged. 'I suppose so. We're in different professions – he doesn't know my business acquaintances either.'

'So, no reason to feel guilty,' Clarice said. 'You can only tell it like it is.'

'I told the officer it was a white car, though I didn't take in the type, but Louise and James, his friend in chambers, seem to share the opinion that I should have seen more.'

'But you weren't expecting him to vanish.'

'Quite.' Charlotte looked at Clarice as if awakening from a

dream, then fell silent for a few moments before speaking again, her voice guarded. 'We argued the evening before; it was about something and nothing – his work, the bloody job – but then this happened . . .' She put her mug of tea down and pressed her hands together hard in her lap, turning her knuckles white.

'So maybe that's the reason you feel guilty. But everyone argues occasionally – it's normal.' As she spoke, Clarice remembered her own situation with Rick leading up to their estrangement, weeks of bickering about the time each prioritised for their work.

'Yes,' Charlotte stared at her, 'but later you make up, apologise, whatever . . .'

'It must be upsetting that you didn't sort it out,' Clarice said. 'Why did Guy not just invite Charles into the house?'

'He said it was a serious business meeting. I thought, as he wasn't catching a train to London until midday, they'd drive to the Ludlows' farm shop. They have a café that opens at seven, so it would have been quiet. Do you know it?'

'Yes, of course, the best coffee shop. I love their organic veg and sausages. It's only about twenty minutes from here, isn't it?'

'Quite,' Charlotte repeated, in her precise manner. 'When Guy uses the word *serious*, it means that two small children running around would not fit the bill. It might have been different if Tara had been here – she would have kept an eye on them – but she'd had a sleepover at her friend Amy's house in Heathby village.'

'You didn't know what the serious business was?'

'No, but he has been really down about the case he's working on. It's not like him to bring his work home, or to make such a big deal about the need to talk privately, away from the house, but . . .'

'He has done with this one.'

Charlotte nodded, then changed the subject, casting her gaze critically through the kitchen into the open living space. 'I lost my cleaner. With all that's going on, I phoned and asked her not to come in this week. She told me she wouldn't be coming back – but in less polite language!'

'That's awkward.' Clarice sensed that Charlotte felt more emotion about the prospect of finding a new cleaner than she did about the death of her first husband. 'You certainly need help here; it's a big house, and you work.'

'I can't manage without one. Helen came three afternoons a week. She's a bit sour, but she got on with the job.' Charlotte sniffed. 'Helen Ambrose, have you come across her? She has several employers; she's a cleaner, and also works for an agency as a carer.'

'No, is she from Heathby?' As she spoke, Clarice pondered. Cleaners and carers were usually on minimum hourly pay. Had Charlotte, when telling her not to come in that week, offered to pay her regardless? She suspected not, given that the woman was clearly aggrieved.

'She's from Castlewick,' Charlotte said. 'She'd get the bus that goes through Heathby to Skegness – it stops at the junction, ten minutes' walk away.'

'Clarice, look at this!' Angel ran to the table, ending their conversation. She held a drawing in crayon. 'It's Susie, Blue and Jazz.'

'Wow!' Clarice took the blue and brown masterpiece.

'Mine too!' Poppy followed with another drawing of the dogs, in red and yellow.

'She always copies me,' Angel said. 'You've missed out Susie,' she added to her sister.

'Aww,' Poppy groaned, going back to the table.

'It's because I'm the oldest,' Angel said wearily.

'Actually, I'm the oldest,' Tara said with a smile.

Angel thought for a moment. 'I'm the oldest out of us two.' She pointed at Poppy. 'The children.'

'I can't argue with that.' Tara grinned at her mother and Clarice.

'What about you, Clarice?' Charlotte asked. 'Any brothers or sisters?'

'No, I'm an only child,' Clarice stated, remembering how she'd longed for siblings when she was Tara's age. But then again, being an only child had given her a self-sufficiency that had stood her in good stead.

On the journey home, Clarice wondered what, if anything, Charlotte might know about Helen Ambrose. If Helen was on minimum wage, giving up on an employer who paid her for three afternoons a week might have been a rash move. Her mind moved on to phone calls, the one that she had not received from Rick, and the message Louise might have left on the house phone with the contact details for James.

Once she'd parked outside the cottage, she checked her mobile – no missed calls or messages from Rick. Trying to suppress her feeling of disappointment, she went indoors to feed the animals and get changed. There was still time; he might be planning to turn up on time and surprise her. The pleasures of solitude, she felt, had their limitations.

Chapter 8

'He doesn't know what he's missing.' Jonathan beamed broadly at Clarice across the dining table. After his third blue gin, he'd gone on to red wine, with both the starter of walnut pâté en croute and the main of smoked salmon with mussels on a bed of aubergine puree and rocket salad. His voice had developed the faintest slur.

The low-ceilinged kitchen was small, its window overlooking an area of paved patio displaying large pots filled with herbs. Opposite the window stood a large top-of-the-range orange Italian cooker. Above, in a line, like a row of roosting hens, hung bright copper pans with red handles.

'You have such an unsophisticated palate,' Keith said archly, looking at Jonathan's glass. 'You should be drinking white wine, not the bloody red. I bought this dry white especially.'

'Nobody bothers about that nonsense these days.' Jonathan flicked his hand in the air dismissively as he reached over to the bottle to replenish his glass. 'And you know I prefer red!'

'When it suits.' Keith rolled his eyes at Clarice, who gave a non-committal smile in response. Keith's father was English, but he had inherited his French mother's dark brown eyes, tanned complexion and black hair, though Clarice suspected that to keep the colour so dark required a little help. He was in his mid-fifties, but it was still as black as tar.

'Rick's still hoping to get here for the pudding – or some coffee,' she said. She never took sides; the badinage between the two men was familiar. And she knew Jonathan enjoyed white wine every bit as much as red. Their relationship was like elastic, stretched and tested first by one and then the other. When it was Jonathan doing the cooking, it would be Keith's turn to upstage him.

'Poor Rick.' Keith paused his fork midway between his plate and his mouth. 'He does miss out with the hours he works.'

'I'm sorry he's not here as planned. Daisy phoned—'

'That's the sergeant who works with Rick?' Keith interrupted.

'Yes, they've had to go to Leeds to speak to witnesses. Rick was still tied up, but he asked her to call me,' Clarice said. 'Thanks for collecting me, Jonathan.'

'No problem. If Rick doesn't turn up, you'll only have to get a taxi one way, and won't have to worry about collecting your car tomorrow.' Jonathan observed Clarice inquisitively over the rim of his glass for a moment. 'Isn't it the death at the printing works that Rick's working on?'

'Yes, Ben Abbot,' Clarice said.

'So it's a murder case.' Jonathan looked at Keith as he spoke.

'We all know Rick only works on murder cases, clever clogs,' Keith mocked.

Clarice picked up her own glass and sipped her wine without comment.

'Guy still hasn't returned home?' Keith enquired.

'Sadly not.'

'Poor Louise must be desperate for news, and Guy is such a sweet man. He came and did work experience with me a very long time ago. He was still at school, but was quite sure, even then, that he wanted to work in the legal profession.'

'And he's stayed in touch,' Jonathan interjected.

'Yes, I don't see much of him, but he does phone on occasion and suggest a drink.'

'And Charlotte?' Clarice asked.

'Charlotte's a tad on the starchy side for me. My friendship is with Guy. We've always got on well; he says I'm easy to talk to.'

'Did you know he was having problems?' Clarice said. 'Or a crisis that might have forced him to up sticks and go?'

'I haven't seen him for a few weeks – work commitments for both of us.'

'Back to bloody work again – it always takes over. We need Rick in on this conversation!' Jonathan hiccuped before taking another slug of wine and sinking back into his seat. Keith had designed and made a set of generously large cushions to ensure the nineteenth-century yew Windsor chairs were as comfortable as possible.

There was a long silence.

'I'm thinking about Martin.' Keith looked at Jonathan, his voice reflective.

'Yes.' Jonathan put his glass down, suddenly sober. 'Poor Guy, life hasn't always been easy for him. I'm not sure how someone ever gets over the death of a child.'

'Martin was his son?' Clarice said.

'Yes,' Keith nodded, 'his and Charlotte's firstborn – Tara was five then.'

'I didn't know they'd lost a child,' Clarice said. 'Louise has never mentioned it. Martin was the name of her late husband.'

'Yes, they named the boy after his grandfather. I think it's probably too painful for Louise to talk about,' Jonathan replied.

'It was a cot death,' Keith said. 'I don't think Martin was very old – maybe two months. Guy was devastated. He'd gone into the nursery to check and found him dead.'

'That's so sad.' Clarice felt overwhelmed with sorrow, not only for Guy but also for Charlotte and Louise.

'He suffered from depression afterwards,' Keith said. 'He took unpaid leave from his chambers – didn't want it to affect his career.'

'I didn't know that,' Clarice said.

'Don't say anything to Louise,' Keith said quickly. 'When Guy returns, I don't want him thinking I've dropped him *dans la merde*.'

'Of course not.' Clarice wondered how much gin Keith had drunk before she'd arrived. The possibility of him drifting into French increased with the amount of alcohol he'd consumed. He especially favoured obscure swear words learned from his volatile mother, something he wouldn't have countenanced when sober. 'I thought he had a good relationship with Louise – why did he not tell her he wasn't coping?'

'Well . . .' Keith exchanged another look with Jonathan.

'Don't tell me,' Clarice said, 'stiff upper lip and all that?'

'Yes, in part,' Keith said, and there was a pause while Clarice imagined he was considering how much to tell her. 'Louise was overprotective of him as a child – that's Charlotte's opinion. She also has set ideas about how men should behave; she would have told Guy to man up and pull himself together.'

'Guy told you that?'

'Pretty much,' Keith said. 'I also think,' he leaned forward, 'that Charlotte is jealous of the relationship between Guy and his mother. If she wants to wind him up, she teases him, calls him a mummy's boy.'

'I knew Louise and Charlotte weren't close,' Clarice said, 'but it sounds like there's a reason why.'

'Louise knew he'd taken time off work after baby Martin died, but she didn't know how much, nor that most of it was unpaid,' Keith said. 'He thought she wouldn't understand depression, she'd see it as a weakness. It caused friction between Guy and Louise, and Charlotte couldn't see why his mother's good opinion was of such concern to a grown man.'

'Caught between the two of them,' Clarice said thoughtfully.

'It seems so, but it has improved since.'

'Yes.' Jonathan nodded.

'How?' Clarice asked.

'The girls, of course,' Keith said, as if stating the obvious. 'Louise adores her grandchildren and counts Tara as one of her own – she wants to be part of their lives.'

'And,' Jonathan butted in, 'Charlotte enjoys having a baby-sitter who's available at a moment's notice, so they both work harder at being friends.'

'So much better for Guy,' Clarice noted.

Jonathan and Keith looked at one another and Clarice read from their glance that she'd not been told the full story.

'Then they had a problem with Angel,' Jonathan said.

'What was that?' Clarice asked.

'She has a nut allergy.' It was Keith who replied.

'Yes, I know. Louise told me she couldn't eat anything nut-related – I made sure there were none at the cottage when the girls came over.'

'Guy told me that he thought Angel had shared lunch boxes with of one of her school friends. That was how she ate something containing nuts. She wouldn't admit it because she didn't want to get her friend into trouble.'

'Thank goodness it was discovered in time,' Clarice said.

'That's down to Tara,' Keith said.

'Although,' Jonathan joined in, 'there is a lot of uncertainty about what can trigger an allergy; it's not cut and dried. You can't always trace the source. But Tara is so loving with her sisters – so protective.'

'She was lovely when I took the girls home to their mother.'

'Tara found Angel after she'd eaten whatever it was that contained the nuts,' Keith continued, 'and told her mother something was wrong.'

'I hate to say this, but Angel can be a little monkey,' Jonathan said.

'In what way?' Clarice asked.

'She's a tad resentful of Poppy.'

'The green-eyed monster.' Keith nodded in agreement.

'She was certainly playing the big sister with her,' Clarice said, 'but there was no hostility.'

'Mmm, I'd disagree,' Jonathan said. 'I think Tara gets attention as the oldest, and Poppy as the baby of the family. Angel's the resentful one in the middle. I've seen her being rough with Poppy – snatching things from her – and she can play at being ill. Ask Louise, she'll tell you: it's attention-seeking.'

'I'm an only child,' Clarice said, 'so I have no personal experience, but don't you get sibling rivalry with most children of that age?'

'Perhaps.' Jonathan shrugged. 'I can only give my own opinion.' He looked at Keith. 'She took those pills from Guy.'

'Yes,' Keith stated. 'Sleeping pills. Guy said she must have thought they were sweets.'

'Did she admit she'd taken them?'

'No, she told them at the hospital that she couldn't remember.'

'How awful,' Clarice said.

'Guy and Charlotte had the hospital welfare worker on their doorstep.'

'It must have been hell – no wonder Louise didn't tell me.'

'But they're lucky with Tara, she's a rock. She's been so supportive,' Keith said.

'And she's bright,' Jonathan added. 'Guy said she's a whizz with computers, and driving that friend's old banger.'

'I thought she was only fifteen?' Clarice said, puzzled.

'She is,' Keith agreed, 'but she's passionate about wanting to learn to drive. Guy taught her; she practises with Charlotte's old VW on their land. Also a car belonging to a friend on a property that was once part of an airfield. Guy said she's itching to reach seventeen, pass her test and get out on the roads.'

'Another reason perhaps for Angel's jealousy, Tara taking attention away from her with everything she does?' Jonathan suggested. 'After the problem with the pills, Guy said they sat Angel down and had a good talk, no more fibs. They explained that her mum and dad would get into big trouble. She's young, but I think she got the message.'

'When did all this happen?'

'The nut thing was maybe a month ago; the sleeping pills a couple of weeks back,' Keith said.

'No problems since?' Clarice asked.

'None that I'm aware of. Now let's top up our wine and go sit in the garden. We'll have a pause before pudding.'

'Yes, let's,' Jonathan agreed, as if eager to get away from the sombre mood that had fallen upon them. 'We can have our pud and coffee out there with or without Rick.'

As the light began to fade, Keith gave a throaty rendition of 'J'ai pas d'regrets', despite Jonathan reminding him that they had neighbours he'd have to face the next morning.

At 10.30, having left a message for Rick to say she was heading home, Clarice was picked up by Doris Lewis, or Doris the Taxi, as she was known, the only female taxi driver in Castlewick, a beat she'd worked for fifteen years.

'Thank you both so much.' She went first to Jonathan and then Keith for a hug before leaving. As she slipped into Doris's taxi, Jonathan, one arm around Keith's neck, called, 'See you on Saturday!' and blew kisses with his free hand.

Riding home, she reflected what good friends they had been to her. During her months of estrangement from Rick, there had been numerous evenings such as this when one or the other, sensing her despondency, had insisted she join them for supper. Going back over the conversation, she realised that Keith would not have been so indiscreet about Guy had it not been for the quantity of gin and wine he had supped. She hoped he didn't regret it tomorrow.

Chapter 9

At home, she found a text from Rick. *Sorry I missed you – on my way back from Leeds, will stay at number 24 and fill you in tomorrow, sleep tight xx.*

Satisfied that he was safely back in Castlewick, Clarice went through her usual routines, giving the lactating queens extra food and walking the dogs. The night was warm and still, and there was a strange comfort in walking around the silent garden, lit only by the moon and stars. Passing the herb garden, the odour of mint caught for a moment in her throat, making her reflect on Louise's herb business, then her thoughts flew on to Guy and his family. The Corkindales and their problems remained with her as she left the three dogs together in baskets in the kitchen, turned off the light and climbed the stairs, navigating the dog gate at the bottom that she'd put up to prevent Susie from attempting the climb.

Dressed in one of Rick's old T-shirts, she spotted her reflection in the long bedroom mirror. The T-shirt, once a fetching shade of cornflower blue, had over the years lost shape and colour, comfortable for sleeping in when she was alone, but hardly attractive. She made a mental note to include something black and silky in her bag for London, in case Rick did go with her.

Despite the long day, she didn't feel tired; her mind moved, shifting to refocus on events since Guy's disappearance. She got into bed and propped herself against the headboard, pulling her knees up to wrap her arms around them.

Before going out for supper, she'd found a message from Louise on the house phone. It gave the contact details for James; she'd phoned him immediately, delighted when he'd agreed to meet her in London on Friday. Now all she had to do was tell Rick. She hoped his reaction would be positive.

Keith had called Charlotte starchy, which although unkind appeared accurate: nothing about her suggested either empathy or a sense of humour. She clearly had her sights set on particular goals: her career, the children, expensive cars and the impeccable home. Most people would envy her lifestyle. Clarice, pondering for a few moments, rested her head on her duvet-covered knees. Charlotte Corkindale gave the impression of being overly self-contained, curled into a small tight parcel and tied up with string, everything exact and perfect. It could not be easy to control every aspect of her life, keeping it all faultless. If Guy wasn't found and the stress continued and intensified, how quickly might she fall apart? It would not be a gentle process. She was wound so tight that her distress at her loss of control might be the flame that made her combust. And how would that affect the girls?

Clarice wondered what the quarrel with Guy might have been about – something trivial, Charlotte had said.

Her thoughts wandered to Rick not turning up for supper this evening as planned. Their arguments before their separation had generally centred on his job and her charity work. Their themes were superficial – the real dissatisfaction was more about how much each was listening to the other, and the amount of quality time they spent together. She'd once believed that they could almost read one another's minds; from their first meeting there had been no barriers. Still, small arguments had gone unresolved. Hundreds of tiny pinpricks had inflicted pain, allowing the lifeblood to bleed out from the marriage. The relationship had unravelled, first slowly, then gathering pace, until there was nothing left worth saving. The road back to becoming a couple, one entity again, had been excruciating. The rawness of the wounds needed acceptance of fault from both sides, and forgiveness as its healing balm.

How had the Corkindales' arrangement worked out, with Guy in London during the week and Charlotte in Lincolnshire? Could Guy's obsession with his current case have been the trigger; was Charlotte offended by the suggestion that he meet Charles away from the house, without the encumbrance of the children? Clarice had developed an image of Guy as caring and decent. It was difficult to imagine him hiding to punish Charlotte, and it was clear that she was genuinely distressed by his disappearance.

Settling down for the night, Clarice tried to put everything out of her mind. But sleep evaded her, and she threw herself about the bed until she'd become damp and tangled in the sheets. She considered getting up and making tea, or finding a book, but in the end decided to fix her thoughts on Big Bill. All the cats had a favourite sleeping place. Big Bill, the slow-moving, friendly ginger boy, favoured the chair in the corner of the bedroom. He didn't snore, but his breathing was even, gentle and rhythmic, as natural and soothing as the wind, and attuning her mind to its rise and fall, finally Clarice succumbed to a restless half-slumber.

And then suddenly she could see Rick packing, the brown canvas suitcase open on the bed, just as it had been on the day of their break-up, trousers at the bottom, shirts neatly folded on top, underpants and socks around the edges.

'Rick, don't go!' she called to him.

Ignoring her, he continued to pack, slowly and methodically.

'Rick, stop!' she called out. 'Stop!'

Fingers brushed gently against her cheek.

'It's OK, sweetie.'

Opening her eyes, she found Rick's face close to hers on the pillow, his eyes gentle.

'I'm not going. I've only just arrived.'

Daylight hid behind the hardwood shutters like a much-loved friend waiting to be welcomed inside.

'Rick?'

Downstairs she could hear the dogs barking. Big Bill had gone. Howlin', an eight-year-old black and white cat, jumped onto the bed, followed by BB, another of a similar colour.

'I'm surprised the dogs didn't wake you,' Rick said, pulling himself into a sitting position on the bed next to her. 'You didn't set your alarm; it's gone seven.'

Clarice showered and dressed quickly before going out to the barn to feed the cats. On her return, she found that Rick had not only walked the boundary of the garden with the dogs, he had also fed them and the house cats and made a jug of fresh coffee.

'Wow,' she laughed, 'you can come again.'

He paused in the task of pouring mugs of coffee, with a half-smile that turned his mouth up on the left and made his rugby-damaged nose appear to be broader and flat. 'I hope you've forgiven me for yesterday.'

'Don't worry, it's work – it happens.' Clarice crossed to the bread bin, taking out a loaf before moving to the fridge.

'Eggs on toast?' she asked. 'Or maybe tomatoes, or mushrooms?'

'That's a yes, yes and another yes,' he said, going to sit at the table with his coffee.

'All on toast?'

'Yes please,' he said. 'Any baked beans?'

'You *are* hungry.' Clarice opened a cupboard full of tins to pluck one out.

'I'm not sure what time we'll get to stop for some lunch,' he sighed. 'Next time I'm home, I'll cook all the breakfasts.'

'I'll hold you to that,' Clarice said. 'Tell me about Leeds.'

'I wanted to talk to Debbie, Ben Abbot's wife. They'd been living apart just over a year.'

'Is she a suspect?'

'Everyone connected to him is a suspect at the moment.'

'So you saw her?' Clarice asked.

'No, but I was able to talk to her sister, a close friend and her parents. They all agreed that she and Ben were still on good terms, but there's been no sighting of her since Ben's murder.'

'Sounds like you've been given the run-around.'

'Too bloody right!' Rick rested his elbows on the pine table, cradling his mug, and took a deep slug of coffee. 'But tell me about you – how did it go last night? How was the gin?'

'The gin was good, as was the company and the food.'

'It's not like you to sleep so late. Or not to hear the dogs,' he grinned. 'How many gins?'

'I had one, then a couple of glasses of wine.'

'So I'll take that as two large gins and maybe three glasses of wine?' His grin broadened.

'Mmm, that about nails it.' Clarice rubbed her head.

'And what else?'

As she prepared the breakfast, she told him about the conversation about Guy.

'Poor beggar,' he said when she'd finished.

'That was the consensus last night.' She placed the breakfast in front of him.

Rick concentrated on demolishing half the mound of food before he spoke again.

'I can't imagine baby Martin's death ten years ago, or the recent problems with Angel, have any bearing on Guy's disappearance,' he said thoughtfully.

'I wasn't aware he'd had such a problem with depression.'

'No,' Rick agreed as he shovelled the remainder of his breakfast into his mouth, 'I thought that was a recent issue.'

'I think the problems with the children might have just added to the stress if there was a difficulty with the case he was working on.'

'John Bream,' Rick said. 'I've spoken to a friend who knows the barrister on the other side.'

'You mean part of the prosecution team?'

'That's right; Guy's defending Bream.'

'What did he say?' Clarice asked eagerly.

'She,' Rick said. 'Barbara Graham, an inspector who comes

from my original stomping ground in south London.' He paused. 'Do you understand how laundering works?'

'I think so.' Clarice was thoughtful. 'Recycling money that has iffy origins – drugs, prostitution, whatever – to make it legit.'

'That sums it up, but there are three stages: placement, layering and integration.' Rick spoke as if thinking out loud. 'The first part is the hardest – the placement of large amounts through gambling or smuggling, but usually into financial institutions to mix the money with legitimate funds. There are so many legal blocks in place to stop this happening; in this case, Bream's being accused of using overseas accounts in the Bahamas and Panama.'

'What's layering?' Clarice asked.

'Moving the money around to hide its true origins. Integration, the final stage, is the movement of the layered funds, with their source no longer traceable, into the legitimate financial world. In this case, the money never got as far as that. The layering is where Bream came unstuck: someone dropped him head-first into the shit. The money was detected and it led back to him. According to Barbara, the most difficult part – the placement – was cleverly done, making the money untraceable, so why did he cock up on the easier part?'

'Because someone leaked information to catch him out?'

'In part that's likely, but it still doesn't make sense. Why make it so obvious?'

'It's forfeiting that amount of money that doesn't make sense.'

'In what way?' Rick looked intent.

'Would any crook throw away millions just to destroy some-one, however much they hated them?'

'Yes,' Rick agreed, 'I see your point. But there are lots of issues we know nothing about. Has it actually been confiscated by the courts, for example, or vanished completely into those untouchable overseas accounts in Panama and the Bahamas? Barbara says the defence team believe it was Mick Housman who set up the scam – Bream's partner in crime until they had a mega falling-out. They know the amounts involved and the trail, but Barbara hasn't said how much they managed to get their hands on.'

'Can Housman's involvement be proved?'

'The case was due to come to court next week, with Guy pursuing that line, but the trial will now have to be delayed. Barbara said they're desperate to establish who this Charles is.'

'No leads?' Clarice asked.

When Rick didn't answer, she stared at him until, looking shifty, he averted his eyes downward.

'It probably won't go anywhere.'

'I'm not going to tell anyone,' she persisted.

'There's someone called Charles Tidswell, though he's never called Charles, always Chad; he's a mutual friend of Bream and Housman.'

'Have they asked Charlotte to try to identify him?'

'No, it's still being investigated, but by all accounts Tidswell has an unbreakable alibi for Monday morning. So it doesn't sound like he's our man.'

Clarice looked quizzical.

'He was with his wife,' Rick said. 'His father-in-law was in hospital after an operation for stomach cancer. The family were informed that his condition had worsened; he died later that morning.'

'That sounds pretty solid.'

'It is, but there is one thing, Clarice.' His voice sounded stern. 'You are not to go poking your nose into this. My understanding is that Housman is not someone you'd want to upset.'

'More reason to think he's had a hand in Guy's disappearance.' Clarice was truculent.

'Maybe,' Rick said. 'But I don't want him setting his sights on you – he is a total piece of work.'

Clarice didn't reply; instead, she wondered how to bring the meeting with James Wright into the conversation.

'I'm serious, Clarice,' Rick said.

'Yes, I know you are.'

They looked at one another, neither speaking.

'There's something else.' Rick's voice was grave, and Clarice looked at him with concern. 'The local police will be paying Charlotte a visit. It's better that you know; I expect she and Louise will be upset.'

'What kind of visit?'

'It's standard procedure,' Rick said. 'They'll search every inch of the house and grounds.'

'I doubt he could be hiding there. The kids would blow it, and open-plan design isn't conducive to hiding a corpse!'

'I don't imagine he is, but given the circumstances they have no choice.'

'Is there anything I can do?' Clarice asked.

'No,' he said. 'Just carry on being a good friend to the family when they need you.'

'Yes, of course.' She paused, looking at him intently. 'Are you sure you can come with me tomorrow? I need to be at the gallery early. If you can't, I'll take the train to meet the others in the morning.'

'I'm glad you asked.' Rick's shifty look was back. 'It might be better if you go down by yourself – I'll join you there for the opening. I'll be at the gallery by six.'

'Don't make promises you can't keep,' she said, smiling but serious.

'Are Bob and Sandra moving in?' he asked, ignoring the provocation.

'Yes, so they won't be coming over today. They're arriving early tomorrow, at six, and staying overnight. Georgie's calling in today, though, late afternoon, to talk about the Sunday fund-raiser.'

Ten minutes later, as Rick prepared to leave, Clarice went out to the car with him.

'You've got plenty on without worrying about Guy,' she said, noting that despite his nourishing breakfast, he still looked tired. 'Take care of yourself.'

'And you,' he smiled, kissing her gently.

As she stood watching the car disappear up the incline, Clarice could feel the warmth of the sun on her back. She had a headache – self-inflicted: too much alcohol last night – and she felt edgy with the familiar nerves before an exhibition. She also knew that she should have told Rick about the arranged meeting with James. But, she rationalised, she had not lied, just omitted to mention it. When – if – he arrived tomorrow, the meeting with James would already have come and gone, and she could just fill him in.

Chapter 10

After Rick's departure, Clarice went into the workshop. She had been making progress on recent designs, pots similar in size to those that were part of the London exhibition. The new pieces would incorporate different colours, and she had plans to change the surface texture. It was generally her favourite part of the design process, working out the shape, height, surface and colour, and then timing the firings to test-fire the colour combinations. It required all her attention, allowing her to imagine the process, and the pieces when completed. She used her camera to record the various stages of development, with notebooks close at hand in the workshop. But today her progress was slow, her attention unfocused, wandering back to the conversation with Rick.

It didn't sound possible that Charles – Chad – Tidswell was the man Guy had left home with on Monday morning. Also, if Housman was as smart as Rick believed, would he have drawn attention to himself by organising the disappearance of a defence barrister? It would only delay the trial. Another barrister would be briefed to take over the case. Or perhaps that was part of the plan, if Guy had upset Housman in some way that necessitated his removal.

Glancing at the clock, she decided to call it a day and return to the cottage. It was nearly eleven, the dogs needed to go out again, and she was making no progress. Her mind was soft and tangled, like a ball of knitting wool. She mentally admonished herself again. The hospitality of the previous evening had been excellent, but she was regretting the second gin and the third and fourth glasses of wine. She smiled, remembering Keith singing, then cringed recalling that at one point she'd lost her inhibitions and joined in. Her singing voice was not an asset. She retained a childhood memory of Mrs Cooper at her junior school suggesting she give up on her ambition of joining the school choir and concentrate on the subjects she'd showed promise in, art and literature.

Going outside, she spotted Louise's dark green Land Rover arriving. She watched Louise go to the passenger doors to bring out first Angel and then Poppy.

'Clarice! Clarice!' The children chanted her name as they ran towards her.

'I'm so sorry for just dropping by,' Louise said. 'I did try you on your home phone and then the mobile.'

'Sorry, I forgot to take the mobile with me,' Clarice said. 'Nothing wrong, I hope?'

Louise didn't reply; instead, she nodded her head meaningfully at the children.

'Where's Susie?' Angel demanded.

'Where do you think?' Clarice replied.

'In that house.' Poppy pointed towards the cottage.

The barking of the dogs grew louder as they approached.

'Shall I let them out? They'd like to see you.'

The girls went immediately to their grandmother, and

Clarice put Susie on a lead, then the two adults set off to walk the boundary of the garden whilst the girls, having given an ecstatic Susie a hug, ran back and forth with Blue and Jazz.

Louise began to speak in a low voice. 'I didn't want to talk in front of the children. The police are going to search the house and grounds this morning. It seems quite ridiculous – it's obvious Guy's not hiding there.' She frowned. 'Charlotte asked if I could take the girls away for a few hours. She didn't want them to see what was going on.'

'Is Tara still there?' Clarice asked.

'No, she was already with Amy, her friend in Heathby village. At least the police officers were thoughtful, seeing if she wanted to make arrangements for the children before they started.'

'Searching the house is just normal police procedure,' Clarice said.

'Yes, I know, but it's still hard. I felt awful leaving her there on her own – she's not as hard-boiled as people imagine.'

'Do you want to go back to her?' Clarice asked. 'Leave the children here?'

'Don't you have plans?'

'No, I've got Georgie coming in later, but I'm here all day.'

'I thought, with the exhibition . . .' Louise hesitated. 'If you're quite sure you don't mind?'

'No, it's no problem. Go back to her and put your mind at rest. I'll make a sandwich for their lunch, if that's all right.'

'That is so kind,' Louise said, and for a moment her bottom lip quivered. 'No nuts!' she added.

After Louise had left, Clarice asked the girls what they'd like to do. Playing with the dogs was top of the list, so, holding onto an envious Susie's straining lead, she strolled with her around the garden whilst the children charged back and forth, throwing balls for Jazz and Blue.

The sun was high and bright in a cloudless denim-coloured sky, a soft breeze playing over the wildflower meadow. Once the girls grew bored with the game, Clarice took them into the cottage to make sandwiches.

'Are you going to grind something?' Angel asked, pointing at the pestle and mortar on the kitchen worktop.

'No, not today,' Clarice smiled. 'Does Mummy do that?'

'Yes,' Poppy interrupted, 'and Daddy and Tara.'

'Do they cook?'

'Yes.' Angel pushed herself in front of her sister to regain the conversation. 'Mummy says we all have to eat, so we must all be able to cook.'

'Quite right,' Clarice agreed.

'And Grandma has lots of herbs and things at her house,' Poppy said.

'She has an electric grinder, silly.' Angel spoke sharply.

'She has one of *those*, like Mummy.' Poppy stared up to the worktop.

'She won't use that if she has an electric one,' Angel insisted.

'You tell lies.' Poppy closed her mouth and crossed her arms as if getting ready for a battle.

'Now, girls,' Clarice said in her best schoolmarm voice, 'no falling out while you're here. I want to tell Grandma how good you've been.'

'See,' Angel said to Poppy, 'no falling out – and I don't tell lies.'

'Angel,' Clarice said, her voice admonishing.

'Can I have mayo, please,' Angel asked, suddenly the perfect guest.

'Me too,' Poppy joined in.

'Copycat,' Angel hissed under her breath.

'Come and sit at the table,' Clarice instructed, 'and afterwards we'll go and feed the cats and kittens – but only if you're on best behaviour.'

There was complete silence as the girls ate their sandwiches.

Later, inside the cat barn, Clarice passed them dishes from a table, getting them to take the food to the queens and the older kittens. The children wanted to stay and play with the smallest kittens, but Clarice explained that, at only a few days old, they were too young. She promised to invite them back when the kittens were older, to throw ping-pong balls for them to chase.

When they had finished, they went across the garden to the workshop, where she brought out crayons. While the children drew, she explained how she gave the cats and kittens their names. Roma's five kittens, she said, did not have names yet; could they help her think of two boys' names and three girls' starting with the letter R? Two hours later, they each had drawings of the kittens to add to Grandma's kitchen wall collection, the names written below: Rihanna, Raquel, Rebecca, Robert and Ray.

They were sitting outside drinking home-made lemonade as Louise drove down the incline . 'I hope you were good girls,' she said as she reached the group.

'Yes, Grandma.' Angel and Poppy spoke together. They told her what they had been doing, describing the cats and kittens in detail.

'And,' Poppy said, 'I had cucumber in my sandwich.'

'Was it good?' Louise asked. 'You don't normally like that.'

'No, Grandma, it was horrid, yucky puke,' Poppy said, her face solemn, 'but I was polite and I didn't spit it out.' She stuck out her tongue and moved it as if vomiting.

'Well,' Louise said, 'that sounds like a real improvement.'

After Clarice had shut the dogs inside the house, Louise buckled the children into the back of her Land Rover.

'Thank you so much, Clarice, I do appreciate it.'

'It was a pleasure,' Clarice said, meaning it.

'I hope Angel behaved with Poppy; she sometimes gets jealous and can try to bully her.'

'Nothing serious,' Clarice said. 'She was just playing the older sister.'

'I'm sorry about the cucumber; I should have mentioned that Poppy's not a fan.'

'It was a shame she didn't tell me, but I loved her description of it,' Clarice said, smiling. 'How did it go with Charlotte?'

'I wouldn't rate it as a pleasant experience, but we both accepted it as part of the process in the end.'

Clarice nodded.

'Are you seeing James tomorrow?' Louise asked.

'In the afternoon. He couldn't have been more helpful – we've arranged to meet for a coffee at a place close to the gallery.'

After Clarice had promised to pass on any information, Louise departed. Going back into the cottage, Clarice worked through the exchanges between the sisters in her head. There had been small outbreaks of hostility, but nothing serious. Their behaviour was, she imagined, perfectly normal for their ages. She rarely had anything to do with children and was surprised by how much she'd enjoyed her time with them. Rick, while always kind to the offspring of visiting friends, had from the onset of their relationship been clear that he had no desire for children of his own. They both had demanding careers, plus the added pressures on their time running the animal welfare charity. Still, while Clarice felt her nurturing instincts were fulfilled by her work with four-legged waifs and strays, she occasionally wondered if, had she unintentionally fallen pregnant, Rick might have come to terms with and enjoyed fatherhood. She'd never know.

Chapter 11

Georgie Lowe arrived at teatime as planned. She was forty-five years old, but looked much younger, with a pretty heart-shaped face, brown urchin-cut hair and an abundance of freckles. Although small in stature, she always reminded Clarice of a long-legged Afghan hound, bounding in with glee, hair flying. Today she was wearing paint-encrusted overalls with a pink plastic tiara.

'What have you come as?' Clarice asked, watching her friend roll on the tiled kitchen floor with the three dogs.

'I'm a painter and decorator, can't you tell.' Georgie burst into her familiar peals of laughter. She was, Clarice considered, the most voluble of all her friends.

'So what's with the tiara?'

'Have I still got that on?' Georgie put her hand to her head. 'It belongs to Jessica, keeps the hair out of my eyes when I'm wielding my paintbrush – I'm doing ceilings, so I'm always looking up and down.' She demonstrated, tossing her head dramatically back and forth.

'I thought Alan did all the decorating?'

'He used to, but I've asked him so many times that I've given up waiting.'

'That pink's quite vibrant,' Clarice said as she scrutinised the paint on Georgie's overalls.

'Yes, pink ceilings, and I'm going to have blue wallpaper with diagonal rows of tiny pink rosebuds in the lounge and hallway. If Alan bleats, it'll teach him to show a bit of interest when I give him a colour chart, and to move off his backside to give me a hand.' Georgie laughed again and put her arms around Susie.

'Is Jessica fully recovered?' Clarice asked, picking up her mug of coffee. 'She didn't pass it on to Seth?'

'Yes, she's OK now – one of those forty-eight-hour bugs. She's with a friend this afternoon. And Seth's fine. I hardly see him unless he wants feeding – a bit like his dad.'

'Will she be coming on Sunday to Jayne's garden opening?'

'No, Alan will be home, so I'm completely free on Sunday.' Georgie looked slyly at Clarice. 'I know who this beautiful dog belongs to.'

'Yes?'

'Louise's son Guy – it's his dog.'

'How did you know?'

'She was with Louise and the three grandchildren at the open day at Sutcliffe Manor last year.'

'You do have a good memory.' Clarice held out the biscuit tin.

Georgie got up, her freckled face pink with exertion, to take the tin and join Clarice at the table. 'Is it true Guy's done a runner with someone he works with in London and dumped Charlotte and the kids?'

'Wherever did you get that story?' Clarice said with surprise.

'Mrs Elliott at the baker's – that's old Mrs Elliott, the one with the sticky-out teeth, not the young one, Janice, the daughter-in-law.' Georgie overlapped her bottom lip with her teeth in imitation of a rabbit.

'What utter rubbish – pure drivel.'

'If it's not true,' Georgie looked sly again, 'what's the real story, and why have you got Susie – and what happened to her leg?' She leaned her elbows on the table, staring intently at Clarice before biting into a biscuit. Blue pushed herself close to her, depositing a wet brown sock in her lap.

'Whatever's going on is none of my business,' Clarice said. 'But please set Mrs Elliott straight and tell her that Guy has *not* left Charlotte for a woman he works with or anyone else.' She suddenly realised that with the police visit earlier in the day to Lark House, the whole of Castlewick would probably know Guy was missing now. In this small rural community, gossip spread like wildfire.

'They must have told you something,' Georgie sounded disappointed, 'or why would they ask you to look after their dog?'

'If someone had told me something in confidence – and I say *if* – I wouldn't be much of a friend if I ran around repeating it.' Clarice sounded exasperated.

'But it's only me, Clarice – I wouldn't breathe a word to anyone else.'

Clarice stared at Georgie, her lips parted and eyebrows raised in an expression of mock shock.

'What?' Georgie said. '*What?*'

As Clarice tilted her head to one side and continued to stare, Georgie started to laugh.

'OK, OK,' she said, 'you know me too well. I should call you Sherlock or Miss Marple – if something's going on, you're always the one to ferret it out. But what's the point of me being one of your best buddies if you can't feed me the juicy bits first?'

'Georgie,' Clarice laughed, 'you are wicked.'

'That's why you love me.' Georgie munched another biscuit, crumbs flying as she spoke.

'Let's talk about Sunday – the fund-raiser,' Clarice said. 'Have Rosalind and Chrissy volunteered to help?'

'Yes.' Georgie pouted. 'I can't afford to turn helpers away, but I do wish they were less competitive.'

Clarice smiled. There had been several skirmishes between the two women, both in their fifties, and other volunteers, notably Sandra. The pair always reminded Clarice of her school days: Rosalind superficially sugar-sweet, pretty and smart; Chrissy, her shadow, dumpy and quite dull. Rosalind coveted Georgie's position as chairperson of the fund-raising committee, though her support base was restricted to Chrissy at present. Clarice was concerned that the conflicts might one day get out of control and turn into something bigger, splitting the committee.

'It's up to you, Georgie, as to whether you accept their help. You're the chair – if they're causing trouble, tell them they're surplus to requirements.'

'I'll think about that,' Georgie said meditatively. 'Let's see what Sunday brings. If they behave and just do the jobs I've allocated, fine. Rosalind's such a huge snob she'll be excited to be part of a fund-raiser in Lady Jayne's garden.'

'You don't think she'll be resentful it's not something she instigated.'

'Yes, I can see her wishing it was one of hers, but that's her problem. She is so incredibly self-aggrandising. When she organises something, every minute of every meeting has to be given to reiterating over and over the plans and timetable.' Georgie pulled a sour face. 'The meeting goes on for hours, and then every volunteer under the sun has to be at the event.'

'Yes, I know,' Clarice said. 'Even if there's bugger-all for them to do other than stand around.'

Georgie smiled. 'Is there anything important I should know after your meeting with Jayne?'

Clarice filled her in on the arrangements agreed earlier in the week. Georgie finished her coffee, then stuck a biscuit into her overall pocket as she got up to leave. 'For the journey home,' she said. 'I'll phone if I think of anything we've missed.'

Clarice nodded, knowing that she would phone any number of times before Sunday, panicking about minor issues.

'One thing.' Georgie spoke as she was leaving. 'If Guy *had* run away with a pretty girl in the office, nobody would be too surprised.'

'Why's that?' Clarice kept her voice non-committal.

'Charlotte's so snobbish and stiff, keeps everyone at arm's length, while Guy is laid-back and easy-going.'

'Perhaps it's a case of opposites attracting.'

'Maybe.' Georgie was thoughtful. 'The kids are certainly lovely.'

'Yes,' Clarice agreed. 'Louise might bring them on Sunday – she said Tara will help out if you're short on volunteers.' She didn't add that Louise was trying to take their minds off their father's disappearance.

'That's great, Tara's a poppet. I wish Jessica was more like her.'

'Charlotte must be doing something right – she seems to be a great mum,' Clarice said.

'Mmm, I suppose. It's a shame Tara's so chubby and plain compared with the other two.'

'I don't agree,' Clarice said. 'She's got a sweet face. Angel and Poppy might go through a chubby patch when they get to fifteen too.'

Georgie didn't answer; instead, she came to hug Clarice before adjusting her tiara as she passed a mirror and blowing kisses to the dogs.

Watching her car as it departed, Clarice felt that the house had experienced the blast of a whirlwind. With Georgie's departure, all was suddenly calm. She always spoke her mind, never editing her thoughts beforehand. Like a piece of machinery with the function button jammed, whatever idea came in was immediately spewed straight out. And although she was often brash and cheeky, Georgie Lowe was never dull.

Chapter 12

Bob and Sandra arrived early the following morning with an overnight bag, which Bob immediately took upstairs to the spare bedroom. Blue and Jazz, who understood the logic of this action, went into a frenzy of hopping, twisting and yelping. They waited for him at the bottom of the spiral staircase, dancing joyfully, then followed him into the kitchen. Susie, who had no understanding of the ritual, but did not want to be left out, copied them.

'Do you think they're pleased to see the back of me?' Clarice laughed.

'No, darlin',' Sandra said, 'but it makes us feel very welcome.' She had already filled the kettle for her first cuppa. She looked, as always, immaculately groomed, every strand of hair neatly brushed and hairsprayed into place, her tan foundation and pink lipstick fresh, ready for her to confront any obstacle the day might put in her way. 'How did it go yesterday?' she asked.

Clarice told her about the children's visit. She'd spoken to Louise late the previous evening: the presence of the police at Lark House had not gone unnoticed. Louise assumed it had been discussed around the area, putting the information that Guy was missing firmly into the public domain.

'Poor Louise,' Sandra said. 'Must be doin' her head in.'

Clarice noticed she had not mentioned Charlotte, and the memory of the twitching, frightened woman she'd talked to a few days earlier came into her mind. It was sad that what people saw as Charlotte's stand-offish behaviour had not endeared her to her neighbours. At this challenging time, when she needed support, she must be feeling vulnerable.

'It's hard for them all,' she said.

'Yeah, poor little kiddies.'

'Rick couldn't get back to drive you both to London?' Bob asked.

'No, he's meeting me at the gallery at the opening of the exhibition.' Clarice noticed the look that passed between her friends. 'He can't help it – it's work,' she said defensively.

'It's the job.' Sandra shrugged. 'That ain't never going to change.'

'It's just gone six,' Bob said. 'Feeding time in about an hour?'

'I've had these three round the garden.' Clarice indicated the dogs. 'They won't wait an hour now that their day's started.'

'I'll feed them,' Sandra said.

'Come on, I'll drive you to the station,' Bob said. 'Save leaving the car there and paying for parking, and hopefully Rick will be bringing you home.'

'Are you sure?' Clarice asked. 'You haven't had your first cuppa yet.'

'He can have one when he gets back,' Sandra said, 'and we'll do the cat barn together.'

Bob picked up Clarice's overnight bag, and a second bag in which she'd packed all the items she'd need at the gallery.

'Hang on, Bob.' She collected a bottle of malt whisky from

the dresser to put into the second bag. 'A thank-you present,' she said by way of explanation.

The sun was already warm. The balmy air, perfumed with the scent of flowers and herbs, reminded her of her late-night wander in the darkened garden. Driving up the incline to the main road, she glanced back, holding on to the early-morning serenity, mindful of the bustle of London, the traffic and the jostling of bodies too close together. On the opposite side of the carriageway, as far as the eye could see, stretched a landscape filled with golden fields of wheat jigging in the breeze.

As they headed into Lincoln, the traffic increased, with lorries, farm vehicles and commuters filling up the road.

'Are you looking forward to it?' Bob asked.

'I will be once it's set up,' she said. 'This is the bit where I worry in case something's got damaged in transportation.'

'It'll be fine,' Bob said comfortingly. 'It's just last-minute nerves.'

Clarice thought about Bob and Sandra's daughters, wondering if they appreciated their parents' kindness. Neither Michelle nor Susan appeared to make contact unless they wanted something. Sandra said they were busy with their own children, but Clarice sensed disappointment that the relationships were not closer.

'Thank you for house-sitting and looking after all the beasties,' she said. 'I really do appreciate it.'

'We enjoy it.' Bob smiled. 'We both hated the idea of retirement, all that time stretching ahead and bugger-all to fill it. Polly is Sandra's favourite at the moment.'

'She does seem to have fallen for her,' Clarice agreed.

'Once we've found a good home for her, Sandra will be happy.

We can't have another cat. We had our Vera from a kitten. When the end came, it took Sandra weeks to stop crying.'

'I know she'll never take another one herself,' Clarice said. 'She enjoys caring for all the charity waifs and strays, though, and it's rewarding seeing them go out to start new lives.'

At the station, Bob carried Clarice's bags, waiting while she bought a ticket before leaving her on the platform. Once on the train, she stowed the bags in the baggage spaces and found a seat. It was the wrong time of day to be travelling. The other passengers, she imagined, were daily commuters with business in London. She realised that she had been fortunate to acquire a seat; many were left standing.

She decided to use the time to work out what she'd ask James when she met him later. Resting her head back, she closed her eyes, trying to filter out her surroundings. Especially irritating was the closeness of her neighbour, a small, whippet-like man, who seemed to have expanded since taking the seat next to her. She reminded herself rationally that the claustrophobia she always experienced, especially in elevators, was the reason for her discomfort. Perhaps next time she'd grab the aisle seat, rather than being trapped on the inside, next to the window.

She began to sift elements of Guy's mystery into three categories: what had occurred, what was guesswork, and things about which she had no idea.

In the first category, Guy had gone to meet a man called Charles, and the reason he had not returned home was linked to the case on which he was currently working. She corrected herself. That last part was guesswork – the connection between Guy's disappearance and Bream was far from certain. That Guy had believed Bream to be innocent was definite: the information had come from Louise, supported by DI Barbara Graham. The reason for his certainty was the trail from the money laundering leading directly to Bream's door. She needed to dig further on this with James.

Returning to the first category, the fact that Guy was suffering from depression or anxiety was definite. Both Louise and Charlotte had agreed, indicating his work on the Bream case as being the cause. On a more personal level were his concerns about Angel's behaviour and his falling-out with Charlotte. Usually these would not have been relevant: children play up and couples argue. But given his mental state, had one or both been enough to push him over the edge? If this was the case, perhaps James might have an idea where he would be holed up.

The man beside Clarice started a telephone conversation. His voice was strident, slicing through Clarice's thoughts. She opened her eyes, switching off her inner world. Glancing at her watch, she anticipated another half an hour to London, then the Tube to the gallery. She thought of Rick, hoping he would be there this time as promised. Then she remembered, not for the first time, that her birthday was only just over a week away. Last year they had been separated, so the day had come and gone without notice. This year she wanted to do something special with him. A marker in the year that signified that they were a couple again. Rick usually joked about it well in advance, signalling that they would be going out somewhere nice. But not this time. He had so much on his mind, he'd clearly forgotten. And she didn't want to add to his burdens by reminding him.

Chapter 13

The journey by Tube to Bond Street was effortless, apart from the usual crowds on their way to work, and tired-looking people returning home from night shifts.

Walking into the gallery, she was greeted by Jerry Caldecott. 'Well timed, Clarice.' He spread his arms wide to indicate the boxes and plinths scattered around the floor.

'Is that Clarice?' Ros Ford came out of a door marked *Private* at the back of the gallery, behind which was the small kitchen. Next to it, a black door led to a secure area, with reinforced steel doors, used when there were exhibitions of precious items of silver or jewellery.

'Where's Rick?' Ros asked, her voice giving away her disappointment. 'I thought he was giving you a lift.'

'Change of plan,' Clarice said, 'but he should be here later.' Ros, in her late forties, had a running gag with Rick that if Clarice were ever to kick him into touch, he should phone her as a first replacement. Clarice suspected she was only half joking: her fellow ceramicist seemed a little too hopeful that she might one day fall into a large hole and disappear. Ros had been unaware of their estrangement, only finding out after they'd been reunited. Clarice suspected she might have been in touch to commiserate with Rick otherwise.

The fourth member of the group, John Jackson, came in behind her.

'Hi, Clarice!' He kissed her on both cheeks. 'I've just got rid of the wheels in the hotel car park.'

'Thanks for bringing the work in, John.' Clarice waved her hand towards the bubble-wrapped shapes she knew contained her vases. 'It's so kind of your dad to lend you his van for the day.'

'Yes, and thanks from me too,' Ros echoed.

'Dad didn't mind, and I was bringing in my own work as well as yours.' John looked at Clarice. 'I heard you say Rick was coming up later. Grace is coming for the opening too, with the children, and we're going to make a night of it: go for a meal, stay overnight and drive back tomorrow.'

John and Grace's children, both in their early twenties, had agreed to act as waiters, serving and handing out the drinks and canapés at the opening.

'Are we doing the usual?' Jerry, a small, wiry man in his mid-thirties, turned slowly around to take in the gallery space.

The room was L-shaped. At the top of the L, next to the main entrance, was a desk and two chairs. The glass entry and large windows allowed light to flood in. The walls had been freshly painted in white, the usual background for gallery walls, so as not to distract from the pieces on show.

They looked at one another; used to working together, they had a routine of discussion so that everyone was satisfied with the allocation of space and there could be no later recrimination that one person had taken the most prominent display positions.

'I've made the coffee,' Ros said. 'We can walk around and decide who's going where.'

The other three nodded.

Forty minutes later, the group separated into two pairs, Clarice with Jerry, John and Ros working together.

Jerry had brought two glass and steel showcases in which to display his collection of miniature ceramics. It was a two-person job to assemble them. Clarice held the steel frames in position, while Jerry screwed them together. Before inserting the glass sides and tightening up the gaps, they placed one of the tall cabinets into its designated window space. They then set to work cleaning the glass of fingermarks before sliding the shelves in. The second case had an allocated space in the middle of the gallery.

Once finished, they joined John and Ros, who had been manoeuvring plinths around the gallery. The exhibits, still bound up in bubble wrap, were in a line against a wall.

'What do we all think?' Clarice asked, looking around, hands on hips.

'That one is too high to be at the front.' John pointed. 'We need to move it.'

'And,' said Ros, 'we need to work out the heights when the work is in place, so that whatever's at the front doesn't dominate.'

There followed further discussion and moving and measuring of plinths until finally, they all agreed that they were satisfied. Each maker then went to their own work to unwrap it and begin the task of displaying.

Sitting on the floor slowly removing bubble wrap from her precious pieces, Clarice checked each to ensure the journey had not damaged them. When she'd assured herself they were intact, she felt a sudden inward sense of relief. She realised that for several hours she had not thought about Guy Corkindale or Rick.

Having finished the unwrapping, she compressed the bubble wrap into one box and went to look for her bag. Checking her mobile, she found a message from Sandra, wishing her luck with the exhibition and telling her all was well at home.

'Are we going to the usual sandwich bar when we've finished setting up?' John threw the question out to the room.

'I want to check in at the hotel and get rid of my overnight bag,' Clarice said.

'Can't you do that later?' Ros asked. 'The opening is at six – we don't need to be back here until half past five.'

'I've got to meet someone beforehand,' said Clarice. 'I'll come here straight after.'

'Oh,' Ros said. 'Not a boyfriend – a secret tryst?'

'I don't do boyfriends, I have a husband,' Clarice smiled.

'No problem, come and join us if you have time,' Jerry said reasonably.

They all went back to setting up. Price lists, CVs and statements were put up on the walls, the discarded packaging and boxes were cleared away into the back room, wine glasses were arranged on a table near the desk, white wine and cartons of orange juice put into the kitchen fridge.

As they finished their tasks, the mood changed, their intent and purpose dissipating, leaving only peace. Having been focused on their own work and its arrangement, they suddenly became fully aware of one another's. The serious business behind them, they walked calmly from one display to another, discussing the processes, talking about the problems of drying, firing and glazes. Clarice felt drawn to Jerry's new work. He appeared to have created a futuristic city inhabited by soldiers, monks and bizarre animal-like creatures. They poured out of the open showcase, down ladders onto the floor of the window space.

'That'll certainly stop people in their tracks.'

'I hope it brings them inside,' John said.

They moved together to stand near the entrance and survey the room.

'Looking good,' Ros said.

'Did you bring the visitors' book, Clarice?' Jerry asked.

'It's on the desk,' Clarice said. 'And the canapés will be delivered at five thirty.'

There was a moment of silence, followed by a collective sigh of satisfaction.

They were ready.

Chapter 14

After checking in to the hotel, Clarice took her bag up to her fourth-floor room. The hotel was part of a chain, expensive because it was in central London, but cheap in comparison to other more upmarket places in the area. She liked that the hotels in the chain, no matter what part of the country they were in, were identical in room format and provision of service. Clarice had an eye on her expenses and simply wanted a bed for the night. The bedroom had a double and a single bed, the bathroom a shower, all clean and adequate.

Leaving her bag of toiletries in the en suite, she took from her overnight bag a short, strappy silk slip. Looking at it, she thought about the shapeless blue T-shirt, her nightwear at home – this was a definite improvement. It brought Rick to mind, and after going through her bag to look for her mobile phone, she realised she'd left it at the gallery, on the corner of the last plinth she'd set up. It was annoying, but the gallery was locked, and it would be safe there until her return.

After a quick shower and a refresh to her make-up, she changed into the green linen suit and black suede pumps she'd wear for the rest of the day.

She arrived at the café ten minutes early, planning to take a seat in a corner to wait and watch for James's arrival. But as she walked in, a tall, thin, dark-haired man who'd already bagged a quiet corner table stood up and looked hesitantly at her.

'Clarice?' he said.

She smiled as she walked towards him, holding out her hand. 'James.'

'I feel like I'm on a blind date,' he grinned.

She laughed, the ice between them broken.

James insisted she sit and wait while he went to order a coffee for her.

'They'll bring them over,' he said on his return. 'Tell me what you already know about Guy's disappearance, and I'll try to fill you in on bits you don't.'

Clarice explained briefly what Louise and Charlotte had told her. 'There isn't a lot to say. Both Louise and Charlotte are desperately upset,' she finished.

'Understandably so,' James said. 'I had a visit on Wednesday from the police – they're looking into his disappearance.'

His voice was exact and clipped, with traces, Clarice thought, of a South African accent.

'I'd known Guy before we started working together. He's a thoroughly good bloke,' he said. 'You mentioned that both his wife and mother had concerns because they thought he might be depressed?'

Clarice nodded.

'I've been worried about that too; he has had bouts of depression previously. The main period was ten years ago, when his son died – a cot death. I was concerned that he was moving back into that territory when he didn't want to come into work.'

'He stayed in his flat?' Clarice asked.

'No, he didn't want to come to London at all; rather, he would hide away in Lincolnshire, working from home as much as he possibly could.'

'Was it the Bream trial, do you think?' she asked. 'Was there something about the case that was giving him cause for concern?'

Her coffee arrived, and as she added milk, she watched James lean back for a moment thoughtfully.

'It's something I've kept asking myself since he disappeared. I'd say yes and no.'

Clarice waited.

'There's no getting away from the fact that the prosecution team have a solid case against Bream,' James went on. 'Accounts were set up to deposit funds and move it around. The money is from drugs smuggled into the UK – misery money.'

'The trail leads to Bream?'

'Yes, the accounts were set up by him – or by someone posing as him, which was Guy's theory.'

'Housman?' Clarice queried.

'Yes, they were involved together for years. The falling-out was inevitably about money,' James said. 'The path leading to the movement of the funds went so directly to Bream that Guy was sure Housman was the person responsible. He had the most to gain from Bream being in the frame for it.'

'But I don't understand why Housman would be prepared to lose millions just to see Bream put inside. Nobody's that rich.'

'He wouldn't lose millions. The amount the police have traced and seized, in actual cash, comes to under four hundred thousand. According to the records kept of the movement of the money, what they have managed to get their hands on is only the tip of the iceberg. They will never get to the accounts in Panama and the Bahamas. And anyway, it will already have moved accounts.'

'I see,' Clarice said, understanding. 'What you're saying is it was worth losing several hundred thousand to get Bream convicted.'

'That amount's nothing to a man like Housman. Guy and I discuss our cases, in confidence, of course. The money involved amounts to a fraction of one deal.'

'And Guy felt quite strongly that he'd built a good case?'

'Yes, he did.' James nodded. 'But you mustn't lose sight of the fact that although Guy thought this was a set-up, he knew Bream had been a villain in the past, just as much as Housman. The only redeeming factor is that he believed Bream was trying to play it straight; he'd moved on, attempting to leave his relationship with Housman in the past.'

'Yes, I see,' Clarice said again, thoughtfully. 'Is there anywhere Guy might go to ground, a friend, or a place he felt safe?'

'The police asked me the same question. As I said, I sensed he didn't want to leave Lincolnshire. He didn't want to be here in London. He was depressed and anxious, and I think he and Charlotte might have been having problems.'

'The marriage?'

'It was something I picked up on from bits of conversations in the office when he called home. They did argue, but then what couple doesn't?'

'It wasn't all the time?' Clarice asked.

'No, not all the time. Having known Guy for years, I always believed that he and Charlotte were solid. He was someone who'd cracked it – nice wife and kids. The bickering was recent, over the last few weeks.'

'I don't think I've heard anyone say a bad word about him.'

'And I don't think you will.' James looked brooding. 'I cannot for the life of me think who Charles might be, the man Charlotte said he was meeting.'

'That does seem a puzzle.' Remembering that she had told Rick she would not repeat the name of Charles Tidswell, Clarice felt a sense of guilt that she could not share this information with James, who was being so open with her. 'Thank you.' She smiled. 'You've been a great help.'

'No, I don't think I have, but I guess it gives you a clearer picture. Tell me,' he leaned towards her, 'about your work, the exhibition. I've never met a ceramicist before.'

'I haven't met that many defence barristers,' Clarice laughed, before explaining about the exhibition.

'I know that gallery,' he said. 'I'll try to call in while the exhibition is running. My wife, Lizzy, would love it.'

'Good, I hope you both enjoy it.' Clarice copied him in getting up and followed him out into the street. They shook hands again, and he wished her well for the opening of the exhibition.

'If you think of anything else you'd like to ask, please don't hesitate to call me,' he said as they were parting.

'Thank you, James, I appreciate that,' Clarice said, 'and if you hear anything that might relate to Guy's disappearance . . .'

'I'll let you know.'

Clarice stood on the street, watching as he walked away and disappeared round a corner. It was almost five on a Friday evening, and busy. People were streaming past her like sheep following the lead ram, all with single-minded determination to get home for the weekend. She felt suddenly hungry, and turned her back on the crowds, returning to the café to buy a sandwich to take back to the gallery. It would be a long, but, she hoped, stimulating evening.

Chapter 15

Back at the gallery, the other ceramicists had been joined by John's wife and children, Grace, Marc and Emily, plus Sophie, Ros's younger sister, and Jerry's girlfriend Alice.

On my lonesome again, Clarice mused, Billy-no-mates.

'*Love* the new pots,' Grace called as Clarice made her way to where they had gathered.

'Thanks, Grace.' Clarice beamed at her. 'Everyone's work is amazing. John's has changed so much – in a good way.'

'Yes, it has.' Grace smiled with pride. 'It's always evolving. You know the creative process can be painful, but in the end, when it all comes together and this is the result . . .' She swept her arm around to take in the room.

'It's worth the hard work,' Clarice agreed. 'And with any luck we'll all sell a few pieces.'

'I bloody well hope so,' Ros said, joining them. She passed Clarice her mobile.

'Thanks, Ros,' Clarice said. 'I realised I'd left it here.'

'It was ringing, so I answered it,' Ros said smugly. 'It was Rick. He's still tied up with work.'

'Ah, a hazard of the job.' Clarice kept her voice non-committal.

'He said he was still hoping to get here.' Ros spoke as two men entered the gallery carrying covered trays. 'That looks like our order of canapés.' She left Clarice to go and meet them.

What a bugger, Clarice thought. Ros was the last person she would have wanted answering her phone, but it was her own fault for leaving it. She went to the back of the gallery to eat her sandwich and to call Rick, leaving a message when the call went straight to his messaging service.

People began to arrive before the official opening time of 6 p.m., family, friends and clients of the four ceramicists, and by 7.30 the numbers had swelled and the room had become crowded and noisy, forcing all thoughts of her earlier encounter with James from Clarice's mind.

Lady Constance Oliver arrived early. 'I'll be the first in and out. I'm going on from here to meet a friend for supper,' she announced, kissing Clarice. A loyal customer of many years, tall and hairpin thin, she immediately homed in on the display of new work. 'Darling, it's splendid, but *where* do you find the energy? You run that animal rescue place . . .' Having forgotten the name of the charity, she waved her arm vaguely in the air, jingling the gold bracelets competing for space on her bony wrist. 'Plus you have your own menagerie to care for, and that delightful husband. Is he here?' She paused to survey the room.

'No, not yet, he has work problems.'

'Always going to, darling. A career policeman – it makes sense he'll never be home.' Constance broke the word 'policeman' into two, making the words sound earnest and nefarious both at the same time. 'I wanted to have first peek,' she said theatrically. 'You know Carol Burton couldn't come tonight?'

'Yes,' Clarice said. She remembered the two had been at school together and were best of friends but also competitive in their purchases. 'She's coming in tomorrow – I won't be here then.'

'No, darling, you'll be on your way home.' Constance strode to the central plinth to survey the tallest of the vessels. 'I have to have this one!' She clapped her hands like a small child who had received her favourite sweets.

'I'm pleased you like it.' Clarice smiled.

'Let me leave a cheque, darling. Carol is going to hate me.' The beaming smile told Clarice that this would not be a bad thing.

After Lady Constance had left, Clarice greeted Tina and Malcolm, who'd first bought one of her pieces over fifteen years ago and had become friends as well as customers. The pair, who worked together from home in their graphic design business, were both in their early forties and shared a love of books, cinema and the arts. They would come and stay with Clarice and Rick in October each year, and Clarice always associated their visits with the digging-up of the wild horseradish. It grew plentifully on the boundaries of her garden, its broad, flat leaves becoming larger and brown around the edges throughout September. Malcolm would always ask if the spades were in the usual place and head off with Rick to dig up the long, hairy tubular roots, which, after being peeled and grated, were mixed with cream and black pepper and heaped plentifully onto rare roast beef. It was something the men enjoyed doing together, that and the beer-drinking that accompanied the digging. Clarice especially loved visiting Tina and Malcolm at their southern Italian holiday home, a cottage they called the Blue House, on the island of Procida in the Bay of Naples, though Rick's work obligations limited their trips there.

Before leaving, Tina and Malcolm talked about the work in the gallery and their next visit to Lincolnshire, but Clarice sensed that they were disappointed by Rick's no-show. While Malcolm had one last look around, Tina and Clarice found their diaries to write in the date in October for the next intended visit.

'Everything OK between you and Rick?' Tina whispered.

'Yes,' Clarice reassured her. 'The problem is, being a police officer isn't a nine-to-five job, and it's sometimes difficult for him to stick to arrangements.'

Tina looked relieved as they said their goodbyes. But as she smiled and kissed her friends, an image crawled into Clarice's mind, and refused to leave: Rick's packed suitcase, open on the bed.

Throughout the evening she found her eyes drawn towards the door, hopeful that he might finally arrive. He didn't, but other friends and customers did. It was, she thought, a bit like a wedding, where everyone knows either the bride or the groom but not the other guests. She couldn't help feeling a little as if she'd been left at the altar.

As the number of guests began to diminish, Clarice was delighted to see that four red stickers had gone up next to her pieces. Grace and Sophie had been standing at the desk near the door, accepting orders and cheques; the work could be collected on the last day of the exhibition, or by arrangement with the maker. Jerry, having so many small, less expensive pieces, had an unbroken line of stickers against his pieces. Still, Clarice delighted in seeing that all four ceramicists were selling well. It would have been embarrassing for one of them not to have made any sales, though there would be other opportunities while the exhibition was running, since not everyone invited to the opening had been able to make it.

At 9.45, with the last hangers-on leaving, John asked if anyone would mind if he went to take his family to a nearby restaurant to dine.

'Noodles,' he said by way of an explanation. 'Grace can't get enough of them.'

'I think they deserve a treat,' Clarice said. 'They've all worked so hard all evening.'

'And Sophie,' Ros interjected. 'I'm taking her for a drink at that Japanese club in Soho.'

'We'll stay and help you put everything away,' Jerry said, looking towards his girlfriend.

Clarice noted that Alice's response was glacial. The relationship was in its early stages, and she knew that Jerry had promised to take her somewhere special.

'No, Jerry,' she said. 'You and Alice stick to your plans; it's only putting a few boxes away and locking up. Rick's obviously not coming, so I'm going to head back to the hotel.'

'Why not come with us?' Grace said. 'We'll all pack up and then go to the noodle bar together.'

'Thank you, that's kind,' Clarice said. 'But I'm knackered. I just want to get back to the hotel for a hot shower.'

'Only if you're sure?' Grace ventured.

'I am,' Clarice assured her.

'OK.' Jerry led her to the door. 'There's no key to lock; it's all easy-peasy. For both the main and the security room doors the code is four numbers, 1964. Press the red button once and put the numbers in, then press the blue button.' He touched the bank of light switches on the wall. 'Just leave this one up

– security says it keeps that row of tiny lights on.' He pointed to the wall running the length of the gallery.

'Anything else?'

'Yes, push the bolt across at the bottom of the main door while you're alone in here. And if you're going to put those boxes in the storeroom to clear space for tomorrow, push one of the heavier ones with full bottles inside the door so it doesn't shut. It closes quickly and there's no internal handle.'

'I'll do that.' Clarice felt a frisson of fear at the idea of the security door closing and trapping her inside. 'I guess the air would run out?'

'No,' Jerry said. 'I asked about that: there is a vent. It doesn't let much in but it's sufficient for someone to survive.'

They walked back to the main door, where everyone had gathered their bags and coats, ready to leave. Clarice managed to catch John for a moment and give him the thank-you gift of whisky.

'You shouldn't spoil him.' Grace was suddenly beside him as the present changed hands.

'Oh yes she should.' John grinned cheekily.

After they had all gone, Clarice switched off most of the lights, plunging the place into semi-darkness. Then she poured herself a glass of wine and returned to the front of the gallery to relax in the padded chair by the desk. From there she watched groups of passers-by, dressed up for a night out, and let go of the frenetic activity of the last twenty-four hours.

Just after 10.30, she got up to wash and dry the glass before returning it to the cupboard. She moved the boxes of full and empty bottles from the gallery into the kitchen, then placed a box containing full wine bottles inside the security door. It was

110

then that she heard the noise, a movement in the gallery, and with a sense of shock, she realised that she hadn't slid the bolt on the main door.

She stepped out of her shoes and crept soundlessly to the half-open kitchen door. As she listened, she heard the sound of footsteps in the gallery. She walked back to the boxes and quietly slid one of the empty bottles out by the neck, then returned to her position by the door. Slowly opening it, bottle raised, she braced herself to spring forward. A shadow loomed ahead of her, and she saw the outline of what looked like a massive creature.

There were only two possibilities, the first being that somehow an enormous grizzly bear wandering the streets of Mayfair had negotiated the door to get inside.

She went for the second option. 'Rick,' she called.

'Ah,' he said. 'There you are. I thought you'd buggered off back to the hotel, but the door wasn't locked.' He looked bedraggled; he'd discarded his tie, and his dark five o'clock shadow had deepened, suggesting he'd not shaved that morning.

'Where did you leave the car?' she asked.

'I've taken it to the hotel and checked in,' he said. 'I left my bag in the room.'

Clarice paused, wondering if she should hit him or hug him. He'd not only arrived too late, but so far, he hadn't apologised.

'Let me just pop these last few boxes into the back room and I'll be with you,' she said, turning to head back to the kitchen.

'I'll help.' He took off his jacket and hung it over the back of a chair.

'Don't worry,' she said. 'There's so little left to do, it'll only take a moment.'

'I insist,' he said, following her, 'by way of apology for being so late.'

She turned to find him behind her, and chose the hug option, putting her arms around him to press herself into his embrace.

'I'm so pleased to see you,' she mumbled into the collar of his shirt.

'Me too.' He kissed her on her forehead. 'Come on, let's get finished and go; I'm starving.'

He began to pass the remaining boxes to her, and she stacked them neatly.

'Don't move the one by the door,' she said, turning, and at that same moment she realised that he was proffering the last of the boxes, the one she'd used to prop the door open.

'Why not?' he asked quizzically.

The door swung shut with a sharp click, plunging them into blackness.

'Rick!' she gasped. 'What have you done?'

Chapter 16

Blackness with the fluidity of water closed in from all sides, filling Clarice with fear, pressing the air from her lungs. She tried to swallow, to breathe, but felt fixed, immobile.

'Why the hell didn't you tell me?' Rick's angry voice in the small space became exaggerated. The sound joined the oppression of complete blackness pushing against her senses. 'You should have said something sooner.'

Yes, he was right. She'd known the door closed quickly. Why hadn't she explained the significance of the placement of the box?

'Where's the safety release for the door?' he asked, and she felt him moving around as he touched the walls and the door frame. 'There might be a way of opening it from the inside in case someone gets trapped in here – like us, now.'

Clarice couldn't speak. She began to count in her head, trying to regulate her breathing. Over and over, without moving or making a sound. Being trapped in a small space in the dark was her worst nightmare. She thought about coffins. A coffin lid closing, with her inside, immobile and dehydrated, and then slow suffocation. But Jerry had pointed out the vent, and there was air; it was just a matter of waiting.

'Clarice?'

She didn't answer, just closed her eyes and continued the internal count.

Rick's voice was suddenly soft. 'Clarice,' he said, and she felt his hands gently on her, pulling her down. 'Let's sit down, sweetie – here, just where we are.'

She followed his movement downward, pushing back against unseen boxes until they were both seated on the ground. She knew he would be aware of her panic. He'd told her once that claustrophobia was irrational, but saying that didn't make it any easier. He had a fear of heights; small spaces caused no problems for him.

'Do you have your phone?' he asked.

She shook her head without thinking that he couldn't see her.

'I guess that's a no. Mine is in my jacket outside on the chair.'

Clarice couldn't respond; each passing second was filled with torment.

'I'm here, Clarice.' He wrapped one arm around her shoulder, keeping her close to him. 'Is that better, or worse – would you rather I didn't hold you?'

'Better . . . better,' she said, pushing the words out, realising that her mouth had become parched. Then the wave of bleakness and panic overwhelmed her again, trapping her breath somewhere inside her body. She put her head on his shoulder.

'All right, sweetie,' he whispered. 'I know you don't feel much like talking to me, so let me unburden myself about this case, the reason I was late getting here. Is that OK?'

She moved her head against his shoulder, realising that he was talking to distract her from panic and from the dawning comprehension that they would have to stay in this small black space until someone came into the gallery the following morning.

'Today has been a perfect shit storm,' he said. 'The team checking CCTV have come back with nothing new on Ben's movements on the day he died. The murder weapon has not been found – no surprise there. The witness statements all confirm what we already knew: Ben was well liked, he didn't have any enemies. But although it's early days in terms of the investigation, there's already pressure from above for me to show that I'm making headway.'

Although Clarice drew closer to him as she listened, part of her wanted to pull away. There was no movement of air, and she could feel the sweat on her back, making her linen jacket damp. She was sitting uncomfortably, her knees pulled in under her chin, her skin felt prickly, and all around her the stacked boxes seemed to press in on her. Still, lurking in her confused mind was the idea that if she concentrated hard enough on what Rick was saying, it might divert her from the fear she was feeling.

'The first question is why he would have been in the factory on his own. The press is never operated by one person on their own, and certainly not in the middle of the night.' Rick paused, as if laying out his thought process before Clarice, and in doing so, re-examining the case. 'The Abbot business was set up by Ben's father, Harold Abbot. It's well run, and they have a good turnover. The old boy died less than two months ago and left the business in equal part to Ben and his brother Mike, who's the elder by four years. Both brothers were married, Mike to Catherine, with two sons. Ben to—'

'Debbie,' Clarice's voice was a low whisper.

'Yes, you remembered. I went to Leeds to meet her, but I couldn't find her. I spoke to her best friend, her sister Pauline and her parents. It was a useful exercise. And here is a parallel to Guy Corkindale – nobody had a bad word to say about her.'

Clarice found herself nodding.

'Everyone said that she's a lovely, decent person. They liked Ben, and were sad that the relationship hadn't worked. Her mother told me that she thought they would've eventually got back together.'

When he paused for a moment, Clarice felt his body tensing.

'We hadn't made any progress, and I was thinking the day was going to be a complete non-starter, and then it got worse.' Rick was morose. 'A body was discovered yesterday by a dog walker, hidden in dense undergrowth at Fulby Woods, on the other side of Lincoln. There'd been an attempt to bury it, but there're a lot of foxes and other creatures, squirrels and the like, foraging for food, and it hadn't been hidden deep enough. We're waiting for official identification, but it's pretty certain to be Debbie.'

Clarice felt an undercurrent of distress, linked to her estrangement from Rick, connecting her like a twisted thread to Debbie from Leeds. A woman she didn't know, whose husband was dead – and now, it seemed, so was she.

'Poor Debbie,' she whispered.

'Although the business was left equally to the two brothers,' Rick continued, 'there was a clause in the old man's will – it's one in common use – that if either of his sons didn't survive him by three months, the remaining son would inherit the whole lot.'

'You think Mike did it?' Clarice asked.

'Yes, I do,' Rick said. 'But I can't prove it. I've had them at the station, Mike and Catherine; they were supposedly together at home the night of Ben's murder. There's no incriminating computer or phone use to suggest they were responsible – nothing to connect them to it.'

'And Debbie?' Clarice asked. 'Do you know yet how she died?'

'Nope, not yet, it's still with pathology,' Rick replied. 'Another parallel with Guy: it feels as if Debbie and Peppy just disappeared without a trace.'

'Peppy?'

'The dog, didn't I mention him?'

'No – what kind is he, what breed?' Rick had her attention now.

'He's four years old, a long-haired harlequin dachshund, a lovely dog according to the parents and her sister, and Debbie adored him. The last sighting of Debbie was from her neighbour's security camera, on the same night Ben died. She drove away with Peppy in the car. A couple of sightings on CCTV, then we lost her.'

'The dog would be easy to recognise; he wasn't in the woods when she was found?'

'No, he's still missing. He'll feature in the information given to the media. Debbie's death changes everything. We're establishing a timeline . . . when she died . . .' Rick sounded preoccupied. 'Hang on, I'm just going to undo my shirt – it's bloody hot in here. If we're going to be here until they open the gallery tomorrow, we might as well be comfortable.'

She felt him move about as he unbuttoned his shirt and pulled it away from his body.

'Do you want to get rid of some clothing?' he asked.

'I'll dump my jacket,' she said. Unbuttoning it, she found her fingers sweaty and clumsy, her hair clinging damply against her face.

After Rick had helped her to remove the jacket, she felt his body shift and heard him fumbling around in the boxes. There was a click that sounded like the lid of a bottle being unscrewed.

'Here,' he said, and he passed her what she realised was a plastic bottle of mineral water.

'Thanks, Rick,' she said, bringing it to her lips with shaking hands. She drank from the open top before pouring some of the liquid over her head, and was still trembling as she felt Rick slide his arm around her shoulder again.

'There is one thing Debbie and Catherine had in common,' he said, suddenly thoughtful again.

'Yes?'

'The dogs. Catherine has five.'

'What type?' Clarice was interested again.

'The same as Debbie's – dachshunds, but all short-haired and plain brown.'

'Interesting.'

'In what way?'

'Why they should both choose the same breed. They were only related by marriage. It's not as if they'd grown up sharing a family pet.'

'Pauline, Debbie's sister, said that Catherine saw Debbie as a rival. Everything Debbie had, Catherine wanted – cars, houses – only bigger and better. Catherine had always had dachshunds. Debbie got to know the breed through her and wanted one. But Pauline said Catherine was annoyed. She thought Debbie was trying to outdo her, although Debbie wasn't like that at all, apparently. Peppy was long-haired and a harlequin, not the regular brown colouring, so a cut above the average. Smarter than Catherine's dogs, in other words.'

'Sounds a bit petty,' Clarice commented.

'Yes,' Rick said, 'but quite capable of making Catherine envious.'

'But envy's not usually a reason for murder. If it was, half the population would be in court for attacking the other half.'

'That's true.' Rick raised his bottle to drink more water. 'Catherine maintained that Debbie had killed Ben and done a runner. Assuming the body is Debbie's, it looks like that's not the case. The bottom line,' he spoke with conviction, 'is that the case pivots on avarice – old man Abbot's money. Mike wasn't satisfied with his half-share; he wanted it all, but the person driving the situation forward, I'm sure, is Catherine. She's clever and streetwise, and – I believe – also very greedy. Now I just have the not-so-simple task of finding proof.'

There was a pause as they both digested his words. Then, 'The trousers will have to go.' Clarice felt him stand up, and after several minutes of rummaging and movement, she heard a soft plop as he threw first his shoes then his trousers to one side.

There was a pause, Clarice sensed more movement and wondered if he was stretching his arms.

'Better,' he said as he sat down. 'What about you, do you want to take some more clothes off?'

'No thanks,' she said. She might succumb in another hour or two, though she knew realistically that one item of clothing less would not make her feel much better.

As she pondered on the thought, the room was suddenly

flooded with light as the door opened. It completely blinded her, and she raised her hand to shield her eyes.

'Clarice?'

She struggled for a moment to work out what had happened before identifying John's voice. She opened and closed her eyes several times while slowly getting up; she felt Rick next to her doing the same.

'Are you all right, Clarice?' Grace came into focus, small and rounded, with dark features, at that moment the most beautiful person Clarice had ever seen. John stood beside her with the children, Marc and Emily, who were peering open-mouthed at the spectacle before them.

'Thank you,' Clarice stuttered as she recovered her wits. 'We got locked in. What time is it?'

'Um.' John looked at his watch. 'Gone half twelve. We were on our way back to the hotel, and Emily noticed your bag and mobile phone on the front desk as we passed the gallery.'

'I tried the door,' Grace cut in, 'and it wasn't locked.'

'Thank you so much.' Rick spoke from beside Clarice. 'I accidentally locked us in. We thought we'd be here until opening time in the morning.'

'It was my fault,' Clarice interjected. 'He was helping me, and I didn't tell him not to move the box.'

She glanced at Rick for the first time since their release: a hirsute giant, naked apart from underpants and socks, dripping from a combination of sweat and mineral water. It struck her that his pants and socks were the same shade of blue, and though she realised that it was an incongruous thought, she still couldn't help wondering how that could have happened, given that Rick was the most unkempt, untidy person she knew. She had a sudden mental picture of herself in her lacy black bra and green linen trousers, her wet hair plastered to her head, and looked again at the startled faces of the children and their parents' expressions of bemusement. Grace gave an awkward smile, perhaps aware of Clarice's embarrassment.

'Nice bra,' she said.

'Thanks,' Clarice muttered, before picking up her jacket and shrugging it on. Walking into the gallery, she was hit by the cooler air, and a sense of relief; Rick, now fully dressed, followed.

'We'll need to mop the floor and tidy up back there,' she said as an afterthought.

'No you don't,' Grace said. 'Go back to the hotel – we'll clear up.'

'I can't let you do that,' Clarice protested.

'Please go.' John smiled as he spoke. 'While we've been enjoying our noodles, you've been locked in here. We won't see you at breakfast, but I'll give you a ring at home tomorrow.'

Grace walked to the door with Clarice. 'Have a good journey home tomorrow.' She gave her arm a friendly squeeze.

'You too,' Clarice said. 'And I shall enjoy stretching out in the hotel bed tonight, thanks to Emily's eagle eyes.'

'It was worth all the work – the opening, I mean. Lots of sales, and such good vibes.'

'Yes, that part of the evening was brilliant,' Clarice said. She gave Grace a hug as she left, thinking how the sight of her and Rick in their underwear must have provided a memorable finale to the night. It wasn't a vision she cared to dwell on.

Chapter 17

Outside on the street, Clarice gulped in the suddenly sweet London night air. Through the window she could see Rick in conversation with John. She imagined he was complaining about there being no way to exit the storage room once the door had closed.

When he came to join her, she tucked her hand through his arm, and light-headed at the sudden freedom, they started the short walk to the hotel.

Rick confirmed that he had spoken to John about the security room. 'I thought it might be breaking health and safety regulations, not having an internal handle.'

'What did he say?'

'He said that it was something he'd brought up with the gallery owners, but it's classified as a security safe or at the most a big cupboard. They pointed out that it had an air vent, which is not an actual requirement for a cupboard.'

'I think it's best to move on, Rick.' She squeezed his arm. 'I'm just so glad you were with me.'

'Me too,' he said, putting his hand over hers, 'even if I did go on a bit about the Abbot case.'

'You didn't go on.' She was aware that he'd talked about the case to distract her from the panic caused by her claustrophobia. 'I'm amazed that you got here at all after the day you've had.'

As they walked, Clarice thought about the contrast between city life and home. At this hour of the morning, sleepy Castlewick would be silent. Here in central London, noisy groups of people, some unsteady and loud, blocked the pavement and spilled into the road, a steady stream of taxis passing by. She realised she was looking forward to going home the next day.

At the hotel, Rick asked if she minded him using the shower first. After she'd watched him go into the bathroom, she turned and noticed the silk slip on the bed. She remembered leaving it there earlier, before the meeting with James and the exhibition. With all that had happened, it felt like a very long time ago.

On his return, he was still towelling himself.

'We haven't had time to talk,' Clarice said tentatively.

'About?'

'I arranged a meeting before the exhibition with James Wright, Guy's friend and colleague, a quick coffee. I'd hoped if you'd been here, you might have come with me.'

'Ah.' Rick stopped towelling. '*He* was your secret tryst?'

'My what?' Clarice showed her surprise, then remembered where and when she'd recently heard the expression used. 'Bloody Ros!'

Rick smirked. 'Why did you not tell me sooner?'

'I was too stressed: I just forgot.'

'OK, I forgive you.' He sat on the bed next to her. 'Fill me in then.'

She was pleased he hadn't accused her of keeping secrets. She related the conversation she'd had with James, and for a moment he was thoughtful.

'We knew Guy and Charlotte had had an argument the night before he disappeared, but it sounds like the relationship problems were more serious than a tiff,' he said.

'The problem with his depression is a recurring theme, isn't it?'

'But it also keeps coming back to the Bream case. If things at home weren't going well, he might want to be out of the house to escape Charlotte's company. But you say James implied that Guy didn't want to hide away at the London flat; he wanted to stay in Lincolnshire.'

'Yes, that's right. I did have one other thought,' Clarice said. 'James didn't have a clue who this mystery Charles was, so how could he have been a business acquaintance? Guy's business is his work as a barrister, and James is a friend and colleague who's privy to details of all the cases he worked on. I'm not aware that Guy had any other separate areas of work.'

'That occurred to me, and it makes the fact that Guy didn't want Charles in the house more of an issue. Maybe he didn't want Charlotte to ask him about the relationship.'

'Do you think we might have been looking at this from the wrong angle?' Clarice asked.

'Go on,' Rick encouraged her.

'I was mentally categorising all the issues into three groups on the journey here. Those that are definite, the areas of guesswork, and those where we don't have a clue. I've always put Guy into group one; he's a good person, honest and decent. But,' Clarice paused, 'our family and people who care about us only ever have good things to say. If something happened to push Guy over the edge, is it possible that he might have been making money from dubious connections?'

'Do you really believe that?'

'Mmm, I'm not a hundred per cent convinced, but I think it has to be a consideration. Not everyone starts bad, but anyone might wander over to the wrong side because of a change in circumstance, and Guy does mix with a lot of criminals.'

Rick nodded. 'His computer has come back clean; there's nothing on it that shouldn't be there.'

'I didn't realise the police had taken it.'

'It's the one from his home; it was in the bag that he left behind. Having said that, there might be another we don't know about.' Rick sounded cynical. 'If someone is up to something dodgy, they'll naturally try to hide it.'

'Anything else?' Clarice asked.

'They didn't do a house-to-house because there are no near neighbours, but they have checked the CCTV of the garage next to the café where Charlotte said they might have gone – nothing.'

'They could have gone somewhere else,' Clarice said. 'Charlotte said she thought it probable that they'd gone there, but it wasn't definite.'

'True. Also there's no CCTV on the lane at the back of the café; it concentrates on the garage at the front.'

'I know where you mean; that lane is the route from Guy's home.' Clarice gave a frown. 'So they might have parked at the back – people often do when the place gets busy – and they wouldn't be caught on the CCTV.'

'At that time in the morning the place wouldn't have been busy,' Rick said. 'Why not park in the car park near the garage? It's much closer.'

'Unless they didn't want to be seen?'

'Quite!'

'Do you know if Guy has withdrawn money from his bank account?'

'It's been checked, and his plastic's not been used. Neither has his mobile – it's not been switched on.'

'Mmm.' Clarice nodded. 'Is that everything?'

'Not quite,' Rick said. 'During the initial search, Charlotte couldn't find Guy's passport, but said that it was probably in the house somewhere.'

'And was it?'

'No. Bridget Latimer, the family liaison officer, asked her again yesterday, and she says she can't find it.'

'Could it be at the London flat?'

'It's been searched, as has Guy's office.' Rick's tone of voice told Clarice that she shouldn't try teaching her grandmother how to suck eggs.

A few moments of silence fell between them. When he spoke again, Rick looked stern.

'Look, Clarice, this isn't my case and there are only so many questions I can ask without someone telling me to butt out. If another officer rooted around in one of *my* cases, I'd give them short shrift.'

'Yes, I can see that,' Clarice said, her tone a careful neutral.

'I want to get to the bottom of this as much as you do, mainly for Louise's sake, but ...' he held his hands open, palms upwards, as if exasperated, 'the Abbot case is the one I'm working on.'

'I'm sorry, Rick.'

He looked at her for a moment, then, his irritation digested, said, 'No, don't be sorry.' He gave his lopsided grin and put his hand gently on hers. 'I'm as much at fault as you; I feel I'm being drawn in. I want Guy to be found.'

'Let's hope it happens soon.' Clarice got up. 'It's very late – we should sleep on all this. I'm going to have my shower.'

'Go on then, hurry up.' He smiled at her, and she noticed that his glance had slid to take in the black silk slip she picked up from the bed.

Twenty minutes later, she returned to the bedroom to find Rick spread-eagled across the king-sized bed, snoring gently. With an effort, she managed to roll him one way and then the other, and eventually pulled the duvet out from under him. She knew she wouldn't wake him; he was too far gone. She climbed into bed next to him, and sleep came instantly.

Chapter 18

The following morning, after an early breakfast, they left the hotel and headed home.

As Rick took the turn from Long Road, following the downward incline to the cottage, Clarice felt her spirits lifting.

'Don't forget,' he glanced at her glumly, 'you'll still have to give Louise some feedback about your meeting with James.'

'I hadn't forgotten. I'm not looking forward to it. I think she imagines he might have said something that will unravel the whole mystery.'

'She's desperate,' Rick said.

Clarice nodded, then noticed Bob and Sandra emerging from the cottage, accompanied by all three dogs. 'We've got a welcome-home committee.'

They received an enthusiastic greeting from the dogs before going inside, where Bob and Sandra were eager to know how the opening had gone. Had all the work arrived without damage, what about the other ceramicists, was the evening well attended, had she sold much, were there photographs to show them?

They went outside to sit around the garden table in the sunshine, armed with cold drinks, Susie on a short leash and

Blue and Jazz stretched out on the grass nearby in the scented quiet. The previous twenty-four hours of frantic activity felt unreal, and Clarice was relieved to be back on home territory.

'I've a list of messages,' Sandra said, once she had brought her up to date on the cats, 'and Georgie phoned twice.'

'I'll call back,' Clarice said. 'I've got to speak to Jonathan as well, about Susie.'

'Louise is on the list,' Bob added.

Rick exchanged a look of understanding with Clarice. 'It's time for me to get away,' he said as he stood up.

'Not on a Saturday, surely?' Sandra said.

'He's coming back,' Clarice told her. 'He's only going for a few hours.'

'I need to check in with the team,' he said, bending to kiss her. 'See you later.'

'Are you sure he'll come back, darlin'?' Sandra joked as she watched Bob walk with Rick to the car.

'Yes,' Clarice said without hesitation, 'if he can.'

After loading their car with boxes full of cake stands and old-fashioned tea services for the following day's fund-raiser, Bob and Sandra also departed.

Clarice phoned Jonathan to make arrangements to meet at his surgery mid-afternoon, then called Georgie. The forthcoming event had not thrown up any unresolved issues, but, as Clarice had guessed, Georgie's desire to find out more about Guy's disappearance had moved into top gear.

Clarice made it clear there was nothing she could add to the rumours surrounding the Corkindales. Georgie was disappointed but not beaten. With a juicy morsel of gossip she was like a dog with a bone, tenacious, never giving up.

Clarice had saved the most difficult conversation till last.

'I'm so pleased to hear from you.' Louise sounded edgy. 'Did you find out anything new from James?'

'I'm afraid not,' Clarice said, before filling Louise in on what James had told her.

'It sounds as if we share the same view about Guy's depression – it was down to the Bream case – but it's frustrating that he couldn't shed any light on who Charles might be.'

'He did say that if anything new emerged he'd phone, to keep me in the loop,' Clarice said.

'I suppose that's something, but I just feel so flat. Nothing's happening.'

'It will,' Clarice said. 'We need to believe that the police will pick up on a strand that leads somewhere.'

'I hope you're right. I've read of situations where people vanish and are never found. If we don't find him soon, I might just explode.'

'Don't do that!' Clarice said. 'The children and Charlotte depend on your support.'

'You're right.' Louise sounded tearful. 'What about tomorrow?'

'I thought you might want to give it a miss,' Clarice said. 'If there's so much gossip going around, do you really want to bring the children?'

'Life has to go on,' Louise said.

Clarice remembered their earlier conversation, when Louise had described herself as old-school. Stiff upper lip and keep calm and carry on and all that. Clarice was unconvinced; her own concern was that the children might find it awkward. 'Are you sure?' she asked.

'Yes, if it weren't the holidays, they'd be at school facing other people. It'll be extra help on the stalls, especially with Tara being with us.'

'OK,' Clarice said. 'But if you change your mind, just give me a ring.'

Saturday was one of the two weekly market days in Castlewick. Popular with visitors, the place was always busy on August days when the sun was shining. Several coaches were parked on open ground at the edge of the town. Holidaymakers on day trips from Skegness made their way to the dark blue covered stalls in the square, despite the fact that the market sold nothing more exciting than fruit and vegetables. An added attraction was the wide variety of antique shops, ranging from junk to top quality, for which Castlewick was known. The fish and chip shop and local cafés were busy too, grateful no doubt for the extra trade the market brought.

Driving into the veterinary car park, Clarice saw Jonathan waiting at the open door of the surgery.

'Just the one customer today,' he called as she backed into a space.

'It is good of you to see me on your rest day,' she said gratefully.

'Nonsense, I get emergency visits all the time – animals don't stick to timetables with illness.'

Once she was inside, he gave a cheeky chuckle. 'Dare we mention the H word?'

'I expect yours was as bad as mine,' Clarice said with a smile. She had left a message on Jonathan's phone the day after their supper date, thanking them for a splendid evening and admitting to a hangover.

'Mine was bad, but I think Keith might have overindulged a tad more than us. He was rubbish all the next day, poor boy.'

Clarice noticed he didn't sound overly sincere in his sympathy. Smug was more the word.

'It was a great evening,' she said. 'I shall remember the blue gin.'

'Me too,' Jonathan said as he petted Susie. 'The gin, the wine and the large brandies we had after you'd gone.'

'Ah,' Clarice said. 'I hope Keith didn't have important clients first thing in the morning.'

'The brandy was a mistake, but he did soldier on.'

Jonathan lifted Susie onto the table and she gave him a friendly lick.

'Thank you, lovely girl,' he said. 'Now, let's look at this leg.' He slowly removed the bandage. 'Yes,' he said, switching to professional mode. 'Well done, that's healed nicely. I'm not going to cover it up again. You will still have to be vigilant – make sure there's no chewing – but you've done well keeping her calm. It's not an easy task with a Boxer.'

'She is pretty full-on, but she's behaved well and fitted in with our dogs beautifully.'

'Tell me about the opening – spare no details.'

Clarice went over the course of the exhibition again, surprised when she told him about getting locked in the security cupboard that he didn't laugh.

'That's awful,' he said. 'I know you suffer from claustrophobia – it must have been so frightening.'

'I had Rick with me; it would have been worse on my own.'

He nodded and appeared to deliberate.

'I don't like to mention Guy, but there has been a lot of talk since the police searched the house.'

'It was inevitable – his disappearance was bound to get out,' Clarice said. 'One of the curses of small towns and villages.'

Jonathan lifted Susie back down onto the floor, where she wiggled her back end happily. 'Louise phoned when you first brought Susie in to say that as Charlotte is so preoccupied, any veterinary charges must go on her account. Today is a freebie, though.'

'Thank you, Jonathan, that's kind,' Clarice said.

'Ah.' He raised an index finger. 'You might retract that sentiment when you hear what I'm going to ask you.' He smiled. 'I'm giving with one hand and taking with the other.'

Clarice waited.

'I've been contacted by social services about a house clearance.'

'I see,' she said. 'Do we know how many animals?'

'The woman is a Mrs Helen Ambrose. Lives in a council property on Dutton Lane.' Jonathan had folded his arms and leaned against the examination table. 'As far as we're aware, she has four cats. Usual story, we think she's rescuing them. But nobody who calls ever gets past her front door, so we don't actually know how many there are in there.'

'I know that name,' Clarice said with surprise. 'Charlotte employed Helen Ambrose as a cleaner. She told her not to come in for a bit when Guy went missing. Helen took umbrage and told her she wouldn't be coming back.'

'Apparently she cleaned for other people and also worked as a carer, going into elderly people's homes. The carer work was through an agency.'

'Yes, Charlotte told me. Why have you been asked to clear the house?' Clarice asked.

Jonathan stroked Susie's ears as he talked. 'The daughter of one of her clients thought money was going missing, so she set up a camera. Helen was indeed pinching money, and it's since come to light that she'd been stealing from all the old people she worked for.'

'Don't tell me, to pay for the cats?'

'So sad; she probably thought herself a modern-day Robin Hood: steal from what she perceived to be wealthy older folk to pay for cat food.'

'It is sad,' Clarice agreed. 'People like her start with the best of intentions, perhaps taking in one stray, and then another, and another, then when it gets out of hand, they lose the plot.'

Jonathan nodded.

'Is she going to prison?'

'Bernice, the social worker, says that it's highly likely, due to the amount of money involved; it comes to court on Tuesday.'

'I thought that for a first offence it was usual to receive a suspended sentence?'

'It's not her first offence,' Jonathan said. 'She's done this before as a carer employed by a different agency. The new agency had the correct DBS check done on her but her previous criminal record didn't show up because she'd changed her surname and used a different address.'

'Will she sign the animals over, or does she have family or friends who might want to take one or two?'

'No family or friends. I've told Bernice it will be a requirement that she sign them over.' Jonathan looked severe. 'If she does receive a custodial sentence, she'll go straight to prison, so arrangements need to be in place. Otherwise the inspectors will go in with the police to remove the animals.'

'OK, let me know what happens on Tuesday – I'll be on standby.'

'Thank you, Clarice.' Jonathan looked relieved. 'Will you contact that friend at the charity in Peterborough, in case the numbers are larger than anticipated?'

'Yes, I'll sound him out. I took four cats for him last year when he did a house clearance, so I'm sure he'll be happy to help.'

'Bring them straight here,' Jonathan said. 'I'll check them for any health issues before you hand them over to the foster carers, plus I'll scan them for pet chips.'

'That's great, I'll do that,' Clarice agreed, 'but will you have enough room?'

'Tuesday should be quiet, and there'll be six empty spaces in the recovery room. If there are more than that, I'll set up some cages. We have four collapsible spares for emergencies. If your foster carers are on the ball, the cats will only need to be confined for an hour or two before being moved on.'

After finalising the details with Jonathan, Clarice said her goodbyes. Lifting Susie into the back of the car, she thought about Helen's reaction when Charlotte had told her not to come in to work. Charlotte said it had not been polite; Clarice had thought it was likely to have been provoked by not being paid for the missed week. But now she realised that if Helen had already known about the court date, that would explain why she'd told Charlotte she wouldn't be returning to work. Her solicitor would have advised her that given her previous conviction, come Tuesday she was highly likely to be serving a prison sentence.

As she drove home, Clarice mentally went through her list of foster carers who had spaces and wondered what Rick would say, having already told her she'd taken on too much with the exhibition and the Sunday fund-raiser. At least he would be home later and they could have some proper time together, just the two of them.

As she entered the cottage, the house phone began to ring, and she hastily patted the dogs in passing to reach it before it went to the answering machine.

'Clarice?' She recognised the voice with its hint of a South African accent.

'James,' she said. 'Good to hear from you.'

'Did the opening of the exhibition go well?'

'Yes, thank you. It was busy, lots of work sold – by all four ceramicists.'

'That's great, I'll look forward to seeing it with Lizzy.' He sounded upbeat. 'The reason I'm phoning is that I thought you'd want to know: the police have located Charles.'

Chapter 19

It was almost 7 p.m. There had been no phone calls or messages from Rick, and Clarice tried to suppress her mounting disappointment. She wanted to discuss her telephone call from James, but mostly she just wanted him to come home.

She busied herself in the kitchen, preparing a tuna bake, which she'd put in the oven when he arrived, then moving on to make a salad. Ten minutes later, while she was opening his favourite Australian Shiraz, she heard the car arriving, and her spirits soared with relief.

He came into the kitchen to the frenzied welcome of the three dogs.

'We have a guest!' he called.

Following him in was Daisy Bodey, who had worked with him first as a constable before her promotion to detective sergeant. Slim and athletic, with dark brown eyes and short shiny hair, she always made Clarice think of a sleek spaniel.

'Daisy!' Clarice's voice gave away her delight; Daisy was not only Rick's working partner but a trusted friend. Although she'd wanted Rick to herself, Daisy was someone for whom Clarice didn't mind making an exception.

'Her car is kaput,' Rick said, as he made a fuss of the dogs.

'I'm still hoping it's something trivial,' Daisy said with a wide grin. 'Rick tailed me to Fred's garage, but they won't look at it now until Monday morning.'

'I've asked Daisy to stay over,' Rick said. 'We're working tomorrow morning.'

'Brilliant,' Clarice said. Then, after a pause for thought, 'That Daisy can stay over – not that you're working on a Sunday.'

Rick and Daisy laughed; in Rick's case, Clarice thought, a little too heartily. He'd told her he would be on standby for the fund-raiser in Lincoln, but that had been before the discovery of Debbie Abbot's body.

'We should be finished by midday,' Daisy said. 'I gather Rick's going on to Lady Jayne's to help you out in the afternoon.'

'Well, you're very welcome to stay; we haven't had a catch-up for ages.' As she spoke, Clarice suppressed a spasm of guilt for doubting Rick.

'Rick's been telling me about the Guy Corkindale case,' Daisy said. 'Is that his dog?' She looked at Susie.

'It is. Her name's Susie.'

'You're beautiful.' Daisy crouched to stroke Susie, only to find herself mobbed, the centre of attention of all three dogs.

'A bit of competition for our own two,' Clarice said.

'Yes, I can see that,' Daisy laughed. 'Can I do anything, Clarice – after inviting myself to supper, I should at least help out.'

'Yes, you can get Rick to find some glasses,' Clarice said. 'We can have a drink in the garden while the food's cooking.'

Outside, with only the sound of birds and the occasional car passing on the top road, the garden was still. Rick wrapped

Susie's lead around the leg of the table so she couldn't wander away as Blue and Jazz spread themselves out nearby on the grass.

'I heard from James,' Clarice said when they were all seated, Clarice and Daisy with gin and tonics and Rick with a can of beer. 'He's a friend of Guy's,' she explained to Daisy.

'In the same chambers?' Daisy asked as she leaned back sipping her drink.

'That's him,' Clarice said.

'I've filled Daisy in on the case,' Rick said. 'Who the main players are.'

'Good.' Clarice nodded. Daisy had an analytical outlook and could be counted upon to contribute.

'Bet James told you they'd found Charles,' Rick said.

'You heard?'

'Yes, Barbara Graham knows I'm keeping an eye on the case. She said that it's Charles Tidswell.'

'Yes,' Clarice replied. 'James said they'd thought he had an alibi to account for the relevant time, but it's fallen through.'

'Indeed. Tidswell said he'd been at the hospital with his wife; his father-in-law had died after an operation. But he's nowhere to be seen on the hospital CCTV. He wasn't there.'

'Has he been brought in?'

'He's in Newcastle with his wife's family and has agreed to be interviewed on his return on Monday with – Barbara told me – his very aggressive, slippery solicitor.'

'No rush then?' Clarice said.

'Being realistic,' Rick sounded deflated, 'there's no proof that he is the right Charles. You know how vague Charlotte is about what she saw – all they have is the name, and the fact that he's known to people connected to the Bream case.'

'He wasn't known to Charlotte?' Daisy asked.

'No,' Clarice said, 'and she took little interest in either the person or the car he was driving.'

'But why should she?' Daisy said. 'A busy Monday morning, three kids on holiday, she works herself – and she wasn't to know Guy would disappear!'

'It all seems too black and white,' Clarice said. 'I'm wondering if we might be missing something obvious.'

'What do you mean?' Rick asked.

'The more I dwell on the facts, the more I question Guy's role in his disappearance. Things were not good between him and Charlotte, so he could have spun her a line. The police searched the house and grounds, but he's not there and he's not in London. We're asking if Housman had something to do with his disappearance, because he's a known associate of Tidswell.' Clarice paused to consider. 'But what possible advantage does it give Housman to kill Guy?'

'Are you saying it's more about the family issues?' Rick picked up the thread Clarice was following. 'Guy's depression?'

'We've already gone there, but unless he's had a breakdown, it doesn't fit,' Clarice said.

'If it's that, he'll turn up eventually, alive hopefully,' Rick said.

The three of them looked at one another before drifting into contemplative thought.

'We kept saying that it always comes back to Bream,' Clarice said, 'but perhaps that's what Guy wanted us to believe. That Bream was involved in his disappearance.'

'It's what you said in the hotel in London, about Guy being more deceitful than we believed. It takes us away from Guy being a victim.' Rick pondered. 'Perhaps we need to extend the search further, to look at other villains he's defended. Maybe we're looking in the wrong place.'

'But?' Clarice said.

'But,' Rick picked up on her thoughts, 'it is still a missing person case. Barbara's involvement is because of the criminal connection and Guy's work. Most importantly, I can't go poking around in another officer's case.' And with a meaningful look at both her and Daisy, he changed the subject. 'Has Clarice told you how well the opening of the exhibition in London went? Every one of the four artists sold well at the private view.'

'We've not had much time to chat recently,' Daisy said, her eyes sparkling impishly. Clarice knew that however interested Daisy was in the number of pots she'd sold, she was playing along, following Rick's lead.

'Have I not told you, Daisy?' she said in a teasing voice.

Rick crossed his arms, looking from one to the other of the smirking women. So Clarice began to fill Daisy in about each of her fellow ceramicists, finding as she spoke that what had been a slightly ironic litany became a genuine celebration of their creative endeavours and her pleasure at their success.

After a while, they went inside to eat, and when they had finished, they moved into the living room with their wine glasses. Daisy and Clarice continued to chat animatedly, and it was some time before Clarice glanced at Rick to see that he had left his glass on the side table and spread himself along the sofa to fall asleep.

'Poor sod, he's knackered,' Daisy said kindly.

'You won't be so sympathetic when he starts to snore,' Clarice said.

'We might have both joined him by then – you've had a busy time too, from what Rick's said.'

Clarice moved the conversation on to more interesting things. 'What's happening with you and Ollie Pierce, that nice sergeant in Lincoln? Rick said you were seeing him.'

'Huh,' Daisy shot back. 'Seeing is one word.' She paused. 'Sergeant Ollie Pierce and I are just friends, nothing more.'

'I thought you'd been seen out and about with him?'

Daisy settled herself firmly into Rick's favourite armchair. 'Ollie's divorced, like me, and about six months ago we were talking about a film we both wanted to see. He said, "Let's go as friends" – that's how it started.'

'Do you really like him?' Clarice asked.

'I do. In fact I fancy him rotten. It's been a long time since the divorce, and Ollie is so decent – funny and kind.'

'So what's stopping you moving to the next level?'

'About a week after going to see the film, we were talking about this new Chinese restaurant, and he asked if I would like to go with him. I said, "Is it a date, Ollie?"' Daisy paused, smiling. 'He said, "No, just as friends".'

'So that's how it's continued?'

'Yes.' Daisy sounded dejected. 'We see one another outside of work once every week or two. I always ask if it's a date, and he always replies . . .'

'. . . "Just as friends".' Clarice finished the sentence.

'It's a bit of a joke between us now,' Daisy said. 'I'm seeing him tomorrow night; we're both taking our one-man tents to camp out at the music festival in Leeds.'

'You could forget your tent,' Clarice suggested.

'He's driving – my car's kaput, remember. I think he might notice when he picks me up if I've forgotten my tent.'

'You need a plan, Daisy.'

'Clarice, you're wearing your devious face!'

'I didn't even know I had one of those.'

'Never mind that.' Daisy leaned towards her. 'I'm all out of ideas – tell me what I should do.'

'First,' Clarice glanced at Rick, ensuring he was still asleep, 'we need to pray to St Jude.'

'Never heard of him,' Daisy said.

'He's the patron saint of lost causes. Six months is a heck of a long time.'

'What are we praying *for*?' Daisy looked puzzled.

'Rain,' Clarice said, wearing an innocent smile.

Chapter 20

The following morning, after breakfast, Clarice waved goodbye to Rick and Daisy. The day was warm, with the sun only occasionally disappearing behind drifting, blowsy white clouds. She hoped that it would remain that way into the afternoon.

At midday, after walking the dogs and putting out more food for the cats, she packed a box with tea, coffee, milk and sugar and set out for Lincoln.

The journey was uneventful. Clarice found herself reflecting upon Louise, wondering if she would turn up with the children. While appreciating that she was trying to occupy them through various activities, a busy fund-raiser, with so many people, might be confusing and upsetting for them.

She had a place reserved in the small car park. As she came in through the back gate, she saw Jayne, Georgie, Bob and Sandra working together, setting out the small tables and chairs on the lawn. She paused for a moment to take in the garden. The grass looked as immaculate as before, its velvet lushness combined with the sweetness of the aromatic walled garden magical. On her way across the lawn, she stopped to talk to Jayne and then to Sandra.

'Hope they like my cakes,' Sandra said nervously. 'It's the first time I've put some in.'

'I've eaten lots of your cakes and they'll love them,' Clarice said. 'It's a shame Jayne didn't want a tombola – you always find such interesting things as prizes. And the tombola always makes a lot.'

'Probably a bit common for this sort of gaff, darlin'.' Sandra spoke quietly, glancing sideways at Jayne. 'Don't worry about it.'

'Hi!' Georgie called, and hand raised, her long white legs in yellow shorts, feet encased in pristine plimsolls, she bounded past Clarice on her way into the kitchen.

Within a few minutes, Clarice was in the kitchen too, setting out the items she'd brought with her. As other volunteers arrived, she helped them unpack the cakes to be served with the tea, all the while marvelling at the artistry and ingenuity of the cake makers. There were also donations of chutney, jam, sweets and biscuits for the stalls, and Lady Jayne had contributed home-made lemonade. The floats were ready so that the volunteers had sufficient change and Georgie was busy designating specific roles.

A few minutes later, Louise wandered into the kitchen with Tara, Angel and Poppy.

'Hello, Clarice,' she said. 'What can we do?'

Clarice felt an overwhelming rush of sadness for her friend. She looked gaunt and ill, her smile set like concrete. She took her arm and steered her out onto the lawn. 'Let's have a word with Georgie, she's in charge.'

'Me too,' Angel said, trotting along beside her.

'Yes, you too.' Clarice smiled at her, taking the proffered hand.

'More troops,' Georgie said, joining them as they emerged into the sunshine.

'Yes, where do you want us?' Clarice asked, hoping that Georgie would be able to find roles for everyone.

'You're on the home-made goods stall, Clarice,' Georgie said. 'If people want to ask questions about CAW, I'll point them in your direction. Louise, you can help Sandra in the kitchen, with hot drinks and lemonade.' Georgie was talking rapidly without appearing to draw breath. 'The cake stands still need doing, and Bob is taking the money as the orders come in. Tara, you can be part of the waitress crew taking the refreshments to the tables. There's another crew clearing and washing up.'

'What about me?' Angel's small voice demanded.

'Are they with me?' Clarice asked.

'Yes, Poppy and Angel can be on your stand,' Georgie said.

After taking the plastic tub containing the float of small change, Clarice went to her stall with the children. Georgie was now almost a blur as she flitted from one group of volunteers to another, ensuring that everyone was ready. She'd delegated Rosalind and Chrissy to take the entrance fee at the gate, the perfect role for gossip while people were paying. The side gate was opened promptly at 2 p.m., to a polite and orderly queue that snaked across the front of the house.

'Look,' Clarice said, pointing to the trestle table covered with a bright red gingham cloth, home-made products set out on top. 'We've got our first customers.' She moved into position behind the table. The next table along had flowers and plants, and Louise had brought in several trays of potted herbs.

'What can I get for you, modom?' Poppy, her fingers laced together across her chest and her face fixed in concentration, gazed up at an elderly lady inspecting a jar of strawberry jam. The waiting customers were charmed, but Clarice noticed Angel watching, her lips parted slightly, like a small, fierce animal baring its teeth. She realised it might be easy to feel sidelined by such a charming and pretty younger sister.

The elderly customer presented the jam to Poppy, who took it, then looked at Clarice, unsure what was expected of her.

'Let me see,' Clarice said, checking the price label stuck on the jar. 'That will be three pounds, please. Poppy, can you put it into the bag for modom, and Angel, I'm sure you're good at maths; how much change are you going to give?'

The customer obligingly held her bag open and passed a five-pound note to Angel.

'Two pounds,' Angel said, brightening up. She looked at Clarice, who nodded encouragingly and watched as she put the note into the money box and extracted two pound coins to pass over.

'I've got a good team,' Clarice said.

'You certainly have,' the customer commented before wandering away.

The time slipped past quickly, the children enjoying their roles. When Clarice heard the ringtones of her phone, she guessed it would be Rick.

'All going well?' he asked.

'Yes, all good here, what about you?'

'I've just dropped Daisy at her flat. Do you want me to come and help?'

'You're welcome to come,' Clarice said. 'But there are a lot of volunteers today – I think Georgie overestimated the number of people needed – so there won't be a great deal for you to do.'

'No problem, I'll head for home, walk the dogs and feed everyone,' Rick said. 'Then I can start on supper before you get back.'

'That would be great,' Clarice said. 'With Bob and Sandra being here as well, one of us would have had to leave early to feed the animals.'

'Sorted,' Rick said. 'I'll see you at home later.'

'Are there too many people helping?' Poppy asked, frowning, having been listening to Clarice's conversation.

'No,' Clarice said, 'we have exactly the right number, so I don't need Rick to come and help.'

'I'm glad Josie didn't come then – she's my best friend at school.'

'Did she want to come?' Clarice asked.

'Yes, because I told her Susie wouldn't be coming.'

'Why, is she frightened of dogs?'

'No,' Poppy said, 'just Susie because she bites people. Josie's mummy says she can't go anywhere if Susie's going to be there.'

'Susie doesn't bite people,' Clarice said with surprise.

'It was only once,' Angel butted in, 'and you shouldn't have told Josie about it.'

'Who did she bite?' Clarice asked.

'Tara doesn't want her back. She says it's better now without Susie,' Poppy added dejectedly.

'Poppy!' Angel glanced at Clarice. 'Mummy said no tittle-tattling.'

'No tittle-tattling.' Poppy echoed her sister's words, then: 'We came here with our Daddy.'

Clarice remembered Louise telling her Tara had no interest in dogs. Then marvelled at the way, in the company of small children, the conversation meandered in such random directions.

'Not *here*,' Angel said, 'not to this house!'

'We went to see swans,' Poppy said as if she'd not listened to her sister's comment.

'It was near the tall buildings,' Angel insisted, 'not here.'

'I know what she means,' Clarice said. 'Where the swans gather, Brayford Pool, it's about fifteen minutes' walk from here.'

'We feed the ducks in Castlewick, by the water,' Angel said.

'With Daddy.' Poppy's voice was low.

'And Mummy sometimes,' Angel chipped in.

Clarice tried to imagine Charlotte taking the children to the flat concrete area near the town's only supermarket. Mothers with toddlers gathered on sunny days exchanging pleasantries while feeding the ducks; she'd imagined Charlotte to be too busy for such trivial domestic activities.

The afternoon moved on. Clarice observed Tara going back and forth with a tray bearing refreshment and cakes. As she passed by, she looked towards her young half-sisters and nodded or smiled encouragingly.

'Tara is good at being a waiter,' Poppy said. 'Can we have something to drink?'

'Yes,' Clarice said. 'I should have thought of that myself.'

'Tara's not a waiter, that's a man. She's a *waitress*,' Angel corrected her sister. 'Shall I go into the kitchen and ask for drinks?'

'No, just go over to Tara – look she's on her way back – and tell her what you want. A cup of tea for me, please.'

'Lemonade and a cake for me.' Poppy sang the words, her voice shrill.

Clarice watched as Angel ducked around the end of the table to waylay Tara before Poppy drew her attention to another customer. A few minutes later, she looked back and Tara had gone. Angel had been stopped by Rosalind, bending so that she was at eye level with the child, deep in conversation.

'Stay here, Poppy,' Clarice commanded, and moved quickly to join the pair on the lawn.

'He'll maybe come home this weekend,' Rosalind was saying, her voice a sympathetic stage whisper.

Clarice saw Angel's pale, unsmiling face. It seemed to register what was being said but she appeared frozen, unsure of what her response should be.

'What do you want, Rosalind?' Clarice spoke in a friendly tone.

'Oh, nothing really.' Rosalind looked awkward. 'I was just saying to Angel that her daddy—'

'Yes,' Clarice cut in, 'I heard.' She stared hard at Rosalind until, pink in the face, the woman turned without speaking and retreated to stand with Chrissy.

Clarice strode back to her stall, where Poppy was peeping around the corner of the table awaiting their return. She felt Angel's small hand slide into her own, and they walked back together.

'What did that woman want?' Poppy asked.

'Nothing,' Angel said, 'she was just a nosy-parker.'

'Yes,' Poppy said, then looked at Clarice. 'Mummy called me that when I thought Daddy was still home.'

'When was that?' Clarice asked.

'When I saw Daddy's blue diary upstairs in the study. I told Mummy and she said, "Don't be a nosy-parker".'

'I expect she was worried,' said Clarice.

'I thought Daddy was still home, but he went out and didn't come back, and Susie ran away to Grandma.'

'Mum said he hadn't come back from a meeting, and he'd never left for London. He always takes his diary to London.' Angel became the all-knowing big sister.

'Mummy had been crying,' Poppy said, 'and she never cries.'

'I saw his London bag, like always,' Angel said, 'but he didn't come back.'

'Let me find out about those drinks,' Clarice said.

'Tara said she's going to bring lemonade and cakes,' Angel said, 'and a tea for you.'

'Mummy says *you're* a nosy-parker.' Poppy beamed innocently at Clarice as she passed on her mother's private opinion.

'Your mummy is probably right; I do ask lots of questions.'

'You shouldn't tell her that, it's rude,' Angel said.

'I wasn't rude – was I, Clarice?' Poppy's face fell in disappointment.

'No,' Clarice laughed, 'don't worry, I know you didn't mean it to be rude.'

'We shouldn't be telling people things Mummy said,' Angel protested. 'She wouldn't like it.' It was clear she was regretting opening up to Clarice. The questions about her father had clearly brought back into focus the reality of the gap he'd left.

Good fortune brought another customer, distracting the children from further discussion. Ten minutes later, Tara arrived with the tray of refreshments.

'I didn't know if you wanted sugar,' she said. 'There wasn't a spare sugar bowl, so I've brought some cubes.'

'Thank you, Tara,' Clarice said. 'I don't – but you think of everything.'

'Mugs rather than pretty teacups for the workers!' Tara gave a broad grin and rushed away.

'Why not sit on the grass for ten minutes and have your cakes and drinks?' Clarice settled the girls, passing them their lemonade once they were seated.

'Clarice?'

She turned to find Rosalind close by.

'I'm so sorry if I caused any upset.' Rosalind touched Clarice's arm and let out a small, nervous girly giggle. 'No offence was intended.'

Clarice struggled with the knowledge gained from experience that behind the charming facade, Rosalind was both unkind and troublesome. She forced a congeniality into her voice that she did not feel. 'Painful subjects are best left alone with small children.'

Rosalind's face had regained its earlier flush; she looked around as if to find another subject and her eyes fell on the mug of tea.

'I could murder a cuppa,' she said. 'I asked for tea nearly an hour ago – they must have forgotten.' Her voice was peevish.

'Have that one,' Clarice said. 'I haven't even picked it up – it's untouched.'

'You are kind, Clarice.' Rosalind affected a small dry cough. 'You're a real lifesaver.' She meandered back towards the gate clutching the mug.

As the afternoon wore on, the numbers dwindled. The sun had disappeared behind darkening clouds and, with few customers, the volunteers chattered and laughed amongst themselves.

'How are you two getting on?' Louise approached the almost empty table.

'We've nearly sold everything,' Angel told her with satisfaction.

'That's brilliant!'

'The girls have been a real help,' Clarice said. 'It must be almost home time.'

'Yes,' Louise said. 'I'm just doing a wander around for a litter check before we go.'

'Don't think the types that come to this sort of event are big on dropping litter, fortunately,' Clarice laughed.

'No, but I told Jayne I'd just check,' Louise said.

'Me too, Grandma,' Poppy offered.

'And me.' Angel followed her sister.

The volunteers began to clear what remained, folding the tablecloths and collapsing the tables. Georgie brought out an empty box and Clarice packed the few unsold items into it.

'Can I take that for you?' Bob was suddenly next to her. 'It'll squeeze into our car.'

'Thanks, Bob,' Clarice said. 'I think with the number of people who turned up, we've done very well.'

'Clarice!' Jayne came over to the table, followed as always by Basil.

Clarice sensed unease in her voice. 'Are you all right, Jayne?' she asked.

'You'd better come and talk to Louise. She's in a bit of a state. One of her grandchildren appears to have gone walkabout.'

Chapter 21

As Clarice entered the kitchen, followed closely by Jayne, they found Louise coming in from the entrance hall.

'She's not upstairs,' she announced, her eyes wild with panic.

Sandra, Bob, Chrissy, Tara and Angel had all followed Jayne and Clarice in, and now stood silently in the doorway, looking from one to the other.

'We need to have a methodical search,' Bob said.

'Are there any small places she might hide, in the house or garden?' Clarice asked Jayne.

'Are there just!' Jayne said. 'A house as old as this is great for hide-and-seek.'

'She's not outside.' Georgie, looking flushed, burst into the kitchen. 'I've searched under and behind every bush.'

'Is the side gate open?' Clarice glanced at Chrissy, who shrugged.

'It's locked now,' Georgie said, 'but it was still open until a few minutes ago.'

'What about the gate at the end of the garden?'

'No, that was locked at two o'clock when we started to let people in. We didn't want anyone sneaking in without paying.'

'Where's Rosalind?' Clarice asked. 'She might have seen something.'

Chrissy shook her head. 'She's been in the loo on and off for the last hour – think she's got the trots.'

'Too much information,' Jayne said, twisting her face into an expression of distaste, before turning to Clarice. 'I'll go and double-check upstairs.'

'I'll come with you.' Georgie moved to followed Jayne.

'I'll do room by room downstairs,' Louise said.

'If she's gone out, she won't have gone far,' Clarice said. 'Chrissy, could you help Louise?'

'What about us?' Bob asked.

'I'll go up Steep Hill with Tara, if you can walk down Danesgate.' Clarice thought that the walk downwards, which flattened out to become less steep, might be easier for her older friend.

'I'll go with you, darlin',' Sandra said decisively to her husband.

'I was going to walk down the hill,' Tara said bossily, moving swiftly to the door as she spoke.

'That's fine.' Bob looked at Sandra. 'We'll go up, then.'

'I'll go with Tara,' Clarice said, relieved that the discussion about who was going to look where appeared to be at an end. 'Phone me on my mobile if you find her,' she called to Louise as she left, 'and I'll let Bob and Sandra know.'

Louise nodded.

'And if you don't find her after searching the house, ring the police and report her missing immediately.'

Louise's hand went instantly to her throat, her face distorted with fear. She nodded for a second time.

'We don't know how long ago she went,' Tara said.

'It can't have been very long,' Clarice replied.

Only a handful of shops and cafés would still be open, but there were a few people walking up and down from the hill. Clarice and Tara weaved through them.

'We need to get to her,' Tara moved with long strides next to Clarice, 'before Gran does her nut.'

'Why would she have gone off on her own?' Clarice asked. 'Has she done this sort of thing before?'

'No.' Tara turned her head to give Clarice a long, reflective look. 'I'd expect it more from Angel – Poppy's usually so well behaved – but . . .'

'What?' Clarice sensed Tara was holding back. The two of them had now fallen into a matching rhythmic roll, like a brace of show ponies working together to pull a trap. The conversation continued in controlled bursts.

'While we were clearing up, she asked about us coming to Lincoln before, with Daddy, and seeing the swans.'

'She mentioned that to me too,' Clarice said. 'The quickest route to Brayford Pool from Jayne's house is Beaumont Fee, and then Newland, but she'd never find her way there on her own.'

'No, she wouldn't, but she's only six – she doesn't know that.'

'Let's stick with the plan. Heading west might be the next option.'

Clarice concentrated on their speedy descent of the hill. She considered herself fit, but her stamina level was no match for a fifteen-year-old, and she was getting pain down the left side of her body. She also felt angry with herself. Why had Poppy's mention of her father and the swans not immediately prompted her concern? Surely it should have registered with her, caused alarm. She knew she was unused to the ways of children, but Tara, at fifteen half-child half-woman, appeared to understand her siblings.

As they reached the bottom of Danesgate, the road went in two directions, both leading to Silver Street, the route to the left shorter.

'Let's split at Clasketgate – you go that way. I'll meet you around the other side, on Silver Street.'

Tara nodded, veering off to the right, while Clarice followed the road that led to the main route for traffic going in and out of the city.

Suppose, she pondered, Poppy had asked someone to take her to see the swans. Someone dubious, who saw the small, pretty child as a lucky opportunity. Or she could have walked in front of a car. But then there would be commotion – ambulances and so on. No, that couldn't have happened . . . She had now reached Silver Street. It was busier there, although not as much as on a weekday. She needed to stop for a moment – the sharp pain in her side was like a knife. But what possessed her body was fear. For Poppy's safety, and for Charlotte, Louise, Angel and Tara, all of whom would be devastated, their lives ruined, if harm had come to the child.

Suddenly Tara was in front of her. She had worked around the longer route to reach the same point as Clarice.

'Shall we split up and check Silver Street, then High Street?' Tara asked, hopping from one foot to the other. 'I'll go this way.'

Clarice looked both ways, at the slow-moving traffic and the distant pedestrian area. 'No.' She stood still, thinking, calming herself. 'She hasn't been gone long, and she's only got little legs. Let's go back, you go the way I came, and I'll do your route. See you back where we separated before.'

'OK.' Tara looked dubious.

'Then I think we should go back up to the house, checking at the back of the flats and offices, and in each of the gardens and driveways.'

Tara nodded, and in a moment was gone.

A few minutes later, Clarice arrived back at Clasketgate to find Tara waiting for her.

'Shall we take opposite sides of the road going up the hill to check the gardens?' Tara asked.

'Good plan.' Clarice nodded, just as her mobile rang.

'What's going on?' Rick spoke without preamble, his voice full of concern. 'I had a call from the office about Guy's daughter. The constable knew that CAW was your charity, so she phoned me.'

Clarice told him what had happened.

'Bloody hell, how did she get out of the garden without being seen?' His voice was tight with anger.

'I don't know,' Clarice said. 'But I'm with Tara, searching. We can have this conversation later.'

'OK, I'm on my way.' He spoke the words and was gone. She imagined him running from the house to his car.

She stood quite still, and for a moment felt she might give way to tears. The feeling of helplessness, distress and defeat threatened to engulf her, but sensing Tara watching she pulled herself back. Tara was being so controlled, which must be difficult for someone of her age. She was likely to follow Clarice into emotional meltdown if Clarice led the way.

'Let's just check there, Tara.' She looked at the office building they'd circled on the way to Silver Street.

They split again, Tara disappearing to the left, Clarice to the right. They had quickly become a tight unit, working together for a common goal.

'She's here!' Tara's voice was shrill with excitement.

Clarice ran past the main entrance of the building to where a group of green and black bins stood in a line, with full dustbin bags next to them on the pavement. Behind were steps and a side door, and on the steps sat Poppy. Spread on her lap was a paper napkin from the fund-raiser, in the centre of which sat one of Sandra's squashed currant buns.

Tara sat down on the step next to her. Clarice went to sit on the other side.

'Do you want a bite of my bun?' Poppy asked her sister, her voice unconcerned, oblivious of the panic she had caused.

'Thanks, Poppy,' Tara replied, using the same tone, 'I had one earlier.'

'They look like flies.' Poppy prodded a currant. 'Don't think I can eat it.'

'Leave it then, we'll drop it in that bin,' Tara said.

'Mummy will tell me off for wasting food.' Poppy's lips dipped at the corners.

'If you don't tell her, she won't know.' Tara took the bun and napkin from her and went to a bin to drop them in.

Poppy smiled at Clarice, her tone conspiratorial. 'You won't tell Mummy?'

Clarice shook her head. 'I can keep secrets.'

Poppy gave a satisfied nod.

'Where were you going, Poppy?' Clarice asked gently. 'We've been looking everywhere for you.'

'I walked down the hill to feed the swans with the bun. I thought my daddy might be there. But I couldn't find them, and my legs got tired.'

Clarice patted her hand, and Tara sat back down and put her arm around the child's shoulders.

'You had us all worried,' Clarice said, watching Tara, as she gave her sister a gentle squeeze.

Awash with relief, she tapped out a text to Bob, Louise, Georgie and Rick.

We have found Poppy at the bottom of Danesgate, she is safe, and well. We are going to walk back up the hill now. Please tell the police she is safe.

Chapter 22

Clarice and Tara walked up the hill with Poppy between them holding their hands. Above, the dark sky rumbled with distant thunder. Looking at the gardens they passed, Clarice realised the impossibility of their search had they not found the little girl so quickly. Each garden had a multitude of foliage-covered areas and dark hiding places.

After they had gone a short way, she spotted a welcome party led by Louise rushing down Danesgate towards them. A moment later, a car arrived and stopped. A door opened and a young female constable climbed out.

'Hello,' she said kindly. 'Are you Poppy?'

The child looked up unsmiling and nodded.

'I'm Adele.' The officer bent down to Poppy's level. 'That lady,' she pointed at a second officer getting out of the car, 'is called Kerry. It's all right, you're not in trouble. We were just worried about you.'

'My dog's called Susie, she's a Boxer,' Poppy informed her.

'A good name, I like it.'

'Clarice is looking after her.' Poppy looked up at Clarice. 'Susie's had a poorly leg, but she's nearly better now.'

'You must be DI Beech's wife,' Adele said to Clarice.

'There aren't too many people about called Clarice,' Kerry added, smiling.

'Poppy!' Louise arrived and rushed towards her grand-daughter. Adele moved out of the way as she threw her arms around the child.

'I don't know if I should hug you or smack your bottom,' she said through tears.

'You wouldn't know how to smack my bottom, Grandma.' Poppy laughed as she wriggled out of the bear hug. 'You think it's wrong – you'd never do that.'

'Mummy and Daddy don't smack us either; nobody is allowed to hit us.' Angel, who had arrived holding Georgie's hand, took over the conversation from her sister. 'You're *very* naughty, Poppy. You are in *so* much trouble.'

'Let's not worry about that just now.' Bob, the last member of the welcome group, arrived slightly out of breath. 'Let's go back to the house, and everyone can calm down.'

Smiling, Louise took Poppy by the hand and Angel went to Tara, and the group turned and started to progress slowly back to the house.

They looked from behind like a solid colourful mass, their brightly coloured summer clothing expanding and contracting as they stopped and started, progressing at the speed of the slowest member.

Clarice stood for a moment with Adele. 'It's a shame you've had a wasted journey,' she said.

'No, not wasted.' Adele was watching Poppy as she walked with her grandmother. 'It's frightening when something like this happens, and we'd rather be called out early. It's best to get help quickly.'

'Yes, that's what my husband always says. Ah ...' Clarice paused to look at the white BMW estate coming up the hill towards them, 'talking of my husband ...'

The car stopped and Rick got out.

'I picked up your text,' he said. 'I was already on my way. She's all right?' He nodded towards Poppy's departing back.

'Yes, she's fine, quite unconcerned when we found her – unaware of the upset she'd caused,' Clarice said. 'She'd gone to find the swans; she'd been to see them before with her dad.'

'I'd better be going,' Adele said to Rick. 'Nice to meet you, Clarice.'

'Yes, likewise.' Clarice nodded.

They stood side by side watching the police car disappear up the hill.

'Bet that was scary.' Rick put his arm around Clarice's shoulder.

'Too bloody right.' Clarice remembered the feeling of helplessness. 'I was terrified of what might've happened, thinking of all the worst-case scenarios.'

'Makes you realise how frightening it must be to be a parent.' He kissed the top of her head. 'Do you want to go back to the house?'

'Yes, let's make sure everything's OK. My car's there as well,' Clarice said as they walked to the BMW. 'I doubt Jayne will ever want us back after this.'

Back at the house, Jayne let them in.

'We're all in the kitchen. Sandra's made everyone a cup of tea,' she told them.

Rick came forward, bending to kiss her on the cheek.

'Well,' she exclaimed cheerfully, 'this afternoon's certainly looking up.'

'Tell me what's been going on,' he said, and Clarice noticed that Jayne had taken his hand to lead him into the sitting room rather than the kitchen, perhaps for a one-to-one chat. She smiled. There was no doubting that when required, her husband knew how to turn on the charm.

'Clarice!' Georgie stopped her before she reached the kitchen. She looked agitated.

'Everything OK?' Clarice asked. 'At least as OK as it could be after all the panic?'

'No, it's not!' Georgie glanced back furtively at the group just out of earshot, and Clarice remembered the way Susie twitched and wriggled when trying to get attention.

'What's happened?'

'It's Rosalind,' Georgie said. 'She's been in and out of the loo, and Chrissy says it must be food poisoning.'

'Where are they?' Clarice scanned the garden.

'They've gone. But the only thing she had to eat all afternoon was one of Sandra's buns.'

'Rubbish,' Clarice said, exasperated. 'She wouldn't get food poisoning from a bun she ate this afternoon; it must have been something she had last night. That blasted woman is more trouble than she's worth.'

'Yes, I agree,' Georgie said, 'but I had to tell you, and I didn't want Sandra to hear. She'd be upset. They've had run-ins in the past, you know.'

'She would probably have given Rosalind a good talking-to.' Clarice raised her eyebrows.

'Anyway,' Georgie looked smug, 'I've just polished off the last of Sandra's buns – my fifth. And I've had no problems,' she whispered, pointing downwards, 'in that department.'

'Five?' Clarice said. 'I'm surprised you haven't been sick – talk about eating the profits.'

'It's just my metabolism. I burn up food.'

Clarice watched her bustle away to rejoin the group, then turned to find Louise gathering her jacket and bag, still looking tearful.

'I'm taking the children home now,' she said. 'I hope I survive Charlotte.' She sniffed and rubbed her hand across her face.

'Have you spoken to her?' Clarice asked.

'Yes, I phoned after I'd contacted the police and she said she was coming over, but I called her again when we knew Poppy was safe. She was so angry, Clarice, her tone of voice was really nasty.'

'Probably the shock. Once she realises that Poppy's OK, she'll just feel relieved.'

'No, it was more than that. She said I'd made things far worse for the girls, and that it was bad enough that their father had disappeared without one of them being killed.'

'What? That's a bit extreme.'

'She was ranting. I could hardly get a word in.' Louise's hands trembled as she lifted them in agitation.

'That just sounds like a distraught mother. Poppy wandered away, which was awful, but these things happen – nobody abducted her!'

'You didn't think it was a good idea for me to bring them, and you were right.' Louise was crying now, rubbing away the tears with a paper napkin.

'Come on, Gran.' Tara had appeared. 'You don't want to upset Poppy and Angel.' She spoke kindly, standing close to Louise, her hand resting consolingly on her grandmother's back.

'Yes.' Louise blew her nose noisily. 'You're right, Tara – and thank you again for finding Poppy.'

'It was just good luck.' Tara looked towards Clarice.

'It was more than that,' Louise said.

'Thank goodness it's all ended well,' Clarice said. 'I'm sure Charlotte will agree with that.'

After gathering the children, Louise left by the rear entrance. Clarice, Rick and Jayne joined the group in the kitchen for another twenty minutes until Sandra began gathering cups and plates. Georgie found a tea towel and Clarice and Bob washed up while Rick took the chairs and remaining boxes out to the cars.

When they were ready to leave, Clarice went to thank Jayne, who, in her pink floral cotton dress, eyes sparkling with good humour and not a hair out of place, looked relaxed and unflustered.

'It's been an eventful day,' she said.

'It has, Jayne, but we've raised quite a bit.'

'Yes,' Jayne said, 'Georgie told me. I am pleased.'

'I'm sorry about all the trouble with Poppy,'

'My dear,' Jayne rested her small hand on Clarice's arm, 'that was not your fault; these things happen. I was telling Rick about a similar incident with Jeremy, my youngest son, when he was only a baby. Please don't worry about it – all's well now.'

As Clarice walked with Rick to the cars, the promised rain started, a thin drizzle increasing as they went the length of the garden.

'At least it held off for the afternoon,' Rick said.

'Not good for camping.' Clarice looked up at the darkening sky.

'Yes, I'd forgotten that Daisy's gone to that festival with Ollie.'

'Maybe the rain's held off in Leeds.' Clarice smiled. 'So, tell me what happened with Jeremy.'

'Jayne was flying to New York to meet up with her husband,' Rick said. 'She was excited at the prospect of seeing him, and imbibed rather too much in the first-class departure lounge.' He paused for dramatic effect. 'It wasn't until she was on the plane, thinking about a nap, that the stewardess came to ask if she might have left something important behind in the airport.'

'Hellfire – not baby Jeremy?' Clarice said.

Rick gave a cheeky grin before diving into his car to escape the rain.

Chapter 23

The next morning Clarice found her progress in the workshop slow, the events of the previous day heavy in her mind.

Following the fund-raiser, Bob and Sandra had beaten them back to the cottage. By the time they'd unloaded the chairs and boxes, fed the cats and walked the three dogs, it was after seven in the evening. Rick had insisted they stay to share the fish pie he'd prepared earlier in the day.

The conversation had centred on the events of the day, mainly Poppy's disappearance, but also Louise's anguish. None of them, they all agreed, would have relished returning the children to an angry Charlotte.

As the guests left, Sandra, over a foot shorter than Rick, had stood on tiptoe to pat his cheek affectionately. 'Lovely, darlin',' she said. 'Thanks for the food and chat. I'm so glad I didn't need to fart around making a meal at home.' Bob, just an inch taller than his wife, gave him a manly bear hug.

Once they were alone, Clarice had fought the urge to burden Rick with the minutiae of the fund-raiser. Now that his mask of congenial host had been removed, his face was wan with fatigue, and his mind, she realised, was still focused on the Abbot case.

She had thought it unkind to keep him up talking. Today, after a large breakfast, he'd left early with another long working day ahead of him. But before he'd gone, Clarice asked if he was likely to hear from Inspector Barbara Graham with updates on the interview.

'Charles Tidswell?' he asked.

'You said he'd be back from Newcastle today. I hope his legal brief isn't *too* slippery so that Barbara can discover if he was the same Charles who Guy left the house with.'

'It will be what it is,' he said, his voice resigned. 'Remember what I've said.'

'It isn't your case.'

He responded with a knowing look, which Clarice took to mean he was glad she'd got the message.

Now, looking around her workshop, where she'd been for an hour and achieved nothing, she decided to go back to the house, let the dogs out for ten minutes and then make herself a sandwich.

As she finished eating, she heard a car arriving, its tyres crunching over the pebbles coming down the incline. The dogs, going to the door, began barking. Susie, now an entirely accepted member of the pack, was between Jazz and Blue, giving it her all. Clarice was pleased to see Louise walking towards her, but as she opened her arms to welcome her, Louise dissolved into tears. Clarice held her close until her sobs subsided, then guided her past the welcoming dogs into the kitchen.

'Now,' Clarice picked up Louise's hand, 'tell me.'

'Where to start?' Louise began to cry again, but gently. Clarice suspected from the heightened colour of her face and the puffiness around her eyes that she had been crying for some time.

'Charlotte?' Clarice asked.

'Yes, but ...' Louise was trembling. Clarice waited. 'Milo died last night.'

'Louise, I'm so sorry.'

'He was such a good age, and as you know, so doddery,' Louise said. 'I did love him, he was such a dear little chap. And he went gently, in his sleep.'

'That's something,' Clarice said. 'A peaceful end to a very happy life. He was so lucky to have had you.'

'Before that, when I took the girls back yesterday,' Louise continued, 'Charlotte was so cruel. I know I'd let her down, but ...'

'Was she unpleasant in front of the children?'

'No, she pushed them into the house, then walked with me to the car. I really thought she was going to hit me.'

'What did she say exactly?'

'That Poppy could have been killed, and I was never to be trusted again to take care of them.'

'Give her time, Louise,' Clarice said. 'She was probably in shock. Imagine if someone had been looking after Guy when he was Poppy's age, and he had wandered away. How would you have reacted?'

'The same, probably,' Louise said slowly. 'We were just going around the garden checking for litter. I took my eyes off them for a minute or two, and then she was gone.'

'It was at the end of the event,' Clarice said. 'There was no one on the gate, and we were all in a flurry of clearing-up, otherwise someone would probably have seen her wander out.'

'Yes, I've been over it a million times since yesterday,' Louise said, regaining control of her emotions.

Clarice went to pick up the kettle. 'Tea or coffee?' she asked.

'Tea, please,' Louise said. 'I'm sorry, I've done it again. This is the second time I've turned up here without checking to see if you're busy.'

'Don't worry about it. Poppy's been in my head all morning – it was upsetting for everyone, and now you've had to cope with losing Milo as well.'

'I felt awful getting Tara into trouble.' Louise's eyes glistened with fresh unshed tears.

'How did you do that?'

'When Charlotte pushed the children indoors, she said to Tara, "I'll speak to you in a minute," and her voice was really mean.'

Clarice watched as she again wiped her eyes, and waited for her to continue.

'I said, "Please don't tell Tara off, she was brilliant – it was her and Clarice who found Poppy".' Louise looked wretched. 'Charlotte said that at fifteen Tara was more than old enough to have taken responsibility for helping me keep an eye on them. And that with both of us there, they should have been safe.'

'I understand where she's coming from,' Clarice said thoughtfully. 'I was thinking yesterday how helpful and grown-up Tara is, but perhaps Charlotte forgets she's still a child in some respects. She can't be expected to bear the responsibility. We were all there, Louise, and none of us saw Poppy leave. These things happen – children do naughty things, nothing is ever a hundred per cent foolproof.'

'Yes.' Louise hung her head, dejected.

'Have you spoken to Charlotte today?'

'No, I've been to Lincoln.'

Clarice looked puzzled.

'You'll think I'm an idiot.' Susie, who had come to sit next to Louise, rested her head in her lap, fixing her large brown eyes on her face.

'Go on,' Clarice said.

'There's a homeless hostel there. I took a photograph of Guy to show them.'

They sat silently for a few moments while Louise stroked Susie's ears. 'Nothing,' she said finally. 'Guy had never been there.'

'I guess you had to try,' Clarice said.

Louise nodded. 'The man at the shelter was so kind, it made it worse really. I couldn't stop crying, and when I got back home, there was a phone call.'

'From Charlotte?' Clarice spoke hopefully.

'No, I wish it had been. It was Bridget Latimer, the family liaison police officer.'

'What did she say?'

'They're going to have something on the news asking for sightings or information about Guy – it'll be on tonight.'

'That's good. It might bring someone forward, help to find him.'

'Apparently Charlotte asked Bridget to phone and let me know.'

'Maybe you need to ring Charlotte, make the first move?' Clarice said. 'Remember, a big part of the reason for both of you being so upset about Poppy wandering away is because Guy's still missing.'

'I've not really slept since he went. One day I had a son and the next he'd suddenly ceased to exist.' Louise looked at the untouched mug of tea in front of her, then at Clarice.

'Did Bridget say if Charlotte was going to take part in the appeal; if they'd include members of the family?'

'No, it seems Charlotte was asked but she said no.' Louise stared hard at Susie, her eyes confused. She wasn't taking it all in, Clarice suspected. The events of the previous day and the visit to the homeless shelter had been too much.

'Drink your tea, Louise,' she said gently.

Chapter 24

'I'll be home by eight.' Clarice had managed to catch Rick on his mobile, and was speaking to him on the phone in the upstairs office.

'I should be back by then,' Rick replied. 'Are you sure you want to go with Louise? I mean, will it really help?'

'Just for a few hours,' Clarice said. 'I said I'll watch the news with her – it'll be on both the regional stations – then stay for a little while afterwards. She really has had one hell of a day.'

'Charlotte should have asked her to go to hers to watch it together.'

'It's bad timing, after their falling-out.' Clarice could hear the background office noise of voices and a phone ringing. 'How did it go with Tidswell?'

'Not great. I'll fill you in later. But most importantly, you must have a quiet day tomorrow,' Rick said with determination. 'Your feet haven't touched the ground in the last few days, what with London and the fund-raiser, and Bob and Sandra aren't coming in till Wednesday.'

'They deserve some time away from here,' Clarice said. 'They've done more than their fair share. Sandra said she had to do their laundry; she was running out of clean knickers. Just as well Georgie didn't know or she'd have offered to lend her some of her thongs.'

Rick sounded intrigued. 'Really – do ladies actually share that sort of thing?'

'No, of course they don't. Can you imagine Sandra wearing a thong?'

'I'd rather not go there,' Rick said. 'But you're right, Georgie would probably offer. They're doubtless all lurid pink.'

'Who knows,' Clarice said, feeling they'd talked enough about her friends' underwear. 'Anyway, I'd better go.'

'OK, take care. Give Louise my love, and I'll see you later.'

Going back down the stairs, Clarice felt guilty. She had been devious in deflecting Rick away from his concern that tomorrow should be a quiet day. She'd not told him about the possible house clearance. Having already given Jonathan her word that, if necessary, she'd spend the morning moving any animals from the house, she could not renege. She'd managed to rope Georgie in as a standby, just in case, but she hoped Jonathan's information was correct and there were only four cats.

At 5.30, Clarice was in Louise's sitting room, the window open, a gentle movement of air carrying through the room. Looking at the empty chair, she knew that it would be some time before Louise could come in here without thinking about Milo.

'He was such a lovely old chap,' she commented when Louise caught her glancing at the chair.

'I think it was Milo who kept me sane,' Louise said. 'I knew I had to keep going for him. He still needed to be looked after.'

'And you must look after yourself properly, or you'll become ill.' When Louise didn't answer, Clarice continued, 'The girls, too. I know you and Charlotte have fallen out, but you both love Guy and the children.' She remembered Keith and Jonathan's comments at supper, about Charlotte being jealous of the relationship between mother and son and calling Guy a mummy's boy.

As the TV news began, Louise sat on the edge of her chair, leaning forward, eyes fixed on the screen, a tissue squeezed between her fingers. Clarice felt a sense of helpless frustration. If Guy's disappearance was due to misdemeanours on his part, she might find it hard to refrain from violence against him on his return. It was excruciating to watch the slow collapse and decline of this gentle, considerate friend who loved him so much.

The appeal came right at the beginning of the regional programme. It was predictable, showing images of Guy and asking anyone with information to contact the police on the given number. When the broadcast had finished, Clarice sensed a flatness in Louise, as if she had expected something else.

'Let's hope it brings some leads,' she said.

'I do hope so,' Louise said. 'Thank you for coming back with me. I won't need to watch the news later tonight.'

'Do you want me to make you some tea, or a sandwich?' Clarice asked.

'No thanks, Clarice, it will give me something to do after you've gone. You've been more than kind.'

'Well, if there's anything else, let me know.'

There was an uneasy silence, as if the older woman was weighing something up.

'What is it, Louise?' Clarice asked when the silence dragged on.

'There are two things. The first is Susie. Now that I haven't got Milo, I should bring Susie here. But can you manage for another couple of days? She does seem settled.'

'No problem,' Clarice said. 'After everything you've had to cope with these last few days, I understand completely. Collect her whenever you feel ready.'

'The second thing – and please do say no, I realise that you probably won't need the help, but can I come with you tomorrow?'

'To the house clearance?' Clarice was surprised.

'I know you usually take Bob and Sandra, but you mentioned you wanted them to have a rest after everything they've done over the last few days.'

'They'll probably be cross when they find out about it. I've asked Georgie to be on standby.' Clarice looked at Louise for a few moments. 'You do know whose house this is?'

'Yes, I know,' Louise said, 'but you would be doing me a big favour. I can't bear rattling around the house all day hoping the phone will ring with good news. I haven't even got Milo to distract me now, and I won't be having the girls. And I didn't really *know* Helen; we were just in the same room maybe four or five times when I went over to see Charlotte. We exchanged pleasantries, nothing more.'

'What about your business? You're usually frantically busy at this time of year taking orders and getting deliveries out.'

'Apart from paperwork to keep on top of things, which I tend to do in the evening, Ian and Judith have taken over. Judith told me – very kindly – that my mind's not in the right place. I'm making mistakes.'

'It sounds like the business is in good hands.'

Louise nodded. 'After all this time, the two of them are more like friends than employees.'

'Well, I'm delighted you want to help,' Clarice said, 'but I never know what I'll find until I get into the house. I've been told four cats – that's the best-case scenario. They might be badly malnourished, and the house might be filthy. It could be upsetting.'

'You won't be expected to clean it, will you? You'll just take the animals out?'

'Yes, if it all goes ahead, I'll be met there by the social worker, with the signed paperwork. I'll have cat baskets with me, and I'll take any animals straight to Jonathan.'

'I've got a large car,' Louise said hopefully.

'If you're sure you're up to it,' Clarice said, 'that would be great. I'll phone you in the morning, probably about half past eleven, when the social worker gives me the nod.'

'Thank you, Clarice,' Louise said, still clutching the tissue between her fingers. For a moment, she looked a little less lost.

Driving home along the quiet lanes, Clarice mulled over Louise's offer. It was a kind one, but she wasn't sure it was really going to be an appropriate time-filler. It might even be quite upsetting for her. She wondered if she should phone Charlotte to try to bridge the divide between the two women, or would they both consider her to be interfering? When Rick got home, she might ask him for his opinion if he wasn't too tired, but first she'd need to tell him about the house clearance, and that Tuesday probably wasn't going to be a peaceful day.

Chapter 25

'Why the hell did you say yes?' Rick ranted.

There had been no time to tell him about the house clearance. Having arrived home first, Rick had taken a call from Jonathan.

'*No*, that's a simple word. "Sorry, Jonathan, but no." That's all you needed to say.' He was, Clarice realised, furious.

'It's never simple,' she said. 'There aren't any other charities that have a gap at the moment. It's summer, kitten season – everyone's busy from spring onwards.'

'And don't we know that?' Rick pointed in the direction of the cattery. 'We have a barn full of cats and kittens. The more we take in, the more food we have to find for them, not to mention home visits and fund-raisers. And how many have you got with foster carers? Fifty cats and eleven dogs, didn't you say at the last count? It just goes on, and on, and on, and you look knackered.'

Clarice fought the urge to respond in kind; he looked worn out, having gone from one busy case to another, and he often slept badly. She'd felt him tossing and twitching in his sleep last night. When not at home, she knew he ate junk food.

'I should have mentioned it sooner,' she conceded.

'Yes, you should.' Rick, Clarice realised, was only halfway through his tirade. 'And when I said on the phone that you needed a quiet day tomorrow, what did you do?'

'I didn't tell you.'

'Not only that, but you tried your diversionary tactics. All that crap about Sandra's laundry – and you think I'm so dumb that I won't notice.'

'Rick,' Clarice moved her head to indicate where to look, 'you're upsetting the dogs.'

He followed her gaze to Jazz and Susie, both sitting upright, necks back, chests out, heads moving from Rick to Clarice as if watching a tennis match. Blue, sitting further back, had a squashed tissue box clamped in her jaw but was peering up at them nervously. In the sudden silence, she took the opportunity to run to Rick and offer her soggy present.

'Thank you, Blue.' Rick, glowering at Clarice, knelt to pat the dog, only to be jumped on by the other two.

'Can I get you a drink?' Clarice asked.

'Yes.' Rick rubbed his hand over his short, bristly hair, anger spent. 'I'll have a glass of red wine.'

'It's salad tonight,' Clarice said as she moved towards the kitchen.

'Did Charles Tidswell come up with another plausible alibi?' Clarice asked forty-five minutes later. The conversation had been slow and stilted.

'He appears to have one; his solicitor asked that it's to be treated with discretion.'

'What did he say?' Clarice was intrigued.

'Apparently, while he was supposed to be at the bedside of

his dying father-in-law, supporting his wife, he was with his mistress, who just happens to be his wife's best friend.'

'Ah . . .'

'It's being checked. Barbara Graham said they have the girlfriend's details. She could have been paid to give him an alibi, but . . .'

'She doesn't think so?'

'He was very cocky, confident in a way that made the interviewing officer feel it's probably the truth. He hadn't wanted it to come out, but neither did he want to be held accountable for something he'd not done.'

'So he's in the clear.' Clarice felt disappointed.

'Not entirely.' Rick smirked. 'While he was playing Mr Cocky, he told the interviewing officer that he knew both Bream and Guy Corkindale very well. And that he could tell him a thing or two about both that would make his hair curl if he had any – Barbara said that her officer is bald. Unfortunately, the sharp solicitor cut in and shut Tidswell up.'

'Does Barbara really think Guy was involved in something dubious with Bream?' Clarice asked.

'It could suggest dodgy dealings, or Tidswell could be trying to wind Barbara's officer up for dragging out his girlfriend's details.'

'Sounds a real sweetheart.'

'You've got it.' Rick nodded. 'How did it go with Louise?'

Clarice was relieved their conversation was becoming more natural. The falling-out had tightened her stomach with anxiety. She relayed what Louise had told her.

'Poor thing,' Rick said. 'The homeless shelters would have been part of the routine check. The manager would have been shown photographs already; the FLO would have told her that.'

'She might only have told Charlotte, or Louise might have forgotten. She's getting confused with all the stress.'

'Taking her with you tomorrow on the house clearance isn't a great plan. If she's flaky, she might be more burden than help.'

'It's difficult,' Clarice said. 'For me, Helen is completely faceless, so I'll be detached, but Louise knew her, if only slightly. She might find it uncomfortable, depending on what we find, but she was practically begging me to take her with me. I guess the days must be dragging for her.'

'Mmm.' Rick looked at her for a few moments, the anger of earlier having dissipated. 'Sleep on it and have another think tomorrow morning; you won't know if it's going to go ahead until late morning anyway.' He paused. 'And I think if you can, it's best to avoid getting between Louise and Charlotte – take a step back.'

But Clarice found she couldn't sleep. Rick next to her appeared to have no problem, but she was kept awake by the events of the last few days.

There was no mention in the morning of the argument, and Rick left early to meet up with Daisy in Lincoln. Before he went, she asked about the Abbot case.

'More of the same,' he said. 'A matter of chipping away at everyone involved to find something that might break their story and lead somewhere.'

'One thing occurred to me,' Clarice said as they walked to Rick's car. The day had started dull, but now the sunshine was pushing through.

'What?'

'It was what you told me in London about the dogs. Have you found Peppy?'

'So,' his eyes twinkled, 'you *were* listening to me. No, he's not been found.'

'I always listen to you,' Clarice smiled.

'Tell me what you were thinking.'

'Although Catherine, the sister-in-law, doesn't sound a particularly nice person, she is a dog lover, I gather – big-time. Yes?'

'Go on.' Rick looked interested.

'She has five dogs of the same type; if she and Mike did murder Ben and Debbie, the thing you need to do to crack the case is to find Peppy.'

'Her neighbours and Debbie's family both confirm that Catherine has five dogs, all brown and short-haired. I've been there and seen them myself; there's no long-haired harlequin.'

'Have you checked with Catherine's vet?'

'To find out what?'

'Given that she's a huge fan of the breed, and you said she was jealous of Debbie having Peppy, I don't think she would be able to bear to get rid of him.'

'What you're saying is that Peppy might have been right under our noses when we visited their home,' Rick said thoughtfully.

'Sadly, dogs get old and die. The vet would know when the last one died, and Catherine would have the paperwork if they replaced it with another dog – back up to five again. It's possible to cut the fur on a long-haired dog to make it short – a bottle of brown dye would sort out the colour.'

'They wouldn't be so stupid,' Rick said. 'Keeping him would be like putting a noose around their own necks.'

'When people fall in love with animals, they can be as passionate and competitive as parents. They wouldn't want to lose him, and in any case, getting rid of him would be hard.'

'Well, it's certainly worth checking with the vet; I'll get Daisy onto it today.'

Watching him leave, Clarice thought he suddenly had the air of a man on a mission. Although it probably was idiotic keeping a dog that could tie them to the murder, Clarice knew that animal lovers often went with the heart rather than the head.

Going back into the house, she wondered what the day would bring. She was not looking forward to the house clearance and felt nervous about the prospect of Louise helping. But she couldn't reject the offer of help; it would be too unkind. And who knew, it just might help her friend.

Chapter 26

The phone call came late in the morning. Bernice Turner introduced herself as the social worker supporting Mrs Helen Ambrose.

'I'm assuming the vet has filled you in about the cats?'

'Yes, I've been waiting for your call,' Clarice said. 'Has the court case finished?'

Mrs Turner explained that it had, and that Helen Ambrose had been given a two-year custodial sentence. She'd acquired a signature on the document given to her by the vet: ownership had been relinquished on any animals found and removed from the house. Initially, Mrs Turner explained, Mrs Ambrose had wanted an assurance that she could have them back when she'd finished her prison sentence.

'That won't be possible,' Clarice said.

'I realise that – you're not running a commercial cattery. The vet told me the same.' Mrs Turner paused as if considering. 'The earliest I'm able to meet you at the property would be twelve forty, if that's convenient for you.' Clarice observed that the woman's voice held a sniff of distaste whenever she mentioned cats.

'Have you been inside the house?' Clarice asked.

'No!' Mrs Turner was emphatic. 'I can't go anywhere near a cat. I have an allergy.'

'That's unfortunate,' Clarice said.

After agreeing the time, she called Louise, silently hoping she might have changed her mind about wanting to help.

'If there are only four cats, I'll have enough room in my own car for the baskets,' she explained.

'Oh, I don't mind if I have a wasted journey. At least it'll get me out of the house.'

Clarice felt guilty that Louise sounded so pathetically grateful.

Clarice arrived five minutes early, and parked in the narrow street outside number 48. The semi-detached houses had been built in the 1940s; the small front gardens had a short pathway to the entrance door, mostly contained by a tidy, well-maintained hedge or fence. The houses had been modernised with uPVC windows and doors, some more elaborate and expensive than others. Many displayed colourful window boxes. Clarice assumed the two rows facing one another across the narrow road were a mixture of council houses and privately owned, under the right-to-buy scheme.

Opposite number 48, a tall, thin man with a beaky nose pierced the relative quiet with a power trimmer as he cut his hedge. The only other noises were the shouts of children coming from the gardens at the back.

Number 48 had no fence or hedge. It was conspicuous amongst its prettier neighbours by the absence of anything that might draw the eye – flowers or a neat lawn. The path was swept, and the area that might have been grassed was covered with gravel. The windows were spotlessly clean, with beige net curtains thick enough to deter anyone hoping to be able to peek inside.

A ten-year-old brown estate car pulled up to the kerb and a small, stout middle-aged woman with short, wispy hair emerged. She wore a baggy dress with leggings that, Clarice noticed, were the same shade of mud brown as her car, and she peered around her through large spectacles.

'Is it Mrs Beech?' she said, approaching Clarice, who recognised her Lincolnshire accent from the earlier phone call.

'Yes.' Clarice shook the proffered hand. 'This is it?' she asked, looking at number 48.

'It is.' Mrs Turner glanced across at the man cutting his hedge. 'Here you are.' She handed Clarice a key ring with one key.

'What about her furniture and possessions?' Clarice asked. 'Do you want to go in with me to check?'

'No.' Mrs Turner sneezed loudly, before fishing in the pocket of her dress to pull out a tissue and blow her nose. 'One of my colleagues was here yesterday. Mrs Ambrose gave him several boxes of personal items that were going to a relative for storage; what's left will be cleared as rubbish.'

'I understood she didn't have anyone,' Clarice said.

'There's a brother, but his wife doesn't get on with Helen. They said they would store the items as an act of kindness but that she must find somewhere else to live when she gets out.' Mrs Turner glanced again at the man opposite, who had paused from his task to stare at them. 'Helen didn't get on with her neighbours either.'

'Won't she come back here?' Clarice asked.

'No, the house is being taken back by the council. The rent has gone unpaid for over six months; they were already working on evicting her.' Mrs Turner sneezed again. 'I managed to get them to agree to hold back until five p.m., to allow time to get the cats out. I'll wait here in the car until you've finished, then I'll drop the key back to the housing department.'

'Did your colleague confirm the number of cats in the house?'

'No, I didn't speak to him. I'd left the office by the time he returned, and he wasn't in this morning.' She sneezed again. 'I expect you deal with cats every day.' She took a step back, as though Clarice's proximity might be hazardous.

'Yes, and dogs,' Clarice said.

Mrs Turner took another step away. 'Are you going to be on your own?'

'I'm expecting a friend, a volunteer,' Clarice said.

As if speaking of Louise had magicked her presence, her dark green Land Rover pulled in behind Clarice's car.

'And here she is.'

Mrs Turner turned and escaped back to her car.

Louise looked as if she had dressed down for the business in hand. The faded jeans with worn knees were what Clarice imagined she wore when potting up her herbs. Clarice filled her in on what the social worker had told her, then opened the front door.

The first thing she noticed was an overpowering smell of bleach and disinfectant. Although the top part of the front door had a mottled coloured glass panel, it was dark inside. The wallpaper looked as if it was from the 1970s, perhaps when Helen had moved in. She must have arrived as part of a family;

a three-bedroom council house would not have been available to a woman on her own. What had happened to make her life plummet out of control?

Louise, who had followed her in, closed the door. 'That smell's overpowering,' she gasped, voicing Clarice's thoughts.

'I expect we'll stop noticing after a while,' Clarice said. 'It's the opposite of what I was expecting. Helen obviously had a heavy hand with the cleaning fluids.' As she spoke, she moved forward. There were two doors on the left, another directly in front, and a staircase with carpeted treads to the right. She opened the nearest door, and stepped into the room she imagined would have been where the family might once have gathered to watch TV together in the evenings.

Apart from two old wooden dining chairs and a single wardrobe, there was no other furniture. The faded wallpaper was of a similar design to that in the hall. The woodwork, although clean, was chipped and tired, and a washed-out wool rug sat on the bare floorboards in the centre of the room. In a basket in a corner, a ramrod-thin black cat sat upright, staring. A Siamese reclined on top of the wardrobe; the head of a scruffy tabby cat appeared from inside to join the wary watchers. The room had four trays containing clean cat litter, and dishes of varying shapes and sizes held wet and dry food and water.

'She's left the place in good order.' Clarice was surprised. 'I think she must have been an obsessive cleaner.' She had reached the black cat, and as she leaned forward with her hand extended, the animal let out a small squeak and lifted its head to butt her hand. 'You're a very friendly fellow.' The cat responded with a louder squeak.

'How do you know it's a fellow?' Louise asked.

'I don't, I'm just making small talk.' Clarice smiled.

Not to be outdone, the Siamese let out the high-pitched yowl familiar to its breed.

'Look, Clarice.' Louise pointed upwards, and Clarice saw a second tabby, who head-butted the Siamese before standing next to it to survey the guests. 'This could be the four.' She sounded hopeful.

'Let's have a good look around first,' Clarice said.

Returning to the hall, closing the door behind them, they went upstairs. The stair carpet showed its age, with worn and bare patches made thin by years of use.

There were four doors off the landing. An open one showed the bathroom. Walking past, Clarice noticed that it had been stripped of towels and there remained only a sliver of soap and a deodorant spray next to the sink. The other three rooms must be bedrooms.

In the first was a double bed, a chest of drawers, a chair and a wardrobe, the bed made with worn pink sheets and a candlewick bedspread. Helen's head had left a dent in the pillow, and the sheet and coarse grey ex-army blankets were thrown back, revealing a tunnel where a small body would have lain.

'It's not quite so bad in here,' Louise said.

'No,' Clarice agreed, turning to look. The room had a stale odour due to lack of fresh air, and a light flowery smell, perhaps from deodorant. She wondered how much this visit was distracting Louise from her incessant focus on Guy.

'Are you all right with this?' she asked.

'I'm OK. The house is spotlessly clean, but so bleak, barren of any warmth or personality.'

'She must have been in a bad place.'

Louise nodded, and Clarice imagined that after her own recent traumatic experiences, she might be drawing a parallel between herself and the unfortunate Helen. A woman whose life had gone badly awry to reach this desolate pass.

'We need to check under the bed and anywhere else a cat might hide.' Clarice walked around the bed towards the window to peer underneath. There were dustbin bags of clothing and shoes, but nothing else. Glancing outside through the net curtains, she could see Mrs Turner sitting in her car, her phone pressed to her ear. Across the road, the beaky-nosed man had been joined by two other men and a woman, all watching the front door of number 48.

'Nothing in the wardrobe,' Louise confirmed.

They moved on to the next room, another double bedroom, but without a bed; only food, water and litter trays. Clarice counted another four cats: two ginger, one black and a heavily pregnant tortoiseshell.

'Oh!'

She heard Louise gasp as she followed her in.

'Four more,' Louise said, 'so eight so far.'

'Hello, young lady.' Clarice spoke to the tortoiseshell, who hissed in response. 'I wonder,' she said, 'if Helen locked her in with some of the male cats when she was coming into season.'

'She might not have realised she was female.'

'It's incredibly rare to find a male tortie; they're generally always female,' Clarice said.

Louise looked puzzled.

'It's to do with chromosomes,' Clarice explained. 'To get that colouring, the male needs an extra strand in his DNA.'

Louise nodded, looking around the room. 'How many cat baskets did you bring?'

'I've got ten, but if that's not enough, I'll need you to go to Jonathan's – it's only five minutes away.'

'No problem,' Louise said, turning back to the door.

In the final bedroom, large enough for only a single bed, they found a lone elderly white-faced black cat. Downstairs, a room that might once have been the dining room contained three cats.

'We've got twelve so far,' Clarice said, 'so it's a trip to Jonathan.'

'OK,' Louise said.

'Last room.' Clarice opened the door.

Apart from an electric cooker and a fridge, the kitchen housed an old Formica table draped with a faded checked cloth, on top of which stood boxes of cat biscuits. The wall cupboards, all open, showed a mismatched collection of cups and plates.

'I think here and the bedroom is where Helen would have spent most of her time; there's at least a table and chair.'

'What's that?' Louise asked.

Clarice had stopped to peer into a large cage. 'Looks like two hamsters. She's put in plenty of food, anyway.'

'No cats?'

'No. We'll go around once more after we've finished and make sure we haven't missed anything.' She bent down to lift the tablecloth; from the blackness under the table, two round, frightened eyes stared back. 'Hello.' She spoke gently. 'That's a good place to hide.' The response was a noise like the rhythmic beat of a soft wire brush against a drum skin. She realised that the small dog was frantically wagging its tail but not moving to come out. 'I'll be back later,' she promised.

'Is it a dog?' Louise asked.

'Yes,' Clarice said as she slowly lowered the cloth to allow the animal to regain its safe space, 'but it's quite frightened, so we'll come back once we're done with the rest.'

'So what's the plan?' Louise asked once they were back in the hall.

'I'm going to ring Jonathan and tell him you'll be going in with the first six cats,' Clarice said as she took out her phone.

Once she'd spoken to him, she went to the front door. 'We need to get all the cat baskets from the car. Jonathan is going to give you two more. When you come back after dropping the first lot off, we can divide the remaining animals between our two cars.' She paused, ensuring Louise was absorbing all the information. 'While you're gone, I'll do a phone-around of the foster carers; once Jonathan has checked the cats over, the carers will pick them up from the surgery. There's one near Skegness who doesn't have use of a car – I'll need to drive over.'

'I can do that,' Louise said.

Leaving the house to collect the baskets from her car, Clarice noticed that many more neighbours had appeared in their front gardens. Some were pretending to weed, while one woman was cleaning her windows; all had their eyes focused on number 48.

'We've got an audience,' Louise observed.

'Mrs Turner said Helen didn't get on with the neighbours,' Clarice said. 'They want to see what comes out, and it looks like we're part of the show.'

Chapter 27

After loading Louise's car with the first six cat carriers, Clarice went back into the house and searched every room again. She also looked on every surface for a note from Helen Ambrose in case she'd wanted to pass on information, about the animals, but there was none. The original head count had been correct, and now Clarice began working through her list of volunteers on standby. Her first phone call was to Colin, who ran a similar animal rescue charity in Peterborough. He agreed to take four cats.

After finishing the calls, she went to her car, returning to the kitchen with dog treats. Lifting the tablecloth again, she lowered herself down beside the dog. His eyes as before were filled with confusion and fear, and she began talking slowly and quietly while offering the treats. Twenty minutes later, he had emerged to sit on her legs. He was small and rough-coated, white with black patches. The left side of his face was white, with the ear flopping down. In contrast, on the right side, his black ear stood erect, the colour extending down over his eye to form another patch.

'The eyepatch makes you look like a pirate,' Clarice told him when she eventually picked him up to go out to the car, once she and Louise had loaded all the remaining animals into the two vehicles.

After locking up the house, she found Mrs Turner sauntering back to her own car.

'Needed to stretch my legs,' she said. 'Are you finished?'

'Yes,' Clarice said, giving her the key. 'My friend has just taken the second group of cats to the vet to be checked, twelve in all in the end. I'm about to follow her with a dog and two hamsters.'

'Twelve – my goodness! She told me she just had four.'

The neighbours, sensing the show was over, had started to drift back inside their homes. In her car, Clarice spoke quietly to the small dog, who was hiding in a blanket at the back, separated by a dog guard. 'We're on our way,' she told him and was rewarded with the emergence of one erect black ear.

The hamsters, destined eventually for a local group known to Jonathan that took in rodents for rehoming, sat quietly in their covered cage in the back seat.

'What breeds do we think are in the mix with this one?' Jonathan asked as he examined the dog at the surgery. 'A bit of Collie, the black and white?'

'And definitely some Terrier type,' said Clarice, who was holding the dog on the table while Jonathan looked into his ears.

'He's quite overweight: too much food and, I imagine, a lack of exercise.'

Georgie had already left, taking four cats to Colin in Peterborough, a three-hour round trip. They'd been passed by Jonathan as being in good condition, though they were unchipped, so their original owners would be untraceable. Georgie had been in her usual exuberant form, saying that Colin had told her she could look around his rescue centre. Clarice wondered what the kindly but shy Colin would make of the whirlwind that Georgie's presence engendered.

'How old do you think he is?' Louise asked Jonathan.

'Always a guesstimate.' Jonathan paused after finishing looking in the dog's ears. 'He's not old – between two and three to judge by the condition of his teeth – and he's nervous, but that's not surprising if he never comes into contact with people.' He stroked the dog's head. 'You can only get braver, Pirate. You can't be a wussy-woo with a name like that.'

Louise laughed, and Clarice felt warmed by the sudden sound.

'What about the rest of the cats?' Louise asked.

'Well,' Jonathan moved away to allow Clarice to pick up Pirate, 'from the original twelve, two are chipped, the Siamese and one of the tabbies. Cora, my assistant, has phoned the numbers held for the owners, both local, and left messages, so leave those two here with me in case someone wants to come and claim them.'

'That leaves six,' Clarice said. 'I'll take the pregnant girl, Annie, and Pirate.'

'And the other five?'

'The two foster carers will be over within the next couple of hours. They're friends and will decide between them who takes which ones.'

'What about the Skegness carer?' Louise asked.

'We won't need to make that trip today,' Clarice said. 'Although if the two chipped cats aren't claimed by their owners, we'll need to take them over there tomorrow.'

'Successful mission,' Jonathan whispered, holding his hands in the air dramatically. 'And they've all been wormed and flea-treated – my contribution, Clarice, no charge.'

'Thank you,' Clarice said. 'That is so generous.'

Pirate put his head to one side and leaned away from Clarice's shoulder towards Jonathan.

'You are a dear little fella.' He cupped the dog's head in his hands.

'He is looking for a home, Jonathan,' Clarice said sweetly.

'I'd have him in a heartbeat, but Keith is quite adamant we shouldn't have another one.'

'I remember Lennie,' Louise said. 'Such a cute little creature.'

'Yes, he was seventeen when we lost him, over four years ago.' Jonathan was thoughtful. 'Keith was heartbroken, so that's it for us.'

'That happens a lot,' Clarice said, thinking of Sandra and her cat.

'You'd met Helen then?' Jonathan said to Louise as they were preparing to go. 'At Charlotte's?'

Louise shrugged. 'I never had a proper conversation with her, just hello and how are you. It feels awful now.'

'Why?'

'That she was living hand to mouth, in that state – she must have been so terribly lonely.'

'But you weren't to know,' Jonathan said.

'No, I suppose not, but it was as if she was invisible.' Louise looked at the perplexed expression on Jonathan's face. 'She was at Charlotte's house to clean and I didn't chat because I was always too busy.'

'That's just normal,' Jonathan said.

'I understand what you mean, though,' Clarice said. 'As far as we can tell, Helen had nobody: she didn't get on with her brother's wife, the neighbours disliked her, and I doubt that she had any friends.'

'Perhaps I could have made more of an effort to be friendly,' Louise said. 'If Helen only ever mixed with people who used her as a tool – a cleaner or a care worker, struggling along on minimum wage – it's no wonder she found her purpose in life through the animals she took in.'

'Well, we don't know her background, her history,' Clarice pointed out.

'I know, but if she'd been anyone other than the cleaner, I'd probably have taken more notice of her.' Louise looked downcast. 'She's just started a prison sentence, and when she gets out, she won't have a home to return to.'

Clarice glanced at Jonathan, who was listening intently to Louise. She sensed that he – like her – was concerned that because of her own torment, Louise was deeply troubled by Helen's situation. Guy's sudden disappearance had left her emotionally raw.

As they left, Clarice asked Louise if she'd like to follow her home for a cup of tea. 'Or maybe you've had enough for one day and want to head for home.'

'No,' Louise said, 'I'd love to come.'

'Can I put Annie in the back of your car, away from Pirate?' Clarice asked.

'No problem.' Louise went to her car and opened the rear passenger door. 'Jonathan's such a big fan of *Coronation Street*, isn't he?'

'Yes, he's called this one after Annie Walker, the pub landlady from years ago.'

'At least it saves you thinking of another name.'

'Too right,' said Clarice, leaning into the car with the cat basket. 'Is this Poppy's raincoat?'

'It is.' Louise picked it up and held it out. 'I was going to ask you to do a huge favour and drop it in to Charlotte.'

'You should take it yourself.' Clarice used the voice she saved for encouraging shy semi-feral cats. 'A great opportunity to speak to Charlotte and get over the argument.'

'No, I can't.' Louise pushed the coat at her. 'Please take it for me. I can't face Charlotte yet.'

An hour later, Clarice had settled Pirate with a basket, food and water in the storeroom leading from the kitchen. In the cat house, she prepared a large wooden box, with a round hole for the cat to enter and exit, adding soft blankets inside and food and water by the exit outside. Pregnant cats often wanted to hide, and Annie had gone straight inside.

Sitting in the kitchen, she and Louise finished their cups of tea.

'He's dead, Clarice.' Louise spoke in a voice devoid of emotion, as if stating a dry fact.

'You can't know that.' Clarice was taken aback by the blunt statement.

'I can, I'm his mother.' She put her hand to her chest. 'I can feel it here. There's no way he would disappear like this and not get in contact.'

'Unless he's had a breakdown.'

'Yes.' Louise's voice cracked. 'I never thought that I'd be relieved at that possibility, but it would be so much better than the other option.'

'Try not to give up hope.' Clarice felt wretched, the words

the only ones she could dredge up, for her gut instinct was that Louise was right. She couldn't say it out loud, though, and certainly not to his mother. All she could do was think what more could possibly be done to find him.

Chapter 28

After Louise had left, Clarice went into automatic mode, feeding the animals and walking the dogs. Annie, who had been pacing around the room, gave a few hisses to caution that she was not a girl to mess with before going back into her hideaway to settle. Jonathan had warned that the birth could be within the next two days – he thought only two kittens – but that Annie seemed in good condition and should have no problems.

After being fed, Pirate turned in circles in his pile of bedding to make a nest. Clarice sensed his eyes following her every movement adoringly. She warned herself, as she had done on so many previous occasions over the years, that she must not become too attached to him. If she kept every cat and dog she fell in love with, she'd run out of space and not be able to continue to foster or bring in needy and damaged animals. Her role was to provide a stepping stone for the animals. To give them a place of safety where they could thrive and become healthy and confident, ready to find someone who would take them on as a valued and much-loved member of their family. It always felt heartbreaking to pass them on, but it was rewarding to watch them being adopted into a lovely home.

In the cottage, she checked both the house phone and her mobile. There was a message from Jonathan. Both owners had reclaimed their chipped cats. He reminded her that she had an appointment with him for Susie on Thursday at 4 p.m. Making her way outside, Clarice set to weeding the vegetable garden, something she could not put off, as well as a welcome distraction.

Later, with no message from Rick, she poured herself a glass of red wine and went back outside, followed by the dogs, to sit at the garden table. The evening was still and silent; the sky, streaked with red and yellow where the sun would soon set, gave hope that tomorrow would be another sunny day, and the world was at peace. It was in direct conflict to her disconcerting sense of internal turmoil. A feeling that she was ineffectual and helpless, dealing with something it would be impossible to resolve. She looked at Susie, sitting close to Jazz, and her mind went again to Guy's disappearance, and Louise's shock at her safe world shifting. There was now a rift with Charlotte, and the latest blow was the loss of her companion Milo. Poor Louise. So many troubles at once.

The sound of tyres crunching on the pebbles jolted her back to the present. As Rick's car swept into its regular spot outside the cottage, the three dogs barking to signal his arrival brought her to her feet. Watching him getting out of the car, she felt a sense of relief that he had come home, not stayed overnight at number 24 as she'd imagined he might. Taking Susie on the lead, she allowed the other dogs an opportunity to converge on Rick.

'You're ahead of me on the wine tonight,' he said, slinging his arm around her shoulders as they walked to the house, the falling-out of the previous day forgotten.

'Lucky me,' she said.

'Tell me about today.'

'You first. Any progress with Peppy and the vet?'

'Not in the way you'd suggested. The dogs Catherine has are her own, not Debbie's, but she's a member of a club that supports the breed, and we've been given contact details, so we might get something from them.'

He dropped his jacket over the back of a kitchen chair and took the glass Clarice held out to him.

'Your turn – how many cats did you find in the house in the end?'

Picking up the bottle, he followed her back out into the garden, closely trailed by Blue carrying an old canvas shoe. Once seated, Clarice unloaded all that had happened that day.

'You never know what you'll find with a house clearance,' Rick said when she'd finished. 'And now we've yet another house guest – this Pirate creature.' He raised his eyes. 'But poor Louise . . .'

'Wait until you meet Pirate; your cold heart will melt. I've told Louise not to give up hope, but I felt like a hypocrite. I don't believe there's much to be optimistic about.' Clarice felt overwhelmed again by a feeling of helplessness.

'I'd have agreed yesterday. I think Tony Simpson was finding brick walls whichever way he turned, but I spoke to him this morning and there's some progress – the appeal brought forward a response.'

'Really? Tell me what he said.'

'Don't get your hopes up too much. There was the usual dross, time-wasters because they'd seen it on the telly, but there was one interesting response from Watford that they're following up.'

'I've never heard Louise talk about Watford. There's no connection as far as I'm aware.'

'The sighting might be false – someone who looks similar. It was called in by the owner of a trendy bar. The man he thinks might be Guy has been in twice in the last few days.'

'On his own?' Clarice asked.

'No, with a very attractive woman,' Rick said, looking for the reaction in Clarice's face.

'Ah,' she said.

'Yes, ah indeed. They've been in early in the evening to sit quietly over a glass of wine – they never stay to eat. He said if it's not Guy it's someone who looks remarkably like him. Tony's going there tomorrow – the bar has CCTV.'

'Maybe he has a doppelgänger.'

'Please don't tell Louise; I don't want to give her false hope.'

'I won't tell anyone,' Clarice said, 'but I'll keep my fingers crossed.'

Louise and Charlotte would be furious if they found Guy had put them through the hell of his disappearance because he was too cowardly to come clean about a girlfriend. But Clarice knew that whatever he had done, Louise would forgive him. Charlotte would be another matter.

Chapter 29

'You should have told us, darlin',' Sandra said when Clarice had explained about the house clearance the previous day. 'We'd have been glad to help.'

'The good news is that all the animals are healthy – one cat needs a dental, another has a thyroid problem, and there are two unneutered toms, but it all can be dealt with.'

'I don't suppose even with her thieving she would have had enough to pay vet's bills for all those animals,' Bob said.

'She couldn't afford to pay her rent,' Clarice said, 'never mind vet's bills.'

Sandra sat with her empty tea mug on the table in front of her. Nestled on her lap, Pirate looked back and forth from Sandra to Bob and Clarice and then down to the three large dogs reclining on the floor, sated after walks, food and visitors.

When Clarice had taken the dogs around the garden for their early-morning walk, she had done an extra lap with Blue and Jazz. After carrying Pirate for the first half of the walk, she'd put him down to introduce him. Her own dogs were accustomed to visitors, and after an initial sniff, they took little notice of the small, unobtrusive interloper.

Inside the house, she had carried Pirate until Susie's elation at meeting the new boy had abated, her focus of interest turning instead to her breakfast. When Bob and Sandra arrived, an hour later, they were immediately charmed by the newcomer.

'He's losing his shyness,' Clarice stated, watching Pirate cuddling up to Sandra.

'I really do wish you'd phoned us,' Sandra said. 'After all that stress on Sunday you could have done without more yesterday, and Louise, the poor woman, must be at bleedin' rock bottom!'

Clarice made more tea, and they discussed again the events of the Sunday fund-raiser.

'Georgie said that Rosalind was blaming my cakes for giving her the trots!' Sandra said with indignation.

'That's nonsense, your cakes were delicious. Forget about it.' Despite knowing that Georgie couldn't keep a secret, Clarice was annoyed that she'd told Sandra about Rosalind's claims. For Georgie, the thrill of having a tale was in the beefing up and retelling. It took a while to reduce Sandra's sense of outrage.

Clarice suggested that they go over to the cat house to meet Annie. Sandra went straight to Polly, who, despite her reticence with most visitors, emerged immediately from her box when she heard her voice.

'Don't forget Doreen's coming over to visit,' Sandra said as Clarice turned to leave.

'No, I know June Blake's away for a couple of days. I've set up a cosy box for Doreen in here, away from the cats.'

'Rick won't be too happy.' Sandra laughed. 'He doesn't really like ferrets.'

Clarice smiled, remembering the expression on Rick's face the last time Doreen had come to stay. 'I don't have much choice,' she said. 'June does a lot of fostering for us; the only thing she ever asks is that I look after Doreen for a few days twice a year.'

'Well,' Sandra said, 'if she's in here and you don't go handling her too much, you might get away with it. Rick doesn't have to know.'

Sandra was devious, Clarice thought as she walked to her car, but she was right: if Rick didn't know about Doreen, there would be no harm done. Checking that Poppy's raincoat was on the back seat of the car, she toyed with the idea of just turning up at Lark House. In the end, she decided to ring first – Charlotte was not the type to appreciate someone just dropping by. Charlotte sounded pleased to hear from her and said she would welcome a visit.

It was a beautiful day, and Clarice drove slowly, enjoying the undulating landscape with its abundant swaying crops, the cloudless light blue sky and the warm breeze through the open window. She felt the stirring of pleasure again on arriving at the gateway to Lark House, looking at the straight drive leading to the concrete, steel and glass building, the curve of the river running along the boundary, the pleasing confluence of nature existing side by side with modernity.

As she parked the car, the front door of the house was thrown open and Poppy and Angel ran to meet her.

'Have you brought Grandma? Is Susie with you? How are the kittens?' One question followed another as the girls took her hands and pulled her towards the house.

Charlotte came to greet her with the familiar air kiss. 'Come in, Clarice. Coffee? It's Java.'

'Yes please,' Clarice said, thinking that Charlotte was always specific when offering beverages. It was green or Earl Grey, Java or Colombian – never just tea or coffee.

While Charlotte went into the kitchen, Clarice tried to answer the questions being fired at her. She had seen their grandma; Susie was doing well; the kittens were getting bigger.

'You *are* using their proper names?' Angel said bossily. 'The ones we gave them.'

'Yes, of course,' Clarice said, 'and we have a new cat called Annie who'll soon have babies too.'

A new batch of questions came thick and fast. Who had named the cat, how many babies might there be, when exactly would they arrive? And when might Susie return home?

Clarice tried to answer them all honestly and finished by telling the girls that Susie was going to the vet the following afternoon so she would know then how much better she was.

As they talked, Tara came downstairs. 'It's not all about that dog again, is it?' She glared at her younger sisters.

'We want Susie home.' Angel was adamant. Poppy nodded in agreement.

'Enough of that, Tara,' Charlotte cut in. 'Susie is our family pet. When she's well, she'll come home.'

Tara stared at her mother as if she was fighting to suppress a retort.

'Is it true about Helen, our cleaner?' she asked, suddenly altering course. 'Amy's mum said she's gone to prison for stealing from people she worked for.'

'Unfortunately,' Clarice glanced at Charlotte, 'that's true.'

'She didn't steal from us,' Charlotte said abruptly, before insisting that Tara take the younger children into the garden. It was clear she did not intend to discuss her ex-cleaner any further. 'Stay here,' she added, pointing to the lawn, 'where I can see you.'

Clarice wondered whether there was something she wanted to talk about out of earshot of the children. The insistence that they should remain where she could see them suggested that she was still traumatised by Sunday's events.

They sat in the kitchen with their coffee. Clarice sensed that Charlotte was ill at ease. Previously thin, she had lost more weight, her loose-fitting blue linen trousers and top failing to mask her fragile frame.

'Is Louise still terribly upset?' she asked.

'Yes.' Clarice nodded and noticed Charlotte casting her eyes immediately downwards at the bluntness of her response. 'She's had other problems.' She told Charlotte about Milo's passing and Louise's visit to the homeless shelter.

'Poor Louise.' Charlotte sounded tearful. She tore a piece of kitchen towel from the roll with shaking hands. 'I shouldn't have been so angry with her, but I was horrified that she'd lost Poppy.'

Clarice was taken aback by the emotional response. 'I'm not a mother,' she said, 'but I can understand why you're so upset.'

'You never get over the death of a child.' Charlotte dabbed her eyes.

'Martin?' Clarice said.

Charlotte looked up quickly, startled. 'Yes . . . You learn to live around it, but it's always there: the date that he would have started school, what his favourite subjects might have been. Guy and I had friends who had a child called Adam; he would have been almost the same age. Guy never talked about what our son might have been like at the various stages of childhood, but I knew when he looked at Adam that it was painful; he was always thinking about Martin.'

'You said *had* friends,' Clarice said softly.

'I let the friendship slide. Adam was only two weeks younger than Martin . . . It was too difficult for all of us.' Charlotte blew her nose noisily. 'I know how Louise must be feeling. Guy is an only child, and her fear about his welfare and state of mind must be killing her.'

'She would like to see you,' Clarice said. 'Do you think you could forgive her?'

'There's nothing to forgive.' Charlotte turned her head to stare out of the window at the three children. Tara was sitting on the grass staring at her phone, Angel was collecting daisies and Poppy was running in a circle, arms outstretched, around her two siblings. 'I overreacted. Louise would never knowingly have allowed Poppy to leave the garden on her own. It's every parent's nightmare, that feeling of panic when they turn their back for a few seconds and the child has gone.'

Clarice was surprised by Charlotte's forbearance; she had not anticipated such understanding. Coming here, she'd been prepared to plead Louise's case.

'How did you feel about the television appeal?' she asked.

'I couldn't take part. It would have been too awful.' Charlotte shrugged. 'There's been no positive feedback. No sightings.'

'Nothing more on Charles?'

She shook her head, her eyes downcast again. After a moment's silence she said, 'Angel and Poppy keep asking about Susie. Could you bear to have them visit again?'

'It would be a pleasure.' Clarice smiled. 'Would tomorrow suit? I do have to take Susie in for her final check-up with Jonathan, but not till the afternoon.'

'That sounds good to me. They haven't stopped talking about

the kittens.' Charlotte's face was blotchy but now tear-free. 'Do you think Louise might like to come too?'

'I'm sure she'd be delighted. I know she has an appointment with the dentist in the afternoon, but . . . might you phone her? If she collects the girls in the morning, I'll drop them back and travel on to the vet.'

'Perfect,' said Charlotte, topping the cups up with the remainder of the coffee.

'You must say when you want Susie back,' Clarice said. 'I'll miss her, but she is your dog. Louise can't take her yet; she needs time to get over Milo.'

'If it's no trouble, could you hang on to her a bit longer? It's just, with so much going on, I'd rather concentrate on getting from one day to the next. The girls keep asking when Daddy's coming home.' Charlotte looked to be on the point of crying again.

'It can't be easy,' Clarice said. Still, it might be more beneficial for the two younger children if their dog was back with them. They clearly loved her, and she could become their focus while the search for Guy continued.

'Who did Susie bite?' Clarice looked at Charlotte as she asked the question, and noticed a flash of fear in her eyes, a slight jolt passing through her stick-like frame.

'Bite . . . who told you that?' Charlotte said.

'The children were talking about it on Sunday, that Susie bit someone. I wouldn't have thought she had it in her.'

'As a pup, she nipped a man's ankle. It was a trivial incident. And once when Tara was playing the grumpy adolescent, I asked her to walk Susie. Tara yanked her really hard, and Susie retaliated. It was nothing, but children have a way of blowing things out of proportion.'

'Ah,' Clarice said. 'That's why Tara sounds unenthusiastic about Susie's return.'

'Yes, I'm sorry about that. You've probably realised Tara isn't an animal person.'

'Yes, I remember Louise telling me she wasn't; not just dogs, but cats, rabbits . . . whatever.'

Charlotte nodded without comment.

Clarice still found it odd that Susie would have nipped or bitten anyone. It would have been so out of character. And surely Guy would have mentioned it to his mother.

Charlotte quickly changed the subject, and they carried on talking until Clarice said she needed to go. Once outside, Charlotte told the children that they would be visiting Susie the following day.

'And Grandma?' Angel folded her arms defiantly across her chest as she spoke. Clarice wondered how much of Charlotte's guilt had been caused by the children's desire to see their grandmother.

'I'm going to phone your grandma to ask her to come,' Charlotte replied.

'Hurray, hurray!' Poppy yelled, and Angel joined in.

'Thank you for bringing my raincoat back,' Poppy said before Clarice left. Looking over her head, Clarice met Tara's smile and realised that her big sister had reminded her of her manners.

Driving home, she mulled over Charlotte's story that Susie had bitten Tara. Despite Tara not being a big dog lover, she couldn't imagine the girl suddenly yanking the dog around and causing such a reaction. Why was Charlotte lying, and what was she trying to hide? There had been little mention of Guy, and Clarice had sensed discomfort when asking about the television appeal. But maybe she was reading too much into Charlotte's reactions. How was she supposed to respond when her life, much like Louise's, was currently hell? At least if the two women became friends again, they could offer mutual support.

Chapter 30

'*How* much?' Clarice asked.

It was Thursday morning, and Jonathan had called to give Clarice some good news.

'I've just put the phone down from Mrs Dickens and wanted to let you know how much she appreciated your finding Biggins,' he said. 'She's had Siamese cats since childhood and thought she'd never see him again.'

'When did he go missing?'

'Eighteen months ago. He was sleeping on a seat in an outside enclosed run in her garden – she lives next to a busy road, so he wasn't allowed to wander.'

'So much for Helen rescuing him. It sounds like she stole him from a loving home.'

'Dreadful,' Jonathan snorted. 'Lucky he was chipped.'

'Five hundred pounds is a large amount,' Clarice said. 'A charity walk often doesn't raise that much – she's been very generous.'

'She wanted to know who the cheque should be made payable to, so I've given her the charity details.'

'Thank you, Jonathan. I'll write once I've received it to thank her.'

'You know Louise and Charlotte have made up?' Jonathan said.

'Yes, Charlotte phoned Louise yesterday evening, and then Louise phoned me. She's bringing Poppy and Angel over here later.'

'I'm so glad. They need each other.'

'I agree,' Clarice said. 'I'll see you this afternoon with Susie.'

Later, in the cat house, Clarice checked on Annie, who she found pacing around her box before disappearing back inside. There were no other signs that the kittens' arrival was imminent. After finishing all her tasks, she returned to the cottage. Bob and Sandra had called earlier, helping out for a couple of hours before leaving to visit one of their daughters.

Louise arrived with the children late in the morning. Observing her as the girls played with the dogs, Clarice felt a sense of relief. She looked more relaxed, her attitude apparently more positive.

In the centre of the group, Pirate copied the other dogs. His liveliness and enthusiasm suggested he had found some hidden well of confidence, and Clarice was delighted by the improvement. She noticed that he particularly enjoyed being stroked by the children. While he was the smallest, his bouncy character made up for what he lacked in height.

'I'm trying to be more upbeat for the girls,' Louise told Clarice. They were sitting together watching the children playing in the sand that Clarice had piled onto the end of the terrace, together with various buckets, containers and spades. She thanked Clarice for encouraging Charlotte to contact her.

'It wasn't down to me,' Clarice said. 'I think Charlotte was ashamed that she'd been so horrible to you, and the children were asking about you and when they might be able to see you.'

'They must love me almost as much as Susie,' Louise said.

'It's a close call, but almost,' Clarice laughed.

'We're all going into Lincoln tomorrow morning.' Louise's face had brightened. 'There's something on at the arts centre for children, and we can have lunch there.'

'That's great.' Clarice was so, pleased that Louise was being included in the outing.

'The sand is a good idea,' Louise remarked.

'I was going to suggest Skegness, it's not that far, but I know the children wanted time with the dogs, and dogs aren't allowed on the beach during the summer season.'

'So the beach has come to them!' Louise smiled.

'I hope Charlotte isn't going to be cross because they've got sand in their hair and clothes.'

'I told her about the sand – they're both wearing old clothes.'

'What do you know about Susie biting people?' Clarice asked.

'Charlotte said you'd asked, and that the girls had talked about it.' Louise looked puzzled. 'But I didn't know anything about it. Charlotte said she'd nipped a man in the garden when she was a pup, and more recently Tara because she'd yanked her hard.'

'That's what she told me,' Clarice said.

'I'm surprised Guy didn't tell me. We've never had secrets from one another. He was so careful about Susie's behaviour because of the children. And I would have passed on the information – you'd have wanted to know about that before you agreed to look after her.'

'I might have misjudged Susie's personality,' Clarice said. 'All dogs can reach a limit of what they will tolerate, and sometimes it's fight or flight, but I didn't think she had a biter's temperament.'

'Charlotte said it was only a little nip.'

'Perhaps she just got overexcited,' Clarice mused.

While Clarice was in the house making sandwiches for lunch, she reflected on Louise's words. Louise viewed her relationship with her son as open and honest. Yet Keith had said that Guy hadn't told her about the extra leave he'd taken from his chambers after the death of his son. And if the sighting in Watford turned out to be Guy, he'd kept that relationship a secret from both his wife and his mother. What else didn't they know about him?

As they ate their sandwiches in the garden, the conversation was all about the dogs and cats, Poppy asking several times when they could take Susie home. Clarice assured her that it would be soon, before taking them to check on the food for the cats and kittens.

When they'd finished, Poppy asked, 'Can we see Annie, before we leave, the one who's going to have babies?' Her voice was plaintive; she clearly wanted to spend more time with the cats.

'They aren't called babies,' Angel corrected her. 'They're kittens.'

'We know what she means,' Louise said, 'and remember Clarice doesn't usually let little girls and boys in there when the kittens are so young. Think of it as a privilege because you've been so well behaved.'

'Annie is about to give birth, so she needs to be left in peace,' Clarice said.

Later, Louise told the children to be on their best behaviour while she helped Clarice to transfer the booster seats to her car. They had gone back to play with the sand and waved briefly before returning to their task of filling buckets.

'Thank you again for all you've done,' she said, hugging Clarice close to her. 'It's good of you to take them home. I hate going to the dentist, but it's my six-monthly check-up.'

'I should be the one to say thank you. I don't know how I would have managed yesterday without your help. And I'm going in that direction, so will drop them off on the way to visit the vet.'

'I was glad to be of use,' Louise said, 'and it made me take stock.'

Clarice looked at her as she glanced back towards the children.

'About what's important,' Louise continued. 'Seeing the vile state of Helen's place made me realise that if you sink too low, it's hard to get back up.'

As she strapped the children into their seats, Clarice realised that Susie's presence in the back of the car was having an unsettling effect. Angel was kneeling on the back seat, fiddling with the dog through the bars.

'Stop winding her up,' Clarice said. 'Let her just settle quietly.'

'Why can't she stay at home with us now?' Poppy asked as they were driving.

'She will come home soon,' Clarice said, 'but today, after I leave you, I'll be taking her straight to the vet – it's what I agreed with your mother and grandma.'

'Will she come back when Daddy comes home?' Poppy asked.

'It will be when the vet tells me she is better and doesn't need to go back to see him,' Clarice said, relieved when they turned into the driveway that led to Lark House.

Charlotte had emerged to greet them and was waiting as Clarice went to let the children out.

'Have they been good?' she asked, helping Poppy down.

'They couldn't have been better.' Clarice smiled.

'We met a pirate,' Poppy said. 'He had a black patch over one eye.'

'A dog,' Clarice mouthed to Charlotte.

'Most pirates wear a black eyepatch,' Charlotte said.

As they moved away from the car, the bars holding Susie in the back suddenly came loose, and Susie burst over the back seat and out of the open door.

'Angel,' Clarice said, 'did you move the sidebar to allow that to open?'

Angel, looking down at her feet, did not reply.

'Susie's come home!' Poppy shouted, jumping up and down with uncontrolled glee.

Once out of the car, Susie didn't stop, running hard first towards the house, then, her body whipping to turn to the side, starting the ascent to the wooded area behind it.

Chapter 31

'I hope she doesn't damage that leg,' Clarice said with concern. 'She's meant to be taking it easy.' Leaning quickly into the car, she took a leash from the glove compartment and followed the route Susie had taken.

Running around the side of the house, she could hear the excited voices of the children behind her, but Susie was already out of sight. The gradient beyond the patio was initially gentle, the garden on a level surface that progressively changed to a slope as she advanced away from the house. Following the incline, the foliage was at first sparse, large distances separating the shrubs and trees. As she continued, it became more thickly wooded until she drew near to the copse and the sense of enclosure increased.

She called Susie's name before pausing on the edge of the dense woodland. Running uphill on a hot day had made her legs ache and left her sweaty and panting. She stood still, breathing slowly to regain her composure. Looking back, she saw the children following, sprinting ahead of their mother, who moved with long strides at a less frantic pace. It was silent, apart from the movement made by the wind in the grass and trees. The little girls' high voices had been dulled by distance.

Clarice imagined Guy coming up here to enjoy the beauty and tranquillity after a busy week in London. From this vantage point she could see the house more clearly, the sun sparkling on the glass and steel; the acres of lush green garden, some of it tamed and given over to lawn, other parts cultivated with wildflowers and specialist grasses, designed to give the appearance of random natural beauty. The house stood central and dominant, like a perfect diamond within the greenery of an emerald cluster. The wide, serene river snaked around to the right of the woods, curving beyond the beech hedge boundaries, passing the wide entrance and disappearing under the road, reappearing on the far side. Along its banks were dense areas of summer flora. And, Clarice noticed, a small, square paved area with what looked like a metal table and chairs. She imagined the family sitting at the river's edge, taking tea.

Bringing her mind to focus on the situation, she realised that something was wrong. Why was Susie not barking? Clarice had got to know the personality of the dog over the last few days. When gleeful, she was bouncing, joyful and loud, as if she had a trampoline beneath her feet rather than solid ground. Could she have fallen and hurt herself, or perhaps gone further than the containment of the boundaries?

Clarice called out as she moved between the trees, some young saplings and others fully developed ash, maple and cedar. She tried to remember how many acres Louise had told her the woodland covered: three or four? At regular intervals she passed stacks of wood neatly cut in identical lengths. She wondered if they paid a woodsman, or if it was something Guy enjoyed doing himself. She couldn't imagine Charlotte engaged in the business of cutting old branches and sawing them up.

The close grouping of the woods gave way to an avenue of pale greyish-brown ash trees, standing opposite one another like tall, elegant giants with extended limbs, reaching out above her head to form a domed archway. The sun appeared in abstract, like sparkling shapes, or golden shards of glass, glinting through the greenery.

She scoured the woods around her, listening for the slightest noise, feeling like an interloper in this unique place. Her thoughts went to Guy. The haunting loveliness of the surroundings made her feel a poignancy she'd not succumbed to before, and Louise's anguished face the previous day flashed into her mind. Here in this private heaven, she wondered once again why Guy would run away from his wife, children and mother and leave all of this behind. It didn't make sense.

And then, as she moved from the shade of the trees into an open space, passing a less organised pile of cut branches, with some scattered further from the main stack, she saw Susie. She was sitting twenty feet away, looking silently down over the driveway, house and gardens. Coming up quietly behind her, Clarice murmured her name, imagining that the dog might startle at her presence and bolt. Instead, Susie turned her head to look at her with soft, puzzled eyes, then calmly turned back to continue to stare. Kneeling, Clarice clicked the lead onto the dog's collar. Following Susie's eyeline, she realised she was staring across the river, to the main gateway at the end of the long drive.

'She's waiting for Daddy.' Angel's voice from behind made her aware of the presence of the two girls.

'Yes,' Clarice said. 'I can see that.'

Further back, both hands gripping a tree, stood Charlotte, her eyes fixed on her children, her face immobile but streaked with tears.

Chapter 32

They walked back down to the car, the two girls ahead, and Clarice with Susie on the lead walking with Charlotte. Susie was subdued, her energy spent, and Clarice was relieved that she could not detect a limp.

Charlotte brushed her face repeatedly with the back of her hand, and for a long time did not speak. When they were just under halfway down, she halted to look back.

'He loved to go there.' She had not succeeded in stemming the flow of tears and now allowed them to run unabated, sniffing as she talked. 'It was one of the reasons we chose the location: the woods were special.'

'Did Susie go with him?'

'Always. She was a bit of a nuisance, though. When she got bored, she'd disturb one of his oh-so-neatly-stacked piles of wood. We used it for the stove.'

'Once Guy's back, he'll go there again,' Clarice said. 'If he's had a breakdown, it'll take time for him to mend, but maybe the woods will help him recover.'

A silence fell. Charlotte moved her lips, but nothing came forth, her eyes revealing bafflement and confusion.

'Did he do all the maintenance work himself?' Clarice asked, her voice soothing.

'Not all, but most,' Charlotte said slowly, struggling to regain her composure, her misery transparent. 'It was the time factor; he employed people for bigger jobs. When he came home from London, being here was quite the opposite from his working life, the quiet, being with the children, and spending time outside.'

'Do you help with the garden?' Clarice asked.

'Nobody could know less about gardening than me.' Charlotte sounded indifferent, her thoughts elsewhere. 'But Guy enjoyed it, and we employ a man part-time to help.'

'I was just thinking,' Clarice said, 'walking through that archway of trees, it has a unique serenity. I can't imagine anyone ever wanting to leave.'

Charlotte shook her head, her eyes cast downwards, unable to answer.

'I'm sorry Susie escaped. Perhaps it was a bad idea dropping the girls on the way to the vet.'

'It was Angel being wilful,' Charlotte said. 'She . . . they all three miss their father so much.'

'It's a difficult time. They're all going through the same emotions: Louise fearing for her son, the children for their dad. And you too, Charlotte.'

'Yes, I miss him.' She wiped her face one more time and sniffed hard as if determined to get herself under control. Clarice looked at her anew. This was not the ice queen she had come to expect.

'The hardest thing, I think,' Clarice said as they started to move down the incline, 'is the not knowing. We all tend to fear the worst, to build up the darkest picture.'

'Yes, I get that,' Charlotte said.

'When Guy didn't return from his meeting, it must have been hard to hide your concern from the girls.'

'You don't have children, Clarice.' Charlotte lifted her fingers in front of her face in a fan-like movement, almost as if she was creating an imaginary mental barrier between them. 'Part of a child's behaviour is in response to whatever has their attention, but part is automatic, the familiarity of routine. It was normal for their father to go away on Monday morning – during term-time, he left the house before they did. They think of this as the norm.'

'But the business associate visiting the house and Guy disappearing wasn't part of their norm,' Clarice persisted, aware that Charlotte was avoiding the question. 'It must have been difficult for you.'

Charlotte's eyes were suddenly cautious. 'As far as the children were concerned, he did go out as normal on a Monday morning. Angel saw his bag in the hall, the one they call his London bag. They didn't know the full story until I told them.' Charlotte paused for a moment. 'As you say, it was hard to hide my concern that Guy had vanished.'

Clarice nodded, aware that she had pushed too hard. It was clear Charlotte didn't want to talk about the events of that morning.

'I feel so much anguish for Louise. Even if they're mad or bad, a mother's instinct is to protect her children,' Charlotte said, looking at her own.

'Do you think Guy's done something mad or bad?'

'Not necessarily.' Charlotte looked lost, detached. 'But I know it's what people will think when he doesn't come back.'

Clarice wondered whether she knew that her husband was involved in something illegal, or entangled in an emotional relationship. Why, if the possibility were not alive in her mind, would she have used those words?

They had reached the car, where the children were waiting.

'I'm sorry I let Susie out,' Angel said. 'I just wanted her to come home.'

'It's OK,' Clarice said as she lifted the dog into the back of the car, 'and I promise I won't try to keep her. I know she's your pet, and she'll come home soon.'

Driving away, she could see the motionless gathering watching her car disappear along the driveway. Susie's escape to that private, personal place had had painful consequences. It had stripped Charlotte of the last of her civilised veneer, the pretence that she was coping with the emotional fallout from Guy's disappearance. Like Louise, she had given up hope. She believed Guy was dead. Her unravelling had begun, and the possibilities of where that would lead were terrifying.

Chapter 33

Arriving twenty minutes late for her appointment, Clarice found that Jonathan had already moved on to another patient. When she did eventually see him, she apologised for being tardy and explained what had happened.

'How awkward.' Jonathan's expression was bewildered. 'You'd have imagined Susie would have tried to get into the house.'

'I thought that, but then Charlotte mentioned that she always went with Guy up into the wooded area, following him about.'

'That's true. Keith told me that it was like Guy's private domain up there. He was very neat and tidy – a bit like Keith himself – a tad anally retentive. All the felled branches were cut to a set size, the woodpiles all the same dimensions. Striving for such perfection in a log pile would have driven me bonkers. Still, I guess Charlotte might be similar; they couldn't live in that open-plan glass house if either was a messy type.'

While they talked, Jonathan had knelt on the floor next to Susie and examined her leg. 'Let's take her outside so I can see her walking about.'

Once Clarice had done a couple of laps around the yard,

Jonathan called her to a halt to say that he was satisfied. Susie's sudden exuberance had caused no further damage.

'She can go home with a clean bill of health.' He beamed at Clarice.

Driving home, Clarice mulled over the problem of Charlotte not wanting Susie to be returned. She'd felt like piggy-in-the-middle between the children and their mother earlier. She'd hoped Charlotte might have said something when Angel had made it clear she wanted Susie home; her silence had been uncomfortable. Could it be because she felt Tara would be annoyed, or was it just too much for her at present to care for the dog? After all, it was clear that she was having difficulty coping.

At home, Clarice checked her mobile to find two messages from Rick. In the first, he said that the man in Watford, although similar in looks, was not Guy. A mixture of relief and disappointment washed over her and she moved on to the second message.

'We've found Peppy, and it links straight back to Catherine and Mike. The woman who now has him came from the list the vet gave us, of dog owners who are members of the dachshund club.' Rick sounded jubilant. 'She lives in Peterborough; Catherine's been paying her to keep him until what she called family business issues are resolved. They're being brought in any time now, so don't wait for me to eat, I don't know what time I'll be back. If it's too late, I'll stay overnight at number 24. I'll text you if I do.'

Listening, Clarice smiled. At last, some good news – although not for Catherine and Mike.

Later, after she had eaten, she went to the barn to check on the cats. She was delighted to find that Annie had produced two tiny, perfect ginger kittens.

'Well done,' she said gently to the cat, stroking her head with one finger. Annie surprised her with a look of pleasure and no growls before going back to washing her new family.

After returning to the house to feed the animals there and walk the dogs, Clarice went to work weeding the flower beds, Blue and Jazz spread out on the grass, Susie, her lead attached to the table leg, copying them. Nearby, Pirate flipped onto his back and stuck his full, round stomach contentedly upwards to be warmed by the sun before falling asleep.

Once she had finished her task, she stayed outside, sitting at the table, the dogs spontaneously gathering close. The evening was still and tranquil, the birds having ceased their chatter, a charmed moment in time before the sun dropped behind the horizon and the world became not only silent but dark.

She thought about the reasons why people went missing. Abuse of some kind, or the breakdown of a relationship; debt, a death, suicidal thoughts due to depression, or unhappiness that created a need to escape to make a new life. The cot death had been too many years ago to be obviously significant now, and there was, as far as she was aware, no abuse, either physical or psychological, between the couple or directed at the children. The last of the possibilities, that Guy had been unhappy and had run away to start a new life, might be deemed selfish. She herself had felt angry with him as she'd watched Louise struggle to keep a grip on the day-to-day reality of her life. But was the extreme act of running away a decision he could control? And would it not follow that the longer he was away, the harder it might be to return? She thought about the people Guy had left in limbo: his wife, mother, children, friends and colleagues. If he'd died, they could have followed the rituals and procedures that went with death: cards, messages of condolence, arranging the funeral and grieving. Over time they would have come to terms with the loss, let go and, eventually, moved on. The cruelty of his disappearance had taken them to unknown territory. The stress and chronic sorrow would continue, unmitigated.

But there was still something that did not fit, that niggled. Revisiting the information and conversations, Clarice had a sense of gliding, fluid and artless – but then there it was again, the thing that jarred. What was it? She reached into blackness . . . Louise believed Guy to be dead, although a tiny part of her still held out hope that he wasn't. For Charlotte, it was a done deal, a certainty – but why? And there was something else, something about which she had never been convinced. Charlotte and Guy both owned upmarket, expensive cars, so surely Charlotte would have a certain amount of knowledge of various makes. Why had she been so vague about the kind driven by Charles? The reason why there had been nothing on the CCTV at the farm shop café was because Guy had not gone there; indeed, he had never left home. Charles was a fiction invented by Charlotte. Or perhaps Guy had talked about his work and mentioned a Charles who was a rogue, so Charlotte had used him to deflect attention from what had really gone on.

At that moment, Susie raised her head, turning her large, sad brown eyes to look at Clarice. Clarice visualised Charlotte again, the movement of her hand, the downward cast of her eyes: constructing walls between them, forming barriers to hide the truth. The small, petty lies, about Susie biting, and why she didn't want the dog back. Guy's bag in the hall. Charlotte had packed that herself, leaving it out for the benefit of the children. She thought about the half-finished untidy stack of wood near where Susie had sat, remembering Jonathan passing on Keith's observation that Guy was obsessive about each pile having to be identical. He would never have left a wood pile like that.

Susie had taken Clarice to the location where Guy had died. Charlotte had watched from nearby, unable to bring herself to enter the clearing. And walking back, she'd lost control, because of the memory of what had happened in that place. There was no doubt in Clarice's mind that Charlotte was devastated, traumatised by what she had done. It was there that she had murdered Guy.

She took the dogs around the garden once more before returning them to the house. Going to the cattery, she checked on all the inhabitants. Annie opened her eyes briefly to observe Clarice peering into the hiding box before returning to sleep.

It was late as she tidied up the kitchen. Feeling restless, she made herself some tea. As she dropped a chai tea bag into her cup, Charlotte's voice came to her, always so precise about the type of tea or coffee on offer, as about most things.

It was nearly 11 p.m. when, still sitting in the kitchen, she heard a car driving down the incline from the road. The dogs joined together in barking as she went to the door. Since Rick had not phoned, he must have decided to return rather than staying at number 24.

'It's all wrapped up,' he said as he came through the doorway, looking tired but cheerful. 'I don't need to get in early tomorrow, so I thought I'd come straight home.'

'I'm glad you did. So tell me everything,' she said. She was itching to unload her thoughts about Charlotte but didn't want to spoil his moment of triumph after the long, gruelling days of working all hours to get to this point.

After he'd made himself a coffee, they moved into the living room, and he started to speak. Mike had yielded first, after much hedging, owning up to his part in the murders. When she realised the game was up, Catherine blamed her husband, reducing her own role to that of a passive onlooker. 'But we'd already heard Mike's version,' Rick said, 'and believed him.'

'What I don't understand is why they didn't just leave Peppy at Debbie's home,' Clarice said. 'They could quite legitimately have offered to take him when Debbie disappeared.'

'I think they might have done that, but Peppy never left Debbie's side,' Rick said. 'He even slept on her bed at night. When they lured her out to meet them, by saying that Ben had been in an accident, she had Peppy with her. Her neighbours have security cameras, which cover Debbie's place – they installed them after a break-in.'

'Yes, I remember you told me that: it was the last sighting of Debbie, leaving the house with Peppy. It all sounds so premeditated!'

'Yes, all about the money.' Rick was silent, lost in thought for several minutes, then: 'What about you, how did it go with Louise today?' He relaxed back into his favourite armchair, stretching out his legs.

'It's a long story,' Clarice said. 'I'll tell you what happened from the beginning, but the ending is that I believe Charlotte murdered Guy, and I'm pretty sure I know where she hid the body.'

Chapter 34

The next morning, they drove in convoy to Lark House, Clarice in her Range Rover, with Susie curled up behind the dog guard, her head raised to watch the passing fields. In the second car, Rick had DC Rob Stanley as his passenger, the constable who'd worked with him on numerous cases. Finally, a silver-blue estate driven by Inspector Tony Simpson, accompanied by the family liaison officer, Bridget Latimer.

Bob and Sandra, arriving to help in the cat barn, had clearly been intrigued by the arrival of the cars with police officers, but knew well enough not to ask too many questions; they would find out what was going on when Rick deemed it appropriate. Sandra whispered to Clarice that June would be along later to leave Doreen, the ferret. Clarice nodded as both she and Sandra looked sideways at Rick, ensuring he'd not heard.

The previous evening, after Rick had listened to Clarice's theory, he'd gone through the details several times, looking at it from every possible angle. His air of tiredness fell away, and he'd swiftly become sharp and alert. By then it was after midnight, and they were both drinking chai, their talk interspersed with silences in which Clarice knew Rick was contemplating the situation.

'I'm not saying I disagree with your logic,' he had said eventually, 'but telling my chief that I want to follow up what my wife is suggesting because a dog has shown her where the body is . . .' His voice trailed away.

'Yes,' Clarice agreed, 'I can see that might be awkward.' She had met Chief Inspector Charlie Johnson on several occasions, and found him arrogant and insincere. He was also a keen player of office politics: if the outcome on a case was good, he'd take the credit, but if something went wrong, he'd be sure to shift the blame onto another officer. In his mid-fifties, he was short and slim, dapper in his uniform. She had an abiding memory of watching him at a social event passing a mirror and catching sight of his reflection. Unaware of her presence, he had straightened up, sucked in his stomach and smiled admiringly at himself.

'I need to make him aware that if you're right and he doesn't follow it up, he's going to look like an inept halfwit.'

'Maybe alter that wording a little.' She smiled as she spoke. 'Just a little.'

Listening to her husband speaking to the chief early the following morning, Clarice had to concede that he might take up politics himself. He had not phoned Charlie until 7.30, judging that by that time, although still at home, he would be on his second coffee, thinking about the day ahead.

'I entirely agree with the point you're making, sir.' He spoke smoothly. 'I was thinking that we didn't actually search that area – and if the body is found there later, it will look bad . . . No, that's what I thought. There's been no progress at all: a complete dead end, no new leads.'

He swivelled in the chair, turning to smile at Clarice leaning against the door frame of the room they called the office, drinking her own second coffee.

'Yes, that's the information I have. The family – Mrs Corkindale, her mother-in-law and the children – are in Lincoln for the morning, due to have lunch there . . . If that's what you think, that sounds like a plan. I know that if the body does turn up it's no longer going to fall into Tony Simpson's remit, but like you, I believe he'll want to be with us. He's been on the case since the start.'

When he hung up, he turned to Clarice again. 'It's happening this morning. Charlie wants to go in immediately. The family may have decided to stay at home, or they might return while we're there, so he wants Bridget on hand too. I know that neither Charlotte nor Louise likes her, but that's their problem – she's good at her job.'

'I don't think it's personal. They'd hate anyone in that role; they can't help seeing her as intrusive rather than supportive.'

'If we find what we expect to find, life is going to get more painful for Louise and the children. She'll need to accept any support that's on offer.'

On arriving at Lark House, Clarice parked in the shade of a tree, away from the other cars, aware that the white Mercedes with Charlotte's personalised number plate had, as on previous occasions, been left near the house. After going to the main entrance with Tony and Rob, Rick returned a few minutes later, joined by Bridget.

'I had to be sure nobody was at home,' he told Clarice. 'It would be awkward if we were wandering around and hadn't announced our presence.' He nodded in the direction of his

DC. 'Rob will stay here with Bridget in case the family returns unexpectedly.'

Clarice went to the back of the car and attached a leash to Susie's collar. Recognising where she was, Susie moved her legs up and down as though trying to scale an invisible staircase. Desperate to get out, she wriggled as Clarice lifted her from the car. Once on the ground, she immediately pulled forward, with Clarice hanging onto the leash. She followed Susie around the side of the house and up the incline towards the private wooded area, Rick and Tony at their rear. Out in the open, the sun felt hot against their backs, and as the gradient increased, she could hear Tony panting behind her.

'Susie's keen,' he gasped, his ordinarily pale complexion now reddened, his accent pure Yorkshire.

'She knows where she wants to go,' Rick said.

It was not until they walked between the trees that formed the avenue that Tony spoke again. 'By, it's lovely up here.'

'Beautiful,' Rick responded. 'I can understand why Guy took pleasure in coming here.'

Clarice, who had paused briefly to listen, felt herself tugged forward again as Susie pulled hard to move on. They continued until they arrived near the small, untidy stack and scattered branches, which Susie passed on her way to the place where she had stopped on the previous visit. After glancing momentarily at Clarice, she turned her full attention to stare out towards the entrance gate.

Clarice watched as Rick looked at the cut branches and those strewn nearby, clearly thinking about what she'd told him the previous evening. Then he joined her where she knelt next to Susie, bending to line himself up above the dog to take in her view.

'She's looking at the gate, isn't she?' Tony spoke as he came to stand next to Rick.

'That's what I thought at first,' Clarice said. 'She's certainly looking in that direction, over to where the river curves. Louise told me it's quite deep there. I think that's where you'll find Guy's body.'

She heard Tony's sharp intake of breath. 'So where do you think he died?'

Clarice looked at him. 'Up here, killed while he was working.'

'So this could be our crime scene?' He turned a full circle to cast his eyes all around.

'There are no trees on the way down,' Rick said, leaning to look down the steep slope that led to the river.

'It wouldn't have been hard to roll him down there,' Clarice said.

'Was there anything else, apart from Susie's behaviour, that made you think Charlotte was lying?' He gave her a penetrating stare.

'Poppy said that on Monday morning she'd thought Guy was still at home because he never went to London without his blue diary. He put events in it over the weekend to add to his online diary at his chambers. He tried to avoid logging in to work too much over the weekend, apparently. And it was a kind of double security, to have both an online and a paper diary, in case anything happened to either one. Later, Charlotte told the girls that he had gone out with a business friend and had not returned. I think she packed Guy's bag, but with all that had happened, she forgot to put the diary in. Leaving the bag at the bottom of the stairs, where Angel saw it, maintained the sense of routine. She wanted everything to appear to be normal for the children.'

'Or,' Rick said, 'Guy packed his own bag and, just this once, forgot to put the diary in. What made you believe it was significant?'

'I only thought about it being relevant after Susie did her runner and came up here,' Clarice said. 'Poppy said that when she told her mother that Guy was still at home, Charlotte told her not to be a nosy-parker. And Angel then said she'd seen the bag "like always". It suggests that Charlotte had added the diary so it looked like a normal Monday departure.'

She looked from Rick to Tony. 'I've come to realise that small children bounce artlessly from one thing to another. Their thought processes appear free-flowing and unstructured, like a balloon let loose in the wind. It is so easy not to believe what they are saying, or to believe that they're mistaken. It's for that reason that I didn't properly interpret what Poppy said, the truth about the order in which things had happened. That Guy and Susie both vanished at the same time.'

'Yes,' Rick said, 'I can see that.' They looked again at their surroundings, the beautiful woods silent but for birdsong, their eyes then drawn back downhill to the river.

'We're soon going to find out if it was significant,' Tony said warily. 'It's interesting that the dog stays here – she doesn't go down to the water.'

'Yes,' Clarice said. 'She's fixed on staring at that point where the river bends.'

'Guy's body would have to be weighed down,' Rick said as he took out his phone. 'I need to report back to Charlie and get the team up here and into the water.'

Tony nodded, forcing his hands absent-mindedly deep into his jacket pockets, lost in contemplation as Clarice turned to gently move Susie away and take her back down the hill, with each step remembering the same journey from yesterday with Charlotte. Although if she was right and Guy's body was in the river, for Louise and the girls it would be an end to one journey and the beginning of a new and even more painful one.

Chapter 35

Despite the heat, with both the driver and passenger windows open, the inside of Clarice's car was reasonably cool. She lifted the dog into the back; Susie, worn out, laid herself amongst the blankets and stretched out yawning.

Rick, after following her from the woods, was in deep conversation with Tony. They'd been joined by Rob and Bridget. There were times when Clarice felt close to Rick's world; she could watch from the sidelines and, as she did with the rescue animals, work out the behavioural problems and psychology involved. On other occasions, she felt she was on the outside. She was the boss's wife, and unless it was a social occasion, she was in the way. Today, watching the tight little group, was one of those times.

As Rick glanced over towards her, she raised a hand in farewell. He lifted his own in acknowledgement before turning away and immediately becoming engrossed again in conversation.

'Looks like it's time to head home,' Clarice told Susie as she turned the key in the ignition.

She'd gone less than two feet when she saw Louise's Land Rover driving through the entrance gateway of Lark House.

It continued along the driveway past her, coming to a halt next to Rick and Tony's cars. It was just before noon; the family must have decided to skip the planned lunch. Charlotte, who had been in the front passenger seat next to Louise, was out of the car the instant it halted.

'What's going on?' Her voice, shrill with anger, carried across the driveway. Susie raised her head enquiringly in recognition.

Clarice could see Rick holding up his police ID, and she could hear the deep rumble of his voice, although not what was said. She switched her engine off, getting out of the car.

'I don't want my children here,' Charlotte said, pointing to Louise's car. As she turned her head, she spotted Clarice under the trees. 'Wait!' she commanded, her voice stern. Her stick-thin frame, in mustard-yellow pedal-pushers, matching T-shirt and white plimsolls, moved at speed across the tiled driveway.

'What's going on, Clarice?' she asked. 'They say they need to search again, the woods and the water. They've already done their searches!' Her eyes were piercing as she positioned her face inches from Clarice's.

'She's got nothing to do with this!' Rick called as he followed Charlotte. 'If you have questions, direct them to me.'

'Then why would she be here?' Charlotte threw the words over her shoulder before glancing at the dog, now sitting up in the car.

'Why is Rick here?' Louise had joined them.

Charlotte looked confused.

'Rick is Clarice's husband,' Louise told her. 'Remember, I've told you she's married to a police detective inspector?'

'Yes . . . yes,' Charlotte stumbled over the word, 'I do remember.'

'Mum,' Tara had got out of the car, 'what's happening?'

Charlotte stared around the gathering circle, her expression increasingly panicked.

'Louise,' she said, as if coming to a decision, 'please do me a favour and take all the girls home with you. The police want to do another search – more police officers are apparently on their way here to look in the river.'

'But they know Guy's not here.' Louise looked incredulously from Charlotte to Clarice. When nobody responded to her statement, she continued, 'I don't want to leave you on your own,'

'I won't be alone. Please do what I ask.'

Louise moved her eyes around the group, then came to a decision. 'Come on,' she said, putting an arm around Tara to guide her back to the car.

'No, I'm staying.'

'Tara, do as you're told.' Charlotte's authoritative tone implied that she was in charge. 'Louise, I'll phone you later. I need to speak to Clarice.' She put a hand on Clarice's arm and moved her away from the circle.

'Clarice?' Rick, his face unreadable, looked at his wife.

'It's OK; I'll go inside and talk to her,' she said.

'I'm not comfortable with this.' He had moved near her to hiss the words.

'It will be OK, Rick.' Clarice spoke quietly. 'Please trust me on this.' Moving quickly away, she saw annoyance in her husband's eyes, and realised he was fighting the temptation to say more.

As they walked past Bridget, the FLO spoke quietly to Charlotte. 'I'm here, you can talk to me if you like – why not let Clarice go home?'

'Bugger off,' Charlotte responded, without either turning her head or breaking her stride.

Although Clarice's legs were moving, her brain seemed disconnected, affected by the high levels of emotion from all those present. Despite having been in the shade, she felt suddenly hot and sticky, her T-shirt attaching itself to the sweat of her body.

'Clarice, Clarice!' The penetrating wail of a child came from outside. She recognised Poppy's voice as Charlotte, still holding her arm, drew her into the house and closed the door.

Inside, it was suddenly cooler, but despite all the glass, it seemed dark after the bright sunshine. Charlotte released her, then turned to look at her.

'What have you told them?' Her voice was clipped, straight to the point.

'What I believe to be the truth.' Clarice held her gaze until her eyes dropped.

'You know, don't you?' Charlotte looked deflated, as if suddenly the confidence had been emptied from her.

'That Guy never left here? Yes, I've worked that out.'

'It was Susie, yesterday.'

She nodded.

'I knew it wouldn't work, Susie being here; I hoped that when Louise got over Milo, she'd take Susie in – she was always Guy's dog really.'

'Charlotte!' It was Clarice now who was sharp.

Charlotte looked at her, silenced by the tone.

'Just listen to yourself, plotting and planning about what to do with the dog. What about the body in the river – the corpse of your murdered husband? Did you think it could just stay there forever?'

'No, no ... I don't know.' Charlotte lifted her arms to press the palms of her hands to either side of her head, visibly shaking. 'I've been living in a nightmare. I didn't set out to kill him, it was never a plan. We'd been arguing and I lost it. I hit him once – just once – with the spade, and he was dead ...'

The door suddenly opened and Tara darted into the room. Clarice and Charlotte, caught off guard, stared as she slammed it shut and slid the bolt across. For a moment she stood transfixed before hurtling forward.

'Mum!' she screamed.

Charlotte grabbed her, holding her tight.

'I told you to go with Grandma,' she said as she rocked the girl back and forth.

'Grandma's taken the girls. I didn't want to go with her. It's about Dad, isn't it? That's why they're here – the police?' Tara forced the words out between sobs, her face red and bloated.

'I have a confession. Clarice knows, but you'll find out soon.'

Tara stepped away from her mother, her eyes filled with terror, her lips parted.

'I killed Daddy. He's in the river. The police already know. I have to tell the truth.'

'Noooo!' Tara's unbroken scream went on and on, and she clutched at her mother. 'It's a lie – it's not true.'

'It is true, Tara. What I've done ... I didn't mean it to happen. I lost it; for the first time in my life. I lost it big-time.'

Tara stood back, staring at Charlotte. Then she suddenly put her hands over her ears and closed her eyes, like a younger child playing a game: I can't see or hear, so nothing bad can happen.

'It's not true, Mum, stop, stop, stop, stop!' Her voice was like a high-pitched whistle that had jammed, going on and on.

There was a noise from the door, and Clarice heard Rick's voice.

'Clarice, open the door.'

Charlotte gently removed her daughter's hands from her ears. 'I need you to be my brave girl,' she whispered. 'I know you were sometimes jealous thinking the little ones got more attention, but I've always loved you equally.' She put her fingers under Tara's chin to raise her head. 'You must help Grandma with Angel and Poppy. What I did wasn't premeditated – it will make a big difference that I didn't plan it. I might not even get a custodial sentence.' She spoke each word slowly, separating them. It was as though she was trying to make Tara fully comprehend the information, to give her some hope for the future.

'No, Mum,' Tara moaned. 'I can't bear it.'

'I'm so sorry. Grandma and the girls are going to find out what I've done, and it's unforgivable. You have to help me by being strong for the three of them. Can I trust you to do that for me?'

Tara, unable to speak, tears rolling unchecked down her face, nodded as she pressed herself against her mother again.

'Clarice, can you hear me?' Rick's voice again. 'Let me in.'

Clarice went quietly to the door to slide the bolt and open it. As Rick stepped in, his face full of thunder, she stood in his path, her hand raised, silently imploring him not to explode with anger. He looked at the mother and daughter, their bodies locked together, both sobbing, before he nodded at her.

Chapter 36

It felt like time had slowed down. Clarice imagined everything and everybody moving in slow motion. Tony, Bridget and Rob were together in a cluster at the door; Rick went back outside and spoke quietly to them. Tony and Bridget walked off to the cars, presumably to await the arrival of the rest of the team, whilst Rob's solid frame remained to fill the open doorway. Rick came to stand next to Clarice.

'What happened in here?' he asked.

'Charlotte will tell you herself,' Clarice said.

Hearing the conversation, Charlotte turned, still with her arms around Tara, as if reluctant to let her go. 'I expect Rick is going to arrest me now?'

Rick looked at Clarice questioningly. He had not heard the confession, but Clarice knew he'd worked it out.

'I have no evidence yet on which to base an arrest,' he said, 'but I am going to caution you, and we'll take you to the station.'

'Noooo!' Tara wailed as she clung to her mother. 'Don't go with them, Mum.'

'Why don't we go and sit in the kitchen,' Clarice said, 'just for a minute.'

Without replying, Charlotte guided Tara into the kitchen and sat her down, then pulled another chair close for herself. Tara immediately bent forward to rest her head in her mother's lap. The girl had transformed. It was as if the confident teenager had dissolved, to be replaced by a fluid replica, her movements liquid and slow, the tears unbridled.

Rick joined them to stand next to the table.

'Do you want tea?' Clarice asked.

He looked daggers at her. Clarice knew he would not be diverted from the job in hand. Tea drinking was the last thing on his mind.

Charlotte shook her head. Clarice thought again of her previous precision about tea varieties.

The sound of vehicles arriving in the drive made Rick and Rob turn their attention in that direction. Rob, who had an unobstructed view, nodded towards Rick. Charlotte, watching, pulled herself erect.

'I confessed to Clarice that I killed my husband,' she said quietly, looking at Rick. 'It wasn't planned. We'd been arguing for weeks; I lost it and hit him. I am so very sorry for what I did. It wasn't premeditated, but I'll have to learn to live with it.'

'How did you kill him?' Rick asked.

'I picked up his spade and hit him with it.'

'Where is that spade?'

'Stop it, Mum, why are you saying that, stop it,' Tara sobbed broken-heartedly, allowing the words to fall into her mother's lap.

'Shh,' Charlotte soothed her daughter, stroking her hair. Then, as if she had suddenly regained control, 'It's hanging on the wall, the first one inside the gardener's shed, by the door.

It has a blue band around the handle. Anything else I say will be in the presence of my solicitor.' The ice queen was back in the room.

'Did you hear that?' Rick spoke to Rob, and the sergeant nodded.

'Ask Kenny to go to the shed and find the spade. Then get Bridget to come in here.' Rick turned back to Charlotte. 'The family liaison officer will go with your daughter and DC Stanley to your mother-in-law's home – she needs to be informed of your arrest.'

Tara raised her head to look from one to the other. As she moved from her lap, Charlotte stood up.

'Go to your grandma's, Tara.' Her voice was stern.

'I'm not going with that Bridget woman.' Tara spat the words out. 'I'll go with her.' She pointed towards Clarice.

'I'll take her.' Clarice looked at Rick as she spoke, to gauge his response.

Rob had returned with Bridget, and Rick went to speak quietly to them. 'Wait here,' he told Charlotte, before turning to Clarice and motioning her to follow him. Charlotte sat down again and took Tara's hand.

Outside, once out of earshot, Rick let rip. 'What the hell do you think you were doing? I made it perfectly clear that I wanted you to stay out of this. You went into that house – by yourself – with a murderer, and allowed a fifteen-year-old girl to lock herself in with you. And then suggesting tea! It's not a bloody tea party, Clarice, we're working on a murder investigation. It's my work you're poking your nose into. It's not your job to take Tara to her grandmother's.' He tipped his head back in silent exasperation.

'I'm sorry, Rick, I just went with my instincts. I thought—'

'Do you want to make me a laughing stock? When I say how something is going to happen, that's it, that's how it works. Why can't you just do as I say? I made myself perfectly clear. Now you've made me look a fool in front of junior officers.'

'I promise that wasn't my intention. I just wondered how it would look if you took Tara kicking and screaming from the house. She won't go with Bridget, and if you mismanage her, it will be harder to interview her mother. The girl does know me.'

'Yes, and it won't take her long to realise that it was you and Susie who gave the game away for her mother. How do you think that will play out in your future popularity stakes?'

Rick was thoughtful for a few moments, and Clarice could see he was calming down. 'OK, you can take her, but wait till Rob and Bridget have left. We need to give them a head start, time to talk to Louise.'

'You know Louise's reaction will be the same as Tara's – she won't believe it, and neither will the little ones.'

'Yes, I know that, but she still needs to know.' Rick looked to where another car was arriving. 'Daisy's here, I need to brief her. She'll accompany me and Charlotte to the station.'

Clarice went back into the house. Daisy replaced Rob in the doorway while Rick spoke on his phone outside. The room was pervaded by an oppressive silence. Charlotte, true to her word, did not speak again.

When Rick returned to the kitchen, he looked at Tara. 'OK, Clarice will take you to your grandmother's now.'

'I'm not going without any clothes,' Tara said truculently.

Clarice looked questioningly at Rick, who seemed to be weighing up the request.

'Go with her, Daisy,' he said at last. He instructed her to pack two bags, one for Tara and another for her sisters.

They returned fifteen minutes later to a kitchen still frigid with silence, each carrying a bulging bag. Daisy placed hers beside Clarice before resuming her position by the door. Tara went to stand next to Charlotte.

Charlotte cupped her daughter's face and kissed her forehead. 'Remember what you promised. I depend on you.' Tara nodded, her reddened face still wet, her eyes bloodshot.

Clarice's eyes met Daisy's as she walked out, only the slightest flicker of acknowledgement between them. Daisy was wearing her professional police officer's face. She would know that Rick wanted Tara to leave before he officially arrested and cautioned her mother.

Walking towards the car, Tara was silent. Before they reached it, she stopped abruptly, and Clarice followed her gaze as a constable passed by carrying a clear plastic bag containing the spade with the blue band around the handle. After he'd gone, Tara lowered her eyes to stare at the ground and continued to the car. In the passenger seat, next to Clarice, she appeared to shrink, to fold physically and emotionally, as if by minimising herself she might hide in plain sight. In the back, Susie gave a gentle whine, looking around in confusion.

'I'll soon have you at your grandma's house.' Clarice spoke softly.

Tara did not respond. She was staring, her eyes large and fearful, as they came to the bend in the river near the drive. Two white police vehicles, one with the back doors open, the other with a trailer attached, were parked on the bank. On the side of one of the vehicles were the words LINCOLNSHIRE

POLICE – UNDERWATER SEARCH UNIT. A group of men were bringing plastic sheeting to be placed next to a small inflatable and carrying equipment to the water's edge. One was wearing a dark wetsuit.

They paused as Clarice drove past, and she returned to a sense of everything moving in slow motion, as if she was fighting to wade through waist-high mud. Beside her, Tara had clamped her hands over her eyes, as if trying to block out what was happening. As they drove away from Lark House, she eventually moved her hands to rest in her lap, but her eyes were still closed. It had been a terrible day, and it was not over yet.

Chapter 37

Clarice didn't attempt to breach the silence that had wrapped itself around Tara. The death of her stepfather and her mother's confession to his murder had stripped the girl of any remnant of composure. Like a hare dazzled and trapped in the beam of the headlights of an oncoming car, she was frozen. On the threshold of womanhood, her future had altered course; she would need to come to terms with terrible circumstances beyond her control and comprehension.

Reaching a divide in the road, Clarice pulled over to the grass verge to allow herself time to think. When she arrived, Louise, having been told of Guy's fate, would be in an extreme state of distress. While Susie could easily wait in the back of the car with the windows open, if the children were outside they would want her to be allowed out. Given Tara's aversion to the dog and her present understandable despair, taking Susie to Louise's might create an unpleasant situation, something Louise did not need.

'I'm going to drop Susie at my place,' Clarice said as she pulled the car out to move back onto the main highway, 'then we can go onto your grandma's, OK?' She felt a momentary pang of guilt; she had said nothing to Rick about stopping at home. She hoped, after their recent run-in, that he would understand the logic of her dropping the dog there first.

By the time they arrived at the house, Susie was already standing up, recognising the surroundings, her tail swishing in excitement.

'I'll only be a minute,' Clarice said. Tara turned, staring blankly at her before returning to her thoughts.

Clarice attached the leash and walked the dog inside. Bob and Sandra had already left, but they were greeted by Blue, Jazz and Pirate, who was now part of the regular welcome-home crew. She left them to receive Susie back into their midst, like a long-lost friend.

When she went back outside, she could no longer see Tara in the passenger seat. She scoured the area around the vehicle, but there was no movement. The shock was instant, followed by nausea. She'd been gone for less than five minutes. In the time it took her to run to the car, her mind had spiralled downwards in panic. How was she going to explain to Louise that she'd lost her granddaughter? How would she tell Rick that the daughter of a murder suspect had absconded? But then, with a surge of relief, she saw that Tara was where she had left her, her upper body bent so that her face was touching her knees, arms wrapped over her head.

'Tara.' She spoke the girl's name as she got into the car. 'Are you OK?'

'What do you think?' Tara's voice was muffled but hostile; she did not sit up. 'It was Susie's fault!'

'What was?'

'You know.' Tara turned her head to face Clarice. 'Mum told

me yesterday about her running up to the woods, and how you all followed her up there.'

'Susie didn't kill your father,' Clarice said. 'How could anything be her fault?'

'Whatever happened to him, it isn't right for Mum to go to prison. If Susie hadn't run away to Grandma's . . . if you and Grandma weren't friends . . . if Angel hadn't let Susie out of the car . . . it all keeps coming back to that bloody dog.'

'No, Tara, it comes back to your dad losing his life. You're getting things mixed up.'

'I want to go to Grandma's now.' Sounding petulant, Tara sat up and pulled her seat belt across to snap it down. 'And he wasn't my dad, he was my stepdad.'

And Louise is your step-grandma, Clarice thought, but she said nothing in response as she drove silently away from the cottage.

Pulling into Louise's driveway half an hour later, Clarice remembered arriving here from Jayne's in Lincoln, when Louise had first told her Guy was missing. Nothing had changed in this perfect setting – the smells of cut grass, flowers and herbs, the sunshine and the loveliness of the surroundings – and yet nothing remained the same. Tara left the car without further discussion and went into the house.

Rob's car was still in the driveway, and Clarice considered for a moment whether to knock at the door and ask to speak to Louise. But it might disrupt an ongoing discussion with Rob and Bridget, or make the two younger children want to come out to ask questions about Susie. She sat in the car for five minutes, to allow time for Louise, having seen Tara's arrival, to come outside to talk to her. Then, with a mixture of melancholy and despair, she reversed to turn the car around. She felt an overriding sense of guilt. It was she who'd instigated the search for Guy's body in the river. Would Tara, after the devastation of her mother's arrest, move the blame from Susie to herself?

'Clarice!' As she pulled out into the lane, she heard her name being screeched against the backdrop of birdsong, and glancing in the rear-view mirror, she saw Louise running behind the car. She stopped and got out.

She was hit with the force of her friend's body as she threw herself against her. Much like Tara had done earlier with Charlotte, Louise clung to her, unable to speak. Rob appeared, looking concerned.

'Where are the girls?' Clarice mouthed the words to him over Louise's shoulder.

'With Bridget.' Rob jerked his thumb back to indicate the house.

'It's OK, Rob,' she said. 'We'll be inside in a few minutes.'

He nodded before returning to the house.

'Clarice . . .' Her voice broken, her body shaking, Louise was racked with sobs. 'They were there to get Guy. He's been in the river all this time.'

'Yes,' Clarice said.

'But . . . Charlotte, I can't believe it. Were you there – did you actually hear her say that she killed Guy? Did you *hear* it?' Louise's eyes were manic.

'Yes,' Clarice said, and watching her friend's face, she realised that although she'd been told of Charlotte's confession, she had not until this moment believed it.

'She killed him, my boy?'

Clarice could not answer, but Louise, looking into her eyes, recognised the certainty.

They stayed facing one another for several moments, in acceptance of the truth. Louise was suddenly calm, and Clarice felt relieved that the screaming had ceased. But – the thought floated like a bubble through her meandering deliberations – why shouldn't she scream? Her son had been murdered.

'I told you he was dead,' Louise said. 'I could feel it here.' She placed the palm of her hand against her chest.

'Let's go back in,' Clarice said gently. She turned Louise around, and they moved through the garden and into the house. Stopping just inside, she asked, 'Do the girls know?'

'No,' Louise said, 'they're upstairs with Bridget. The sergeant spoke to me alone.'

Rob was waiting in the living room, standing awkwardly by the unlit woodburner.

'OK?' He looked at Clarice.

'I'm going to sit with her for a little while,' Clarice said, then turning to Louise: 'Is there someone you'd like to come to be with you? Your sister, perhaps?'

'No,' Louise said forcefully. 'Bridget has already asked me that, but there is nobody. Guy, Charlotte and the children – they're the only real family I have.'

'Can I make you a drink, some tea?'

'No, no thank you.' Louise sounded flustered. 'I didn't realise Tara was home until I heard her talking to the girls upstairs.'

'You need to think what you're going to tell them – the little ones.'

'It's all right, Gran.' Tara had come into the room, followed by her younger siblings.

'Is Susie here?' Poppy asked Clarice, her gaze sweeping the room.

'No, she's at my house.'

'Why did you come to our house when we went to Lincoln?' Angel asked.

'She came to visit Mum,' Tara said, eyeing Clarice as if daring her to contradict.

'Can you bring Susie back here to Grandma's for us, Clarice, *please*?' Angel wheedled.

'Please, please.' Poppy joined her sister's chorus.

'*No*,' Tara said forcefully, 'not until Mum is better.'

'Our mum's poorly,' Poppy said. 'Tara said we're going to stay here with Grandma until she's better.'

Clarice and Louise's eyes met, and Clarice felt the shock of the lie reflected back.

'When can I see Mum?' Poppy asked.

'When she's better,' Tara said bluntly.

Louise went to make tea and Clarice followed.

'It's just Tara's way of coping,' she whispered to Clarice in the kitchen. 'To pretend nothing has happened, to keep everything as normal as possible.' She glanced towards the sitting room. 'Though Bridget has suggested the girls should be told the truth as soon as possible. And she's recommended a child counsellor who will be able to support them.'

Clarice nodded, looking at her friend as her face twisted with emotion.

'I've told Bridget that all three children will be staying here with me; they have no one else. I won't allow them to be taken into care.'

'What did she say?'

'Just that someone from social services will be getting in touch.'

As she talked, Louise walked from one side of the room to the other, a trapped, distressed beast, her cage the small square of the kitchen, her hands moving in agitation as she spoke. But there was no way out of her situation. Her son was dead and her grandchildren were essentially motherless.

It was hard to leave. Two hours had passed and Rob and Bridget had already gone, Bridget saying she'd return the following day. Louise, while not welcoming the offer, had not rejected it either.

'I wish you'd let me call someone – your sister or someone else. I feel awful leaving you here on your own with three children,' Clarice said as they stood in the lane next to her car.

'It's for the best.' Louise's expression was wretched but now controlled: business as usual. 'I sense Tara has a lot of anger she needs to let go of – towards her mother.'

'Yes,' Clarice agreed, 'but I think she'll blame the whole world – starting with the dog – before she can deal with the anger for Charlotte.'

As she climbed into the car, she caught sight of Judith Roberts walking from a polytunnel, followed by Gavin, the youngest of Louise's employees, bearing a tray of herbs. Judith raised a hand by way of a hello, and Clarice waved back. She was relieved the pair were far enough away to avoid the necessity of engaging in small talk.

She drove home with the window open, feeling the warmth of the breeze against her face, breathing in the smells of summer. But her last image of Louise remained fixed in her mind, walking away with her shoulders back. It was as if by being externally rigid and upright in her bearing, she might hold up her broken spirit.

Alone, Clarice allowed her own facade of peaceful control to slide like a damaged animal moving into cover, her face twisting as she drove, the tears she'd held back running down her face unchecked.

Chapter 38

Later, at home, Clarice sat with Annie, drawing a sense of peace from the cat's calm demeanour. Annie's motherhood instincts had kicked in, and the kittens were thriving. While she didn't treat Clarice's arrival with unrequited joy, there was no longer any hint of a hiss. Clarice knew it was her role as the provider of food that had engendered Annie's tolerance of her presence.

She let her mind wander as she watched Annie bathing her infants with long, leisurely licks, trying to remember what she herself had been like at Tara's age. Adolescence was not something she'd ever crave returning to, with a foot in both camps, neither a child nor an adult. In some ways, Tara appeared to be quite mature, and it was easy to forget she was only fifteen. Having promised her mother she'd support Louise and her young sisters, Tara clearly believed that delaying telling the girls the truth would help. It might have been a mistake for Charlotte to give false hope, though there was no doubting she would have the best of lawyers. Still, a custodial sentence was unavoidable. How well was the relationship between Louise and Tara going to work out? Angry and confused, Tara might make life even more challenging for her step-grandmother.

It was after nine when Rick arrived home. They had a supper of home-made tomato soup with crusty bread from the freezer, before going into the living room to take up their familiar seats: Clarice stretched out on the sofa, Rick adjacent in his armchair.

'You did all you could,' he said to Clarice once she'd filled him in on what had happened after they had parted earlier in the day. 'You can't govern the relationship between Louise and Tara; they're both raw and hurting, and it sounds like Tara is in denial about her mother's involvement. They're going to have to sort out their way forward themselves.'

'I keep feeling I've let Louise down,' Clarice said. 'I know it's illogical.'

'You're right, it's nonsense. How could it have been better for Louise not to know the truth – to go on hoping that Guy might walk back in one day?'

Clarice smiled weakly, understanding the wisdom of his words. But it did not ease her sense of responsibility towards her friend. Was there something she could have done that might have helped?

'So . . . did they find Guy's body easily?'

'Yes, it was wrapped in a green tarpaulin, tied up with rope and weighted down by four canvas bags filled with large stones from the garden.' Rick's voice was sardonic. 'Double-knotted, very neat and tidy. And he had a blue bathroom towel wrapped around his head.'

Clarice gave him a look of incomprehension.

'Don't ask,' Rick said. 'Maybe she didn't want to look at his face again. The post-mortem will be tomorrow.'

'Charlotte's very precise – even, it would appear, in the hiding of a corpse.'

'It was all exactly as she said we'd find it,' Rick said. 'Down to the folds in the tarpaulin and the last double knot. There's no doubt it was her. Only the person who disposed of the body could know all the tiny details.'

'Did you interview her?'

'No.' Rick stroked Ella, the diminutive tabby cat. She'd moved in on him the moment he'd sat down, beating Muddy to the coveted place on his lap by a few seconds. 'Daisy did the interview; I knew that if I hadn't ruled myself out, Charlie would have said something. I told him about our friendship with Louise, and he agreed that it would be inappropriate for me to interview Charlotte. He sat in with Daisy and said that he'd officially oversee the case.'

'Did she keep up her ice queen mode?' Clarice asked.

'Yes,' Rick said. 'It was what we'd expected. I was in the viewing room watching the interview. Her solicitor, Jake Barton, is a long-time friend of the family. Before Charlotte and the children came along, he and Guy played tennis together on Saturday mornings. Keith knows him well.'

'What did you find out?' Clarice shifted on the sofa, squashed between Blue and Jazz, with Susie and Pirate nearby on the floor. The daylight was fading outside, and through the open drapes, long shadows were stealing towards them across the room. The first patterings of rain started to hit the windows.

'She didn't reveal specifically what the argument had been about – the final one. She did say that they'd been arguing a lot recently, which fits with what his colleague James said.'

'But what about?' Clarice asked.

'She said it was husband-and-wife stuff – it was personal, no more.'

'Mmm,' Clarice pondered. 'It must have been something explosive to bring on that kind of violence. She comes across as such a cold fish. I think "husband-and-wife stuff" doesn't seem at all adequate.'

'Daisy did push hard in the interview, but Charlotte wouldn't say any more than that, and Jake Barton wasn't going to allow Daisy to take it further. But he was very eager to reiterate Charlotte's assertion that it was unplanned, there was nothing premeditated about it. She'd lashed out, only once, in anger.'

'Why did she not call for an ambulance after she'd hit him?'

'She said that when she realised he was dead, she panicked.' The sardonic tone crept back into Rick's voice. 'If you buy that.'

Clarice pulled down the corners of her lips. 'I don't know her that well, but I find it hard to believe. And where were the children while all this was going on?'

'Tara was at the home of the friend she goes to quite often – Amy – best friends and all that; the two younger children were in bed, locked in the house.'

'Getting him into the water and then filling the bags to weigh him down must have taken time,' Clarice said, 'and she'd have been soaked.'

'Yes,' Rick agreed. 'Daisy went over those issues. Charlotte said she left his body up in the woods until she'd fed Angel and Poppy. After she'd put them to bed and was sure they were asleep, she went back out. She covered his head with the towel, then wrapped him in the tarpaulin before manoeuvring him downhill. She found the canvas bags and filled them with rocks and stones to weigh the body down. The point in the water where she left him was chest high.'

'Good grief,' Clarice spoke with passion, 'what emotional

control – to behave normally, feeding your kids when you've just killed their father. And plan what to do with his body while you wait for them to get to sleep. Do you think she read them a bedtime story?'

Rick gave a shrug, sharing her disgust.

'I imagine that might have been when Susie did a runner,' Clarice said.

'She said Susie hung around for quite a while watching, but when she called, she wouldn't go to her. When she noticed that the dog had gone, she had to think quickly, which is why she invented Charles.' Rick looked at Clarice reflectively. 'I think we were both doubting his existence.'

'When I followed Susie up to the woods yesterday, Charlotte was genuinely devastated,' Clarice said. 'I was worried that all the good work on Susie's damaged leg would be undone with that sudden burst of speed, but I knew it couldn't have been what Charlotte was upset about, with a dog she's indicated she doesn't overly care for.'

'Anything else you want to add, Mrs Beech?' Rick made a pretence of using an official tone.

Clarice smiled momentarily before her face became serious again. 'As it happens, there are a couple of things.'

'Go on,' he encouraged.

'The first is that Charlotte said Susie hung around but wouldn't go to her when she called.'

'Yes?'

Hearing her name, Susie, who had been dozing, opened her eyes and lifted her head to look fleetingly at Clarice. Sensing that nothing was in the offing, she stretched her legs and returned to her slumber.

'What are you thinking?' Rick asked.

'It was clear that Charlotte didn't want Susie back; she waffled on about thinking that when everything had settled, Louise might take her in.'

'Yes, you told me that, when she first confessed to the murder.'

'Susie saw Charlotte killing Guy,' Clarice said. 'She was Guy's dog – what if she'd tried to protect him? The cut on her leg might be from Charlotte lashing out at her with the spade. Jonathan said it might have been made by something metal.'

'That makes sense,' Rick said. 'Although confessing to killing your husband but not wanting to admit you gave his dog a cut on her leg seems odd.'

'I agree,' Clarice said, 'but so is filling Tara's head with stories of Susie leading us to find Guy's body. It's set the child's mind against the dog. Tara thinks it's all Susie's fault that Guy is dead – not her mother's.'

'And what's the second thing?' Rick asked.

'I saw the spade being brought from the shed.'

Rick nodded.

'From what I've learned about Guy, he was pernickety. Jonathan described his extreme fussiness as anally retentive. The cut wood had to be set lengths, and the piles each perfectly in order, and Charlotte echoed how orderly he was. I believe he'd use the correct tool for a job. So why would he use an edging spade up in the woods? That's what it was. He would have used it in the lawn and flower garden area, but not up there.'

'What you're saying is that Charlotte must have taken it up there herself,' Rick said, 'intending to kill him.'

'Charlotte told me nobody could know less about gardening than her,' Clarice said. 'And when you asked her where the spade was, she told you it was the first spade hung up in the shed.'

'It was the nearest to the door,' Rick said. 'She just grabbed the first one.'

'So how was Guy's murder not premeditated?' Clarice opened her hands, palms up. 'It's a long walk from that shed, around the side of the house, up the hill, through the archway of trees . . . She would have had a lot of time to think.'

Later, lying in bed, Clarice found she couldn't sleep. She forced herself not to move restlessly, knowing Rick had to get to work early, but her mind whirled with all the new information. Rick had been fidgety, but eventually succumbed to sleep, as finally did Clarice, only to wake at 6 a.m. groggy and tired. After break-fast, as she watched him drive away, it felt to her as if Charlotte's protestations that Guy's death had not been planned had dissolved in the overnight rain.

Chapter 39

The following morning, both the local radio and television early breakfast programmes reported the recovery of the body of barrister Guy Corkindale. Also that his wife Charlotte had been arrested and charged with his murder and was currently in police custody. Ten minutes after listening to the news, Clarice received a phone call from Georgie, her voice dramatic and hushed as she tried to elicit further information. Clarice told her that she knew no more than what was on the news. After replacing the receiver, the phone rang again almost immediately; this time it was Keith, who was genuinely devastated by Guy's death. They arranged that, after he had dealt with the business of the day, he'd call in to see her later in the afternoon.

Clarice tried to distract herself. The crops in the vegetable garden were in abundance, with aubergines, beetroot and cauliflower doing well; also the early apple and carrot crops, revitalised by the overnight downpour. But nothing there sparked her interest, her spirits weighted down for a man she'd hardly known.

Inside the workshop, she held onto the vain hope that work might be the answer. Laid out on the drawing table were the designs she'd recently worked on, four large ceramic containers. She needed to consider colours and glazes, usually one of her favourite tasks. But today she couldn't focus on the images spread before her, her thoughts flying in diverse directions. Later today, Rick might have the details of how Guy had died. Steve, the pathologist, who had been asked to get the results to them as quickly as possible, was renowned for his professional thoroughness; he would not be rushed. And there might be problems if further analysis of body parts or substances was required, to delay him delivering his conclusions.

Another call came at 8.30 a.m. Although it was a welcome distraction, Clarice's reaction at seeing Louise's name appear on her mobile screen was one of apprehension.

'I'm so sorry to bother you,' Louise said. 'I'm expecting Bridget later . . .' Her voice trailed away.

'You're not bothering me,' Clarice said. 'What's happened, are you OK?' She sensed Louise's anxiety.

'Did you see the breakfast news?'

'Yes,' Clarice said. 'It was inevitable, although that's no help to you.'

'There's a policewoman sitting in a car in my driveway; it was good of them to send someone. I don't want to be bothered by press.'

'No,' Clarice agreed, 'you don't need any more problems.'

There was a long silence, and Clarice wondered if Louise had hung up.

'I'm worried about Tara.' She spoke eventually. 'I do think Bridget is the best person to support us, she's trained and experienced, but Tara has taken against her. I think it's because her mother doesn't like her.'

'So Tara might feel she's being disloyal by accepting support from her?'

'Yes, but it isn't only about her; she thinks that neither the girls nor I should have anything to do with Bridget.' Louise sounded defeated.

'That puts you in an awkward position.'

'And she's told me she wants to visit her friend, says she's suffocating here.'

'Is it Amy – the best friend?' Clarice asked.

'Yes, Amy Lyndon,' Louise said. 'It must be hard being stuck here with me, but I've only had a few hours to get used to the fact that my son is dead, and I was up all night, I couldn't sleep. Sorry, I don't mean to whinge.'

'Stop apologising,' Clarice said. 'You've every right to be upset, and you need to take all the help that's on offer. Tara is old enough to understand what you're going through – she can't treat you as her taxi service, and you can't leave the young ones on their own.'

'I've told her that,' Louise said. 'I've pointed out that she's been here for less than twenty-four hours, and that when Charlotte is sentenced, she'll be here permanently. We'll have to find a way for it to work for all four of us, school and so on.'

'How did she take that?' Clarice could guess at Tara's response.

'She told me that I was being silly, her mother would be home soon; that she'd never been in trouble before and what had happened was a crime of passion. She said that Guy must have deserved it!' Louise could not keep the shock from her voice. 'My son did not deserve to be murdered.'

'That's an awful thing for you to hear,' Clarice said. 'She probably believes it, because Charlotte told her she didn't intend to kill him – she lost control during an argument, and lashed out.'

'That's what the policeman said,' Louise replied. 'Although I could never see Charlotte losing control like that.'

Clarice had a mental image of the edging spade being carried from Guy's garden shed in a clear plastic bag.

'It's going to take time for Tara to accept what's happened,' she said, trying to push the image from her mind.

'I realise she's finding it hard to cope . . .' Louise's voice cracked, and Clarice guessed she was crying.

'Take it one day at a time,' she said gently. 'First of all, you need to give yourself some time to adjust. You're facing the worst possible experience for a mother – losing your child.' She paused while she considered. 'Is there any chance, given the circumstances, that Amy's mum might come over to collect Tara today? It'll mean you can have time with Bridget without Tara being present.'

'I hadn't thought of that. I don't know her mother. And I'd find it awkward to talk to her . . .' Louise's voice trailed away.

'Lyndon's not a common surname; I'll look the number up and speak to her mother on your behalf. She can only say no.'

Fifteen minutes later, after a difficult conversation with Beth Lyndon, Clarice called Louise back.

'Tell Tara that Amy and her mother are on their way to pick her up. Beth says she'll drop her home to you at about five p.m.'

'That is kind.' Louise sounded relieved. 'I didn't expect her to bring her back as well.'

'It would be a good idea to make sure Tara's ready to go as soon as she arrives,' Clarice suggested. 'Beth sounds nice, but she had lots of questions.'

'I don't feel strong enough for chit-chat.' Louise sounded exhausted. 'Thanks, Clarice. I'll phone you later.'

Clarice sat with her phone in her hand for some time after ending the call. She had expected that the relationship between Tara and Louise would become difficult, but she hadn't imagined it would go downhill quite so quickly. After half an hour of pondering, she decided she was too edgy to get any work done and returned to the house.

Chapter 40

Bob and Sandra arrived later in the morning. There were two appointments in the afternoon for would-be adopters, both of whom had already had a home check, to look at available cats. Bob and Sandra were adept at matching the cats and their quirks with sympathetic adopters.

Sandra's main interest today was in meeting Mrs Marie Walsh, a woman who had specifically asked to see Polly. Clarice realised that while part of Sandra hoped the visitor would turn out to be lovely in every way, another part was thinking how hard it would be to say goodbye. She'd become too attached.

The three of them had lunch together, sitting in the kitchen, the four dogs around them on the tiled floor. The discussion inevitably centred on the news that Guy's body had been found and Charlotte arrested. Clarice, feeling drained by recent events, contributed very little.

'With you being so close to Louise, it must be difficult,' Sandra said, perhaps sensing that she did not want to talk.

'Clarice doesn't need us to keep going on about it,' Bob said. 'I expect Georgie's already phoned trying to pump her for gossip.'

'I'm not doing that!' Sandra was outraged, turning to Clarice. 'You don't think that, do you, darlin'?'

'No, Sandra, I don't. You're a good pal – both of you. I'm just not very with it today. My head's somewhere else.' Clarice smiled weakly. 'And yes, Bob, Georgie did phone. She means no harm. Anyway, I can't complain about other people gossiping; I'm pretty nosy myself. Gossip's part of country life.'

'What's getting to you, darlin', is that you can't help her,' Sandra said.

'You're right,' Clarice said. 'She has to somehow find her own way through this. I can only imagine how terrible it must be to lose a child. She feels so lost.'

Bob veered the conversation onto the cats, and Clarice noticed furtive husband-and-wife glances as he and Sandra tried to engage her with something other than Guy's murder. When Mrs Osborne, the first of the two prospective adopters, arrived, the pair left the cottage to go with her to the cat barn.

'She wasn't interested in the older ones; she wanted two of the kittens,' Bob said when he returned.

'I thought she might,' Clarice said. 'She did get an excellent report from the home visitor. She works from home, so they'd have company, and there're no busy roads nearby. She'll be fine. Did you give her dates?'

'Yes,' Bob replied, 'the usual – that they can go out when they're ten weeks old. I told her that if they're quite small it would be twelve weeks. She's keen on Robert and Ray; she's going to come back again to see them when they are bigger.'

'It's always nice if they go out in pairs,' Sandra said, then turned at the sound of a car engine, signifying another arrival. Reaching into the back pocket of her jeans for her lippy, she applied it with one hand while watching out of the window as Mrs Walsh got out of her car. The woman would have to be perfect in every way before Sandra would agree to her taking Polly.

Bob went out with his wife to greet the newcomer. On his return, he seemed unable to settle. The pad with the list he'd been making for animal food that needed reordering lay open on the pine dining table, seemingly forgotten. His hand crept up to scratch his hairless head, an absent-minded gesture of agitation.

'They've only been in there for fifteen minutes,' Clarice said. 'It'll take longer than that for her to get to know Polly.'

'Sandra was up and down all night worryin' about that cat.'

'It's good someone has expressed an interest, and you know she'll be pleased if Polly finds that special person,' Clarice said.

Bob shrugged. 'She generally doesn't take it so much to heart.'

'They're all important, but the more vulnerable or damaged they are, the more they get under your skin,' Clarice reminded him.

'A cuppa?' Bob suggested. It was his way of dealing with problems.

'OK, but let's go and sit outside to drink it, and wait for Sandra there.'

Half an hour later, Sandra left the cat barn with Mrs Walsh, smiling and talking. She waited until the car had disappeared from the drive before joining Bob and Clarice.

'So?' Bob asked when she reached them.

'Very nice woman.' Sandra spoke slowly. 'Polly wouldn't go to her, but it's early days, and I think she'd be patient. She's coming back to sit with her by herself – if I'm there, Polly just comes to me.'

'Good,' Clarice said. 'I'm leaving you to have the final say.'

'Thanks, darlin',' Sandra said. She turned to her husband. 'Now, are you making me a brew?'

'Certainly, my love.' Bob winked at Clarice as he went back into the house.

After sitting in companionable silence for a few minutes, both of them watching the small birds busily coming and going from the bird table, Sandra said, 'I think I know a bit of what Louise might be feeling. Guy was her baby.'

Clarice nodded slowly. 'She did call him her boy yesterday.'

'It doesn't matter how old my girls get, in my head they'll always be my babies, and if I had to, I'd kill to protect them. You don't know your feelings will be that fierce before you've had kids.'

'So what are you saying?' Clarice asked, looking at Sandra's preoccupied face.

'She might be feeling guilty,' Sandra said. 'I know he was a man, not a child, but still, your feelings don't change.'

'She has no reason to feel guilty,' Clarice said, then, after a moment of hesitation, 'But he was still her boy.'

'And even though the only person to blame is the one who murdered him, I bet Louise has lots of what-ifs.' Sandra cast her eyes down, looking forlorn.

Clarice leaned forward. 'You are a wise old thing,' she whispered.

Sandra shook her head. 'Less of the bleedin' *old*, if you don't mind.'

Chapter 41

After Bob and Sandra had left, Clarice went back inside to make basil and butter biscuits for Keith's visit later, as well as getting started on a loaf of bread.

When Keith arrived, he was sombre. But as they chatted outside in the garden, his mood seemed to lift. He waved his long, elegant fingers in the air as he spoke, sharing tales of the cheerful times he'd had with Guy when he'd first come to his solicitor's office, a shy young man on work experience. He also spoke of Guy's sadness at the death of his baby son, then of him moving on to better times with his girls.

'He always included Tara,' Keith said. 'He considered he had three children.'

'That was the impression I had from both Louise and Charlotte.' Clarice nodded. A comfortable silence fell between them, and she looked at him thoughtfully. 'You could help Louise.'

'Me – how?' Keith asked immediately.

'She really needs her friends now,' Clarice said, 'and I was never a friend of Guy's. We bumped into one another at local events when we were young, but all I know about him is what

I've learned from you, Louise, Charlotte and James. It would be lovely if she could share memories of Guy with people who could reciprocate; she'd enjoy hearing you talk about him.'

'I'd not thought of that,' Keith said. 'I was going to send her a card, but if you think I might help, of course I'll go and see her.'

'Yes,' Clarice said, 'I do.'

A short while later, Clarice's mobile rang. Realising it was Louise, she moved away to take the call, pacing back and forth as they talked. As she was saying goodbye, Keith was suddenly at her side.

'Can I say a quick hello?' he asked.

Clarice spoke to Louise, and after a moment's hesitation, she agreed. Passing Keith the phone, Clarice went into the house to fetch water to top up the dog dishes, and on her return found him still talking, Pirate perched on his lap.

'I told her I'd call in to see her, but I'll phone first.' Keith looked tearful after the call ended. 'I'm sure Jonathan will want to go with me; I'll speak to him later.'

'Good,' Clarice said. 'Tara's plans have changed; she's staying overnight with her friend Amy, so Louise will be able to talk freely.'

Pirate stood up and placed his paws on Keith's chest, then brought his head up so their noses touched.

'He isn't that affectionate with everyone,' Clarice laughed.

'He's just got great taste.' Keith was mockingly haughty.

Sitting in the sunshine drinking peppermint tea, they continued to chat until the welcome committee announced Rick's arrival. Pirate remained with Keith.

Clarice waved as Rick climbed from his car to be mobbed by Blue and Jazz. Susie looked on with envy, her leash wound around the leg of the table. With all that was going on in Louise's life, adding to her woes by losing Susie again would be unforgivable, and Clarice still did not trust the dog not to run away.

'Look at you,' Rick said as he came to the garden table. Upside down in Keith's lap, Pirate responded with a wiggle and a squeak.

'Was that your happy noise?' Keith asked, enchanted.

'He certainly sounds happy,' Clarice said. 'He usually joins the pack to welcome Rick home, but he obviously doesn't want to leave you.'

'I think he likes me,' Keith told Rick proudly.

Rick nodded his agreement. 'Would you like something stronger than tea?'

'Or to join us for something to eat?' Clarice added.

'That is so kind, my darlings, but I'm driving, and I should get home. Jonathan is *slaving* in the kitchen.' Keith sounded reassuringly theatrical once more. He stood up, gently placing Pirate on the ground. Pirate yawned and trotted back to the other dogs, now all gathered around the table. They welcomed him back into the circle by sniffing every part of him with enthusiasm.

'He looks like a plump little sultan with his harem of girlies,' Keith chortled, watching Pirate standing confidently in the middle of the pack.

'Come and have supper soon,' Clarice said as she gave him a goodbye hug. 'I'll arrange a date with Jonathan.'

She and Rick stood watching as Keith's car drove away up the incline.

'Did it go well today?' Clarice asked.

'Very badly for Charlotte,' Rick said grimly. 'I'll tell you while we get supper sorted.'

In the kitchen, Rick topped and tailed green beans that Clarice had picked from the garden before Keith's arrival. Beans always brought Mary, her late mother, to mind. The house had been enlarged and modernised since Clarice's childhood, but it was in this kitchen that she'd help her mother prepare salads while chewing on the odd raw bean. The food Mary had cooked had come straight from the garden, wholesome but plain. But she had introduced her daughter to the pleasure of herbs. Back then there had not been the variety Clarice now grew, but helping her mother in the garden and the kitchen had given her her initial spark of interest in both gardening and cooking.

Today Clarice peeled prawns and made up a vinaigrette dressing. At the same time, Rick moved on to washing and cooking the pink fir apples, an early crop of their favourite home-grown potatoes.

'She's been charged with murder, so we don't have a time limit,' Rick said. 'We need to interview her again, but that will be after Steve's delivered the full autopsy results. With Guy's remains having been in the water for so long, it's made things difficult. But Steve says the timescale Charlotte gave does tally. Guy died in the late afternoon of the Sunday. And he's awaiting the results of toxicology tests.'

'Do you think Charlotte drugged him?'

'Toxicology is just part of the process. We need to cover all the bases, especially since there was no water in his lungs, meaning he was dead when he went in. He did regularly take something to help him sleep, so that might be in his system – if tests show there are unusually large quantities, that would raise questions. Hopefully the toxicology will come back with the final autopsy results for Monday morning.'

'Then you'll interview her again before she goes before a judge?' Clarice asked.

'When it does go before the judge, she'll be placed on remand. She won't enter a plea, just give her name and address, then she'll go to the women's prison in Derbyshire.'

'No chance of bail?' Clarice asked.

'The prosecution team would object.'

'She'd hoped for manslaughter – you're saying the final charge will be murder?'

'That has yet to be decided officially, after the test results come back and Steve's signed off the autopsy. But it's stacking up. We'll ask her again about what happened when she hit Guy, and about the spade she killed him with.'

'It won't be easy for her – the prison,' Clarice said quietly.

'It isn't for anyone, but . . .' Rick's voice trailed away.

'She did admit to the killing,' Clarice said. 'She hasn't tried to run away from it – she put her hands up.'

'No,' Rick said, 'that's not entirely correct. She confessed once she was caught out, not before. She'd hoped to get away with it, and with all that malarkey about the fictitious Charles, she wasted a lot of police time.'

Clarice had cut chunks of fresh bread to go with the prawns. Rick carried everything to the kitchen table, and Clarice brought cutlery from a drawer in the pine dresser. They sat with the dogs, as was usual, laid out on the kitchen floor around them.

'Why do you believe they won't accept the manslaughter plea?' Clarice looked closely at Rick, sensing he was holding something back. 'It can't just be about the spade.'

'No.' Rick spoke quietly.

'Tell me?' Clarice asked.

'It won't come out officially until Steve delivers his autopsy report.'

'So tell me unofficially – you know I won't repeat it.' Clarice moved her food around absent-mindedly with her fork. In her mind, something felt unbalanced, like a tray of shiny steel balls tipping first one way and then the other, about to overspill into disaster. She sensed something nasty was coming.

'The blows from the spade were close together, almost on top of one another. On first inspection, it looked like Guy had been hit only once.'

'But he wasn't.' Clarice spoke with a sudden feeling of nausea.

'No,' Rick said. 'Steve says that he'd been hit twice. The first blow was from an angle above him from the back – he believes Guy was probably kneeling or bending when he received it. He might have been occupied working, not aware that Charlotte had crept up on him. And he wasn't expecting it – there are no defence wounds, his head was tilted as if he was looking down.'

'And the second?' Clarice asked when Rick paused.

'The second was deeper and the angle suggests it was delivered while Guy was lying on his front, incapacitated from the first strike – a chopping motion from above.'

'It was murder,' Clarice said, the words hanging in the air between them.

'Yes,' Rick repeated, his dark brown eyes staring at her unblinkingly. 'It was murder.'

Clarice looked again at the food, and realised she no longer had an appetite.

Chapter 42

'I can't believe it's a whole week since the fund-raiser,' Clarice said to Rick. The sun was full in a cloudless blue sky as they sat in the shade of the cottage.

'And I can't believe I've got a whole day off.' Rick looked from Clarice to Daisy and Ollie Pierce.

'I'll drink to that.' Ollie raised his glass of freshly squeezed orange juice.

Daisy had phoned as Clarice and Rick finished lunch to ask if they might call in on their way back from a visit to Castlewick. Having not had a chance to catch up with Daisy about her personal life, Clarice quickly grabbed the opportunity. The first thing she'd wanted to know was why she and Ollie were food shopping together. It boded well.

'How did the concert go last week?' she asked Ollie now.

Daisy had gone inside with Rick to look at something on his laptop. It had been agreed that there would be no discussion about work or the Corkindale case, but Clarice suspected that whatever Rick wanted to show Daisy would be related to the interview with Charlotte, and relevant for the following day.

'The concert was great,' Ollie said, 'or at least what we saw of it.'

'Did you get there late?'

'No.' Ollie looked around with a bemused expression at the circle of four dogs, Blue the nearest to him, with her chewed red rubber ball. On the garden table, Big Bill stretched out his ginger body as if guarding the jug of orange juice. 'It took ages to set up the tents, it was raining, and the wind had got up. When we eventually managed to get to the stage for the band we wanted to see, the sound wasn't great because of the weather.'

'Did you stick it out?' Clarice asked.

'We went into the bar for a drink, but when we got back to the tents, I'd got a leak, my tent had flooded, and neither of us could find our torches.'

'A wasted journey then?' Clarice said.

'No.' Ollie gave a big grin. 'I wouldn't say that. I really enjoyed being with Daisy.'

'She is lovely,' Clarice said. 'Great company.'

Ollie nodded. 'Tell me about the animal charity.' He looked around again at the assembled group.

Clarice told him about CAW, and her work as a ceramicist, and he explained his role in traffic. Although their paths had crossed briefly at social gatherings, it was the first time they had engaged fully in conversation. As they chatted about people they knew in common, Daisy returned.

'Rick's on the phone.' She smiled as she sat down next to Ollie.

'You've got a call from Louise,' Rick said as he rejoined the group. 'I had a chat, and now she's waiting to talk to you.'

'Hi,' Clarice said when she reached the phone. 'You beat me to it; I was going to call later.'

'I needed a friendly ear, nothing special,' Louise said.

'Is everything OK?' Clarice asked.

'As OK as it can be.' Louise's voice was pragmatic. 'Bridget's been great; she was so helpful yesterday. I told her what I was going to say to Angel and Poppy, and she said she thought I had the right approach.'

'In what way?'

'I felt it was important to tell them that Guy was dead, without further delay. Tara threw me, saying their mother was ill.'

'I agree with you,' Clarice said.

'Also, I think it confuses children to use terms like "passed", "lost" or "gone to sleep". Although I've told them that when people talk about their dad, they will use those expressions.' Louise sounded pensive.

'It sounds like you'd planned it carefully – how did it go?' Clarice asked.

'Angel was silent and thoughtful; Poppy was in tears. I know we've got a long way to go while they come to terms with what's happened.'

'I'm so sorry you're going through this.' Clarice felt tearful herself.

'Not as sorry as me,' Louise responded quickly. 'But it's what you said before about taking it one day at a time – that really applies now with the children.'

'What have you told them about their mum?'

'I said she's helping the police,' Louise said. 'It was easier with Tara not being there. I tried to answer everything as honestly as possible. Bridget's put me in touch with a counsellor, because of the complexity of the situation. She said each time they want to know something, answer them; keep things short, but be truthful.'

'That sounds sensible advice.'

'The conversations now are all about the funeral – the coffin, the service, who will be there,' Louise said. 'Although I've no idea when it can take place. Bridget said she would let me know when the police are going to release Guy's body.'

'What are you doing today?'

'Jonathan and Keith have just left.' Louise sounded more upbeat. 'It was so kind of them, and the girls adored them. Poppy has decided that Jonathan is Father Christmas without his beard. She said he must be doing his summer job, visiting children. They brought some colouring books.'

'I'd never have thought of that one,' Clarice laughed, 'but she's spot on. What about Tara?'

'She came back with Amy, and they've been upstairs in her room all day. Tara came down to say hello to Jonathan and Keith, but that was it. She's turned into a monosyllabic fifteen-year-old. But who can blame her in the circumstances?'

'Is Amy's mum collecting her?'

'Yes,' Louise said. 'Tara's going back with her again tonight. She'll be home at teatime tomorrow. Thank goodness for the school holidays.'

'Is there anything I can do?' Clarice asked.

'I was wondering if you might have time for us tomorrow, to get together with Susie for a couple of hours,' Louise said. 'Angel and Poppy are missing her and Tara won't be here when you come. I'm hoping she won't be so hostile towards Susie, though. She's had some space, spending time with Amy, so maybe we can take Susie back soon.'

'No problem,' Clarice said. 'I'd intended to ask if you thought the girls might like to see her. Would you prefer us to come to you, rather than bringing them here?'

'Come here. Maybe we could visit you another day – see those kittens.'

'I'll be over in the morning, about ten. Is that all right?' Clarice asked.

'Perfect,' Louise said. 'See you then.'

Back outside, Daisy said it was time for her and Ollie to go. Clarice hung back with her as Rick and Ollie walked to the car.

'I'm glad the concert went well,' she said as they crunched over the gravel.

'Me too,' Daisy said, giving Clarice a hug, and although she couldn't see her face, Clarice could read a smile in her voice.

'Tell me about Louise,' Rick said once they had returned to the table.

Clarice obligingly filled him in on the conversation.

'Your turn,' she said. 'What was the something you wanted to show Daisy?'

'The tox results came back today. There were acceptable levels of medication in Guy's system; he'd not been given an overdose.'

'At least that's some good news,' Clarice said hopefully, watching his face.

'It is one thing less to talk about, but we still need Charlotte to understand that we won't accept that what happened was a spur-of-the-moment loss of control.'

'The interview is going ahead tomorrow?'

'Yes, but Daisy's in court in the morning on another case.

I want the continuity of her doing the interview, so it'll be in the afternoon.'

They sat for a while enjoying the tranquillity of their surroundings.

'There is one thing I'd like to know.' Rick broke the silence.

Clarice looked at him.

'I've been following the Daisy and Ollie saga for weeks. It seems to me they're more than just friends now. What broke the deadlock? The concert sounded like a disaster, but they both said it was great. I gather the shopping trip was so he could buy ingredients for something he's cooking tonight – she's staying over at his place.'

'Your guess is as good as mine,' Clarice said, her face deadpan. 'Though Daisy did mention he was cooking.'

'Come on, Mrs Beech, spill.' Rick crossed his arms in a gesture that suggested he was preparing for a wait. 'You know Daisy will tell me eventually, on some long, boring car journey, but it'll take her three weeks to work around to it.'

'Apparently Ollie's tent sprang a leak and was full of water. It was pitch black and they'd misplaced their torches, so Daisy invited him to share with her.'

'Her tiny one-person tent?' Rick considered it. 'Well, that would certainly have been cosy. Lucky it rained.'

'Yes,' Clarice said.

'There's more to this,' Rick said suspiciously. 'What part did you play?'

Clarice held back for a minute, making him wait. 'I did suggest that Daisy should try praying to Jude, the patron saint of lost causes.'

Rick continued to stare at her.

'I also suggested that she use a penknife and hide the torches.'

'You what?' Rick was incredulous. 'Daisy took a penknife to the poor bloke's tent?'

'No, she didn't, as it happens.' Clarice smiled, her eyes mischievous. 'She said a pair of nail scissors did the job just as well.'

Chapter 43

The next morning Clarice walked her usual circuit, the outer boundary of their three-acre gardens; it was an unexpected bonus when Rick was able to join her before leaving for work. Susie stayed close to Clarice on a lead, Blue ran back and forth carrying her ball, followed by Jazz and Pirate.

A light breeze tempered the heat, unusual so early in the day. The weather forecast gave rain warnings for later, and now wafts of air moved the long grasses of the wildflower garden to caress Clarice's legs, bare below her favourite calf-length jeans. Overhead, small clusters of candyfloss-pink clouds drifted slowly. But despite being in the midst of so much loveliness, her mind was in turmoil again.

'Do you think Louise will want to take Susie back any time soon?' Rick asked, breaking into her reflections.

'It depends on Tara,' Clarice replied. 'Louise said yesterday that she hopes it will happen soon. Susie being here isn't a problem, is it?'

'Not at all,' Rick said. 'We have to fit around Louise's needs at present; she has enough to deal with. It's just I remember you telling me after Guy disappeared that the younger children might benefit from Susie's presence.'

'I still believe that,' Clarice said. 'I think having a lively dog in the house would be a diversion. When Charlotte goes to court and isn't given bail, Tara will know her mum isn't coming home any time soon. It might change her idea about who's really at fault.'

'I'll be talking to Daisy before the interview with Charlotte – Charlie's sitting in again.' Rick stopped for a moment to look around, and Clarice felt he might be thinking, as she was, how the early-morning beauty surrounding them contrasted with the ugliness of Guy's death.

'Charlotte was adamant she only hit Guy once,' she said, bringing his attention back. 'I wonder why she would say that. She must have known it'd be exposed as a lie.'

'She'll change her story when she's been told the results of the post-mortem.' Rick's voice was unemotional.

Clarice waited, watching him. He seemed convinced Charlotte was an out-and-out liar. He hesitated, as if digging deep to answer.

'Perhaps she thought she could get away with saying that because it *looked* like Guy had only been hit once, with the strikes being almost one on top of the other. And of course, if we thought that, she might get away with manslaughter.'

'No, I don't buy that.' Clarice's response was instant. 'Charlotte's far too bright – she would know how exhaustive the post-mortem would be in a murder case.'

'Clarice.' Rick sounded exasperated. 'She has confessed, and her perfect description of where the body was found and how it was tied up makes it impossible for it to have been anyone but her. What other explanation is there, apart from her losing it so completely she really does believe she only hit him once?'

'I don't know, but there must be one.' Clarice spoke with conviction.

They were quiet walking back to the cottage, both deep in thought. When it was time for Rick to leave, Clarice went to the car with him and wished him luck.

'Thanks,' he said absent-mindedly, his mind already in another place, working on the pattern of questions to be asked at the interview. 'Speak later.'

Walking back into the house, Clarice realised it was still only 8.30. Bob and Sandra would be coming over later, but she felt unsettled.

She checked on and fed the cats, then looked in on Doreen, who appeared delighted to see her. She stayed for fifteen minutes throwing a ping-pong ball that Doreen batted around the large enclosure with the energy of a young kitten rather than a middle-aged ferret, before eventually tiring. Climbing onto Clarice's lap, she received an absent-minded cuddle before Clarice departed, her mind still weighed down by the earlier discussion with Rick.

Later, after driving up the incline to reach the road, she slid a CD into the car player to listen to T-Bone Walker singing 'Stormy Monday' as she followed the line of caravans and cars with fully laden roof racks heading to the coast. The rhythm of the music and the beauty of the day allowed her mind to untwist, and she found her thoughts rebounding between the present and the past.

It had been December when her father had died unexpectedly of a heart attack. Two years older than Angel, Clarice had had no concept of the meaning of death, and had found it impossible to believe she'd never see him again. Her main recollection was of confusion. Friends and neighbours were still excited about the forthcoming festivities; people were carrying on as normal, wrapping presents and laughing, when her world was completely changed, her father suddenly absent, her mother bereft. Sometimes she'd been distracted, only then to feel guilty that for a short time she'd forgotten. It had been a time filled with sorrow, and she knew now that the experience had changed her. At that young age she'd discovered a love of poetry, its words and rhythms able to reach inside her to bring some peace.

Looking at the sun-bleached crops on either side of the road, her thoughts drifted as she drove, and the first lines of an Emily Dickinson poem crept into her mind: *As imperceptibly as Grief / The Summer lapsed away*. Would Guy's children feel the same cynicism about the loveliness of nature in the summer as Clarice did about the merriments of December? At least her father's death had been natural. Charlotte's involvement in Guy's would mean double the grief – she would be lost to them in prison. And they would also have to cope with the idea that someone they loved had killed someone else they loved. How would they ever come to terms with that? And with her?

As Clarice turned into the narrow lane that led to Louise's home, she considered again what Rick had told her about the pathologist's findings. It didn't make any sense, and a few minutes later, as she parked, the niggle was back, a mental itch she couldn't scratch.

Chapter 44

Louise came outside to meet her; once inside the house, Clarice let Susie off the lead.

'Find the girls,' Louise whispered, and Susie bounded ahead of them to the kitchen.

'It's going to be a lovely surprise for them,' Louise said as the air filled with squeals of joy.

'Has she come back to live with us?' Angel asked when Clarice and Louise joined them in the kitchen. Both Angel and Poppy had their arms around Susie like limpets clinging to a rock. Susie's tail swung joyfully in delighted appreciation, tongue lolling, eyes bright with delight.

'It's just a visit today, but she's your dog and she'll come back one day soon,' Clarice reassured her.

'When?' Poppy demanded.

'We can't say,' Louise cut in, 'but it will happen, I promise, and you know Grandma never breaks her promises.'

'It'll be when Mum comes home,' Angel said, turning into the knowing big sister.

Both girls appeared to weigh up and consider Angel's conjecture before looking at one another and nodding.

'Are you drawing for Grandma?' Clarice asked as she walked over to the kitchen table. At one end was paper and crayons; the other was tidier, with an open laptop.

'*I'm* drawing,' Poppy said, slipping her small hand into Clarice's big one. 'Our daddy is dead.' She spoke the words in a whisper, as if divulging a shameful secret to herself.

'Yes, I know, and I'm so very sorry.' Fighting to suppress the sensation of a giant rock crushing her chest, Clarice knelt on the floor beside her.

'Grandma will have told her that.' Angel came and stood close; Clarice imagined that it was so as not to be left out. As Poppy wrapped her arms around her neck, Angel did the same.

'Big hugs,' Clarice said, opening her arms wider. 'Where is Grandma?' Louise, who had been standing at the door watching, came over, her eyes brimming with unshed tears, to join them, kneeling to be part of the hug.

'Clarice?' Angel's voice as she emerged from the cuddle held a question. Clarice waited. 'Why are you stinky?'

Clarice looked from her to Poppy, who was holding her nose in mock horror. Louise, through her tears, had suddenly dissolved into helpless laughter.

Later, they moved out into the rear garden and the children erupted onto the lawn, chased by an ecstatic Susie.

'I'm so pleased to see you. Thanks for bringing Susie over,' Louise said.

'Even when I cuddle Doreen the ferret before I leave home?' Clarice pulled a face and sniffed.

'Yes, even if you are a bit niffy.'

'I think Susie's enjoying the reunion as much as the girls.'

Clarice smiled, watching the frenetic activity. 'Is Angel using your computer, by the way? I gather that Poppy's the only artist today.'

'It's keeping her occupied,' Louise said, 'but it's Tara who's the real computer nerd. Guy taught all the girls how to use it; he said computers were a necessary tool. It's not mine; it belongs to Charlotte.'

'Does it live here then – for use by the children?'

'It didn't used to. Tara brought it with her in the bag she packed before coming here.'

'She must have put it in without Daisy seeing her,' Clarice mused. 'You said it belongs to Charlotte?'

'Sort of.' Louise spoke precisely, clearly trying to be accurate. 'It was used by all the family, Guy as well, and it's the one he used to teach the children on.'

'Don't you think—'

'I know what you're going to say,' Louise interrupted. 'It might have something important on it – for police purposes – but I promise it doesn't. I've checked it myself.'

'But you're not an expert with computers, and there might be something on it the police are interested in.'

'That's true,' Louise agreed. 'I get by with computers because I have to, but I can't do the things Guy did.'

Clarice sat quietly for a moment considering.

'Have you checked out any previous searches?'

'I wouldn't have a clue how to do that.'

'They may have been wiped, but . . . Can I take it with me, would you mind?'

'No, I don't mind. Although now that Charlotte has con-fessed to the murder, I'm not sure there's much point.' Louise looked flustered. 'I should have thought about giving it to the police. Quickly, put it into your car now while the children are occupied. I don't want them asking questions about what you want it for. The password is susie123, all lower case.'

Clarice quietly went into the kitchen and took the laptop out to her car, putting it out of sight under the passenger seat. Then she returned to rejoin Louise, who was back in the kitchen. Once she'd cleared the table, made tea and poured orange juice, Louise called for the girls to come in. Susie bounded through the door, tail still swinging, the children attached. While they drank the juice, the dog took up position on the kitchen floor, near the table, resting her head on her paws; much as she did in Clarice's kitchen.

'Are the kittens big enough now for us to throw ping-pong balls for them to chase?' Poppy asked.

Louise laughed. 'You only saw them a few days ago; they won't have grown much in that time.' Clarice felt momentarily warmed by the sound of the laugh, a salve for the frayed anguish lurking just beneath the surface of the small gathering.

None of them heard the car stopping outside, or the door opening.

'What's *she* doing here?' Tara was suddenly in the room, pointing accusingly at Susie, her face stretched into a scowl. 'I told you not to bring her here.' She spewed the words towards her grandmother.

'She's our dog,' Angel said.

'She's trouble.' Tara's face was pink with anger. 'She's the reason Mum's not here.'

'Don't be silly, Tara.' Louise stood up. 'The dog is not to blame for the predicament your mother is in.' She looked at her watch. 'It's only eleven. I wasn't expecting you until teatime.'

'You mean you thought you'd sneak the dog in and out behind my back?' Tara spat. 'Amy's mum wanted them to go out to visit Amy's grandma.'

'She's our dog, Tara!' Angel repeated shrilly as she left the table to confront her sister. 'We want her here all the time.'

'Tough,' Tara said, taking a step forward. 'You're too young to understand the trouble that bloody dog has caused – *and* she's smelly.'

Clarice felt a moment of guilt as Tara wafted her hand across her contorted face.

'Tara!' Louise's voice was sharp.

And then, suddenly, Susie moved to stand between Tara and Angel, staring unblinkingly at the older girl. The hackles along the length of her spine stood erect as she emitted a long, low growl. Tara backed slowly away towards the door.

'Susie!' Clarice rose, her firm voice cutting across the growl. 'Come!'

Susie gave Tara another long look, but obeyed. As her hackles dropped, she stood looking up at Clarice's face, awaiting the next command.

'There you are,' Tara said. 'If ever you needed proof that she can't be trusted.'

Louise looked from Susie to Tara with a stunned expression. 'She's never done anything like that before.'

'She has – just ask Mum. She bit someone who came in the garden once.' Tara threw up her hands in exasperation, her voice hinting at tears. 'And that's the second time she's had a go at me. She bit my arm.' She turned and flounced from the room; a few moments later, a door banged upstairs.

'Susie!' Poppy ran to the dog, who, all signs of aggression

gone, was once more the friendly tail-wagging family pet. Angel joined her sister to bury her face in Susie's fur.

'I don't understand what just happened,' Louise said to Clarice.

'Let everyone calm down,' Clarice said in a weak attempt to sound relaxed. 'We didn't know Tara would be back so soon. I'll take Susie home with me.'

Outside, as Clarice put Susie into the car, Angel, her voice obstinate, said again, 'She is still our dog.'

'Yes,' Clarice agreed. 'She is still your dog.'

Above the heads of the children, she met Louise's eyes, and read fear and panic there. Driving away, she realised that there would now be a question in Louise's mind about Susie's behaviour and whether it was safe to leave her with the children. She would not want the dog to return as part of the family if there was the slightest chance she would bite someone. But how to tell Angel and Poppy, having already given her word?

At the end of the lane, Clarice stopped the car, looking in both directions; there was no traffic, all was still. The sun skimmed the golden landscape, while behind her, in the back of the car, Susie sat upright, her forehead furrowed by her puzzled look as she gazed back in the direction of the house.

Turning the car onto the main route home, Clarice drove slowly. In contrast, her mind raced. It was there again, that itch she couldn't reach; what was it she'd missed? It had to be somewhere, in a conversation or an action. Trying to be methodical, she started with what had been said at the supper with Jonathan and Keith. They'd discussed Guy coping with depression while coming to terms with the death of his infant son; Angel being ill, endangering her life by eating nuts and pills. But it had not been Angel herself who said she'd shared her lunch with a school friend, or eaten her father's pills while believing them to be sweets. Keith had said that Guy had told him both those things. Neither was a fact; they were both assumptions. Poppy had said to Angel, *You tell lies.* Clarice had sensed at the time that Poppy did not necessarily mean it to relate to the pestle and mortar, but to something else. Possibly to their parents' disbelief of Angel's version of events. But what if Angel hadn't been lying – it would take everything in a completely different direction.

There was James's belief that Charlotte and Guy had, until recently, had a good marriage, and it was only in the last few weeks that they'd had problems. Guy's desire to remain at home in Lincolnshire fell into the same time frame. Her thoughts moved around Tara, Angel and Poppy, the conversations, things they'd said, and finally came to rest upon what Rick had said about Charlotte. *Her perfect description of where the body was found and how it was tied up makes it impossible for it to have been anyone but her. What other explanation is there?*

She pulled to the side of the road, turning the engine off. Susie, who had lain down, stood herself back up and looked around. Sliding Charlotte's laptop out from under the passenger seat, Clarice opened it up and switched it on. She looked at it, hesitating for a moment, before putting in the password.

'I'm searching for four words,' she said aloud to the dog, who responded by putting her head on one side. Going into the history option, she waited with bated breath for the list of previous searches to load.

Her eyes met those of the dog. 'Clever girl,' she said, imagining that Susie's soulful look expressed a deep sense of something unfathomable.

Then, knowing that if Rick were busy he would read a message rather than play a voicemail, she typed: *Charlotte did not murder Guy – phone me.*

Chapter 45

'Come straight here,' Rick said, 'with the laptop.'

Clarice leaned against her car, all its windows open to allow movement of air for Susie, who watched her closely. She'd been impatient for Rick to reply to her text; the waiting had felt interminable, but she realised that he'd responded within five minutes.

'I've got Susie in the car. I won't be able to leave her – it's too warm – and I'm scruffy, still wearing what I had on earlier.'

'Don't worry about it. Come straight here. Daisy's only just arrived back from her court case, so the interview was delayed. I need to tell her what you've just told me, and try to talk to Charlie. He's going to *love* this.' Rick's voice dripped with sarcasm.

'Sorry . . .' Clarice's voice trailed away.

'Don't be sorry. I'm glad you've told me. Better now, before Charlotte's interview.'

'I'll let you go,' Clarice said. 'See you soon.' He hung up and was, she imagined, dashing about bringing Daisy and Charlie together.

Half an hour later, she found him impatiently awaiting her

arrival in the headquarters car park. She held the laptop while he lifted Susie from the back of the car, then handed it over in exchange for the dog leash. On the way into the building, they talked again about what she'd told him earlier. Going up the main staircase, he stopped suddenly, looking her up and down.

'What?' she said, anticipating what he was going to say.

'What the hell is that smell?' He looked accusingly at Susie. 'Has she rolled in something?

'No.' Clarice continued climbing the stairs. 'It's from Doreen.'

'Who?' She saw the dawning of recognition in his eyes.

'June Blake's ferret.' She shrugged, attempting to make it casual.

'Clarice!' Rick's voice expressed his exasperation. 'Hellfire!'

Ten minutes later, they were sitting in a small grey office with the window open and a fan oscillating, moving the air slowly around the room. It did little to bring the temperature down or disperse the smell. Kerry, the constable Clarice had met on Steep Hill when Poppy had gone walkabout, had brought in a dish containing water, and Susie was lapping at it noisily.

'I think the dog's well and truly sorted.' Chief Inspector Charlie Johnson smiled as he spoke, an attempt at geniality. In contrast, Clarice sensed, bubbling under the calm exterior he was feeling quite the opposite. She was messing up his murder case, one he'd considered was neatly tied up. 'Clarice, would you like to tell us what you think you've discovered?' He patted her hand, which rested on the small green table between them, next to Charlotte's grey laptop.

If Rick sensed Clarice stiffen as she moved her hand to rest it in her lap, he didn't show it. But Clarice caught the swift, cautious glance that Daisy shot in his direction. They would, she realised, know she'd recognise when she was being patronised.

'It began with a discussion,' she said, looking directly at Charlie.

He nodded encouragingly.

'I was at supper with friends who know – knew – Guy well, just after he'd gone missing. The discussion was centred inevitably around his disappearance. Guy's sadness at the loss of his baby son some years ago, and how badly he was affected by it. He took extended leave away from his chambers.' Clarice paused to observe the set expression on the chief inspector's face. 'More recently Guy had had problems with his daughter, Angel, who has a nut allergy. She'd supposedly eaten something with nuts from her friend's lunch box and had a bad reaction. Later, she took some of her father's sleeping tablets – it was assumed she thought them to be sweets. On both occasions it ended with her in hospital. I also found that Guy was reluctant to leave home; he wanted to stay in Lincolnshire.'

'James Wright, his friend in chambers, told us that,' Daisy interjected.

'Yes,' Clarice said. 'And James also said that Guy and Charlotte were arguing a lot recently. He'd heard Guy talking to her on the phone and assumed the marriage was in trouble.'

'Well, it certainly must have been for his wife to hit him with a spade and hide his body in the river.' Charlie's lips had set into a tight smile as he stared unblinkingly at her. 'Which she has already confessed to.'

'Yes, she did move Guy's body into the river,' Clarice said. 'That was how she knew, to the last detail, the way the body had been wrapped and weighted down. But she didn't murder him. She was protecting her daughter. Tara killed Guy.'

'And you believe this because of,' Charlie crossed his arms, 'something on this?' He looked at the grey computer.

'The laptop was used by Charlotte and Guy. Guy taught the children how to access it.'

'Then why wasn't it brought in when he went missing?' Charlie's voice was accusing. 'And what motive would the stepdaughter have for the killing?'

'It wasn't brought in because we didn't know of its existence,' Rick interrupted. 'We only knew of Guy's work laptop, which we had. And Charlotte Corkindale wasn't then a suspect in the murder of her husband – it started as a case of a missing person.'

'Someone – presumably either Guy, Charlotte or Tara – searched on this computer.' As she spoke, Clarice opened it – it was already set to its home page, with a screen saver of Susie on the lawn at Lark House – and they watched as she went into the search history.

'Munchausen syndrome by proxy,' Charlie read aloud. The heat made the small room feel oppressive; they looked at one another, but nobody spoke. Charlie sniffed the air, and Clarice saw Rick's lips twitch.

'As I'm sure you're aware, Munchausen syndrome is a deep-seated mental illness,' Clarice said. 'The sufferer wants to gain attention and does it by faking illness. And Munchausen syndrome by proxy, known as MSBP, is when the sufferer inflicts illness on someone vulnerable in their care – often an elderly person or a child.'

Charlie's voice was waspish. 'And you believe that Tara has this mental illness, and Charlotte Corkindale is trying to protect her by confessing to the killing herself.'

'I think Tara overheard her mother and stepfather arguing about her. Either he or Charlotte googled to find out more about the illness; or perhaps Tara googled it herself.'

'Which,' Rick said, 'is why Guy didn't want to leave home.'

Clarice enjoyed a moment of satisfaction at the expression that flitted across Charlie's face. As the seeds of doubt began to germinate, the certainty of his previous convictions was demolished like bricks turning into dust.

'Guy feared Tara had this illness, and that while he was working away, she might do something else to hurt the younger children,' she continued. 'In both previous cases, the nut allergy and then taking the sleeping pills, Tara supposedly came to the rescue and saved Angel. What I believe really happened was that she gave her sister the nuts and the pills.' Clarice paused for a moment, seeing she now had Charlie's complete attention.'

'How do you think she did that? Surely the child – Angel – would have known that she had an allergic reaction to nuts.' Charlie had lost his inscrutable expression and now leaned forward, his face animated.

'It's a guess on that one,' Clarice said, also leaning in. 'Tara enjoys cooking, and when preparing food often uses a pestle and mortar or an electric grinder. It would have been easy for her to grind the nuts and then the sleeping pills to hide them in Angel's food or drink.'

'Yes,' Charlie nodded, 'I see.'

'Angel insisted she didn't eat either the nuts or the pills,' Clarice went on, 'but she wasn't believed. However, I think Guy had worked out what was going on, and the arguments with Charlotte were because he wanted to confront the problem.

Perhaps to take Tara to seek medical attention. Charlotte might have disagreed with him, or else couldn't get her head around mental illness. It's still taboo for many people.'

'Which,' Rick said, 'would have put Guy in an impossible position.'

'Yes,' Clarice agreed, 'and it showed that Charlotte either had complete faith in Tara, unable to believe she would harm her sister, or that she couldn't bear to confront the reality. Logically, if Tara is the murderer, she must have told her mother she only hit Guy once, and Charlotte again trusted her, accepting that she'd been told the truth.'

'The two strikes were almost on top of one another.' Rick spoke directly to Charlie. 'The pathologist said that at first glance it appeared the victim had received one blow. It was only on close inspection that it became obvious that there were two. Tara might have thought she'd get away with it; she didn't want to admit to her mother that she'd hit Guy twice. So that's what Charlotte confessed to.'

'You're reading a lot into four words in the search section of a computer,' Charlie said, but his tone lacked conviction.

'It isn't just what's on the laptop,' Clarice said. 'There are other things – like when Poppy disappeared at the fund-raiser, for example.'

Rick nodded and looked at her, waiting for her to continue.

'Poppy had talked about her father taking her to see the swans at Brayford Pool. It would be a confusing route for a small child from Lady Jayne's house, but we believed that although she didn't know where she was heading, she'd still gone looking for him. When we discovered she was missing, we went to search for her. I asked Bob and Sandra to go down the hill because I thought it might be easier for them. But Tara was adamant she would be the one to search downhill.'

Charlie was listening intently.

'It goes back to what I said to you,' Clarice looked at Rick, 'that young children are spontaneous, and can appear random in what they say and think, so we don't always take it in or believe them. But there is often a pattern, a logic we don't detect at first.'

'You were talking then about Poppy having seen the diary in the wrong place,' Rick said. 'Because Charlotte must have packed Guy's London bag, and she'd forgotten the diary; she said Guy always packed everything into that bag on Sunday evening, the night before.'

'Yes,' Clarice agreed. 'And Poppy was sure that the swans were down the hill. But why not uphill, unless the suggestion of going downhill had been planted in her mind? She wouldn't have known Brayford Pool was down the hill – it is in fact west of Lady Jayne's home.'

'So Tara sowed the seed,' Rick said, 'so that she would be the hero again, the one who saved her sister?'

'Yes.' Clarice nodded.

'Didn't Tara have an alibi when Guy disappeared?' Daisy looked intently at Clarice. 'She'd stayed overnight on the Sunday at her friend's house.'

'At a guess, I think that after Tara killed Guy, she immediately went back down to the house to tell her mother. For Charlotte to protect Tara, she needed to do two things. The first was to get her away from the murder scene, the second to hide Guy's body. I think if you ask Amy's mother, you'll find Charlotte phoned late on Sunday afternoon to ask if Tara could go over there and stay the night.'

'We didn't realise Tara not being at home on Sunday evening had relevance,' Daisy said. 'We were focusing on Monday morning.'

'Yes, we've all had our sights firmly fixed – as Charlotte wanted – on Monday morning as the relevant period. It was only when I realised it was Sunday evening that other things fell into place.' Clarice looked at the three faces; nobody spoke. 'Poppy thought Guy was still at home because she saw his diary. She said to me, "I thought Daddy was still home, but he went out and didn't come back, and Susie ran away to Grandma".'

'What point are you making, Clarice?' Rick asked.

'It's the thing that's been bugging me,' she replied. 'I kept going over the details but couldn't work out what it was.'

'Go on,' he encouraged.

'Once I'd grasped that it was Sunday evening we should be looking at, not Monday morning, I realised that Susie was out for two nights rather than one. When Poppy said that Susie had run away, she meant that when she got up on Monday morning, neither her dad nor the dog was there; they'd both gone.'

'Yes,' Charlie said, 'that makes sense.'

'Why did Charlotte put Guy's body in the river?' Daisy asked.

'Because she was in a state of panic. She couldn't carry it to the car; it was too heavy to move that far. The river was the most obvious place. Remember, she thought she might have had more time before the police had to be informed.'

'What do you mean, more time?' Daisy persisted.

'It was Susie who gave the game away.' Clarice looked down at the dog.

'Yes,' Rick said, 'she saw what happened.'

'Susie followed Guy around when he was working in the woods, but she'd never attempted to run away. She was always his dog and stayed close to him. Charlotte said Susie had bitten Tara once because she was rough with her. I think that what actually happened is that Susie saw Tara killing Guy and tried to stop her, grabbing Tara by the arm. Tara then retaliated by hitting Susie with the spade, causing the gash to her back leg.'

'Then she ran away?' Rick said.

'Not immediately. She must have been hanging around the woods for two nights. When she turned up at Louise's house, Charlotte knew she had to report Guy's disappearance. I think she might have intended to hold back and wait until someone he worked with in London called to say he'd gone missing. It would have distanced her and their home if he had disappeared somewhere en route to work; she wouldn't have needed to invent Charles.'

Charlie looked from Clarice to Rick and Daisy; there was a stillness before he said, 'Anything else, Clarice?'

'Tara's been adamant that Susie should not be allowed to go to Louise's, but I took her there this morning. When Tara returned unexpectedly, her reaction was extreme. It resulted in a stand-off between her and Angel, and Susie stepped between them to defend the little girl. After seeing Tara attacking Guy, she doesn't trust her. Tara knew Susie would be a problem; that was why she didn't want her at her own house. Charlotte colluded with that by asking Louise to take the dog.'

Charlie shifted his chair backwards, folding his arms thoughtfully. The voices of officers outside in the car park drifted upwards through the open window.

'I've listened to what you have said about MSBP.' He looked

from Clarice to Rick. 'That may be relevant with concern to Tara's half-siblings, but if she did sneak up on her stepfather and hit him with the spade, there was never any possibility that she could come to his rescue and save him, was there? It couldn't be put down to MSBP; it would be premeditated murder!'

'Yes.' Clarice nodded.

'Do you have any thoughts about her motive?'

'Apart from the fact that she knew the game was up regarding what she had done to make Angel ill, there were a couple of things her grandmother said that stuck with me.'

It was Charlie's turn to nod as he leaned forward to listen attentively.

'Louise told me Guy had said to her that if he wouldn't allow Tara to do something – I imagined she meant him imposing normal parental boundaries – she would paint her birth father, Paul, as an absent hero. He died in a car accident in Australia when she was a baby. Tara believed that if he'd still been around, he would have supported her every whim.'

'You mentioned that to me,' Rick said. 'You said Louise asked you not to repeat it to Charlotte.'

'Yes,' Clarice agreed. 'I think Louise thought Charlotte would have taken offence. Nobody could be allowed to know about their possible flaws or problems. It didn't match Charlotte's image of her perfect family.'

'You said there were a couple of things?' Charlie cut in.

'Tara told Louise that if Charlotte had killed Guy, it would have been because he'd done something to deserve it.'

'Because,' Charlie said, 'Tara herself thought Guy deserved to die.'

'Charlotte talked to me about loving someone who might be

either mad or bad,' Clarice said softly. 'At the time I thought she meant Guy, but I now realise she was talking about Tara.'

For a long time nobody spoke, the clicking of the oscillating fan the only sound, the heat of four bodies in the small space overwhelming. Beads of sweat showed on Charlie's forehead. He drew the back of his hand across it. Clarice could feel his agitation. Sensing a change, Susie stood up to watch her face intently.

'Well.' Charlie also rose, and Clarice walked Susie around the desk to stand opposite him. Looking down at his hot, damp face, she knew it would be difficult for him to patronise her with a six-inch height disadvantage.

'Thank you for coming in, Clarice,' he said. 'You've given us much to consider.' He looked at Rick and Daisy. 'Mrs Corkindale is expecting to be interviewed, and I think we need further discussion.' He held out his hand to Clarice, who shook it, then glanced down at Susie and sniffed again.

'I'm *so* sorry about her,' Clarice apologised. 'She rolled in something before we came here.'

'Ah.' Charlie smiled, as if suddenly enlightened. 'I wondered what that strange smell was.'

Clarice again noticed the twitch at the corner of Rick's lips; Daisy was staring down at her shoes.

Driving home, Clarice mulled over the discussion. She had said what she had gone to say and was now surplus to requirements. She would have liked to have been allowed to stay to hear the outcome of the interview, but instead she would have to wait for Rick's call to fill her in on their reaction to the new information. She felt her stomach twist with anticipation.

Chapter 46

The cottage felt strangely quiet after all the activity of the day. Clarice went immediately upstairs to shower and dress in a clean T-shirt and jeans. Back down in the kitchen, she put the clothes she'd been wearing into the laundry bag propped against the washing machine.

A line of four dogs followed wherever she went, Blue leading the pack, Jazz behind, then Susie and finally, bouncing along at the rear, Pirate. She did not appear to notice them. Sensing her sombre mood, Blue was watchful and low-key. As top dog, she was the one the others copied.

Clarice had taken her mobile with her to the bathroom. She rechecked it for the umpteenth time before picking up the receiver for the landline, only to be disappointed to find that Rick had not rung.

Taking an apple from the fruit bowl on the kitchen table, she sat down and bit into it. It was only just after 2 p.m.; so much had happened that day, it felt much later. She could hear the ticking of the grandfather clock against the wall near the door. Its polished walnut veneer always connected her reflections to her father, its previous owner. That she was now older than him when he'd died often came to mind.

From the top of the pine dresser, where she knew she would find Ella, the smallest of her cats, came a gentle muffled hiccuping sound. Like all the household cats, apart from Ena, who had come via Jonathan, the shy tabby was named after a blues musician. The top of the dresser was where she invariably spent her afternoons.

The four dogs now sat in a semicircle watching Clarice intently for any signs that a walk, play or food might be imminent. After five minutes, Blue sighed loudly before going to the laundry bag and emptying the contents, item by item, onto the floor. She threw glances at Clarice, but her actions caused no comment. After fishing around in the pile, she selected a lone brown sock, bringing it across and ceremoniously placing the offering on the floor next to her mistress.

'Thank you, Blue,' Clarice said distractedly, before coming to a decision. Getting up, she went to the fridge and began to empty its contents onto the table. After removing each of the glass shelves and washing them, she replaced everything neatly.

As she closed the fridge door, the landline phone rang, and she pounced with the alacrity of a young cat to pick it up.

'Clarice?' The voice was not the one she had been anticipating.

'Louise,' she said. 'Is everything OK? Has Tara settled?'

'No.' Louise spoke rapidly. 'She asked where I'd put the laptop. When I told her I'd let you take it, she went ballistic.'

'But she's calmed down now?' Clarice asked, her voice hopeful.

'I thought she had. She went outside with the girls, and now

314

I can't find them. They've gone off somewhere. Please tell me I'm making a fuss about nothing.' Louise sounded panic-stricken.

'They can't be far away,' Clarice said. 'How long ago did you last see them?'

'Maybe twenty minutes.'

'Are you sure they're not somewhere in the garden?' Clarice's mind raced, mentally making a journey along the polytunnels, around the outer edges, thinking of the large space that comprised the garden.

'I've been everywhere. What worries me is that Tara had obviously tried to start my car; the keys were still in the ignition. As you know, my Land Rover is quite old and temperamental, and she obviously couldn't get it going.'

'Thank goodness for that. But they can't have gone far; you're fairly isolated there. Could she be heading home? The route Susie would have taken when she turned up on your doorstep must be familiar to all the girls.'

Suddenly the ringtone of her mobile cut through the conversation. Picking it up, she saw Rick was the caller.

'Hang on, Louise,' she said, 'that's Rick on the other phone. I'm going to put you down for a minute.'

Without waiting for a reply, Clarice clicked onto the call, running from the kitchen into the sitting room so Louise wouldn't overhear.

'Rick?'

'It's been a long haul.' He spoke immediately. 'The solicitor turned up late. Charlotte started again by insisting she was responsible for Guy's death. Then her solicitor pushed the crime-of-passion button, claiming that she wasn't a risk and should therefore be allowed bail.'

'Daisy's still doing the interview?' Clarice asked, wondering if Charlie might have muscled in.

'Yes,' Rick said. 'When she asked why Charlotte had lied about how many times she hit Guy, the shock on her face was beyond belief. She wanted to talk to her solicitor alone, so that's where we are currently. We'll be going back in a few minutes.'

'Listen.' Clarice rapidly told Rick what Louise had said. 'I'll have to go; she's hanging on the other phone.'

'Are you going over to her?'

'I'll suggest meeting her at Lark House; I think Tara will have taken Angel and Poppy there.'

'Louise won't realise that they're in danger with Tara.' Clarice heard the alarm in Rick's voice.

'No, she won't. I've got to go, Rick. The car keys for Guy and Charlotte's cars are in the house, where Tara can get her hands on them.'

'I'll see you there.' Rick cut the call.

The sky had darkened while she was indoors, and now the rain came, light at first, then heavier and faster, giving the road a shiny pond-like surface. The windscreen wipers swished, and Clarice, peering through the sudden downpour, fretted that Tara might not have got Angel and Poppy to the house. They could be out in this deluge. Worse still, if Tara had already taken one of the cars, she could be on the road with the girls, an inexperienced driver in a car she'd no knowledge of in heavy rain.

While she concentrated on driving, she allowed her mind to explore the periphery of her emotions. She now knew that the sense she'd had of having missed something had been warranted. She'd got it wrong. That feeling had been most potent in the moment of believing Charlotte had killed Guy. Everything now fell into place. When Charlotte had told Tara, 'I have a confession . . . I killed Daddy,' Tara's response had been, 'It's a lie – it's not true.' It was all there. By saying that she might not even get a custodial sentence, Charlotte had been priming Tara, letting her know she'd take the blame, telling her daughter not to confess to Guy's murder.

Clarice felt an overwhelming mix of pity and sympathy for Charlotte and the agonising impossibility of her situation. Trying to take the blame for Guy's death, but having to trust Tara with her two younger children – she must have been in hell. After Poppy had gone walkabout in Lincoln, Charlotte must have realised Tara's involvement. Clarice remembered Charlotte's jerky movements when she'd gone to see her. The constant bird-like lift of the head, checking the girls in the garden through the window while they'd talked. How much greater the torment when she entrusted the children to Louise. Charlotte was an intelligent woman and must have been aware that if Tara was suffering from Munchausen syndrome by proxy, a serious mental illness, her promise of good conduct meant nothing. And now, if something happened to either Angel or Poppy while they were in Tara's care, how would she live with it? And how would Clarice?

She felt angry with herself – why had she not put the pieces together earlier, made the connection? She gripped the steering wheel hard, forcing herself to resist the urge to drive faster.

Chapter 47

The turn that led to Lark House was less than half a mile away, and just as suddenly as the rain had begun, now it stopped.

Clarice tried to work out how long it had been since she had spoken to Louise. Louise had last seen Tara about twenty minutes before that. Adding twenty minutes to the telephone conversation and the journey to this point would total forty to forty-five. The walk along the river between Louise's home and Charlotte's took thirty minutes, though probably longer with two small children.

She recalculated the numbers twice. Then, as the turn in the lane came into view, she saw the white flash of Charlotte's white Mercedes. It shot out of the turning at an angle, not slowing, and headed away in the opposite direction. Clarice pressed her foot hard on the accelerator and followed. She had not been near enough to see the driver or whether there were any other occupants, but it would be too big a coincidence for some unknown person to have stolen the car. It could only be Tara at the wheel, and Clarice had no other option but to tail her and hope she might stop. Another white car, this time a BMW, flashed past in the lane coming towards her, and she realised it

318

was Rick, and behind him, a police car. In her rear-view mirror she saw the brake lights of the police car and grasped that Rick must have recognised Charlotte's car and her own, and was turning to follow them.

The Mercedes moved erratically, swinging from one side of the road to the other as it passed a large truck coming towards it on the opposite side of the carriageway. Clarice caught a flash of the angry face of the driver looking in his rear-view mirror. Focusing on the car ahead, she recognised that the gap between them was widening. Her speedometer showed she was doing just over seventy-five miles per hour, a mad speed for these narrow, winding lanes. The vehicle Tara was driving had the capacity for high speeds. Under the control of a fifteen-year-old used only to driving on privately owned land, it was a loaded gun. She was likely to kill herself and her sisters, or an unsuspecting driver who got in her way.

Behind her Clarice could see the flashing light of the police car moving closer, Rick's white BMW still ahead of it. As she took the next bend, she saw a blur of red. Only after she'd passed did she identify it as a post delivery van, careering from the road into a field. It had obviously attempted to avoid a collision as the Mercedes swerved back and forth across the carriageway. Behind it, a convoy of four other vehicles had pulled over to avoid collision with the speeding car heading towards them. As she passed them, Clarice saw the Mercedes veer sharply to the left into a narrow lane leading away from the main road. She knew where it was heading: in the direction of Huntley's quarry.

The realisation forced her feelings of panic to intensify. Her body ached with the effort of concentration and she gasped audibly as she swung the steering wheel to follow. Behind her, the wail of the police siren was getting closer. The sun had reappeared after the rain and was almost blinding. She flipped down the sun visor while batting away an incongruous thought that somewhere nearby there would be a rainbow.

The Mercedes continued up the tight unmade track, and then it was gone entirely from her view. Clarice came around the last of the curves onto a large flat area that extended across the top of the quarry. To her left, she could see the vast open pit, but she was too far from the edge to gauge the drop, the depths to which it would fall. The air hung heavy with dust. As it cleared, the car was visible, stationary, its front wheels over the pit edge, like a massive beast balanced on a toothpick, rocking gently.

She scoured the ground in front of her, her eyes seeking out the hidden areas in the wall of chalk that curved in and out like corrugated iron to her right. Behind her, Rick's motor was now so close that she could see his face in her rear-view mirror. And further back, she could hear the incessant screeching of the police siren. Were all three children still inside that rocking car? As she threw herself out of her own vehicle to run towards the Mercedes, she saw it tilt, and for a fraction of a second the world stood still – and then it was gone.

The sound of the siren had ceased, and the air after the rain felt warm, with nothing moving. The silence was broken by the crash of metal as the Mercedes hit the bottom of the pit, then the noise of the explosion, like a bomb detonating, flames and smoke shooting suddenly upwards.

Clarice, feeling dazed, remained unmoving, watching the fireball. Above it stretched the rainbow she had expected, a perfect unbroken arc of colour. She glanced back. Not far behind her, Rick and Daisy stood motionless, as if frozen. Uniformed officers emerged from the police car. For a few seconds, the only sound was the roar of the flames. Then there was a scream. A long, shrill, primal note, a piercing sound that went endlessly on and on, as Charlotte tried to claw her way past the officers to reach the pit edge.

Chapter 48

A female uniformed officer – Clarice realised it was Kerry – appeared from behind the group to wrap her arms around Charlotte in a bear hug. Daisy turned back to do the same, but Charlotte continued to scream. Rick broke away, going to Clarice, putting his hands on her shoulders.

'Are you all right?' He looked directly into her eyes, his own searching and fearful, his forehead briefly touching hers.

'I'm OK.' She nodded, looking back at the black and grey cloud of smoke now rising from the pit, and Rick turned to follow her gaze.

'The little ones?' he asked, his voice halting.

Clarice felt as though a piece of broken glass had become jammed in her windpipe; she was unable to speak.

Charlotte screamed again, the piercing sound filling the air. Then she began calling Tara's name over and over, like a deranged animal that had become permanently separated from its young. The sound bouncing around the walls of the pit came back as an urgent echo.

And then, from a dark area in the chalk wall, a shout responded to the calls: 'Mum! Mum!'

'Look there!' Rick touched Clarice's arm, pointing as Tara emerged from her hiding place and ran towards her mother. 'She's on her own,' he said, the pain in his voice almost tangible.

At the same time, Clarice's mobile rang – Louise. With trembling hands, Clarice took the call, not knowing how she would tell the friend who had suffered so much what might have just happened to her grandchildren.

'Clarice,' Louise said, 'I've phoned you about five times and left messages. I couldn't start my car after Tara had messed with it. It's Ian and Judith's day off today or they could have given me a lift. I had to run all the way here, and Tara has taken Charlotte's car.'

'I'm sorry, Louise,' Clarice said. 'I was driving. I saw Tara in the car and followed her.' She noticed Rick's head swivel to look at her, listening to what she was saying. Tara had reached Charlotte, throwing herself into her mother's arms.

'Is she OK?' Louise asked.

In the background, Clarice heard a high-pitched sing-song voice.

'Tara is OK,' she said. 'Is that Poppy I can hear?'

'Yes,' Louise said. 'The girls were locked inside the house when I arrived.'

'Are the children there?' Rick cut in, impatient to find out more.

Clarice nodded but found again that she was unable to speak and handed him the phone.

Once he had confirmed that both girls were safe, he hung up and led Clarice over to the small group. Charlotte was rocking Tara, neither speaking.

'I've just spoken to Louise,' he said quietly to Charlotte. 'She's looking after Angel and Poppy; they're at Lark House.'

Charlotte raised her eyes – the eyes of a woman touched by something akin to madness – before bringing a trembling hand to cover her mouth and burying her face in her daughter's hair.

'I looked after them, Mum, like I said I would,' Tara mumbled.

It was over an hour later that Clarice drove away from the top of the chalk pit. Daisy and Kerry had departed with Charlotte and Tara. Other police officers had arrived, and Rick, gentle and concerned, had asked her if she'd allow someone to accompany her home. She had declined the offer. Louise was still in the dark about the facts concerning Guy's death. She wanted to go to speak directly to her friend.

While she called Louise, to say she was on her way, Rick made a call to Bridget, the family liaison officer, who said that she would meet Clarice at Lark House. 'Louise might need some extra support,' he said. Clarice suspected that he also wanted Charlie to be aware that all proper procedures had been followed.

Retracing the route she had taken in pursuit of Tara, she saw the red post office van still in the field. A car and a tow truck were parked at the roadside, and men were standing around talking. It was a little after 5 p.m., and the sun continued to shine; a typical August day. It felt surreal, almost as if the chase on the way there had not happened.

At the main entrance to Lark House, she spotted a car turning through the gate behind her and following her along the driveway.

'Hi, Clarice.' Bridget spoke as she climbed from the car. 'Sounds like your day's been a real stinker.'

The air was filled with shouts from the children running from the house towards them. Louise followed at a more sedate pace.

'Have you still got Susie with you?' Angel asked.

'No,' Clarice said, 'I dropped her home a long while back.'

'Come in.' Louise looked at her questioningly, but held back from voicing her thoughts with the children trotting next to them chattering. 'A nice surprise to see Bridget,' she said to the girls, who both agreed.

Inside the house, Clarice looked again at the perfection of the open-plan space with its vast areas of glass. The house looked unsullied by the events of the last week, the police searches and the comings and goings of the family. A thought meandered through her jaded mind. Would Charlotte still want to live here after everything that had taken place?

Louise made tea and indulged in small talk with the children, her eyes constantly flicking towards Clarice, until Bridget said cheerily, 'If you want to go for a walk, I'll stay here.'

'I'll go with you,' Poppy said immediately, standing up.

'Not you, silly.' Angel spoke bossily. 'Grandma and Clarice want to do grown-up talk, with us not there.'

'Yackety-yack.' Poppy nodded, understanding.

'We can stay with Bridget and have a ginger biscuit,' Angel suggested.

'I don't know if there are any.' Louise smiled, aware of the bribery.

'They're in that cupboard up there.' Poppy pointed.

'It's a deal,' Louise said.

Outside, the two women headed round the side of the house in the direction of the woods. While they walked, Clarice told Louise everything she knew about what had happened to Guy. Occasionally Louise interrupted to query a point. By the time Clarice had finished, they had reached the beautiful avenue of trees. Louise walked to put her arms around the rough bark of the nearest one. Clarice stood silently watching her. It was quiet, with a gentle breeze moving through the leaves, the only sound that of birdsong.

At last Louise turned. Her face was drawn and wretched. 'I dreamed of him last night, bound and wrapped in that wet, sad place, so alone.'

'He's not there now,' Clarice said. 'Let's go back.'

As they came down the incline, Louise said, 'I'm so relieved that Charlotte didn't kill him.'

Clarice nodded.

'I'm upset enough that it was Tara, but it would have been worse it being Charlotte.'

'Yes?' Clarice said, wondering what her reasoning might be.

'Guy loved her so very much. He told me once, not long after they'd got together, that she was the love of his life.' Louise appeared to mull over what she'd said. 'We didn't hit it off immediately, Charlotte and I, but I thought, if my boy loves her, then she must be OK.'

They had stopped to face one another.

'I think I understand,' Clarice said.

'For Charlotte to have killed Guy would have been such a betrayal, but I can understand why she would have done anything to protect Tara. Although I don't believe her judgement was sound – thinking she could trust her.'

Clarice nodded and took Louise's arm as they carried on towards the house.

'Do you think you could take us home?' Louise asked.

'Yes, of course I will,' Clarice said.

'There is one thing I need to do first.'

Driving down the incline to her cottage, Clarice saw that neither Rick's car nor Bob's was outside. Bob and Sandra must have fed the animals and gone home. She wasn't sure whether Rick would return home or stay for convenience at number 24. Louise sat beside her deep in thought, while behind her Angel and Poppy chattered, their voices rising and falling like small, animated monkeys.

'Are we going to see the kittens?' Poppy asked hopefully.

'Not today,' Louise said, looking around as if suddenly aware of her surroundings. 'It's getting late, but I'm sure Clarice will invite you another day.'

In the house, the air was cool. They were greeted with great excitement by the four dogs, while Big Bill, the large ginger cat, wandered in from the living room to survey the scene.

'You'd think they'd been on their own all day,' Clarice said as she read a note Sandra had left for her. 'It's only been thirty minutes. Everyone here and in the barn has been fed, and the dogs have been walked.'

'That's great,' Louise said, watching the children's faces. 'It means we don't need to feed Susie when we get home.'

'Is Susie coming home with us?' Poppy asked.

'Yes.' Louise smiled at her. 'I promised she would be coming home soon.'

'Yay!' Poppy called.

'Grandma always keeps her promises,' Angel solemnly informed Clarice.

Later, driving home after dropping the family off at Louise's, she pondered on the conversation that would probably occur the following day. In the excitement of reclaiming Susie, neither of the sisters had asked about Tara. Clarice could only feel sorry for Louise in having to explain the complexity of the situation.

Chapter 49

When Clarice finally arrived home, she was pleased to see Rick's car on the drive, relieved that he'd decided not to stay at the rented house.

As she approached the door, it opened and the three dogs rushed out to greet her, before following her back inside.

'Hello, sweetie.' Rick, who had been carrying Muddy, put the purring cat down as he went to welcome her with a hug. 'Today's been a nightmare,' he said.

'It certainly has,' Clarice agreed.

'And then there were three.' He bent to scratch Blue's ear.

'Susie was delighted to be back with the children.'

Rick nodded. 'She's where she should be.'

'What happened with Charlotte and Tara?' Clarice asked.

'Let's have a drink first in the garden. It's cheese and tomato quiche with salad for supper.'

'Food?' Clarice followed his gaze. 'You found time to make a quiche?'

'No, but you did, four weeks ago according to the label,' he said with a cheeky grin. 'And there's my very own creation – a bowl of salad to go with it.'

'I'm so glad you've discovered the freezer at last,' Clarice laughed.

They took glasses of red wine outside to sit at the table, accompanied as usual by the dogs. The light from the kitchen fell across the garden. Blue, still carrying the lone sock she'd stolen earlier in the day, flopped down next to Rick. Jazz followed suit. Pirate jumped around between the hollyhocks, attempting to catch moths attracted by the light before becoming bored and squashing his chubby body between the two larger dogs.

'So,' Rick said when they were settled opposite one another, 'it was all pretty depressing when we got back to the station. Tara was confused, unravelling; a doctor came in and sedated her.'

'What's going to happen to her?'

'It was obvious she wasn't well enough to be interviewed; she's been remanded to hospital for a report and treatment.'

'Is she in Lincoln?'

'No, it takes hours of phone calls to find a space for a child. A place has been found for her up in Sheffield.' Rick played with the stem of his glass while he talked. 'She's going to face a long and difficult journey. Someone of her age who'd admitted a killing would automatically be charged with homicide and go up before a crown court.'

'It was murder.' Clarice was adamant. 'Although I believe Tara does suffer from MSBP, she murdered Guy!'

'Even if that is the case, she's still in a fragile mental state, and psychiatrists will be the ones called upon to make the judgement. I honestly don't know what will happen; my guess is that she'll stay in care at a mental hospital where she can be assessed while the CPS looks at all the factors. There will be numerous individuals acting in different roles looking at the psychiatric reports. After scrutinising her case from every angle, a decision will be reached. As I said, it'll be a long journey.'

'Her name will be withheld?' Clarice asked.

'Yes, from the age of ten to seventeen the name of the offender can be known to the courts but must be kept from the public domain.' Rick sounded weary.

'And Charlotte?' Clarice asked.

'First off she wanted to ensure that Tara was OK. She accepted what was going to happen, then asked to speak to her solicitor again.' Rick sipped his wine thoughtfully. 'She withdrew her confession – came clean about everything.'

'Was there anything we hadn't worked out?'

'Nothing major. Guy was on to Tara from the beginning; he'd had his doubts and didn't buy the story that Angel had eaten something a school friend had given her. Charlotte – to her shame, she says – worked on him to make him believe that Angel was telling lies.'

'But then it happened again,' Clarice said.

'Yes, after Angel took the pills, the hospital team asked a lot of questions. They had a duty to ensure that Angel was safe. Guy wouldn't accept that Tara had been Angel's saviour a second time – it was too coincidental – and that's when the arguments started. Charlotte said Tara had overheard her and Guy discussing the possibility that she was suffering from MSBP. Guy wanted to investigate what treatment might be available for her.' Rick sounded gloomy. 'Tara was the one who looked the condition up on the computer – I presume after she'd heard her parents talking about it – and the rest you know.'

'Poor Guy, trying to do his best by her. He loved her as a daughter.'

'Yes,' Rick said. 'But Charlotte admitted that Tara didn't reciprocate those feelings. You were right about her birth father, Paul: she'd turned him into a fantasy figure who could do no wrong. The real-world Guy could never match up. Their discussion about the possibility of Tara having MSBP was the beginning of what Charlotte called the downward spiral. Guy wanted to stay at home to protect the children, and he suggested they seek help for Tara. Charlotte told him he had got it all wrong – she still wanted to believe in her.'

'When did that change?' Clarice asked.

'I don't think she ever believed that Tara was capable of harming her sisters. It was only when Tara came into the house that Sunday afternoon and told her she'd killed Guy that she was forced to recognise the reality of the situation.'

'So Tara took that spade from the shed and went to find him. She had plenty of time to think about what she'd do once she located him in the woods. All that pent-up hatred of the man who couldn't ever measure up to her ideal of a father. And of course she knew he'd worked out that she'd been deliberately harming her sisters.'

Rick nodded his agreement. 'She incapacitated him with the first strike; the second finished him off. The police have everything, all the information.' He lifted his shoulders in a resigned shrug. 'It's over to them, the hospital psychiatrists and the CPS to decide how to respond.'

'Is Charlotte being charged?' Clarice asked.

'Yes, with withholding evidence, concealing a body and wasting police time.'

'Poor Charlotte.' She thought about the Mercedes hanging over the cliff edge. 'I really did think Tara had the girls in that car today. How did she get out?'

'She said she'd put her foot down hard on the brake pedal, but the car was going so fast it skidded to the left, towards the pit edge. Luckily, being on the driver's side, she was able to open the door and throw herself out.'

'Was it part of the plan – to kill herself?'

'As I said, she hasn't been formally questioned. The information I'm giving you is what she told her mother in the car. Daisy was earwigging. From what she said, I sensed there wasn't a set plan.'

Rick stood up, and the dogs followed him. 'Come on,' he said. 'Let's go and eat.'

Clarice picked up her glass.

'I forgot to tell you there were three phone calls before you arrived. Good news on the first. June is getting back early; she'll come over to collect Doreen tomorrow morning.'

'That's great.' Clarice remembered the chief inspector's baffled face when they were together in that small room. 'And?'

'Sandra heard about what happened this afternoon – some gossip from the postie who was run off the road. She was worried, so I've set her straight.' Rick smiled. 'And Keith phoned. I filled him in on everything.' He held the door open to allow her to pass. 'After we'd finished talking, Jonathan asked for a word; he wanted to ask about something. You'll need to call him back tomorrow.'

'It's not another house clearance?' Clarice asked with trepidation.

'No, something else – but it's OK, I think you're going to like it.'

Chapter 50

Returning to the house from feeding at the cat barn the following morning, Clarice saw Bob and Sandra's car pulling off the road onto the drive. The weather was hot but unsettled, and the radio's early forecast suggested that rain might again be possible later in the day.

'Mornin', darlin',' Sandra greeted her as she came in. 'Kettle on?'

'It sure is. Thanks for the note; sounds like you had a busy day yesterday.' Clarice set out mugs next to the teapot. 'And thanks for your phone call. Rick told me you were worried.'

'We were, darlin',' Sandra said. 'Just glad it's all OK and no one got hurt.'

'Anything involving the police gets around Castlewick like wildfire,' Bob said. 'And you belting around the lanes chasing another car at a hundred miles an hour – no chance of keeping that in the bag, especially when poor old Larry the postie was forced from the road.'

'I think a hundred miles an hour is a slight exaggeration.' Clarice laughed. 'I don't think my old car could manage that!'

'Larry always did overstate things,' Bob agreed.

'If you'd filled us in sooner about what's been going on, we might have been able to help – talk it through,' Sandra said.

'Rick probably told her to keep a lid on it,' Bob interjected. 'If it was an ongoing investigation she could hardly go about blabbing to everybody.'

'I'm not everybody,' Sandra shot back. 'I'm Clarice's oldest friend.'

'You're both right,' Clarice said. 'I wouldn't repeat anything Rick tells me, even though the pair of you *are* my oldest and dearest friends.' She imagined Sandra as a small pug with its fine line of hackles soothed – the fur slowly going down back to smooth. 'Anyway, you did help me, Sandra,' she said. 'Although you didn't realise it.'

'How?' Sandra looked surprised.

'When you talked to me about your girls, the fierceness you felt for them, how you would have done anything to protect them ... It made me think a lot more about Charlotte as a mother, trying to protect all three of her girls.'

'I feel sorry for Louise.' Sandra spoke reflectively. 'She's as much a victim as Guy, losing her only child that way.'

'What's going to happen to Charlotte now?' Bob asked.

'It's going to court today,' Clarice said. 'She'll be charged with concealing a body, withholding evidence and wasting police time. The prosecution's not opposing bail. They don't believe there's a risk of her absconding, and it's beneficial for the children to have their mother back with them.'

'Too bloody right. They've already lost their dad, and ...' Sandra paused for a moment, 'their big sister – in a different way.'

They sat around for a further ten minutes before Sandra announced that they would be going just after lunch.

'We had intended taking Polly to her new home today,' she said sombrely.

'Intended? What happened?' Clarice said. 'It was Mrs—'

'That woman,' Sandra said. 'Don't even say her name.'

'She did at least tell us straight,' Bob said. 'Some lead you on then don't turn up.'

Clarice looked from one to the other.

'She spent all that time sitting with Polly, then phoned and said she'd been given a cat by a neighbour who was moving home.' Sandra was clearly cross.

'You didn't believe her?' Clarice asked.

'No,' Sandra said. 'We could write a book on the excuses people give. I think she thought Polly was too much trouble – she admitted she'd decided she'd prefer a younger cat.'

'Well,' Clarice said, 'Bob's right: at least she told us.'

'And?' Bob cocked his head at his wife.

Sandra looked at him for a moment, and then at Clarice.

'If you have no objections,' she said, 'I'd like to take Polly home myself. Bob and I will adopt her.'

'Objections?' Clarice was on her feet in an instant to throw her arms around Sandra. 'I'm delighted! But are you sure – you always said you wouldn't take another.'

'Bob said I should practise what I preach,' Sandra said. 'I complain that no one wants the oldies because they won't have them for long, which is why I've been frightened of adopting her. Then I realised that I really didn't want anyone else to have her – she'd become my cat.'

'That's true.' Clarice grinned. 'So you are now once more a proud cat owner.'

'I'm so glad,' Bob said. 'For weeks I've thought we should adopt her, but it had to be Sandra's decision.'

'I think it's the right one,' Clarice said.

'Will it be OK if we take her home in a couple of days?' Sandra asked. 'There are things I have to do, and I don't want to get her home and then not be there to help her settle in.'

'That sounds mysterious,' Clarice said. 'But take her when you're ready, no rush.'

After a lunch of cheese and biscuits, followed by raspberries from the garden, Bob and Sandra left. Clarice thought it odd that they'd not wanted to take Polly immediately. When pushed, Bob hinted it was something to do with Michelle, their elder daughter. Clarice didn't press the point, knowing Sandra would talk about any problems when she felt ready to do so.

Doreen had been collected during the morning, and watching Bob and Sandra's car pull away up the incline to the main road, Clarice felt a sense of peace. After their departure, she phoned Louise to see how her morning had gone, and was relieved that her friend sounded more upbeat, although she realised she would be putting a brave face on things.

'I've heard from Bridget,' Louise said. 'Charlotte will get bail today, and she wants to come straight here.'

'To visit the girls,' Clarice asked, 'or take them back to Lark House?'

'Bridget didn't know. I think Charlotte was testing the water, asking her to phone me.'

'And?' Clarice asked.

'I told Bridget to bring her directly here and I would have

a room made up for her to stay. The girls miss her, and they all need time to grieve for Guy.'

'And you,' Clarice said. 'It's been a roller-coaster ride with everything that's happened; you've had no time to grieve for your boy.'

'Yes, me too,' Louise agreed.

Clarice pondered on the fronts people put up to exist and get by while internally they might be screaming. Louise had struggled in the last few days to hide her devastation over Guy's disappearance and death while supporting her granddaughters. Clarice hoped she might drop what she'd called her old-school approach and be more open. With what they'd been through recently, perhaps she and Charlotte could support one another to move in that direction.

Jonathan had phoned earlier in the morning: he and Keith would be coming by for a cup of tea at about five. Rick had promised, since he had so many hours owing to him, that he'd try to get back from the station in time to join them. After giving the dogs a walk around the garden, Clarice went to immerse herself in weeding and tidying the vegetable patch.

Chapter 51

It felt as if she had only just started to work through her designs before the afternoon had slipped away. Just after 5 p.m., within minutes of Keith's car having pulled up outside the cottage, Rick arrived to park alongside. A fine but persistent rain was falling, and all three arrivals dashed inside, trying to avoid a soaking.

After the dog welcome committee had done their duties, the guests joined Clarice and Rick around the kitchen table. Clarice poured tea and brought out a cherry cake to go with it.

'My darling girl, that cake is never shop-bought?' Jonathan said archly, his eyes impish. 'You'll get drummed out of the Castlewick ladies' circle when word gets out.'

'I think they'd have drummed me out years ago,' Clarice retorted, 'if indeed I'd ever been accepted in the first place.'

'Don't take any notice of Santa,' Keith said.

Jonathan snorted. 'Isn't that just delightful.'

After Clarice had explained to Rick what Poppy had said about Jonathan, they drank their tea and ate the cake. Muddy came into the kitchen to paw at Clarice's leg, a reminder that it was time for her dinner. As if some silent signal had transmitted from one cat to another, Toots, the long grey, followed Howlin' and BB into the room. Big Bill was under the kitchen table and Ena glowered from the window ledge. As Clarice went to bring out the cat dishes, a scurrying sound heralded Ella coming down from the top of the dresser.

As on the previous visit, Pirate had again climbed unbidden onto Keith's lap, flipping over onto his back to show his stomach.

'What happened to Charlotte in court?' Keith asked, suddenly serious, when there was a lull in the conversation.

Rick explained that she had received bail, and Clarice told them about her conversation with Louise.

'It's good of Louise,' Jonathan said, 'given the circumstances.'

'Do you think Charlotte will sell Lark House and move away?' Keith put into words what Clarice imagined they had all been thinking.

'I don't know,' she said. 'But it'd be hard to continue living there after all that's happened; too many terrible memories.'

'Except there were good ones too. It was a happy place once, and so beautiful,' Keith pointed out.

'Mmm,' Clarice mused. 'I'm thinking about the state Charlotte was in when Susie led us into the woods where Guy died. She was completely distraught.'

'That was before it all came out,' Keith said. 'She might find it easier now.'

'I just can't envisage her staying there,' Clarice said. 'But I keep thinking about Louise. She's already lost Guy, but if Charlotte moves away, she'll no longer be a part of her granddaughters' lives.'

The others nodded sombrely.

'On a lighter note,' Rick smiled as he spoke, 'Bob and Sandra have decided to adopt Polly, one of the elderly cats.

It's a milestone for Sandra; she always said she wouldn't take another one.'

'I see it all the time,' Jonathan said. 'People give and receive an enormous amount of love from their pets. When they depart, it's the same as losing a member of the family.'

A comfortable silence followed while everyone watched Keith, who was absorbed in scratching Pirate's upturned stomach. 'I understand this little chap'll be up for adoption soon,' he said. 'I know you have to wait until he loses weight. Jonathan tells me he'll be on a diet for about three months.'

'He's already lost some,' Clarice said. 'It's all the activity running around with the other dogs. It's better that he loses the weight slowly. I generally feed him separately so he can't pinch food from the others. And I'm delighted to say he's found adoptive owners who can take him early. He'll be going out soon to his new forever home.'

'Hurray!' Jonathan said jovially.

Keith's smile had disappeared. 'You didn't tell me that,' he said accusingly. 'Did you know about it?'

'Yes.' Jonathan smiled. 'Clarice told me the good news.'

Keith scowled.

'What?' Jonathan's voice was innocent. 'What are you talking about?'

'I told you how I felt about Pirate.' Keith was indignant. 'I told you several times. I even showed you a photograph of a dog basket I had my eye on. I thought you might have spoken to Clarice.'

'Did you make sure he was listening?' Rick said, amused. 'You know how Jonathan cocks a deaf one when he's busy.'

'Stop it, the pair of you,' Clarice said. 'I can't bear it.'

Keith looked at her, his expression perplexed.

'It's you, Keith,' she said. 'You and Jonathan are Pirate's new owners; the paperwork is ready for you to sign.'

'Us?' Keith looked at Jonathan. 'We're adopting him?' As if on cue, Pirate rolled to sitting position to touch his nose against Keith's while wagging his tail.

'He heard you,' Rick said as everyone laughed.

'Yes, dear heart,' Jonathan said gently. 'Talk about donkeys and hind legs. It's all you've talked about these last few days; how could I *not* have understood.'

'Thank you.' Keith's voice was emotional. 'I'll go back to the pet shop in Lincoln tomorrow and get that dog bed.'

'It's all done.' Jonathan raised his eyebrows. 'I didn't want to spoil the surprise, so I've hidden it in the surgery.'

'The brown and orange striped one,' Keith said urgently, 'with the hood?'

'The one you photographed on your mobile and showed me – yes,' Jonathan said. 'I made a special trip into Lincoln.'

An hour later, after the guests had left, taking Pirate with them, Clarice walked the boundary of the garden with Rick. The air felt lighter; the rain had broken the tension of the heat. Blue and Jazz ran in circles around them, and from the corner of her eye Clarice spotted Ena trailing them from further back.

'It feels odd only having the two dogs again,' Rick said.

'Pirate couldn't have gone to better owners.' Clarice grinned, thinking of the conversation earlier.

'You'd never guess that Keith is a scary solicitor. Very po-faced and professional when he's in work mode,' Rick chuckled.

'It sounds like you're describing yourself, Detective Inspector

Beech,' Clarice said. 'It's how love affects us all. We've been talking a lot about mother love recently, but Keith and Jonathan – like us – are big dog lovers.'

'And cats,' he said.

'Yes, and cats.'

'And,' he looked cheekily out of the corner of his eye, 'ferrets.'

Chapter 52

'I hope to be back by lunchtime!' Rick called across the kitchen.

'They said they'd be here by then,' Clarice said.

'Don't be late!' He picked up his jacket, moving towards the door.

Clarice restrained herself from reminding him of his own lack of punctuality. 'Why do Bob and Sandra want to talk to us together anyway? Is it something to do with Michelle?'

'They didn't tell me.' Rick shrugged. 'You were talking to Louise; is Charlotte still there?' He stood with one hand on the door handle.

'She said the girls were asking about the kittens. I said I'd give them an update when I go over there; and yes, Charlotte's staying with her.'

'You've had a lot to deal with recently,' Rick said, his tone grave. 'Do you really want to go there while Charlotte's around?'

'If Louise and I continue to be friends I don't think I can avoid bumping into Charlotte. Although,' Clarice said warily, 'it's different for you, leading the team that resulted in her arrest. It would be difficult.'

'Impossible,' Rick said.

Earlier, they had enjoyed a pleasant walk around the garden. The temperature was already rising, promising another hot day, perhaps with more thunderstorms and rain to break the heat. Having fed and watered everybody, Clarice was thinking about doing a food shop before Bob and Sandra arrived. The early-morning phone call from Louise had been a pleasant surprise. She'd immediately rearranged her plans to go to Louise first, doing the shopping on the way back. She would still be home in time to see Bob and Sandra as arranged.

Setting off in the car, she felt disconcerted after the conversation with Rick. She knew he was merely voicing his concern for her, believing she was doing too much. That he'd forgotten her birthday was obvious; there had been no mention of it, and it was only two days away. The rational part of her realised that with everything that had happened in the last couple of weeks, his memory lapse was not unreasonable.

On arrival at the cottage, Clarice was greeted by Louise, followed by the children, both wearing swimming costumes. She received a warm welcome from them and Susie, and was immediately drawn inside and pumped for any new information about the kittens. After she'd given them an update, the girls presented her with crayoned drawings depicting a multicoloured cat with two kittens.

'It's Annie,' Louise said, aware that Clarice might not realise. 'I described her colouring to the children.'

'Mummy has come to stay with us,' Poppy informed Clarice, 'and we've got a new swimming pool. Father Christmas brought it for us.'

Clarice looked towards Louise, who smiled and nodded.

'And we're all on holiday,' Angel added as she danced gleefully around the kitchen with her sister.

As the children chattered to each another, Louise lowered her voice. 'Jonathan and Keith came with the paddling pool this morning; they even brought a foot pump to inflate it.'

'What a pair of sweeties,' Clarice beamed.

'I'll make some tea,' Louise said.

The children drifted outside with Susie, and Louise took Clarice into the living room. Despite the tied-back drapes and the open windows, the place seemed dark; very different to Charlotte's open-plan glass house.

Clarice could not help but recall Milo as she looked at the low chair he'd claimed as his own. Louise noticed the direction of her gaze.

'I haven't got past looking at that chair either,' she said as they sat down.

'He was a part of your life for such a long time.'

'Charlotte's out,' Louise said, as if sensing it might be Clarice's next question.

'You've been very forgiving, inviting her here.'

'What am I to forgive her for?' Louise gave a sardonic laugh. 'Trying to protect her daughter? She didn't kill Guy – if she had, I couldn't have spent a second in the same room as her.'

'And Tara?' Clarice asked.

'I know she's mentally ill, and still a child, but I doubt I would ever want to see her again.' Louise stopped speaking, as if gathering her thoughts. 'Charlotte's gone to Lark House to collect some things for her and the girls.'

'Did she not want company?' Clarice asked. 'It must be hard for her going there.'

'She said she needed to go alone, to face her demons,' Louise said. 'It was her idea to think of this time here together as a holiday. She wanted us all to go away somewhere near the sea, but her bail conditions won't allow it.'

'Neutral territory; that sounds like a good plan,' Clarice said tactfully, sipping her tea.

'And there's Tara.'

'What's happening?'

'Another reason not to go away on holiday. Charlotte wants to go to Sheffield to make sure Tara is being well treated. Her solicitor brought it up at the bail hearing and it's been agreed that it would be beneficial for mother and daughter to continue to maintain contact.'

'It's going to be hard for her trying to split her time between here and Tara.'

'Yes, and we don't even know how long Tara will remain in Sheffield. Charlotte's been told she might be moved somewhere that better suits her needs.' Louise paused. 'She'll never give up on Tara, whatever she's done. And we don't know what solutions the medical people will suggest, or what the courts might decide, or where in the country Tara will find a permanent placement.'

Clarice nodded sadly, thinking of the uncertainty her friend would face.

'I thought that in a year or two, when things are more settled, it might be necessary to move nearer to the hospital Tara's allocated to long-term. Angel and Poppy are still young enough to adjust to new schools, and I wouldn't want Charlotte trying to live in two places.'

'You would sell up here, the house and the business?'

'If it's necessary, yes.' Louise was pragmatic. 'On the positive side, I know Ian and Judith would give me a reasonable price. They've taken over all the work recently, you know; they couldn't have been kinder or more supportive.'

'I sense that there's a "but" coming ...'

'Charlotte is in such a dark place.' Louise's voice gave away her sorrow. 'It's heartbreaking. She told me that Tara's dislike of Guy went much deeper than she'd been aware. Dislike is the wrong word ... despite all his love and acts of kindness, she now realises that Tara's feelings towards him must have bordered on hatred.'

'That must be hard for you to hear.' Clarice put her hand over Louise's.

'It is,' Louise said. 'But Charlotte and I both agree that Tara has serious mental issues. Why else would she try to turn a father she didn't know into a saint and reject the decent, loving man who had always been there for her? She built it up into an obsession, I think. And she was resentful about any time or affection directed towards the younger girls, or even the dog, something I'd long suspected.'

'Family life must have been more difficult for Guy than you realised.'

'Yes,' Louise agreed. 'Charlotte has said she never allowed him to criticise when Tara behaved badly; her motto was "least said soonest mended". The consequence is that she now has the burden of guilt that she handled her daughter's dreadful behaviour so badly. But she can't abandon Tara, and she said she believes she can forgive her.'

'She sounds conflicted; as you said, she's in a dark place.'

'She's in turmoil,' Louise sighed. 'Tara is still her daughter, but because of her actions she's been robbed of her husband, and her two younger children have lost their loving father. Perhaps time will help – we need to see how things pan out over the next year or so.'

They sat quietly for a while before talk turned to Susie, and how well she had slotted into being back as part of the family. Also the welcome Charlotte had received, not only from her daughters but from the family dog. In the background came the laughter and shouts of the children. It reminded Clarice again of her own father's death, grieving but also needing to be a child, to laugh and to play.

The sound of a car in the drive alerted them to Charlotte's return.

'She walked over to the house,' Louise said. 'She said she'd pick up Guy's Jaguar and drive that back. It's newer than my old Land Rover, and the insurance covers her. She'll need something reliable to drive to Sheffield.'

'Shall I make myself scarce?' Clarice said, standing up.

'No, please just say hello and talk for a while. Charlotte needs to face all her demons, not just Lark House.'

'Am I one of them?' Clarice asked.

'Yes,' Louise said, 'I do rather think you are. I hope you don't mind if I leave you two together when she gets in; she may open up to you more easily without my presence, and if I'm honest, there are things I'm not yet ready to hear.'

'One day at a time,' Clarice said, and Louise came to put her arms around her and hold her tightly before she left the room.

Clarice went to the open window to watch the girls in the enclosed garden at the back of the cottage. The bright orange paddling pool was in the centre of the lawn. Angel sat in it with Susie next to her. Nearby, Poppy filled a small bucket and with much giggling poured water over the heads of her sister and their dog. While Angel squealed, Susie put her head back and opened her mouth, her tongue lolling out as she tried to catch the falling shower. Louise appeared with a tray laden with cold drinks for her granddaughters.

'Hello, Clarice.'

Clarice turned to see that Charlotte had come quietly into the room. She must have been observing her as she'd watched Angel and Poppy play in the paddling pool.

'Did you want another one?' Charlotte lifted her cup in the air invitingly.

'No thanks.' Clarice sat down where Louise had been as Charlotte moved to sit opposite. Clarice tried not to stare at her as she walked across the room. Her body, devoid of fat, in black T-shirt and chinos, looked like a moving skeleton. The word that immediately sprang into Clarice's mind was 'anorexia'.

'It's been a strange journey,' Charlotte said after a while. A breeze suddenly came through the open window, and with it the laughter of the children.

'Yes,' Clarice said quietly. She felt wretched at this woman's obvious misery, not knowing how to respond.

'You must have a terrible impression of me,' Charlotte said, 'but in reality, I'm quite ordinary.'

'I do know that,' Clarice said. 'You were put in an impossible position and did your best to protect your children. I know about Tara's illness; it must have been hard to come to terms with.'

Charlotte stared at Clarice before averting her eyes. 'Guy realised before me that Tara was ill, I didn't want to believe him.' She moved her long, emaciated fingers restlessly around the top of the cup. 'If only I'd listened to him at the beginning . . .'

'Hindsight,' Clarice said. 'I thought you were talking about Guy being mad or bad, but I realised later that you were thinking about Tara.'

Charlotte nodded. 'Guy believed . . . he blamed . . .' She struggled to find words and to speak them aloud. 'Guy believed that Tara killed Martin, our boy.'

'It was a cot death,' Clarice said, taken aback by the statement.

'Yes, that was what we were told, but after the two incidents with Angel, Guy said he thought it possible that Tara had killed him.'

The voices and laughter of the children were suddenly joined by the ghost of baby Martin in the room between them.

'How old was Tara?'

'She was five,' Charlotte said, 'but so jealous of the baby. She had full screaming tantrums to draw attention away from him. But I told Guy it was impossible – she couldn't have killed him.'

'You believed that?' Clarice asked.

It took a long time, as if Charlotte needed to decide on her answer. 'The truth is, I don't know any more. I'd never in a million years have believed she would kill Guy. He was her father, if not by blood then by his actions.'

Clarice met her eyes but did not speak.

'At that moment, when she told me what she'd done, I descended into hell . . . I loved my husband so very much.'

She stopped speaking, and Clarice watched her, aware that she was mustering her energy to continue.

'I can't say this to Louise, not yet. I will in time, but I have to get the words – these feelings – out. I was vile to her when Poppy wandered away at the fund-raiser, a complete overreaction, even though I knew it was all down to Tara. I don't deserve the kindness she's shown me.' Charlotte's eyes went to the open window. 'I'd gone into damage limitation mode, taking Tara to Amy's house, inventing Charles. I made up the story about Susie biting someone years ago to try to muddy the waters. Susie was defending Guy; Tara swung the spade at her, cutting her leg. I couldn't catch her or get her to come to me; she just hid between the trees, watching me, out of reach.'

'It was why you didn't want her to come home,' Clarice said.

'Yes, I wasn't sure how she'd behave towards Tara, given what she'd seen. The worst thing of all, after everything that happened, was my believing Tara when she said she'd hit Guy only once.' Charlotte's face contorted in outrage. 'She hit him twice. The first blow stunned him; it was the second that killed him.'

'Yes,' Clarice said.

'I wrapped a towel around his head before I tied him in the plastic sheeting.' Charlotte stumbled on the words. 'Before I rolled him down to the water. I didn't want his handsome face to be scratched or damaged. My beautiful Guy was a gentle, sensitive man, and he showed Tara nothing but love and kindness.' She dissolved into tearful anguish, her hands becoming fists held tightly against her eyes.

Clarice went to wrap her arms around the distraught woman, rocking her gently as she might a child, her own tears falling into Charlotte's hair. Then Louise was there, holding her daughter-in-law, talking soothingly.

It took a while to calm her, but eventually Charlotte managed to raise herself to stand. After squeezing Clarice's hand, she whispered something to Louise and left the room.

'She's gone to her bedroom for a while; she said to thank you, Clarice, for being so kind.'

After Clarice had bade the children goodbye, Louise walked to the car with her.

'There was one thing,' Louise said. 'Charlotte told me Tara was annoyed with you; she said you were nosy and interfering.'

'Don't worry about it,' Clarice said. 'It is, after all, true.'

'She told Charlotte she'd played a trick on you at the Sunday fund-raiser. I am sorry.'

'Why?' Clarice said. 'It's hardly your fault, and anyway I missed it, so it couldn't have been much of a trick. What did she do?'

'Well . . .' Louise looked awkward. 'She took some dog laxatives Charlotte kept for Susie and put them in your tea – a whole pack of eight, apparently, crumbled in.'

'That does explain something,' Clarice said thoughtfully. 'I didn't drink the tea – somebody else did.'

Driving home, Clarice thought about the nuts and the sleeping pills Tara had put in Angel's food. She felt thankful that Tara had not had access to anything more lethal than dog laxatives to put in her tea at the fund-raiser. She'd sensed that the girl might have been wary of her, but hadn't realised how deeply Tara must have disliked her. She wondered what angry, malicious thoughts Tara had been harbouring after the arrest of her mother. She'd insisted that Clarice, not Bridget, drive her to her grandmother's. While she was putting Susie into the house, had Tara deliberately ducked down in the car to try to panic her? If so, she'd succeeded.

Chapter 53

Parking outside the cottage, Clarice felt her spirits lift at seeing Rick sitting at the garden table, nursing a cat and a coffee.

He stood up to meet her.

'No sign of Bob and Sandra?' she asked.

'I'm sure they'll be along soon,' he said.

The dogs stayed close, looking from one face to the other hopefully.

'Shall we?' Rick smiled, and Clarice followed him. After the sadness of her recent encounter with Charlotte, she felt an unburdening of the inner tension she'd carried home with her.

'How did it go with Charlotte?' Rick asked as they wandered along the boundary, with the sun behind them. Clarice told him what had happened.

'I'm glad that my original instinct about Guy was right,' she finished. 'He was a good person, honest and decent, and Charlotte loved him so much. She's in a lot of pain.'

'I hope Louise can help steer her,' Rick said. 'If she's not eating, she'll become ill. Coping with the court case, Tara, and the children isn't going to be easy.'

'I think she's in a safe pair of hands with Louise,' Clarice said. 'I got the feeling that they're still friends, and hopefully they'll move into the future with the children together. They both loved Guy; I'm just glad they have each other.'

'You missed the local lunchtime news.' Rick was smiling but sounded arch.

'Was it about Guy?' Clarice asked.

'It was our mutual friend Chief Inspector Charlie Johnson telling us all about how he solved the murder.'

'Ha!' Clarice shouted, laughing. 'Did you expect anything else?'

'He did allude to the importance of teamwork at one point,' Rick smirked.

'Good old Charlie,' Clarice said. 'He'll never change. Onwards and upwards.'

Blue ran ahead joyfully, having rediscovered a lost treasure, the top part of a canvas shoe. The threat of rain had vanished, and the cloudless azure sky made it the perfect summer's day.

In the house half an hour later, Clarice fixed a salad lunch and checked her watch, fretting about the absence of Bob and Sandra. Rick had gone out into the garden. She went upstairs, to find BB reposing on a bathroom chair.

Walking into the bedroom, she was suddenly transported back to the dream of a few nights earlier. In the centre of the bed the brown canvas suitcase lay open, packed with trousers at the bottom, shirts neatly folded on top, underpants and socks around the edges. Her stomach churned as her mind recoiled from the memory the image evoked.

'You've caught me,' Rick said.

Clarice turned to find him behind her, carrying her empty blue case, which he must have brought from the workshop.

'What's going on?' she asked.

'I've brought your bag. I would have packed it for you, but I'd probably leave something important out.'

'Rick?' Clarice stared at him.

'Excluding home, where's your favourite place?' he asked, unable to suppress a grin.

'We're going to Italy?' she said.

'You look suitably gobsmacked; that's the response I'd intended.' Rick laughed gleefully.

'Are we really going?' she asked, still not convinced.

'Did you think I'd dare to forget your birthday?'

'Well . . .' she began.

'Apart from all the reminders from Jonathan, Sandra, Daisy and Louise, I did actually remember all by myself. Sandra and Bob are going to be house-sitting; it's why they wouldn't take Polly immediately. They didn't want to take her home for two days and then bring her back again for five – too disruptive.'

'Are we going for five days?' Clarice asked, her eyes wide.

'Yup,' Rick said. 'Tina and Malcolm have invited us to use the Blue House – just the two of us.' He smiled at her. 'You'd better get your skates on packing. Bob and Sandra will be here in an hour, and we're setting off for the airport in two.'

Clarice looked at him, speechless.

'There's one thing I have to tell you.' He searched her face as he spoke, as if wanting to see her reaction.

Clarice waited.

'While I was in Lincoln this morning, I went into the property rental office to give notice on number 24.'

'About time.' Clarice beamed. 'There can't be much of your

stuff still there. I'll go over with you to help when you're clearing it out.'

Rick's face lit up with a lopsided grin before he turned to the chest of drawers. 'Better not forget these.' He took out a pile of envelopes.

'What have you got there?' Clarice went to look.

'Birthday cards,' Rick said. 'No peeking; not to be opened until the day.'

'I recognise Jonathan's handwriting on that one.' Clarice pointed. 'How many people were in on this?'

'Everyone,' Rick said. 'You're not the only person who can keep a secret, Mrs Beech.' He paused for a moment. 'Although there is one person who didn't know. She would have told the whole of Castlewick.'

'Georgie,' Clarice laughed.

'Georgie,' he agreed. 'You might want to give her a ring before we leave; she'll never forgive us if she's the only one not to know where we've gone.'

Clarice knew at that moment that the dream of the half-packed case would never again be associated with sad memories. It would in future be part of a wonderful one, of Rick planning a secret holiday for the two of them.

He went to put his hands on her shoulders. 'In just a few hours we'll be in Italy.'

Clarice returned his smile. 'Have I told you lately how much I love you?' she said, and waited for his kiss.

Acknowledgements

I owe a huge debt of gratitude to my amazing agent, Anne Williams, to Krystyna Green and the brilliant team at Constable/ Little Brown, and to Kate Hordern, of Kate Hordern Literary Agency. I feel privileged to have had the opportunity to work with you all.

Thanks to friends during the recent lockdown. I am missing our badminton, the yoga, walks and the pub, but the telephone calls and online meetings have been terrific. Thank you to all my book club friends, who could not have been more supportive.

Thanks to lovely Jenny for allowing me to borrow her daughter Beth's pink plastic tiara – useful to keep the hair out of the eyes when decorating. Also, to the potter, John Snowden, and vet Nigel Turner, for being there if I need advice.

While writing about Clarice and her rescue animals, I remember all the beautiful four-legged creatures Ted and I fostered over the years. For the majority we were a stepping stone, as they were on their way to forever homes. The ones who were never chosen stayed to become a permanent part of our family. Every dog or cat brought something special. Thank you to them, for bringing joy, and enduring memories that continue to enrich my life.